FILTHY LIES

A 'CONOR & STAR' DUET

THE FIVE POINTS' MOB COLLECTION: EIGHT

SERENA AKEROYD

DEDICATION

TO ANNE-STAR.
Who knew you'd get another handle after Snake Eyes?
Thank you.
For everything.
<3

FOREWORD & TRIGGER WARNINGS

HELLO DARLINGS,

Me again!

I hope you're ready for this deep dive into Conor's and Star's lives.

You'll find a little catch-up at the beginning of the book. I'd recommend giving it a read if you haven't just done a read-through of the whole universe. :P

You'll also find a deleted scene that didn't fit into the timeline of Filthy Lies here: https://dl.bookfunnel.com/sv06kgjd0e

It's dark and has sexual assault in it from Star's time as a sex slave.

You'll come across an unusual spelling of a Norse character you may know—I've anglicized it for your comfort.

Jörmungandr - you can read more about this mythological creature here: https://en.wikipedia.org/wiki/J%C3%B6rmungandr

Anyway, it's that time for me to warn you that there are GRAPHIC scenes of violence and a GRAPHIC depiction of death by torture. These are the most violent books yet. Domestic violence—not between Conor and Star!!—is also handled in the story.

Don't forget the second FILTHY LIES hits 500 reviews, I'll be dropping a bonus scene in my Diva reader group!

You can join here to read it when it happens: www.facebook.com/groups/SerenaAkeroydsDivas

I truly hope you fall for Conor and Star.

Much love and happy reading to you all,

Serena

xoxo

Triggers:

- Kidnapping,
- References to human trafficking,
- References to rape/sexual assault,
- References to child sexual abuse,
- Graphic violence

PLAYLIST

If you'd like to hear a curated soundtrack, with songs that are featured in the book, as well as songs that inspired it, then here's the link:

https://open.spotify.com/playlist/52BfeLC2FqwUyzWPjv9v8r?si=
b319d9e7a592479e&pt=05bbccf8308bf8459c384f2ed5512145

And if you'd like to hear Conor's playlist, then here's the link:

https://open.spotify.com/playlist/2WWftBdPeX3UKBsbNOMCtl?si=
0ff79a8ef2f84a8d&pt=ef0fb2b2b51a390a9e8d33041ecb7cad

THE CROSSOVER READING ORDER
WITH THE SINNERS & VALENTINIS

FILTHY
FILTHY SINNER
NYX
LINK
FILTHY RICH
SIN
STEEL
FILTHY DARK
CRUZ
MAVERICK
FILTHY SEX
HAWK
FILTHY HOT
STORM
THE DON
THE LADY
FILTHY SECRET
REX
RACHEL
FILTHY KING

<u>FILTHY DISCIPLE</u>
<u>THE CONSIGLIERE</u>
<u>THE ORACLE</u>
<u>LODESTAR</u>
<u>SILENCED</u>
<u>END GAME</u>
<u>FILTHY RICHER</u>

NAMES OF INTEREST:

NEW WORLD SPARROWS - often abbreviated to NWS. The members are known as Sparrows.

One of three global secret societies of criminals hidden in plain sight, mostly known for sex trafficking. Having infiltrated every aspect of US society, from the government to the courts to law enforcement agencies, they've escaped justice for their heinous crimes for decades.

Old World Sparrows - tied to the New World Sparrows. The oldest organization of the trio. Their territory is Europe.

Eastern Sparrows - the final Sparrow organization. Their territory is Asia.

Éire le chéile go deo - often abbreviated to ECD. The members are known as *cheiles*. An Irish organization dedicated to uniting Northern Ireland with the Republic and removing the British from their land.

Satan's Sinners' MC - a motorcycle club in West Orange, New Jersey. Allied to the Five Points. Led by Rex, the Prez.

Famigghia - Sicilian Mafia. Allied to the Five Points. Led by Luciu Valentini, the Don.

Russian Bratva - Allied to the Five Points. Led by Maxim Lyanov, the Pakhan.

United Brotherhood - An elite Russian version of the Masons. This far, little is known about their shady business dealings.

CATCH-UP

WEDDING BELLS HELL

HORRIFIC FOOTAGE WAS RELEASED yesterday of a drive-by shooting during a wedding at St. Patrick's Church in Hell's Kitchen.

Newlyweds Finn and Aoife O'Grady were on the front steps of the church when a van drove by and opened fire on the couple and their guests.

O'Grady, a renowned expert in the city's property market, has links to the O'Donnelly family—owners of the biggest real estate portfolio Manhattan has ever seen.

Aidan and Magdalena O'Donnelly were in attendance, as were their sons, Aidan Jr., Brennan, Conor, Declan, and Eoghan.

Mrs. O'Grady is currently in intensive care as is Aidan O'Donnelly Jr.

Our thoughts are with Mr. O'Grady and the O'Donnellys at this difficult time.

GOOD MORNING WITH TVGM

IT'S wedding season in New York City and leading the charge are Eoghan O'Donnelly and Inessa Vasov.

The event is set to be star-studded with political heavyweights in attendance such as the governor himself!

O'Donnelly, the youngest of Aidan O'Donnelly Sr.'s five sons, is a veteran who served during Operation: Enduring Freedom and is now a leading executive at the family company, Acuig Corp. While much is known about him, very little is known about his bride, Inessa Vasov.

Rumors abound about how this odd couple met.

This reporter just wishes she'd scored an invitation!

Star Sullivan

I'M SO CLOSE. For the first time in years, I actually feel like I'm getting somewhere.

Okay, so the Irish Mob isn't tied to the New World Sparrows like I thought. I definitely got that wrong and I've brought ten tons of shit down on my head because I've got no choice other than to leave Ohio now, but it was worth it.

God, that code was beautiful.

Even Hunter was impressed when we went snooping through their network on the hunt for answers.

I know that the Five Points will be watching me now so I've decided to head to the Satan's Sinners' MC compound in New Jersey.

Maverick might be an ex but I know he'll have my back, especially when I tell him about Katina. I'm going to have to kidnap her. It can't be helped. I'm not supposed to cross state lines with her without informing the state, but I can't risk burning my alias.

I also can't risk them saying no.

She's JUST started getting better. We haven't had to deal with any nightmares or episodes for months.

Fingers crossed heading to Jersey doesn't change anything.

TEXT CHAT

Kim: Did you hear about what went down in
Brooklyn Beach?

Jun: Nah. What?

Kim: That old fucker Vasov got his knees
capped.

Jun: Ain't like he don't deserve it.

Kim: True lol. But they're saying the Italians
did it. You know what this means, don't you?

Jun: No?

Kim: The Italians and Russians are going
to war.

Jun: Fuck. You best be extra vigilant about
security then.

Kim: Security? Ha. There'll be shootouts in
the middle of the streets! Mark my words.

Jun: Wonder if the Irish will wade in?

Kim: When don't they? Aidan Sr. is a fucking psycho. He'll get involved just to take over more territory.

FIERI HEIR KILLED

GIANNI FIERI, long rumored heir to the Fieri crime family, will be laid to rest today in Green-Wood cemetery.

Fieri, murdered while serving a jail sentence, was the eldest son of Benito Fieri, head of the New York City Italian Mafia.

I told you so...
BLOG

A LITTLE BIRD told me that Aela O'Neill, who returned permanently to the US with her son to take up a position at the Rhode Island School of Design, was seen in Manhattan yesterday.

There have long been rumors about her ties to the Five Points and I can't help but wonder if her presence has something to do with the gang war between the Russians and the Italians.

Sure, there doesn't seem to be a direct correlation, but who knows where the seedy underbelly of this city is concerned?

Back in the 00s, Declan O'Donnelly was engaged to Deirdre Donahue and this little bird also told me that Declan and Aela were an item back then.

I can't help but wonder if her son Seamus is Declan's…
Can you?

GOOD MORNING WITH TVGM

TVGM HAS exclusive footage of the shootout at Coney Island yesterday. Witnesses were astounded to see a gunman open fire on a mother and son visiting the area for the day.

Aela O'Neill was injured in the shooting and her security guard was killed. Police are refusing to confirm eyewitness testimonies that suggest her son, Seamus, only fourteen years old, had to defend his mother.

The gunman was killed at the scene.

FIERI WASHES UP ON THE SHORES OF HUDSON BAY

BENITO FIERI, head of the *Famiglia*, who went missing days ago, has washed up on the shores of the Hudson. Police say his death was suspicious and that he appears to have been executed.

Tensions have heated up in Manhattan with the antagonism between Russian and Italian factions.

With both of his sons recently perishing, the city is left wondering who will take over the *Famiglia*, a faction that has reigned over the city for decades.

THE SPARROWS' network runs so much deeper than I could have ever imagined.

What once started as a bunch of lawmakers and officials trying to fight corruption in the seventies has morphed into a shit show the likes of which I don't think the world has ever seen.

Basically, they hook a mark and threaten to turn them into a fall guy *if* they don't cooperate. It'd be brilliant if it weren't so devious.

They're everywhere now.

Not just in the courts, the FBI, the CIA, the police precincts, and the local government, but even crime factions, FFS.

I knew the Fieri *Famiglia* was their front, but it runs *deeper* than that too.

What a fucking mess.

I'm still on the hunt for information and Conor O'Donnelly has joined me. The Sparrows have infiltrated the Five Points too and his da (that motherfucker Aidan Sr.) is going crazy over the rats in his nest.

Still, I heard from Conor on the DL that Seamus was the target of that shootout in Coney Island.

He witnessed Fieri murder some chick years ago, had a nightmare about it while a friend of his mom was babysitting him (turns out that friend was a fucking Fed on the hunt for evidence to tie Aela to a money laundering op. That Fed also just happens to be a Sparrow), and told her about *that* nightmare which was only triggered by Fieri being on all the news channels as he attended the funeral of that shit son of his. The Fed, a bitch called Caroline, sold him out to the Italians.

Heard she's since been MIA. Wonder what the O'Donnellys did to her.

Hope they made her fucking hurt. Sick bitch, selling out a kid like that.

I already knew the Sparrows were scum, and this just confirms it.

BLOG

AELA O'NEILL MARRIES DECLAN O'DONNELLY in a quiet service at the Isabella Stewart Gardner Museum!!

The Isabella Stewart Gardner Museum is having a fantastic couple months.

Long-lost, priceless artworks have been returned to the fold decades after they went missing in an art heist that fooled bumbling investigators and have been the fodder for many conspiracy theories.

This week, eligible bachelor Declan O'Donnelly married his bride in a private ceremony there.

Photos have yet to be released.

A little bird has told me that Declan's name *is* listed as the father on Seamus O'Neill's birth certificate…

This blogger hates to say that I told you so, but *I told you so.*

TEXT CHAT

Regan: Did you hear about that jewelry shop heist?

James: What about it?

Regan: They're saying Callum, that kid who's friends with Conor O'Donnelly, gave the thieves a heads-up. Even though the jewelry store is under Five Points' protection.

James: Whoa. Unbelievable.

Regan: Sounds like some next-level Sparrow shit to me.

James: It is. I heard that Callum was the reason for that drive-by on O'Grady's wedding day too.

Regan: No fucking way.

James: Yeah. Blows my mind.

Regan: He set them up?

James: Yeah.

Regan: Is he dead?

James: Well, I ain't seen him around lol.
Heard his wife and dad were on the hunt for
him. Any luck since?

Regan: Nope. Those Sparrow cunts deserve
everything they get. I heard they sell people.

James: Yeah. Anything that breathes is up for
grabs with them. Disgusting.

Regan: Did you hear about the Sinners' MC
compound?

James: What about it?

Regan: Got blown up.

James: Jesus. Ain't nowhere safe nowadays?

I told you so...

BLOG

CAMILLE VASOV WAS SEEN with Brennan O'Donnelly at last night's gala in Midtown.

I have no idea what that means but they were looking *very cozy* for a couple who are only supposed to be in-laws.

Yeah, you read that right. Brennan's brother, Eoghan, is married to Camille's sister, Inessa.

Isn't that illegal?

Anyway, I'm wondering if that rumor I heard of them at a marriage license office was true…

Her father has gone missing but that's no surprise.

No one will say it out loud but I'm sure Vasov is the head of the Russian Mob.

Is this little fling between Brennan and Camille a marriage of convenience?

There have long been rumors that Inessa and Eoghan's marriage was an arrangement orchestrated by the families.

No one dares say it out loud, but we all know the O'Donnellys are Five Points. They've clearly had a PR firm in to revolutionize their brand because I doubt Manhattan's female population would be mourning the loss of yet another eligible O'Donnelly bachelor if they knew he was an Irish mobster. Or maybe they would…

CONOR JUST TOLD me that his sister-in-law, Camille, was kidnapped. She's fine now but, obviously, shaken.

There was a power grab at the top. Since Vasov's death, the vacuum has been causing all kinds of shit in New York.

Conor says Lukov and Abramovicz, Vasov's second- and third-in-command, wanted to get their hands on Inessa and Camille's baby sister—fucking perverts.

I hate men.

I swear I fucking hate them.

Well, maybe not Conor.

He makes me laugh.

Jesus, did I really just write that?

GOOD MORNING WITH TVGM

DRAMATIC FOOTAGE RELEASED today of Detective Craig Lacey of the 42nd Precinct holding Mayor Coulson hostage before killing him in a shootout that has stunned the nation.

A dirty cop, Lacey, went out with a bang as he revealed to the world that he was a part of the New World Sparrows.

He alleged that he was being set up as a fall guy.

News on the Sparrows is just starting to filter in, but they appear to be a body of individuals who have infiltrated every level of society.

Yes, it sounds like something from a spy novel, but it isn't.

The president is expected to make a speech on this subject today.

I told you so... BLOG

SAVANNAH DANIELS, newly fired from TVGM and the face of the Sparrows' articles, was sentenced to death by the NWS!

You heard it here first, reader.

I told you so when Savannah released that first article exposing the men at the top of the Sparrows' hierarchies that she was asking for trouble, and this just confirms it.

Still, she was seen with Aidan O'Donnelly Jr. shortly after, so she can't be too upset about almost dying…

NYC CATHEDRAL BURNS IN HORRIFIC ARSON ATTACK

WITH FAITH in the NYPD at an all-time low since the investigations into police precincts has revealed dozens of dirty cops working for the New World Sparrows, the eyes of the world are on the boys in blue as they investigate this heinous attack on the city landmark.

With the terror alert on red and the archbishop himself missing, fear is spreading throughout the city.

In his address to the nation, President Davidson revealed multiple investigations have been kickstarted into the Sparrows' infiltration of our nation's federal, state, and local governments.

The question is… is this retaliation from the Sparrows? Or simply a grievous attack on our city's famous cultural hotspot?

Star Sullivan

I CAN'T BELIEVE Savannah nearly died. When I brought her in on this, I knew she'd be in danger, but I didn't think they'd go this far.

Targeting her in her home? Sieging the O'Donnelly stronghold?

It's like something from a fucking movie.

I feel so bad that I got her into this but she's like a cat—nine lives and the confidence of an Egyptian goddess.

She's fine with going ahead with the release of more Sparrows' articles but I'm concerned for her. How can't I be when Justin DeLaCroix, the fucking Chief Justice of the SCOTUS, is the leader of the Sparrows?!

We've never been closer to eradicating them.

The end really feels like it's near.

I'm praying it is. Not that I believe in God.

I want so much more than this life I'm leading, and I think that's because of Conor.

He's making me want *things*. Things I stopped believing I could ever have.

TEXT CHAT

Bagpipes: Maxim Lyanov is officially the Pakhan of the Bratva now.

Forrest: I'm not surprised. Abramovicz and Lukov were old fucks, and he's scrappy. I wouldn't wanna get into a fight with him.

Bagpipes: Me neither. Brennan told me that Maxim beheaded Lukov and sent it to that girl.

Forrest: Which girl?

Bagpipes: Victoria Vasov.

Forrest: He sent a severed head to a kid?

Bagpipes: Well, she's 15.

Forrest: Ain't exactly ancient. He must be fucked in the head.

Bagpipes: Who could blame him? They say he came up on the streets of Moscow, poor fucker.

Forrest: That's probably why he's so scrappy.

Star Sullivan

I HAVE TO LEAVE.

I have to go deep undercover.

Too much shit is coming together and if Savannah being targeted has proven anything to me, it's that no one around me is safe.

I've got my girl, Kat, to watch over, and now there's Conor. Fuck, nothing can happen to either of them. I don't know what I'd do.

Things are in place, things that I need to make happen.

Conor looped me into some info recently that has changed *everything*. Not only did I not realize he had it in him to torture information out of someone (God, that was so hot), but what he shared with me…

It kills me because he's being so honest and I can't be. Not if I want to keep him safe. Not if I don't want him to hate me.

The First Lady isn't a Sparrow, but she's a part of this branch of the IRA—the ECD. A fucking traitor. In the White House. Sleeping with the POTUS.

It's insane.

But, I also learned that she was key in the planning of Aoife O'Grady's mother's murder and that was how I knew I had my in.

I've been hunting Dagda for years. I know he killed my mom, and I learned that he's related to Aoife.

So with a dash of sugar here and there, I know that I can get Dagda out into the open.

I know that I can get to him because he'll want vengeance for his sister's murder.

And if I can bring down a traitor while I'm at it, then the sacrifice is worthwhile, isn't it?

I hope so.

But it just might mean that Conor will never forgive me if he finds out what I've done…

GOOD MORNING WITH TVGM

AOIFE O'GRADY WILL BE live with us from her flagship store, Ellie's Bakery, in Hell's Kitchen in ten minutes.

Stay tuned to learn how she makes her viral brownies!

With over sixty million hits on TikTok, never mind the original *We Cream for Ice Scream* blog, which took the internet by storm, Aoife O'Grady is officially synonymous with *delicious*.

TEXT CHAT

James: Not sure how I feel about the Italians attending the wedding today.

> Regan: Not sure you have a fucking choice lol.

James: Ain't right.

> Regan: Don't let them hear you call them Italians. They're Sicilians.

James: Don't give a shit.

> Regan: Nice wedding though, wasn't it? That broad, Savannah, might be a psycho but she's hot.

James: And Aidan Jr. ain't? Both nutcases.

> Regan: Long live the Five Points, eh?

James: Long live something seeing as the world is coming to an end. Watching Senior shaking hands with the new Don fucked me up.

Regan: Get over it. New times in NYC. New factions. Fewer deaths.

James: True.

Regan: Ain't all bad.

FIRST LADY MURDERED

NEW YORK IS on lockdown after an unthinkable strike against our democracy.

While visiting Green-Wood Cemetery in Brooklyn, our First Lady was struck down by an unknown assailant.

We've yet to hear from the White House about this tragic death but insiders are saying the president will not be making a speech about his wife's passing—unusual in itself—and that he is asking for privacy for his sons to grieve the loss of their mother. The Secret Service is not commenting on the security breach that led to her assassination.

Turn to page seven for a full review of the life and the accomplishments of the First Lady of the United States.

TEXT CHAT

Lucas: I think I'm losing my mind.

Cade: Why?

Lucas: Paddy O'Donnelly's alive.

Cade: No way. He died in the nineties!

Lucas: I'm telling you I just saw him.

Cade: Impossible.

Lucas: So you're saying I am losing my mind, then.

Cade: Ah, fuck. Nothing's impossible with the O'Donnellys. Maybe he pulled a Lazarus and came back to life.

Lucas: I fucking hope Senior doesn't get resurrected!

Cade: Nah, he's in the pits of hell.

Lucas: Where he belongs.

I told
you so ...
BLOG

AIDAN O'DONNELLY SR.'S funeral was the biggest event of the year.

I told you so didn't get the chance to attend, but footage of the O'Donnelly patriarch's burial has been incredibly hard to come across.

What we know is that *noxxious'* Dagger Daniels was there with his son Camden to support his daughter, Savannah (now married to Aidan O'Donnelly Jr.). One of the younger funeralgoers allegedly fainted at the sight of the internationally renowned singer.

Liam Donnghal, NHL star, was also in attendance. Politicians, New York socialites, and a few Broadway actors were also among the grievers, but I wanted an invitation to meet with the Mounties' prized player who has been *very* quiet since his kidnapping last year.

TEXT CHAT

Regan: We've got a new Filthy King. I was there when Aidan Jr. sliced out that prick's tongue.

James: Yeah, that was grody.

James: Packed a hell of a message though, didn't it? He's less crazy than his da, but that don't say much about him, does it?

Regan: Not in the grand scheme of things.

James: I wasn't actually talking about the tongue thing though. His da's generals just got themselves hanged from freakin' rebar in one of the cement factories.

Regan: WHAT?!

James: Yeah. They were behind that mutiny…

Regan: I heard he got kidnapped.

James: He did. Don't look good but he's making all the Points get tagged now, making them reassert their loyalties.

Regan: Tagged?

James: Inked with insignia.

Regan: When are you getting yours done?

James: This week. No choice.

Regan: Might be a chocolate chip short of a cookie, but he's shrewder than his da.

James: Definitely.

Regan: Rumor is he's taking over the ECD too.

James: Those IRA nutcases?

Regan: Yup.

James: Rumor… or fact?

Regan: Fact.

MURDERER OF THE FIRST LADY IN CUSTODY

DETAILS about the man in question are fleeting, but the Secret Service have revealed that the killer has ties to the ECD—an extremist branch of the IRA.

With President Davidson's close relationship with Ireland, the world waits for news on how both countries will respond to such a brazen attack on US soil.

AT THE RISK of finding myself in the crosshairs of a sniper's bullet, I have to wonder if the recent flood of deaths in the political sphere is Sparrows-related.

We've had more names coming out of the woodwork in recent times, and though some of the politicians appear to have perished in accidental deaths, I won't be afraid to say *I told you so* if news comes out of some faction or other dealing with the Sparrows in this way.

Which faction, though?

It's definitely not the NYPD. The boys in blue are as useless (read dirty) as always and the Feds aren't much better. Everyone knows that the director has ties with the Irish Mob.

One has to wonder… who's next?

PART 1

Some people believe because you come in peace, that you aren't prepared for war.

*   - Unknown*

1

———————

TEXT CHAT

THE REASON - HOOBASTANK

PAST

CONOR: *When did you know that you were good at coding?*

Star: *When I was a teenager.*

Conor: *What happened?*

Star: *Managed to change the password on the alarm system that protected the family house.*

Conor: *Why? To cause trouble?*

Star: *Nah. I was pretty well-behaved back then.*

Conor: *At least you recognize that you're not well-behaved now. Lol.*

Star: *:P*

Star: *Oh, I can recognize it and admit to choosing to veer from the path of righteousness…*

Conor: *Meaning that you were on a righteous path at one point?*

Star: *For sure. You don't enlist for shits and giggles. Surely Eoghan taught you that much.*

Conor: *I figured he wanted out of the Irish Mob lol and Uncle Sam wasn't as big of a pain in the ass as Da is.*

Star: *It amazes me how you all let him get away with the stunts he pulls.*

Conor: *He's our da. Don't have to like him to know he wants what's best for us.*

Star: *You genuinely believe that?*

Conor: *Most of the time.*

Star: *And all you alphabet brothers feel the same?*

Conor: *The what now?*

Star: *Alphabet brothers. Ya know, seeing as your ma was so lacking in creative insight into her kids' names she put them in alphabetical order.*

Conor: *Hey, at least we don't have biblical names. I'll take Conor over a saint's name.*

Star: *Odd priority, but fine lol.*

Star: *Do you love him?*

Conor: *Who? Da?*

Star: *Yeah.*

Conor: *I guess. It's not an easy love though.*

Star: *Meaning?*

Conor: *Meaning that it's a habit. We do as we're told. We go to church. We eat Sunday dinner at the compound.*

Conor: *It's like getting up and showering. You do it because you're supposed to.*

Star: *I rarely do what I'm supposed to.*

Conor: *Please tell me you at least shower?*

Star: *I prefer baths.*

Conor: *Good to know lol. Personal hygiene isn't an issue.*

Star: *Like it matters through a computer screen.*

Conor: *I don't consign you to a computer screen.*

Star: *Meaning?*

Conor: *You sure you want to go there?*

Star: *Go where?*

Conor: *You playing coy?*

Star: *No, lol. What are you talking about?*

Conor: *I'm saying that I don't just think of you when I talk to you.*

Star: *Hmm.*

Conor: *Hmm? What's that supposed to mean?*

Star: *It means, 'Hmm.'*

Star: *It means I'm not sure if that's sweet or unnecessary and it means that I'm not sure if I should tell you that I think of you outside of when we're talking too.*

Conor: *Hate to break it to you but you just told me.*

Star: *I'm aware.*

Conor: *So...*

Conor: *We both think of each other, then?*

Star: *Yes.*

Conor: *So...*

Conor: *Do you understand why your bathing might be of interest to me?*

Star: *I'd imagine because you think of me soapy and wet lol?*

Conor: *Well, yes. And doing other things.*

Star: *Huh. Are we talking about acts that would make you want to jack off? Or are we talking about how I'd break someone's code?*

Conor: *Both. I think you know that either of those would be an attractive mental image for someone like me.*

Star: *Interesting.*

Conor: *Interesting good? Or interesting bad?*

Star: *I can feel your nerves from Hell's Kitchen.*

Conor: *That's probably because I AM nervous.*

Star: *Why?*

Conor: *Because I'm not sure if you would want me to think of you in that way.*

Star: *Hmm.*

Conor: *Jesus, are we back to that?*

Star: *I don't suppose you'd think of every hacker you've come across in the bath.*

Conor: *No, lol.*

Star: *Is it because anyone with tits would do?*

Conor: *No.*

Star: *Why then?*

Conor: *Because you're you.*

Star: *Okay.*

Conor: *Okay?*

Star: *Yes. You can think of me in the bathtub.*

Conor: *You know what that leads to, don't you?*

Star: *Yes. I already said the dirty words 'jack off.' I'm not a nun, Conor.*

Conor: *You only act like one.*

Star: *Sex has always been a weapon for me.*

Conor: *That's very candid of you.*

Star: *I'm a very candid person.*

Conor: *I'm aware of that. This is just more candid than usual.*

Star: *We're talking about you jacking off, Conor. I'm not sure you could handle more candor. I already feel like you're squirming and I don't know why.*

Star: *You're a handsome man. You're experienced. For God's sake, you're one of the city's most eligible bachelors. So why are you nervous talking to me about this?*

Conor: *Because I don't want to push you too far. If I did, I feel like I wouldn't know until I never heard from you again and you were in Siberia or something.*

Star: *You haven't pushed me too far.*

Conor: *Good.*

TEN MINUTES LATER

STAR: *Do you have hang-ups?*

Conor: *From my past?*

Star: *Yes.*

Conor: *We're talking sex, right?*

Star: *Yes.*

Conor: *I'm particular.*

Star: *In what way?*

Conor: *I dislike hand jobs.*

Star: *Seriously?*

Conor: *Seriously.*

Star: *That's... limiting.*

Conor: *It is what it is.*

Star: *Anything else?*

Conor: *Anal play is out. I don't like hands in my hair either.*

Star: *Makes sense.*

Conor: *I've never told anyone that.*

Star: *You trying to tell me I'm special?*

Conor: *I think we both know you are.*

Star: *Maybe.*

Conor: *Do you have hang-ups?*

Star: *From being a sex slave?*

Conor: *Yes.*

Star: *Are you sure you want to know?*

Conor: *Wouldn't have asked.*

Star: *I'm aggressive by nature and I wasn't lying about sex being a weapon. That trait doubled down during that period of my life. That I don't associate sex with pleasure is probably a hang-up.*

Conor: *Do you ever want to meet me?*

Star: *A part of me does.*

Conor: *Just a part?*

Star: *Another part of me knows that I'll push you away at some point and you won't come back.*

Conor: *You don't know that.*

Star: *I do.*

Star: *No one sticks around me. I'm toxic.*

Conor: *Savannah loves you. She left, but she came back.*

Star: *Savannah's different. Katina is too.*

Conor: *Why?*

Star: *I got to them when they were young lol. They're used to me being toxic. At some point, I'll alienate her again. Katina too. I think they'll come back. But I never know for certain.*

Star: *Savannah wouldn't have made up with me if I hadn't shared what went down with the Sparrows.*

Conor: *Don't we always have to justify why we do the things that we do if it hurts other people?*

Star: *Is that how love is supposed to work?*

Conor: *I don't think love is 'supposed' to be easy.*

Star: *If it's a struggle, then what's the point?*

Conor: *Two years ago, I'd have agreed with you.*

Star: *What changed?*

Conor: *I met you.*

2

STAR
IN TOO DEEP - SUM 41

Star Sullivan

SUMMER

"IT DIDN'T HAVE to be this way," I sang as I hauled the limp deadweight along the shiny parquet floor of Midlothian Palace's entrance hall.

Ignoring the lump's groans when we reached the grand staircase, I dragged him up each step, aware that his head cracked against the edge every time.

Sometimes, you didn't have to work harder, just smarter.

"You could have just told me who he is."

A garbled reply was his only response.

In all fairness, Prince Edward of Midlothian couldn't speak freely right now. His face was taped up like the rest of him with cling wrap. He had a few air holes, but I'd squished his features up nice and tight to compress him as much as possible.

The human sausage continued moaning with each step and, by the end, I'd admit, I was starting to moan too—from sheer exertion.

"Never heard of cardio?" I panted when we made it to the midway landing of the staircase where it flattened out before going up to another mezzanine level.

He grunted in reply.

Me? I just planted my hands on my knees and tried to recover my breath.

I'd recently gotten back into the game, and torture was a work of art that required not only skill but a strong constitution. My ass wasn't as fit as it used to be, and I was feeling that at the moment.

When my breathing was under some semblance of control, I turned to face the palace ahead of me. Beautiful, ornate, but the best part? It was currently a dead zone thanks to this clever piece of tech I'd borrowed from Conor—none of the CCTV were working, none of the alarms. The guards were watching rehashed versions of last night's footage, and I had a good ninety minutes before the next man came on patrol.

Ninety minutes to make Prince Eddie talk.

Ninety minutes to break him.

I used to be good at breaking people.

Some people in the CIA called me The Nutcracker, and it had nothing to do with cracking code. But I had to admit, Prince Ludwig and Ke Jintao had held out on me.

This fucker here was the last person who could help me.

He *had* to talk.

I was running out of options.

Leaving the lump on the landing once I dropped down to grab a length of rope from my kit, I headed up the stairs.

It was an open mezzanine, but it suited my purposes.

With two landings that looked out onto the massive hall of the palace, it enabled me to loop the rope around one of the ornate balustrade railings and dangle it to the next floor before I tied it in a timber hitch knot to secure it.

Now that it was swaying vertically, I retreated to the prince's side. Once there, I tugged on the rope then tied both ends into a square knot. With the gap in the middle, I looped it around his feet then tightened it.

With more brute force than I'd like—I was pretty fucking sure I popped a vertebra hefting his weight over the railing—I let gravity do the work for me and watched him dead drop.

If my calculations were wrong, he'd snap his neck and break his face if he collided with the floor.

Luckily for him, my math was never wrong.

His muffled scream was music to my ears as he came to a halt a bare inch from the parquet flooring.

After gently twisting my back to ease the strain he'd caused, I loped downstairs and kicked him in the junk to make him swing.

I hadn't found any evidence that indicated he deserved a sprained penis, but my rep was from damage down below and I was sure the fucker had done *something* in his life to earn it.

"I can keep this up for a while. Turn you in circles and make you drown in your own vomit," I taunted him. "That's before I bring out the knives. You see, Your Highness, I need your help and you *will* give it to me." I kicked him a few more times, watching him sway. "You could end it easily tonight. A simple overdose. No pain. Just death. Or we can play."

This time, I had to go the whole nine yards. If it didn't look like an accident as the others did, then it was tough shit.

I needed answers, and I could admit to myself that I was growing desperate.

But I would not bend.

I would not break.

Allowing my threat to sink in, I retrieved the photograph from my pocket.

For a moment, I stared at it.

Ever since I'd seen it when I was cataloging what I'd found in the motel room of the once-Prez of the Satan's Sinners' MC, Bear, it had been haunting me.

Bear had annotated on the back: *United Brotherhood?*

That was what I'd been trying to figure out.

I'd recognized three of them. Three random officials from three different countries.

One, a high-ranking politician in the Chinese Communist Party. Two were princes, easily renowned for their playboy ways back in their heyday. But it was the fourth one…

I recognized him.

I just didn't know how.

No names were on the back. Either Bear didn't know who they were or he didn't feel the need to make a note of them.

I wished he had.

It would have saved me a lot of torture.

The photo wasn't recent, but the men in it weren't much changed from the corpses I'd left behind. They were sitting in a room together, heads dipped as they conversed. What was interesting was the camera angle—it peered through a gap.

The subjects hadn't known they were being photographed.

"Think about it, Eddie," I mused out loud as I studied the stranger's face. "You can die peacefully or you can keep quiet and I can make you regret the day your mother gave birth to you."

Something mumbled spilled from his lips. I grabbed a hold of him and stopped the pendulum swing of his body, then I ducked and popped two fingers into the holes I'd made in the cling wrap that fed air into his nose. Kinda gross, but torture was messy. I needed more than a couple of Tide PODS to keep my whites *white* that was for fucking sure.

As he lost those streams of oxygen, I felt his panic increase before I retreated, tugging the plastic wrap with it.

That was when I knew I'd done my job right—the panic didn't abate. It *surged.*

"You try to scream or alert a guard, you'll do more than choke on your vomit," I warned as I carefully tugged on the gag I'd stuffed in his mouth.

He gulped down air the moment he could, then he pricked my hope like it was a balloon. Much like the others had, he rasped, "In our Brothers we trust."

My jaw clenched as I accepted what I had to do tonight.

It sure as hell wouldn't be pretty…

"If you want to play it that way, Your Highness, then play we will, but there'll be no winners in this game. That's a promise."

AN HOUR LATER, a bare fifteen minutes before the guard was due to patrol this section of the palace, Prince Eddie finally gave me what I'd been seeking.

Anton Kuznetsov.

At last, I had a fucking name.

Now, I just had to figure out how the hell I knew him.

3

CONOR

FURIOUS ANGELS - ROB DOUGAN

Conor O'Donnelly

"CONOR."

"You're the only person who says my name that way, Riggs. Did you know that? I don't need Caller ID for you."

"You say the sweetest things," she cooed in my ear, making my lips twitch.

"I work hard to be charming," I agreed, scratching my temple where there was an ever-present itch since the fist that had collided with my face a few days earlier had cut skin.

"I remember that conversation."

Agitated, I crossed my arms over my chest. "The one where you told me that people wouldn't like me if I remained a robot?"

"That's the one. It's a life lesson you should have learned before you reached seventeen. With your family, I'm surprised they didn't point it out sooner."

My brow puckered, pulling on the dissolvable stitches on my forehead. "Did you call just to insult me? Because I have enough on my plate as it is."

Her chuckle was infectious enough that it made the corners of my lips tug into a smile. Riggs, *when* the urge struck, always laughed from her belly. I wasn't sure she knew any other way.

"I have a job for you," she said lightly once she'd finished finding amusement at my expense.

"I'm busy."

"You're always busy. But this is Uncle Sam," she reminded me—as if I'd forget my deal with *that* devil. "You can't be too busy for him."

"I've done Sammy Boy enough favors for him to leave me alone for the rest of my damn life. You owe me for finding that bug in the NSA servers. You were begging hackers to come in and explore."

She tutted. "You know how it works."

"I do, but I think it's time to renegotiate."

"You don't renegotiate with the United States," she retorted, tutting for a second time. "Do I need to remind you of what happened when you were seventeen? The reason I told you that you needed a personality transplant?"

I huffed.

"You were the one who decided to go exploring NASA. You were the one who decided that a single visit to a top-secret agency's database wasn't enough."

I grimaced at the memory. At the time, I'd needed to access a satellite. *A now obsolete satellite.* It so wasn't worth the punishment.

Deciding to play hardball, I stated, "I need to leave the country."

Her voice grew sharp. "Why?"

"Not for good. Just for a short period. Maybe a few weeks."

"You know you're not allowed to leave the continental US—" She sighed. "Ah. You want to do a deal."

"You catch on quickly." I rocked back in my seat and stared at the footage one of my monitors played on repeat.

Star sitting right where I was.

In my home.

It was the nearest I'd ever gotten to her. The nearest, sometimes, it felt like I'd ever be.

"For a woman?" she guessed, sounding bored by the idea.

"*The* woman," I corrected.

"They always are," she dismissed.

"Not with me. You know that."

"Do you even date?" She sighed. "Never mind. I'll see what I can do. Where do you need to go?"

"Russia."

I waited for the explosion. It came in the form of a growl. "Why the fuck do you want to go to Russia?"

Riggs, a church-going Evangelist, never swore. That meant I enjoyed it all the more when I made her do it.

As much as we were friendly, she was my handler. Granted, she didn't 'handle' me much anymore. Once every four or so years I tended to hear from her. It was both bad and good luck that she'd called today.

Bad because I had other shit I needed to do.

Good because I needed to get to Star and I hadn't been sure if I'd be able to leave the country without being stopped by TSA first.

A private jet was always an option, and I'd sneaked in and out of our borders via that method of transport in the past, but something about what was going down told me I needed to stay on the good side of the US government.

If that meant doing their bidding for a little while, jumping through some hoops, and dancing to their tune, then I'd do it.

"Well?" she snarled. "Why Russia?"

"I need to retrieve someone from there."

"Retrieve?" She paused. "An evacuation?"

That was the problem; I didn't know. Hell, I didn't know if Star was even *in* Russia. I was going off a bombing in Petrovsky Park and what felt like a wing and a fucking prayer.

I scrubbed a hand over my face then winced when I caught on the tear in the skin on my forehead.

Nothing about the last couple of days had gone according to plan.

Ever since Star Sullivan had entered my life, shit routinely went down the shitter, but these past few months had been worse than ever.

This whole crap fest had started with Katina, Star's foster daughter, who had come to visit me, running away from her home in West

Orange, New Jersey, to find my apartment building so she could tell me that her foster mother hadn't been in contact with her and had skipped a call when she never did that.

I'd promised her I'd bring her home, then I'd taken Katina back to the Satan's Sinners' MC compound where I'd been greeted by the man who was dating Katina's older sister—Maverick. It was only after his fist met my face that I remembered he was the one who was a Green Beret.

The prick might have been retired, but that didn't mean he packed less of a punch.

The fact that I woke up in the hospital with an apologetic MC Prez sitting at my bedside told me that Katina had informed Rex, the Prez, and the rest of the Sinners' MC that I *hadn't* abducted her and had, in fact, been in the process of returning her to her family.

I was still dealing with the migraine that came from my head being bounced off the driveway like a basketball, so this shit with the government was the last thing I needed to be juggling.

That was the problem though—it wasn't like they *asked* me. Riggs didn't call with requests.

She *ordered.*

Rubbing my eyes, I muttered, "I'm not sure if it's an evacuation or not. Someone important to me has gotten herself into some trouble over there. I just need to get her back here. I'm not a flight risk. You know that."

"I know that your family situation has changed," was Riggs' cool answer.

I mocked, "Thanks for the flowers."

"Your father was lucky that you *are* a governmental asset, Conor. It's not a bad thing that he can't create more chaos in the city streets."

The bitch of it was I didn't disagree with her.

My da had used me.

Riggs was just the same.

Everyone used me.

I was a tool.

Some days it was easier to embrace that than others.

Pursing my lips, I argued, "Da didn't keep me here. My brothers are everything to me. You know that."

She harrumphed.

Tired of this conversation, I changed the subject to what really mattered: "What does the government need from me this time?"

"The Secret Service had an internal breach a few months ago." *No shit.* "Our engineers have created a communication platform that we'd like you to test."

I arched a brow she couldn't see and called her out on her BS. "Does this 'breach' have something to do with the First Lady's death?"

"What do you know about that?" Riggs clipped.

"Just what the rest of the country does."

"I'm sure," she scoffed. "When I found out her killer was Irish American, I looked into his ties… His past was scraped clean."

"You can't prove that was me," I taunted.

"No, otherwise I'd have hauled your ass into HQ sooner." She sighed. "Why do you make shit so difficult for me, Conor?"

"I'm not like my baby bro, Riggs. I don't live to serve at America's pleasure. Anyway, I'll gladly test your new communication platform." I'd get my kicks then expose it to that beast of a worm Lodestar had gifted me, one that the Green Beret who'd punched me had crafted from scratch. That would fuck it up in no time. Malware and punches —Maverick's skill set was far-reaching. "But after the testing, I want the okay to head to Russia."

"How do we know you'll return?"

I laughed. "I'm not as self-sacrificing as Snowden. The same rules apply as always, don't they?"

"They do," she confirmed bitterly. "You know, when I started in this game, I never thought I'd be doing deals with criminals to protect them and their families from the arm of the law."

It was my turn to tut. "You said it yourself, Riggs. I'm not a criminal. I'm an asset. Pick me up when you have the okay."

With that, I cut the call.

Though she'd pissed me off with that final rejoinder, I got to my feet and twisted around to stare at the city skyline in the distance.

This penthouse had been a gift from Da, but his gifts always came after I danced to his tune.

I figured with him gone, that wouldn't be an issue anymore.

I'd practically been begging for karma to kick me in the nuts.

Moving over to the window, I watched the city that never slept, trying to find comfort in the hive of activity even at this time in the morning, but it wasn't there.

Turning back to my desk, I stared at the files I'd been combing through for the past couple of weeks. Anything from the politicians the Five Points were setting up to die in 'accidents' to the folder I'd been building on Star—her profile.

Lips pursing when my cell buzzed, I reached for it again and stared at the screen as a message notification flashed up.

Riggs: A car will be there in five.

I smirked.

She hated how much her bosses needed me.

I didn't know if I was as special as they thought I was. Hackers had egos and, sure, I had one too, but from how the US government treated me, I had to be the second coming.

Knowing that I'd be busy for the next few hours at least, I set some programs running and shut others off. I grabbed my main rig, which housed original copies of the worm Star had gifted me—"Best goddamn gift ever," I muttered under my breath—and I set it up in its case.

With that done, I collected my phone and checked my messages.

My brothers were shooting the shit about a hockey match our newly-discovered cousin, Liam Donnghal, was playing in—apparently, he was doing a good imitation of a toddler on the ice.

Then, I saw one from Aaron Goldstein.

Goldstein: McClure took me to a cigar club tonight.

Me: Hope you enjoyed your first date.

My lips twitched as I strode from my office and headed for the bedroom.

> Goldstein: How many times do I have to tell you? I don't swing that way.

That wasn't what I remembered from my short stint in college, but if he had memory issues, then that was his problem and not mine.

> Me: Does he?

> Goldstein: Not sure. Maybe? He's creepy, and not only because he's a zealot and a Sparrow.

> Me: You've got your in though? He wouldn't have invited you to the cigar club otherwise, I assume?

> Goldstein: You assume right. Gaining his confidence to the point he encourages me to become a Sparrow won't be easy, but I'm in this for the long haul.

> Me: Good. Keep me updated.

> Goldstein: Will do.

Having known Goldstein since college, I'd gotten friendly with him while he was an annoying jock who drank too much but who always got his assignments in on time and managed to pass his finals even with a hangover.

As a 'grown-up,' he was a dedicated police officer, one who had a skewed sense of justice—my favorite kind—as well as a man who had big enough balls to go deep undercover while taking a sabbatical from Interpol because he saw the potential here...

A potential not just for promotion but to make the world a better place too.

I had to figure that he knew he could ruin his career by doing this unsanctioned, but I also realized that he was as concerned as I was—who in Interpol was a Sparrow?

Who wasn't one of those dirty bastards?

The New World Sparrows were everywhere and had infiltrated every organization. Nowhere was safe. Not the mafia, the government, the media, or the fucking church.

For all those reasons, that was why he was one of the first people I'd gotten in touch with when Aidan, my oldest brother, had come up with the notion we needed to start bringing officials into the Sparrows—infiltrating to tear the fuckers down from the inside out.

He was the perfect candidate—US-born and patriot-bred—*but* he'd left the US after college thanks to a British grandmother from whom he'd inherited a home in the UK's version of the Hamptons—Sandbanks.

He'd moved to Europe shortly after, gained a job in Interpol, and hadn't returned stateside since.

I forged him a new identity, one based on his old credentials, and he was a shoo-in for a senator's aide with majors in American history and psychology and minors in marketing and politics.

The only reason I knew he wasn't a Sparrow? That skewed sense of justice he had…

Attending college with him had been *interesting.*

A thought occurred to me as I picked out a button-down shirt.

Me: May go quiet.

Goldstein: Why?

Me: Somewhere I need to be.

Me: If I do, my brothers will be in touch.

Goldstein: Should I contact them?

Me: No. They'll communicate with you
when/if the time comes.

Goldstein: What's going on?

Me: Nothing. Just hedging my bets.

Ignoring his other messages, I dragged on a suit after I used the bathroom. My doorbell was buzzing as I zipped up my fly, and I ignored it to continue with my preparations.

Two squirts of aftershave to the left side of my throat and two squirts to the right.

An old vintage Rolex that had been battered years ago was on my left wrist, a new smartwatch on my right that was of my own making because I already had the government sniffing between my ass cheeks; I didn't need to invite them into my life with a mass-produced gadget that was nothing more than a tracker.

With that done, I sketched out a note on my bedroom dresser.

Aidan,

If you see this note, I'm probably dead.

It's okay. It was a long time coming anyway. They always say you can rest when you're dead, and fuck, if I don't deserve a rest.

Anyway, love you, dearthàir.

Kid

P.S. Don't try to look for me. I don't want you ending up in a body bag too.

MY NOSE CRINKLED at the short but not exactly sweet message as the buzzer sounded again.

It was always maudlin to write these goodbye notes but I did it just in case. In the past, I'd tossed each in the trash can, but who knew with the state of the world?

I shrugged into a winter coat, rolled up the cuffs twice on each arm, then strode out of the bedroom, collecting my laptop bag on the way and hitting the intercom as it buzzed once more.

"I get the message," I growled. "I'm coming now."

As usual, there was no response.

Yanking two strands of hair off my head, I bit down on one and held it in place between my teeth and kept a hold of the other as I shut the door, jamming the first lock at the top of the jamb, above eye level.

If someone tried to open it after I left, the hair would fall.

As I locked the door, I heard the multilevel pins spin into place, then I jimmied the handle twice to make sure it was closed. After, I retrieved the remaining piece of hair from between my teeth and rested it on the doorknob.

That done, I walked over to the elevator.

Once upon a time, this had been an open space, but I'd had an entranceway built so that I didn't walk straight into my apartment from the elevator anymore.

Over the past year, I'd learned that giving home invaders an extra workout, even if it only took ten minutes for them to get through the door, was ten minutes in my favor to either arm up, aim for the safe room, or to head to the helicopter pad and leave the building via the fire exit.

A short ride later and I was in the lobby when I saw the car idling outside.

The doorman greeted me softly, to which I nodded without making eye contact. The last thing Denny needed was the US government looking at him askance because I'd been friendly with him.

Knowing their incompetence, they'd try to figure out if I was using Morse code with my eyelashes to give him a message or something.

Making a mental note to apologize for being rude if I made it back home, and figuring Denny would forgive me if I disappeared forever, I headed for the back seat and climbed in.

As the doors locked around me, I merely faced straight ahead as the car pulled from the curb and eased into traffic.

"Don't you want to know where we're heading, Mr. O'Donnelly?"

The query came ten minutes into the ride from the gloomy shadows beside me.

The voice was younger than Riggs'. Female. Accent-less and uninteresting with it, aside from the soft trace of amusement in her words.

My brow furrowed. "Why would I be interested? It'll be another beige-on-beige room in a beige-on-beige office space in a random skyscraper in the city."

"Not tonight, Mr. O'Donnelly," the woman informed me, her tone sly. A croon almost.

"I guess I'll find out when I get there," I dismissed, but I turned my face to stare into the darkness where she was sitting. "Do I know you?"

A soft chuckle was her only answer. A glow from the streetlights flashed into the backseat, illuminating a part of her face.

As she turned to look at me, I got more of a glimpse of her features, but I didn't recognize them. I did, however, see that she'd held out her hand for me to shake.

When I reached out, she murmured, "It's a pleasure to meet you, Mr. O'Donnelly."

"The pleasure's mine, Agent…?"

"Black."

"Agent Black," I repeated. "And where are we heading if it isn't some innocuous building the NSA has set up for me tonight?"

More of that odd humor laced her words as she drawled, "Langley."

4

———————

TEXT CHAT

PAST

CONOR: *Can I ask you a question?*

Star: *Depends.*

Conor: *On?*

Star: *Whether I want to answer it.*

Conor: *Helpful.*

Star: *You know I endeavor to be helpful at all times, Conor.*

Conor: *Guess what I just saw!*

Star: *What?*

Conor: *A pig flying over the Empire State Building.*

Star: *Are you saying I'm a liar?* ੭(੭*˘ᵕ˘)੭*˚

Conor: *I'm saying you're liberal with the truth. And you're no angel if that's what that emoji is supposed to be.*

Star: *I'm a star. I exist in the heavens.*

Conor: *Oh, look. Hell just froze over too.*

Star: *You'd know seeing as you live in Hell's Kitchen. What's it like being next door to the devil?*

Conor: *Surprisingly humid.*

Star: *Figured it would be hot.*

Conor: *More sticky.*

Star: *:P Hit me with the question.*

Conor: *What happened in Afghanistan?*

Star: *There was a war.*

Conor: *Sigh. I mean with you.*

Star: *Ah, you mean how did I end up being a sex slave?*

Conor: *Yes. Precisely.*

Star: *Director of the CIA is a Sparrow. I started sniffing around where he didn't want me sniffing, and I got my ass landed in Sex Slave Central. Trust me, it's not the kind of marketplace you want to visit.*

Star: *Unless you're into that, of course.*

Star: *Are you?*

Conor: *Double sigh.*

Star: *Why are you asking?*

Conor: *You have a lot of long-term plans.*

Star: *I do! It's my favorite thing to do.*

Conor: *Do you bullet journal?*

Star: *Do I seem like the kind of woman who'd bullet journal?*

Conor: *Hey, I don't judge. Maybe you have a kill list and it's decorated with hearts…*

Star: *I'm not a 'hearts and flowers' kinda gal.*

Conor: *Skulls and crossbones then?*

Star: *Lol. You got me.*

Conor: *What? Do you bullet journal?*

Star: *Uh huh. I use bullets to decorate my journal.*

Conor: *You're no fun.*

Star: *I'm plenty of fun.*

Conor: *So, do you have a kill list?*

Star: *Naturally.*

Conor: *Is the director of the CIA on there?*

Star: *Yes. That's a very obvious question.*

Conor: *Nothing's obvious with you. Why isn't he dead yet?*

Star: *Because Reinier isn't a priority.*

Star: *The New World Sparrows need to die. Then, I need to kill my mom's murderer. THEN, I have to reunite every woman, man, and child* *who was treated like a piece of meat by those fucking bastards with their family. THEN, the director of the CIA can die.*

Star: *Ordinarily, Reinier would be at the top of my shit list but, as you can see, I have quite a lot on my plate.*

Conor: *How do you want to kill him?*

Star: *Stick a poker up his ass.*

Conor: *Very angelic of you.*

Star: *I try. *curtseys**

Conor: *Do you even know how to curtsey lol?*

Star: *There's plenty I know how to do. I've met several royal families, I'll have you know. Sheiks are crazy. They pay millions to have rock stars play at their kids' weddings.*

Conor: *They do? I know Rihanna did that once.*

Star: *Sure, very nice income stream.*

Conor: *I'll bet.*

Star: *Got my inspiration from you re the ass poker thing, btw.*

Conor: *Figured as much lol.*

Star: *Thought I'd start with the poker, then I'd slice off his dick. Maybe make him eat it. Or maybe break his back or something.*

Conor: *Why break his back?*

Star: *Duh, so he can suck off the stump.*

Conor: *Wow. I just crossed my legs.*

Star: *He won't be able to by the time I'm through with him.*

Conor: *LOL.*

Conor: *Star? You know that if I can help with your to-do list, I will, right?*

Star: *It's MY to-do list for a reason.*

Conor: *You can't do everything on your own.*

Star: *Says you. You're a one-man band too.*

Conor: *Only because my brothers have zero aptitude for what I do. Even Eoghan, who deals with most of our security, doesn't know dick about coding alarm systems.*

Star: *Is this pro bono assistance or quid pro quo?*

Conor: *It's pro bono, I guess.*

Star: *Why guess?*

Conor: *Because this isn't a favor. This is me wanting to help you bring down those who hurt you.*

Star: *Huh.*

Star: *Conor?*

Conor: *Yes?*

Star: *Do you know I'd stick a poker up that priest's ass if I could? Slice him up real good too?*

Conor: ***sniffles** That might be the most romantic thing anyone's ever said to me.*

Star: *I'm better than Hallmark at writing this shit, aren't I?*

Conor: *You definitely should be working on greeting cards. And homicidal bullet journals.*

Conor: *Maybe when the to-do list is done, you can branch out? Even serial killers need hobbies.*

Star: *Maybe.*

Star: *Conor?*

Conor: *Yes, Star.*

Star: *Do you think I'll complete it?*

Conor: *I have every faith in you.*

Star: *You do?*

Conor: *Yes. And I won't rest until it's complete either…*

Star: *I'm not sure what to say.*

Conor: *How about, 'Welcome aboard the killing train, Conor.'?*

Star: *:D Welcome aboard.*

5

CONOR

YES - COLDPLAY

Conor O'Donnelly

PRESENT DAY

CIA HQ WAS something I'd mostly only seen in episodes of *The Blacklist*. Thus, the fear I was about to be murdered kicked up a notch.

A part of me was certain I was about to be taken to a black site, only I wasn't. I was guided down a multitude of empty hallways and led into a large office where a group of 'engineers' were strumming away at their keyboards as if they weren't making code, but music.

If *noxxious* didn't exist, then this was my favorite kind of track to listen to.

The office housed around thirty technicians. Each of their faces glowed in blue light, their attention fixed on their screens and not on what was happening in the rest of the room.

These guys weren't the usual white-collar morons I dealt with.

They didn't dress in grocery-store suits and look like they were dealing with the aftermath of a wedgie. They were like me. *Regular me.* They wore jeans and had tattoos on show. One kid had a green mohawk; another appeared unsure about the year of our Lord because she thought being emo was in fashion.

A challenge, then.

That was my first take on the situation.

The second was that maybe my ego was bigger than I thought.

Said ego had been bruised by Star's repeated invasions into my code, yet as a result, my work had never been tighter.

It was true that only when your mettle was tested did you know what you were capable of.

And Star was the benchmark by which I measured everything.

She was my peer.

My equal.

My fucking everything.

The thought had my jaw clenching with irritation.

Love was supposed to be nice.

It wasn't supposed to hurt like this.

Absently, and of my own volition, I rubbed at my chest. That was when Black clapped her hands and shouted, "Team, we need Eagle's Claw live in five minutes for testing. Are we still on track?"

The emo kid called out, "We are."

Black, folding her arms across her chest, nodded and fell silent so I did the same, except I leaned against the wall and studied the group.

Then, much as if a school bell had sounded—most of these fuckers seemed young enough to belong in high school anyway—they got up five minutes later and traipsed out.

As one, they all flicked a glance at me.

That was an interesting experience.

Some looks were covetous; others were heated. A few were bitter, and a couple were competitive.

"You're their criterion," Black informed me once we were alone.

I arched a brow. "What do you mean?"

"The OG asset," she mused. "The first of their kind."

Clearly, I'd been slow on the uptake. "They're like me?"

"Yes. Turned to Uncle Sam to get out of jail sentences. The program worked so well with you, Mr. O'Donnelly, that we decided to expand our team."

"Why let me in on that secret?"

"Because it isn't a secret and it's good to know that you're not irreplaceable or unique."

"I never said I was either." I smirked at her. "If anything, every time I get a call from Riggs, *you* define *me* as such."

She tipped her chin to the side. "Star said you were annoying."

My smirk died as I straightened up. "You know Star? Star Sullivan?"

She matched my earlier smirk and topped it with… *silence.*

My left eye flickered at the clever tactic.

Rather than engage her in a topic she'd used to snare me, I demanded, "Why am I at Langley? The Secret Service isn't overseen by the CIA."

"I'm merely your courier, Mr. O'Donnelly. I was told to bring you here, and bring you here I have."

Here was a distinctly unimpressive workspace. I'd have preferred the usual non-entity office the NSA set me up in. At least there, I got windows.

Instead, a whiteboard covered one wall where, in a regular room, there'd have been some escape from the sea of blandness. In front of the whiteboard was a desk, which she pointed to.

"I assume you wish to use your own rig?" she questioned, watching as I walked over to the desk.

I dipped my chin in agreement.

On the surface, I found an envelope with my name on it. Without awaiting further instructions from Black, I tore it open and uncovered a note.

Dear Mr. O'Donnelly,

Operation: Eagle's Claw functions under the highest security clearances.

You are, by this point, aware that your family will pay the price if you decide to:

A: Defect;

B: Sell proprietary information belonging to the United States government to a foreign entity;

C: Manipulate any code you see here and use it for your own purpose and/or gain.

The rules of the game have not changed, Mr. O'Donnelly.

Yours faithfully,

Sheridan Reinier

Director of the Central Intelligence Agency

BELOW, there were details of the comms platform that had been developed by Langley and my task ahead. I scanned them, but my attention returned to the signature.

Reinier—I mentally sneered—*as if I bowed to him anyway.*

The piece of shit was a New World Sparrow, so I didn't know where he got off pretending that he was working to 'secure' the president. And that shit about using or manipulating their jackass code for my own purpose when he was selling his agents as sex slaves if they didn't behave? Where did he get off on that?

Still scoffing, I cast a look at Black. "I'd like to make it known that the rules of the game have definitely changed."

For the first time, her brow furrowed in confusion. "Excuse me?"

I waggled the letter at her. "Your boss. Mr. Reinier. He wrote that, 'The rules of the game have not changed.' That's a lie.

"This relationship was established between the NSA and me. Not the CIA."

"You serve at the government's pleasure, Mr. O'Donnelly."

My top lip quirked up. "Thank God I don't or I'd be wearing a shitty suit like yours as well."

Though irritation flashed in her expression, I ignored her and started going through my mission details more precisely.

With the information in hand, I cracked my knuckles twice, cricked my neck on each side, and began the process of unveiling my laptop.

When it was on the table, I waggled the cord at Black. "Make yourself useful."

While she glowered at me, she did as asked, and once I was plugged in, a few moments of exploring my environs had me taking over the hidden speakers and microphones in the room.

Only when *noxxious* was blaring from the speakers at a volume that was loud enough to make my ears bleed was I ready to start playing.

Because, as the director had said, this was a game.

And whether he knew it or not, I'd already won round one.

6

CONOR

WARRIOR'S DANCE - THE PRODIGY

THREE HOURS LATER

RIGGS' head popped around the door, her brow puckered as she watched me dig into a mega slice of pizza. "Still uncaring about damaging your hearing, I see," she chided.

Immediately, the volume of the music dropped.

I didn't bother pouting—tonight's job was definitely complete.

"I do my best work when my eardrums could burst," I mocked as I devoured more of my snack.

"Three hours, Conor? Really?" She wasn't talking about the pizza.

"What did you want me to do? Take my time?" I quipped, taking another bite that was slathered in pepperoni. "You didn't have to drag my ass to Langley. We wasted time, taxpayer dollars, and increased my carbon footprint by flying me here."

Riggs, to Black, huffed. "He's always this annoying, yes."

She rubbed her ear. "As I've learned over the past couple hours."

"How long was the team working on that?" I questioned.

"We had a team of thirty working twelve-hour rolling shifts for the past ten weeks, twenty-four hours a day." Riggs pursed her lips. "How hard was it to break in?"

"On a scale of the embassy in Mumbai or the attack on JFK Airport?"

She blinked. "That easy?"

I shrugged.

I hadn't even needed to break out the worm to get into the comms platform.

If this was what they were throwing at the president's security, then it was no wonder the First Lady had been murdered.

An annoyed breath rattled from her. "You made notes?"

"Of course." I tipped my chin at Black. "Gave them to her."

"We appreciate your service," Riggs said flatly, sounding anything but appreciative.

"Hey, don't shoot the messenger. Be grateful that the president isn't dead because you guys developed a shitty comms platform." I bared my teeth at her. "You can spin everything positively if you try, Riggs."

She huffed. "See him out, Agent Black, if you would."

Black didn't answer, didn't even nod.

Curious.

Before she could turn and leave, I queried, "Since when did you get pally with the CIA?"

"Since the First Lady's death, inter-agency cooperation is at an all-time high." It was a standard response.

Bullshit.

I narrowed my eyes at them both, well aware that something was going on here and that neither would tell me what.

Lips pursed, I carried on chewing the pizza I'd had Black supply me with before I'd finished worming my way into Eagle's Claw just in case they thought they could deny me food after I beat their asses—I deserved a fucking snack after that hot-shit display of cracking genius —and I watched Riggs depart while Black strode over to me.

"You're not her inferior," I said once I was done chewing.

That had her arching a brow. "Says who?"

"Says me. So why is she bossing you around, getting you to escort me out?"

Black smiled. "Are you ready to leave, Mr. O'Donnelly?"

Not for the first time, that smile put me on edge.

"Am I going to be allowed to leave?" I queried, my voice unnaturally calm.

"There are many exits from this building," she demurred. "We will be leaving via a different one than where we entered earlier."

Uncertain why that both answered my question and didn't, I got to my feet, rubbed my hands on a paper napkin that had come with the pizza box, and I grabbed my laptop bag, which I'd stowed away after I'd completed my task.

Case in hand, I checked the time and saw that it didn't line up with the clock on the wall.

Frowning, I rubbed my forehead and followed Black out of the now-silent room.

The halls were empty.

It was nine-forty AM according to the wall clock. Ten-forty according to my watches.

This place should have always been ticking, but it was nine-forty in the goddamn morning, and there wasn't a soul around.

Over the years of dealing with the government, I'd come to learn that as discomforting as life in the mob was, it was a kinder fate.

The mob would only torture and kill you.

The government would torture you, kill you, erase you, defame your name, malign your family, and maybe toss a couple of your brothers or sisters in jail at the same time.

"Fucking government," I mumbled under my breath. "No wonder I have authority issues."

The greasy pizza started to settle heavily in my gut, making me wish I hadn't eaten the damn thing in the first place.

With every step I took, my level of unease grew as I failed to pass a single soul until, finally, I saw someone.

A guard.

Eyes blank, focus straight ahead. Black suit, black tie, white shirt. Translucent earpiece. Brown hair, a forgettable face.

Black didn't nod at him, just went to the door and opened it.

As she walked in, she held the door for me, her gaze locked on mine in a silent order to follow.

I wasn't a moron—this wasn't a battle I needed to die fighting—so I traipsed in after her.

The second I did, I found a man standing by a wall of windows that overlooked a parking lot.

It, too, was empty.

What the fuck was going on here?

Since when was CIA HQ a ghost town?

Had there been a nuclear strike and I hadn't heard it over *noxxious*?

Black cleared her throat in a quiet prompt as she closed the door. I half expected her to step behind it but she didn't. She remained in the room with us.

"How's your first time at Langley been, Mr. O'Donnelly?"

"May I ask with whom I'm speaking?" I inquired politely once the stranger at the other end of the room finished his spiel.

His answer wasn't forthcoming, so I strode toward the table that filled up most of the cavernous area and set my briefcase on it.

The table had to seat at least eighty people but only the three of us shared the same breathing space.

Because no one had pulled a gun on me yet—*there was still time*—and because I was in a boardroom and not a cell, I dragged out a chair, sank back into it, and kicked up my feet.

Black sighed at the sight, much as she'd done earlier when I'd done the same in that other barren office. "Director Reinier is gracing you with this meeting."

My brow puckered at that.

Reinier.

The director of the CIA.

Here.

In front of me.

The man who'd sold Star out.

For the first time in my life, my brain froze.

Sometimes, it worked so fast that it outpaced my heartbeat, but at that moment, it literally stilled.

Was this what impending death felt like, or maybe I was just dealing with an aneurysm?

But my eyes were working.

My ears too.

I could still taste the spice from the pepperoni, and the air conditioning was on high for some bizarre reason considering we were in the depths of winter, and my nose discerned the faint notes of the aftershave I'd sprayed on earlier.

No, I *was* alive. I wasn't dying.

Had I just entered a room where one of Star's mortal enemies was breathing and existing?

One who was within arm's reach…?

Fuck.

7

CONOR

Conor O'Donnelly

REINIER STOPPED STARING at the parking lot and turned around to face me. His gaze flickered over Black. "How long did it take him, agent?"

"Around one hundred and sixty minutes, director."

"That's… disappointing."

Still with my feet on the desk despite my discomposure, I shrugged. "I thought my work was superb actually."

Reinier's mouth twitched—less in humor and more in annoyance. "I'm sure you're aware that we'd have preferred the platform we've been developing for months to be more difficult to penetrate than it was."

"When you terrify a bunch of kids into making software for you, what do you expect? And what the hell were you thinking about giving them the go-ahead to work on a multicast transmission? What are we? Back in the days of *Myspace*?" I scoffed.

Reinier's nostrils flared. "Agent Riggs warned me of your manners, Mr. O'Donnelly—"

"I'm sure I lived up to them."

"She certainly didn't downplay them. Still, you've been of great service to your country today. The nation can't thank you, but I can."

Like I gave a fuck.

Bored, I drawled, "Do I get a medal?"

"I'm told that Agent Black gave you pizza."

I snorted. "Funny." I kicked my legs down from the table. "Why's the whole place dead?"

"That has nothing to do with you."

"It doesn't? Is Black going to kill me when I get back in that black, nondescript car?"

"No. We still have use of your services."

"Reassuring. Why does the government never ask me to build software for them, only crack it?" I mused aloud.

"Because we live in hope that we will craft something that even the great aCooooig can't crack, and we'd prefer for you not to have an in." Reinier raised a hand, clearly indicating that he wanted me to shake it.

Somehow that, more than anything, had me freaking the fuck out.

Star wanted this man dead.

She wanted him to suffer.

I wasn't even armed.

My only weapons were two fists, the laptop case in my hand, and the pizza that was curdling in my gut which was making me nauseated.

None of those options would satisfy her. But God, though she'd cut me off her team when she'd ghosted me, I was still on her side.

My hesitation was too long. The director cleared his throat at me in a silent command.

Rattled, I strode forward.

In the back of my mind, I became aware that Agent Black was following me. For every step I took, she took one too.

Was this it?

Was she going to shoot me when I was otherwise engaged?

Was the HQ a ghost town so they could sweep my body from the building with no one the wiser?

Confused, on edge, and torn, I held out my hand to take his, but before I could, something brick-like was in her grasp as Black swept my arm aside.

When the tool collided with the director's abdomen, I blinked in shock then watched as the electrical current zapped through his veins, bringing him to his knees.

My own experimentations with electricity let me know this was double the voltage normally used in a Taser gun.

His expression of surprise would have been hilarious if I wasn't perplexed as fuck.

I jerked back, unsure what the hell was going on, and watched as Reinier face-planted into the carpet, still twitching as she continued to tase him. Twice as long as usual.

Bewildered, I turned to Black, half-expecting the same treatment, but instead, she'd produced a gun from inside her boxy jacket and was holding it out for me.

"Though she's ghosted both of us, I know Star would prefer it if you did the honors."

8

TEXT CHAT

PAST

STAR: *Remember I told you that I promised to reunite every trafficking victim of the Sparrows with their families?*

Conor: *I do. You rammed the memory home with the image of making the head of the CIA suck off his own dick-less stump. Lol.*

Star: *I do these things to train your memory.*

Conor: *So kind. The nightmares were just for shits and giggles?*

Star: *You got it.*

Conor: *What about the reunions? That's a hell of a process in itself.*

Star: *I know. But I was thinking... I found Katina because I was tracking a cargo ship. The Sparrows had a manifesto of women on board. If they did that for one shipment, surely they did it for others.*

Conor: *Makes sense. How did you come across the manifesto?*

Star: *More by luck than management.*

Conor: *How?*

Star: *It was a listing on the Silk Road.*

Conor: *You bought it?*

Star: *Yeah.*

Conor: *Who was the seller?*

Star: *Just some kid who'd hacked a phone and was selling on someone's ID.*

Conor: *Did you buy anything else from the same seller?*

Star: *I bought a username and password for an email account, but it wasn't an easily recognizable email service and it definitely didn't work with POP or IMAP protocols.*

Conor: *So, it led nowhere?*

Star: *The email was a dead end, but I figured it was because the information was five years old. The cargo ship manifesto led me to Katina, though.*

Conor: *How?*

Star: *Her mom was on there. When I found her, she'd already been sold, wedded, impregnated, and had died. Katina was in an orphanage by that point.*

Conor: *And you rode in and saved her.*

Star: *Sometimes I think she saved me.*

Conor: *Did the Sparrows deal in Baltic brides?*

Star: *No. Sex slaves.*

Conor: *So why did they sell her then? How do you know there was a sale? Did you find a payment trail?*

Star: *No. I guess I just assumed. Back then I didn't know as much about their activities. Plus, Alessa... You know her, right?*

Conor: *Katina's sister, of course. Another Sparrows' victim. :(*

Star: *Yeah. :/ She confirmed that was what her mom intended. She sent money back home too.*

Conor: *Doubt the Sparrows gave her anything from that transaction.*

Star: *Maybe her husband loved her. I got mine to do anything I wanted. By the end.*

Conor: *Fucks me in the head to think you married your buyer.*

Star: *I killed him too.*

Conor: *That freaks me out less.*

Star: *Good to know lol.*

Conor: *So you want to find more of these manifestos?*

Star: *I was thinking that was a start.*

Conor: *It's a needle in a haystack.*

Star: *I know, but we have the original manifesto. I tracked maybe five of the women, but I got sidetracked with Katina and stopped heading down that path and focused on the Sparrows, not their victims.*

Conor: *Why are you shifting gears now?*

Star: *You said you'd help.*

Conor: *And I will.*

Star: *Plus, I told Dead To Me about this situation.*

Conor: *Why don't you call her by her name?*

Star: *Habit. I'm Lodestar to her and she's Dead To Me to me.*

Conor: *It's such a mouthful.*

Star: *Lol. More like a bunch of letters to type.*

Conor: *What's her real name?*

Star: *Cin.*

Conor: *What did you get her doing?*

Star: *She works with the CIA.*

Conor: *Okaaay. Is this about the pokers again?*

Star: *Maybe. She's more like a satellite of theirs now.*

Conor: *You want her back in the field?*

Star: *That's not doable with her schedule.*

Conor: *Yes, I'm sure her kill-for-hire business is booming.*

Star: *Oh, it is. She was complaining about a gift bag shortage or something yesterday.*

Conor: *That's such a weird thing to do.*

Star: *Everyone has their MO. It's called an MO for a reason.*

Conor: *I picked up on that.*

Star: *Cin has family in the field. Family that's friendly with me.*

Conor: *Friendly enough to spy for you?*

Star: *Uh-huh. We served in Afghanistan together.*

Conor: *Why have you never called on her before?*

Star: *Because Cin hadn't told me what went down with her cousin in Baghdad.*

Conor: *She was in Iraq?*

Star: *Yup.*

Conor: *What happened? Was she a sex slave too? (You know, it's only since you came into my world that these questions have become commonplace.)*

Star: *(My bad.) And no. She was demoted.*

Conor: *Why?*

Star: *She came forward with some information about the mistreatment of prisoners of war under her CO's custody.*

Conor: *And they demoted her?*

Star: *Not technically.*

Conor: *Meaning?*

Star: *Meaning 'demotion' can come in many ways.*

Conor: *So... she was given desk duty instead of active jobs?*

Star: *Yeah.*

Conor: *And she's bitter?*

Star: *Oh, yeah. The Blacks are a family of hardcore soldiers. They've served the country for five generations. Don't even ask them about the Civil War. I swear to fuck they know which of their relatives served where.*

Conor: *Jesus.*

Star: *Yeah, it's hella boring. BUT, they're fuckers you want on your side.*

Conor: *And this other Black is on your side?*

Star: *Yup. If I help her get a promotion.*

Conor: *How do you do that?*

Star: *:d Guess?*

Conor: *Sticking pokers up Reinier's ass and making him suck his stump?*

Star: *You're quick. I'll give you that.*

Conor: *My teachers always said I'd go far.*

Star: *I bet.*

Conor: *What's this Black's name?*

Star: *Temper.*

Conor: *She was christened that?*

Star: *Not everyone's christened, you Irish heathen.*

Conor: *So that's on her birth certificate.*

Star: *Nah. Her full name's Temperance but she's about as temperate as a Category 7 hurricane.*

Star: *So... with Temper on the case, plus you, me, and Cin too, maybe we can uncover something?*

Conor: *You're sure we can trust her?*

Star: *We can. She hates Reinier almost as much as I do. She's a better person than me or Cin though. A real soldier.*

Conor: *Isn't it unwise to trust her?*

Star: *She views the current leadership as enemies of the state, Conor. Who better to help us take them down?*

Conor: *Fair point. Send me the manifesto?*

Star: *Sure.*

Conor: *I'd like to look at the info you have for the email and password too, please.*

Star: *I'll send it over as well.*

Star: *Conor?*

Conor: *Hmm?*

Star: *Thank you.*

9

CONOR

Conor O'Donnelly

"WHO ARE YOU?"

Black clucked her tongue. "We don't really have time for this. Star would probably have told you I was called Temper."

My brows rose as the text conversation Star and I had about a woman called Temper rammed me in the frontal lobe. "You're related to Dead To Me?"

To none of my brothers would I admit that I croaked out those words.

She winked. "First cousins."

Though I was relieved to know that she was on 'Team Star,' I was still confused as fuck.

Reinier groaned and a puddle of piss soon joined him on the floor.

Grimacing and taking a step back, I demanded, "What the hell is going on? Is this a trap?"

"Not for you," she drawled then kicked out her foot and aimed it at the director's head. "God, I've been wanting to do that for a fucking lifetime." She clicked her neck and bounced on her toes before slamming him in the side like he was a football she wanted soaring through the goalposts at MetLife Stadium.

Brow still furrowed, I rasped, "This has to be a setup?" Either that or a goddamn joke.

"Meh, less of a setup. More a fortuitous chain of events."

"Not for him."

"For us. For Star. Definitely not for him." She shoved the gun at me. "Do it. She'll appreciate it."

"She won't," I predicted, pressing my hands back against my chest to avoid the weapon.

Team Star or not, the woman was completely deranged.

How had Star described her?

Yeah, that was it—as temperate as a Category 7 hurricane.

Which, considering Cat 7 was only a hypothetical, didn't say much for this super soldier's sanity.

My refusal had her scowling. "If you're too chicken shit—"

"What is this? Kindergarten?" I laughed. "I'm very comfortable in my masculinity, agent, so you can't peer pressure me into killing him. Star wants him dead, sure, but she's got a plan. No smart man gets in the way of a woman with a plan."

Her gaze locked on me for a handful of moments. "I can't deny you're smart. Tonight alone proved that. They really expected the Eagle's Claw platform to hold up under your cracking."

"This wasn't a part of the scheme?"

"Nah. *This* is improv. Fortuitous chain of events, remember?"

"Nothing is ever that fortuitous," I drawled, peering around the boardroom. "What's going on, Temper? Why am I here? Why did he want to speak to me? The head of the NSA doesn't shake my hand every time I work on a case for him."

She hitched a shoulder. "You're lucky that I wormed my way onto this division at Star's request. That guard outside the door was supposed to take you out."

"For dinner and dancing would be wishful thinking, I suppose?"

"Very wishful thinking."

"I knew my gut was right."

"Why do you think I got you the pizza?"

"Last meal just in case this didn't work out? Except this isn't a plan, is it? It's improv."

She clicked her fingers. "Exactly. They wanted you to be incapable of cracking the platform, then they were going to kill you so you couldn't discuss Eagle's Claw with anyone. The place is a ghost town so no one would see you come or go."

"The coders saw me."

"The coders don't count. You'd be a cautionary tale of what happens when they don't behave. Plus, that kid, the emo one, was supposed to be the next you."

Ego tasered to shreds, worse than Reinier's current state, I scoffed, "How the fuck could anyone believe that piece of shit messaging service would withstand a cracker?"

There was always someone better than you out there—I'd been battling Star for that crown for the past eighteen months and had no trouble sharing it when the situation warranted it, but that code had been a sieve.

I'd have been able to build something better when I was twelve.

Temper shrugged. "They manipulate the media so much that they've started to believe their own fake news. Either that or you're just as good as Star says you are."

That pricked my attention. "She's talked to you about me?"

"She has. But this isn't Kindergarten, remember? I'm not going to tell you if she likes you." Her eye roll told me what she thought about that. "What are we doing with Reinier then?" Her hand tightened around the gun when he groaned and started to wriggle on the floor. "I could always shoot him—"

"He's Star's," I dismissed, reaching for her wrist and holding it firmly in my grip.

She tipped her head to the side. "She's gone AWOL."

"I'm well aware of that," I groused.

"So you want us to hold him captive for her?"

I hitched a shoulder. "I can put out feelers. Maybe if she knows we've got him, she'll come home."

"She isn't a lost cat who'll come sniffing around for kibble,

O'Donnelly! Jesus!" Temper triggered the Taser again when Reinier started flopping around harder than before.

When he released a shrill cry, I spat, "Watch it! The guard will come in."

She sniffed. "If I do this, if I help you keep him alive rather than just kill the bastard, you won't like it. Star won't either."

I glowered at her. "If you 'do' what?"

"Get him away from this place."

"We have to leave him here and she'll—"

Temper shook her head. "I'm burned now. If I don't handle this situation, I'm toast."

I hissed under my breath. "Your improv sucks."

"Yeah, that's why I plan everything down to the detail." She scowled. "Usually."

"Stick to your day job in the future, huh?" I sniped, pinching the bridge of my nose. "Who would you call for help? I can't involve my family in this. They don't even know I have a sideline with the government—"

"You don't bring in kids to deal with this kind of shit," she pshawed.

"Kids?" I snarled. "My brothers—"

"You own New York. Maybe half the East Coast, buddy. I'm talking about the *big* boys."

"The Camorra?" I countered in confusion.

"The Union."

"The who?"

She ignored me. Tucking the gun back in her pocket, she withdrew her cell phone. I watched, finding faint amusement in her naivety as she tipped the screen away so I couldn't see her input the code.

"548804," I stated.

Temper glared at me but stopped angling her phone down. She dialed a number from memory then, to the phone, and not to me, drawled, "In our Brothers we trust."

10

TEXT CHAT

PAST

STAR: *What do you know of Prince Edward of Midlothian?*

Conor: *Is this a random question, or does it have a point? I'm trying to hack into that bank account you sent me yesterday.*

Star: *Can't you multitask?*

Conor: *For a standard bank account, it has a lot of protection. Especially considering it's not based in Switzerland.*

Star: *Ah, the Swiss. I love their intricate blending of abiding and ignoring laws to do whatever the fuck they want for whoever's willing to pay a high enough price.*

Conor: *And people think they're neutral.*

Star: *That's the best part. LOL. Hiding in plain sight.*

Conor: *I have to focus.*

Star: *Focus later. I think I have a way of accessing the accounts I need, just bear with me. So answer my question.*

Conor: *God, you're bossy.*

Star: *You're Irish. You're used to bossy women. It's hardwired into your DNA that you react when a woman bosses you around.*

Conor: *Oh, I react. I just can't react how I want to through a computer screen.*

Star: *That again?*

Conor: *Lol.*

Star: *You're proving it's true that men are obsessed with sex.*

Conor: *I AM a man.*

Star: *I know. You can't help it. Still. Try.*

Conor: *LMAO. You're the one who lets me think about you in the tub. I think I'm controlling myself very well for a man whose BFF is his right hand.*

Star: *Why not your left? I thought you were a southpaw.*

Conor: *I'm ambidextrous.*

Star: *Really?*

Conor: *Yes, another secret only you know.*

Star: *Why is it a secret?*

Conor: *I'm a man of mystery.*

Star: *You're an odd duck is what you are. Not sure if you're a man of mystery…*

Conor: *My ego will never heal from that cutting slight.*

Star: *You need to stop watching so much Bridgerton, dude.*

Conor: *YOU told me to watch it!!*

Star: *I didn't think you'd get into it.*

Conor: *Like you didn't.*

Star: *Nah. Too many crusty genitals for my taste. That dude's hot though. The duke.*

Conor: *I agree. I hope he's the next Bond.*

Star: *When your brother IS a Bond, how can you even like that shit?*

Conor: *You're a Bourne. I like that too. I don't discriminate.*

Star: *I'm more of a Black Widow but without supernatural talents. Damn, I'd have managed to cause some shit if I did.*

Star: *The main issue, of course, is that they put that actress chick in such a girly outfit. Total BS.*

Conor: *That actress chick just happens to be Scarlett Johansson.*

Star: *That's her name?*

Conor: *Lol, yes.*

Conor: *You're hotter than her though.* ^^

Star: *Is that a compliment?*

Conor: *She's like the hottest woman on the planet to most men. So, yes.*

Star: *Hmm. Okay. Thank you.*

Conor: *You're welcome.*

Star: *I suppose you're hotter than the duke too.*

Conor: *Thank you!*

Star: *You're welcome. Now that we've gotten that off our chests, can we talk about Prince Edward of Midlothian?*

Conor: **sighs**

Conor: *You want to talk about a crusty old white guy?*

Star: *I do.*

Conor: *I know he's got a gambling problem.*

Star: *How do you know that?*

Conor: *I own shares in a casino in Macau.*

Star: *Lol, shut up. You don't.*

Conor: *I do.*

Star: *You do not.*

Conor: *I fucking do!*

Star: *Why?*

Conor: *Because.*

Star: *WHY?*

Conor: *Because it's a great investment?*

Star: *Isn't that Triad territory?*

Conor: *They owed me a favor.*

Star: *What did you do? And, hell, WHEN did you do it?*

Conor: *I know it comes as a shock to you, but I did have a life before I knew you.*

Star: *Spill.*

Conor: *Only if you spill in return…*

Star: *Deal. When, why, what, and how?*

Conor: *I leveraged some information about four months or so before you came along and headbutted through my firewalls.*

Star: *Half the story much? And I didn't headbutt anything. I slipped inside like a ninja.*

Conor: *You left a mile-wide gash behind you. Nothing about your entry or exit was discreet.*

Star: *Filthy. Lies.*

Conor: *Filthy. Truth.*

Conor: *Anyway, I thought you wanted to talk about crusty old white guys.*

Star: *I did, but now I'm curious. Back to the topic at hand. What information did you leverage?*

Conor: *The Sparrows were on the periphery of my attention for a while, I think. I'm pretty certain this guy was shafted by them. He proclaimed his innocence and I managed to come across the CCTV footage that confirmed his alibi.*

Star: *That was handy.*

Conor: *:P*

Star: *Don't show me your tongue. Waggle it so I understand. Did you make a deep fake?*

Conor: *Sort of.*

Star: *I didn't know you had those types of skills.*

Conor: *There's plenty you don't know about me lol.*

Star: *I'm not sure I like that.*

Conor: *HA! It's not as if you're an open book.*

Star: *True. Was it falsified or not?*

Conor: *The dates were. I knew he was innocent though.*

Star: *How?*

Conor: *Because Da had killed the guy this Triad allegedly had.*

Star: *Lol! That would do it.*

Conor: *Right? Anyway, the Triads aren't like the Russians and the Italians. They stick to their own and they listen to China way more than even the Russians listen to Moscow. I figured it'd be a good thing to have them in my back pocket.*

Star: *It worked.*

Conor: *Not really. They gave me the shares instead lol.*

Conor: *Smart bastards.*

Star: *How many shares do you own?*

Conor: *Thirty-five percent.*

Star: *Yowza. That's some gift.*

Conor: *He was serving life with no chance of parole. Plus, he was related to the Dragon Head. They're like us—the deeper the ties to the leader, the more status you have.*

Star: *Hmm. Okay. Back to Prince Edward.*

Conor: *What about him?*

Star: *He's on a council of some variation.*

Conor: *That's news to me.*

Star: *Me too.*

Conor: *What makes you think he is?*

picture uploaded

Conor: *Huh.*

Star: *Huh.*

Conor: *You know who these four are?*

Star: *Sort of.*

Conor: *Meaning?*

Star: *I know who three are.*

Conor: *Give me names. I recognize the one who likes to think he's the King of Greece.*

Star: *Prince Ludwig—he's the one to the left. Prince Edward of Midlothian is on the right. Beside him is Ke Jintao. He's a vice chairman of the CCP's National Security Commission.*

Conor: *Who's the last guy?*

Star: *That's the only one I'm struggling with.*

Conor: *Where did you get this photo?*

Star: *You know Bear, Rex's father, left him a motel room key?*

Conor: *Lol, I know who Bear is. The ex-Prez of the Satan's Sinners' MC. Duh.*

Star: *Smart ass.*

Conor: *You know it. His room was filled with Sparrows' intel, no?*

Star: *Yes.*

Conor: *Interesting.*

Star: *You heard of the United Brotherhood?*

Conor: *Sounds like a team who'd play Dungeons and Dragons online lol.*

Star: *I told you not to diss D&D.*

Conor: *I'm not dissing dick. I told you I'll play with you!*

Star: *Just making sure.*

Conor: *You're the one who used to pretend you weren't into that stuff.*

Star: *A woman's allowed to change her mind.*

Conor: *So's a man lol. But to answer your question, yes. I've heard of them. Based in Russia. They fund the Pauks, don't they?*

Star: *Those jackasses who claim they don't work for the state but do?*

Conor: *The United Brotherhood isn't the state. Technically.*

Star: *It's all in the technicalities.*

Star: *I've got a headache from this conversation. I feel like I take one step forward and then something comes to light and everything goes to shit.*

Conor: *You're almost there.*

Star: *Maybe.*

Conor: *I'm guessing Googling a reverse image search didn't pull anything? :P*

Star: *No. Lol. NSA facial recognition software didn't work either.*

Conor: *Dayum.*

Conor: *I wish I could help.*

Star: *Me too. But never mind. I just wanted to check.*

Conor: *What does the United Brotherhood have to do with the Sparrows?*

Star: *I'm not sure. I just know Bear was investigating them.*

Conor: *Want me to put feelers out on them?*

Star: *Not if they've got ties to the Pauks. We don't need those fucking spiders crawling over our shit.*

Conor: *You wound me with your lack of faith.*

Star: *Pfft. I will kick your ass if they uncover your feelers.*

Conor: *That would bring you to my apartment lol. I think I wouldn't be too unhappy about that.*

Star: *Don't even joke about this.*

Conor: *I won't, I won't. Sorry.*

Star: *Never mind. **sighs***

Conor: *Are the United Brotherhood allies with the Sparrows?*

Star: *Bear didn't seem to think so but I'm not sure. I haven't figured out who his source is yet, who was helping him with some of the IT shit.*

Star: *If they're not trustworthy, then all his intel could be BS. Plus, not everything he pinned on his wall of death was correct.*

Conor: *Like?*

Star: *He believed the president was a Sparrow. Their commander-in-chief. We know that was Justin DeLaCroix. The chief justice.*

Conor: *That's disappointing that not everything is accurate.*

Star: *Tell me about it. I almost cried when I saw that. So I have to be careful with what I read. I can't just accept it as fact.*

Conor: *Probably for the best. Though it would speed things up if you could.*

Conor: *I think you need a break.*

Star: *Probably.*

Conor: *Feel like playing* Halo *now?*

Star: *Why not? Not getting anything else done. FML.*

Conor: *We'll get there, Star. I promise.*

Star: *Thanks, Con. <3*

Conor: *:)*

11

———

CONOR

Conor O'Donnelly

PRESENT DAY

FORTY-EIGHT HOURS LATER, after I staggered out of the car, I hovered in place on the sidewalk as it immediately took off.

Denny was back on the door and he called out, "You okay there, Mr. O'Donnelly, sir?"

I squinted at him. "Thanks, Denny. Could you get me a cab?"

His smile was hesitant. "Sure thing, sir."

I cringed at the title.

"It's Conor. Remember?" I mumbled. "Sorry about the other night."

"That's fine, Mr. Conor. Did you watch the game yesterday?"

My lips twisted. "Nah. Did the Rangers win?"

"The Islanders skated circles around them and shut them out."

"Good, good."

His eyes flared. "Everything all right, Mr. Conor? You usually love the Rangers—" Before I had to answer, a cab rolled up in front of me. "Where do you want to go?"

I blinked at him, uncertain of *where* I wanted to be, just aware that I needed not to be at home.

That was why I blurted out Aoife and Finn's address. It felt like a second home in the city, and I needed not to be alone right now.

Head ringing, I sat down heavily in the backseat and waved farewell to Denny as the driver got me away from my building.

As he wended us through the horrific traffic, I accepted that a part of my mind was still functioning. Aoife and Finn's place was where I needed to be, but I sure as fuck didn't want Temper Black rolling me up to their brownstone.

Sure, she could have found their address easily, but I wasn't about to hand over catnip to a lion.

In our Brothers we trust.

Just a nonsense saying, I'd thought at first.

As someone who lived his life by that creed, I'd almost relaxed when she'd uttered those words. Who else did I trust apart from my brothers and sisters-in-law, after all?

But she wasn't talking about regular *brothers*.

About blood.

She was talking about the United fucking Brotherhood.

I rubbed my forehead, not even wincing when I dragged my fingertips over the area that was busted from Maverick's knuckles. If anything, it just merged with the pain that had taken residence in my skull since Temper had drawn me into a *plot*.

And I wasn't talking about a fictional device, either.

This was a good, old-fashioned *plot*.

We pulled up outside the brownstone before I could start to feel sick again. I was a mischievous man by nature, but the last forty-eight hours had rattled me as little else could.

I'd learned long ago never to fuck with the government and that alphabet agencies required cautionary handling. Last night, I'd set fire to both those rules and hadn't even bothered to piss on the blaze I'd started.

At this very moment, I could be an enemy of the state and I wouldn't even know until Homeland Security came knocking on my door.

But worse than all that?

Star was close with someone in a group she'd spoken to me about.

And now I was in cahoots with them.

Cahoots.

Was it any wonder I was nauseated?

I was in the middle of a conspiracy, for fuck's sake.

Almost falling out of the cab after I paid my fare, I tumbled into Inessa, who, like a house of cards, knocked into her baby sister. Somehow, Eoghan caught both of them and propped them upright.

"Watch where you're fucking going, Kid!" he sniped before turning to Inessa and demanding, "Did he hurt you?"

Her laughter was soft. "He just surprised me. You're okay too, aren't you, Vicky?"

Victoria eyed me. "I'm fine but Conor doesn't look fine. Are you hungover?"

I found myself at the center of the trio's attention which, fuck my life, meant… "Is it Saturday?"

Eoghan peered at me. "Jesus, you really *are* hungover."

"I'm not hungover," I snapped. "I've just lost track of my days."

Inessa, kindly, informed me, "Yes, Conor, it's Saturday. Do you remember that Aoife wanted us to come over for lunch today and not dinner?"

I didn't remember that.

"Why?" I queried, brow puckered.

Eoghan grumbled, "Does it matter? Can we get inside? Inessa's freezing."

"I'm not, Eoghan," she chided.

"You are."

"Can we go in before they start doing this again?" Victoria groaned at me.

"Doing what?"

She huffed. "Inessa thinks she might be pregnant and Eoghan is treating her like she needs to be wrapped in cotton and both of them think they're hiding this from me when they're totally not."

Eoghan's and Inessa's expressions would have been hilarious if it weren't for the meltdown that was taking place in my brain.

As they gaped at her, I blurted out a laugh and started dragging Victoria with me up the stairs to the house.

The door opened before we could knock and Aoife was there.

Finn had been a wise man marrying her.

She was a haven, not a…

Fuck, whatever Star was.

And that definitely wasn't a haven.

A headache, yes. A heart attack in the making, *sure*.

"Aoife," I pleaded. "I need a whiskey."

She arched a brow at me. "Fighting fire with fire?"

"No. I'm not drunk." I would be soon, though, if I had my way.

Recognizing that I was being scanned again, I almost turned on my heel and got the hell out of there. I'd expected Aoife to be alone, the house empty apart from Jake as Finn should have been at the office. Instead, my whole fucking family was about to convene at the brownstone.

Ordinarily, it'd be a hoot.

Today, it was a nightmare.

Aoife grabbed my arm as if she knew I was on the brink of running off, and she dragged me over the threshold. "Head into the kitchen, girls. Eoghan, Finn's in his man cave." To me, she ordered, "Come with me."

I didn't argue because she was taking me away from the mass of humanity that was the O'Donnelly clan in full force. The only people missing were my mother and Uncle Paddy, for fuck's sake. I couldn't have gone anywhere worse for some quiet time.

When she guided me into a living room I hadn't been in before, I frowned. "Where are we?"

"Existentially or within the house?" was her droll retort.

"Within the house," I groused.

"It's a guest suite."

"A guest what?"

"For guests to stay in." She studied me. "You're not looking well, Con. I think you should get some rest."

"I'm not hungover," I repeated.

"No, you don't stink of booze. But you look like you're coming off a bender all the same. When was the last time you caught some sleep?" she queried, turning to me. Then, her nose crinkled. "When did you last shower?"

"I don't know," I whispered.

And I didn't.

I just remembered the open space of a field, a shipping container, and a man screaming for his life as he was shoved into the container and then locked inside with packs of MREs and stacks of bottled water.

Then, from out of nowhere, she'd pistol-whipped me and I'd found myself waking up in a jet on a return flight to New York.

Apparently, saying 'goodbye' was too much hard work for Temperance goddamn Black.

When I realized Aoife had been saying my name over and over again, I apologized, "Sorry, Aoife. I'm out of it."

"Conor," she said, her tone careful. "You can talk to me, you know?"

"I'm talking to you now, aren't I?"

"About whatever trouble you're in?"

"I'm not fifteen and dabbling in coke, Aoife," I groused tiredly, tugging away from her hold and scrubbing both hands over my face.

"That wound on your head needs cleaning," she stated. "How did you even get that?"

Hitching a shoulder, I mumbled, "I'll do it later."

"I'll do it now or it'll never get done."

As she grabbed my arm and dragged me into the bathroom, I asked, "Do you manhandle Finn like this?"

"Only when he's being a pain."

"So, all the time then?"

Her lips twitched. "Not all the time. Sometimes, he's very... good."

I groaned. "I don't need to be thinking about you two fucking."

"Who said I was talking about sex?" she scoffed, surprising me by not being flustered.

"That smile said everything," I grumbled as she dragged me to the vanity and propped me against it.

A couple of moments later and thoroughly armed with a first-aid kit, she started cleaning me up after tugging me into a slouched position so she could reach me without having to strain.

As she worked, she stayed quiet, but I knew her brain was ticking. Why wouldn't it be? I was acting out of character. I knew I was.

Maybe that was why I blurted out, "Did you hear about Prince Edward of Midlothian's death?"

She paused in her ministrations. "I did. It was late last year, wasn't it?"

"Yes."

"Were you grieving him or something?"

I got her inference and had to roll my eyes even though they were so dry they scraped against the lids.

"Firstly, I'm not high. I told you that already. Secondly, I'm Irish. We hate the royal family."

"You're about as Irish as this iodine. You O'Donnellys," she said with a chuckle. "What did you bring him up for then?"

Why had I?

"Do you know who the United Brotherhood are?"

"Is that the bank on Columbus and West 67th?"

I genuinely didn't know how to answer that. "I don't think so."

Unless that was their front.

The NSA did shit like that all the time.

I rubbed the back of my neck. "I shouldn't—"

"Shouldn't, what? Tell me anything? Trust me, I'm completely in the dark," she teased. "What do a prince and a bank have to do with anything?"

"Sounds like the punch line to a bad joke," Finn mocked.

I cast a glance at the doorway and found him standing there, one arm against the jamb as he studied us both.

"What happened to your head, Kid?"

I hated that tone of voice. "I'm not nine, Finn."

"You look like you are. I remember that time you came back busted up from fighting with Mark Benedict. Your ma went—" He tensed. Paused.

Aoife heaved an impatient sigh. "You can mention her, Finn. She exists. I'm not unaware of that fact."

"You know I don't like to upset you."

"Then don't freeze up when you mention her name. I know Hitler existed and you can say his name without me bursting into tears."

"There's a difference—"

"Yes, there is, but you freaking out when you mention her is more annoying than upsetting. So finish your sentence."

She ended that with a glower that had me remarking, "I'd do as she says, Finn. She could freeze your balls off with that glare."

Aoife chuckled, and Finn grumpily continued, "Your ma went apeshit over you getting into fights."

"She would, wouldn't she? Her good, *pure* boy suddenly fighting." I let out a bitter laugh. "She had no idea."

Aoife frowned but Finn inserted, "Aoife, leave the grouch with me. I'll get him into bed."

"You're not my type, *deartháir*," I mocked, earning a swat from Aoife on the shoulder and a grumble from Finn as he ambled over and hauled me out of the bathroom as if I were inebriated.

"What's wrong with you?" he sniped in my ear.

"Conor, do you want me to call you when lunch is ready?" Aoife asked, not realizing her husband was whisper-bitching at me. "I made your favorite."

That had me shooting her a loved-up look. The quick movement of my head whipping around had the blood rushing to it as I garbled, "Roasted duck with orange sauce?"

"Yep."

"Consider yourself lucky that someone already smacked your head around or I'd do it for staring at her like that."

Snorting, I leaned more heavily on him as I muttered, "I think I need to crash. Can I eat the leftovers?"

"Of course," she reassured me, but her tone was worried. "I'll set aside a plate for you."

When Finn dumped me on the bed, I half-expected him to go with her, but the pair of them whispered at each other like I was five before she left and he returned to my side.

He dropped down to the other half of the bed, kicked up his heels as he settled back against a pillow, then demanded, "Come on then, talk. Who is it? That Star chick?"

That was when I knew I'd entered a parallel universe.

I started sputtering, but all I could get out was, "You think I have woman troubles?"

"Don't you?"

"No, for fuck's sake."

"I thought she went missing."

"She did."

"Isn't that woman troubles?"

"She didn't run out on me."

That was neither the whole truth nor a lie.

Savannah had told me that she thought the only reason Star would pull away from me was because she'd gotten herself embroiled in Da's death.

That wasn't the same as running out though. At least not in my opinion. And, admittedly, I did tend to cut the witch a lot of slack.

"What's the problem then?"

I flopped onto my back and immediately regretted it when my head pounded. *Jesus, did I have a concussion?* That fucking Temperance.

"If I told you," I clipped, "you wouldn't believe me."

Finn chuckled. "Conor, you're you. I'd believe you just because the shit that happens to you happens to no one else on the planet."

"That's… fair," I admitted with a yawn.

"You should get some sleep," he said irritably. "We can talk later. If the house is empty when you wake up, it's because we've gone out."

I rubbed my eyes again. "Funnily enough, Finn, I think I'd have managed to deduce that by myself."

"Sarcastic ass."

"You know it."

He made to stand, but as his weight dispersed, shifting the mattress, Finn paused. "I heard you mention the United Brotherhood to Aoife."

My eyes popped open. "You overheard that?"

"Yes. Don't bring it up with her again. We can talk about it later—"

Jerking upright, I demanded, "You know who they are?"

"Of course. Anyone involved in banking does."

I heaved an annoyed breath. "This isn't—"

"The bank is a front," he dismissed. "A very powerful front."

"I've never heard of a bank called that."

Hell, after Star had first mentioned the United Brotherhood, I'd searched for it on Google. Nothing had come up. *Nothing.* Certainly no mentions of a fucking bank in Manhattan.

"They're investment bankers. Very niche. We don't come into contact with them as Five Pointers, and as vast as your knowledge base is, Conor, you have to admit that you can cut out things you're not interested in."

I had to concede that point. "Why bother to retain something that isn't important?"

"How do you decide which knowledge is or isn't important at a given time in the future? It's important now, isn't it?"

Another point I had to concede. "Have they approached you?"

"In the early days. Before my association with the O'Donnellys became more known."

"They didn't realize you were Irish Mob?"

"No. After I moved in, your... I mean, Da kept my profile low. Do you remember?"

"I do," I confirmed. "You worked your way up but it was on the down-low, wasn't it? Out of sight, out of mind."

Finn nodded. "He kept me busy with the bookies, only letting me get my hands dirty when he was around, and no one said dick about what happened if he was there.

"My affiliation with the Five Points was undesirable once the United Brotherhood figured out who I was."

"Why?"

"They're pious."

"Pious?" I repeated. "They go to church?"

Finn snorted. "Doubtful. I just mean they consider themselves white hats."

That doubled the ache in my head—I was sure my ears were ringing. In my world, *I* was considered a white hat—I went in and found security flaws.

Blowing out a breath, I rumbled, "Didn't Da believe he wore a white hat?"

"I doubt it. I think Da was many things, but I don't think he'd consider himself as pure as the driven snow."

My hand balled into a fist. "Did you… When they approached you, what did they want?"

"It's like the Freemasons. You scratch my back, I scratch yours."

That made me think of Star. "*Quid pro quo.*"

He hummed. "They're harmless, but they're everywhere in the world of investment banking. It's a shame they realized my affiliation. Would have been a great networking opportunity."

"If they're such good guys, why don't you want Aoife to know about them?"

"Because when you mentioned them, you looked like you could puke. Just because they wore white hats in the past doesn't mean they do now. Aoife's been through enough these past twelve months. I don't want to add to her burden.

"You need to talk about whatever is going on, you talk to me. No judgment, no shit, no griping. I'm your brother, Conor. I can help. Now, get some rest."

I wanted, desperately, to ask him some more questions, but the pull of sleep came at me with the force of Temperance. As he closed the door, my eyelids were already shut and, did I but know it, the nightmares were already beginning to load…

12

CONOR

Conor O'Donnelly

I WOKE up to my nose being pinched.

Then my ear being tugged.

My hand wafted on the mattress as I attempted to stop whoever was gnawing at me while I slept.

My hair was snagged in a starfish hand, grabby fingers that gave me my first clue as to the identity of my attacker, but I stubbornly turned my head aside.

"He won't quit," Finn drawled. "He wants Uncle Kid."

I groaned.

"Uncle Kid is tired, Jake. Very tired."

Jake, ignoring me, started bouncing on the bed, singing, "Smell-ee, Unka Kid, smell-ee." He extended the 'ee' sound until I was sure he was drilling into my eardrums with the syllable.

"You know you need to shower when a toddler says you stink," Finn commented.

Blindly, I flipped him the bird as the bed jostled under Jake's jumps. "The audacity. Jake, I've changed your diapers. You think I stink? You ain't seen nothing, dude."

Obviously unimpressed, a second later, I yowled when those little knees of his landed on my kidneys in payback.

"Stink-ee, stink-ee, Unka Kid!"

Finn snorted. "Be grateful it isn't your junk. He's got no respect for other men's dicks."

"Dick-uh. Dick-uh."

"Ah, shit," Finn complained under his breath as Jake started singing and giggling the word, making it two syllables and not one. "Jake!" Finn raised his voice to be heard over the song I didn't need to hear. "Quit it before Mommy comes and tells me off for using bad words around you."

Jake's soft giggles told me he was well aware that Mommy would tell Daddy off for using bad words and Jake was *here* for it.

With a huff, I rolled over, and because his attention was elsewhere, I managed to scoop him up without him expecting it. He let loose a loud squeal that cascaded into more giggles as I tickled his belly and hefted him in the air until he'd forgotten about bad words.

Squinting at my brother, I asked, "Why are you here?"

"I'm not anywhere I'm not supposed to be."

My squint deepened. "It's too early for philosophical debates."

"I'm not debating anything," Finn retorted, amused. "I'm sitting in *my* guest suite where you passed out *two* goddamn days ago." His head tipped to the side. "Jake was *not* happy about waiting for his Uncle Kid to wake up. Plus, I wanted to check in on you before Aoife did."

"Why would Aoife check in on me?"

He hesitated. "Because she loves you?"

My lips twitched. "I love her too."

"I'll allow it."

I dragged my middle finger along the length of my nose. "What else?"

"We were worried about you."

Hauling my ass to the head of the bed, I snagged Jake into a bear hug then found myself surprised when he settled down too, face nuzzling against my throat, mumbling, "Unka Kid nap time."

Only a kid wouldn't mind that I hadn't showered in four days.

"He's been up since five," Finn reasoned, but his smile was as genuine as it got as he watched his kid.

It was smiles like that I'd kill to protect.

No one had had it easy in my family.

We were rich as fuck but it came at a price.

Until Aoife had come along, I didn't think any of my brothers had really known what happiness even looked like. Then, Aoife had started making that smile appear on Finn's face on a regular basis and we'd realized that we didn't just have to live in misery.

One by one, my brothers had found their women. One by one, those smiles had started becoming a recurring thing.

I was happy to see *their* happiness. Just… was it wrong to want some of that for myself?

"You don't have to worry about me, Finn. I'm a grown-ass man," I told him as I carefully settled my chin atop Jake's head.

I loved my brothers. I'd go to the ends of the earth for them. But for Jake? None of them knew the hell I'd reap for him.

Shit, Shay too.

But Shay was different.

Shay was already formed into the man he'd be one day.

Aela had done a bang-up job with him.

"You're my brother," he stated calmly, the word seeming to slip with more ease off his tongue than usual.

"We're blood," I corrected, wanting to make the distinction.

He cleared his throat. "Yes. Naturally, we worry. Especially after these last couple of months."

I'd lost my shit after Da died. I didn't need him to tell me that. I knew they'd been concerned about me—no sleep, little food, and a lot of work. Grief for me was hectic. Violent.

They just didn't realize I'd been mourning the loss of two people.

My da and Star.

"Things have been rough," I agreed. "But this wasn't about that."

"No. It's about the United Brotherhood and Prince Edward of Midlothian," he mocked. "You have two goose eggs on your head. At least they're symmetrical. You should appreciate that."

My nose crinkled as I reached up to carefully prod them. "I think I might have had a concussion."

He straightened. "And we let you rest? Why the fuck didn't you say anything?"

"Because there was no way in hell I was going to be able to stay awake anyway. Damaged brain or not." Yawning, I closed my eyes. "I'm still exhausted."

"What happened?"

My throat bobbed. "You don't want to know, Finn."

"That bad?"

"Yeah. That bad," I admitted with a sigh.

Silence settled between us as we studied a sleeping Jake.

It enabled me to relax some, to let my brain slowly start to stir to life. I hadn't been firing on all cylinders since the moment Temper had tasered Reinier, had been reacting instead of thinking, but nothing, I slowly accepted, had changed.

Reinier was out of the picture, waiting in the wings for Star to deal with him when she was back in the country.

Temper's position hadn't been burned in the CIA.

When I checked my laptop, I'd know if I had any missed calls from Riggs, but the doors to Finn and Aoife's house hadn't been blown off in a raid while I slept and I hadn't been arrested under the PATRIOT Act, so I had to assume my position as a governmental asset was still in play and I wasn't a wanted man.

That meant I could still go to Moscow—I had permission.

I could see if Star had anything to do with that bombing in Petrovsky Park.

I could pin down my woman at long fucking last because the government had already owed me a goddamn break before they tried to assassinate me for being too good at my job.

It wasn't much of a plan, but it was a start.

Wading around in the mud wasn't enough. I'd made a promise to Katina that I'd find her foster mother, and after the past week, I wasn't going to keep on doing this on my own.

"Don't you want to talk about it?"

Lost in my thoughts, I frowned at him. "About what?"

"The United Brotherhood?"

"No."

"Tough because I have questions. Why did you bring them up with Aoife on Saturday?"

"You ever heard the saying, 'In our Brothers we trust?'"

"No."

So he hadn't gotten in too deeply with them if he didn't know the code Brothers used as a greeting among their own.

For his sake, I was glad.

A knock sounded on the door.

"Come in, babe," Finn called out quietly.

Aoife peered inside, and that same happy smile danced about her lips as she took in the picture of me and Jake together.

I wasn't sure what I'd done to earn Jake's trust, but I treasured it. Always.

A kid's trust was so precious.

I, better than anyone, knew that.

"I have to take a picture," she whispered, stepping over to the bed, phone out, and snapping us before I had a chance to grimace. She moved nearer and passed me her cell. I grinned at the sight even as I wanted to groan at the state of me.

Those goose eggs *weren't* symmetrical. My brother was a goddamn liar.

"Let's not frame that one, huh?"

She snickered. "It's cute. You have matching bedhead which makes sense seeing as he's run screaming from me every time I go near him with a brush. Want me to take him?"

"Nah. It's good."

Her gaze softened. "He loves his Uncle Kid. He did *not* appreciate being kept away from you."

"And I love him."

When Aoife approached Finn and settled herself on his lap, my brother's grin was both smug and contented. As his hands curved around her waist, the deepest, bittersweet, most excruciating dose of envy stirred to life inside me.

It made it easier to say, "I'm going to be leaving the US soon."

Finn stiffened. "What?"

Aoife placed her hand on his shoulder. "Where are you heading? On a vacation at long last?" she teased.

Lying, I nodded.

"What's going on?" Finn griped, clearly not believing that story.

He knew me too well.

"I'm taking your advice, Finn."

"What advice? And why are you taking it on this occasion when you usually ignore me?"

I arched a brow at his agitation. "Why are you so stressed? You weren't this freaked out when Aidan went to Florida for Thanksgiving. Declan's heading to Europe soon—"

"They're them. You're you."

"What does that mean?" I grumbled. "I'm perfectly capable of traveling on my own. I'm not a child."

His unease was annoying, but its source was genuine. "You don't leave."

His words had me blinking. "Huh?"

"You don't leave."

Aoife sensed the rawness in his voice, too, because she cuddled into him. "It's okay, Finn. Conor needs a vacation."

"He's not going on vacation. Conor's a workaholic," he argued, still stiff with tension. "And I didn't advise him to go away. I advised him to go after what belongs to him."

"Which is?" Aoife queried, darting a wary glance between us.

"Lodestar," I said simply.

"That was when I thought she was in goddamn New Jersey! Not fuck knows where," Finn sniped, raking a hand through his hair.

"She's in Russia." I cleared my throat. "I think."

"Russia," he yelled. "You want to go to motherfucking Russia?"

Jake stirred, but he only nuzzled his face deeper into my throat. Finn grimaced apologetically as Aoife tutted him, but even she was starting to appear anxious.

"I don't *want* to go. I *have* to go. I'm sure she's involved in that bombing in Moscow."

His eyes flared wide then immediately shuttered. His fingers raked through his hair again before he started drumming them on Aoife's knee. "Maxim Lyanov is in and out of Moscow."

"You've been watching him?"

"Of course. He has influence over there. Maybe if your ass gets locked up in a gulag in Siberia, I can put pressure on him to have you released."

My lips twitched. "Finn, I didn't know you cared."

His cheeks flushed with color. "Fuck off."

Still smiling, I pressed a kiss to Jake's forehead and gave him a gentle hug.

"Conor?" Aoife asked, her voice quiet.

"Yes, sis?"

"Y-You are coming home, aren't you?"

Finn stiffened. "What are you talking about? Of course, he is."

Ignoring him, I locked my eyes on hers. "Not until I bring Star back with me. She's my penguin," I said simply. "You've all got yours. I want mine so I'm not going to stop until she's here. With me. Understand?"

Her nod was slow in coming but I knew she understood.

A glance at Finn told me he did too.

Begrudgingly.

After the last couple years they'd endured together, how couldn't they understand the importance of being with the right person?

But I was an adult. I didn't need to ask permission to do dick in my life.

Star was mine.

She'd gotten me involved in no less than three conspiracies with repercussions I didn't even want to imagine right now, and I wasn't about to do this on my own.

We were a team. She might have forgotten that because she was an only child and I had brothers coming out of the woodwork, but it was about time that she was reminded of that fact.

Whether she liked it or not.

13

———————

TEXT CHAT

STAR: *Are you angry with your da for cheating on your mom?*

Conor: *Honestly?*

Star: *Why would I want you to lie?*

Conor: *Fair point. Lol.*

Conor: *No. I'm not mad.*

Star: *Why not? You love your ma, don't you?*

Conor: *I do. Even if she is a headcase.*

Star: *To be honest, raising all those boys probably did most of the legwork in making her insane.*

Conor: *True. ;) I, of course, was a saint, but I'm thinking that being kidnapped by Aryans was more of an issue.*

Star: *:/ Forgot about that.*

Conor: *It's not your truth. Some days, it's easy to forget. It was so long ago. But that's the thing about trauma, isn't it? You never know what'll make it rear its ugly head.*

Star: *Very true.*

Star: *I can't listen to music during sex.*

Conor: *It's a trigger?*

Star: *Makes me angry.*

Conor: *Okay. Note to self: never listen to music around Lodestar.*

Star: *Lol. You can at some points, just not sex.*

Conor: *Meaning…?*

Star: *^^*

Conor: *O.O*

Conor: *Moving on… Do you mind me asking why it's a trigger?*

Star: *I don't mind. We're sharing, aren't we?*

Conor: *Sharing IS caring.*

Star: *Uh huh.*

Star: *It doesn't have anything to do with being a sex slave, ironically enough. This started a long time ago.*

Star: *My mom had died and my dad derailed. The record company tried to get him to cancel this massive tour they were doing but he refused.*

Conor: *Noxxfest?*

Star: *Of course you know that lol.*

Conor: *I was pissed that Da wouldn't let me go. Plus, I remember when Gerry Sullivan derailed.*

Star: *Yup. He was stoned out of his mind most of the time. I lost him then, I think. That was like the first phase of us pulling away from each other.*

Conor: *I'm sorry.*

Star: *Don't be. Shit doesn't always work out.*

Conor: *You've lost a lot of people.*

Star: *That's just how it is with me. I probably could have gotten a job at Walmart and I'd have figured out a way to alienate the people around me.*

Conor: *I think you're too hard on yourself.*

Star: *I think it's sweet that YOU think so.*

Conor: *We don't always have to believe in ourselves, but it's nice that those who matter can believe in us FOR us.*

Star: *Maybe. Anyway, there was a code I had to learn.*

Conor: *Like a computer code? Alarm code?*

Star: *No. If he was playing a certain album, he was fucking a roadie.*

Conor: *Is it bad that I want to know which album?*

Star: *Probably. It was Sweet Satan Pie.*

Conor: *That's a sick album.*

Star: *For me, it's sick but it hits differently lol.*

Conor: *:/*

Star: *Hot Fuxx Sunday meant he was getting high. Usually on shit that made his tour bus stink like an opium den.*

Conor: *Jesus. Were you traveling with him?*

Star: *I was supposed to, but I spent a lot of time on Savannah's bus.*

Conor: *That must have been a tight fit.*

Star: *It was. But we made it work. Her family has always been like my family too. Well, it used to be.*

Conor: *Why did you guys fall out?*

Star: *So many reasons.*

Star: *Dad only got clean because of Dagger and Lorelei.*

Conor: *Not you?*

Star: *No.*

Conor: *Damn. How come?*

Star: *They helped him. I guess I didn't.*

Conor: *Meaning?*

Star: *I used to get mad at him. We'd argue like crazy and had screaming matches that'd have all the roadies freezing in fear because Dad had a temper and I inherited it.*

Conor: *I'm surprised there wasn't more gossip.*

Star: *noxxious's management had the staff on tour under NDAs more iron-clad than a medieval nun's chastity belt.*

Conor: *Makes sense with that kind of shit going down.*

Star: *Yeah, but it was from the good old days. Pre-Mom, that was how Dad rolled. I just didn't know that until I walked in on him having a fucking orgy with three groupies.*

Conor: *Jesus!!*

Star: *Hmm. It's great being a rock star, doncha know?*

Conor: *But he let you walk in on that?*

Star: *I should have learned the code earlier.*

Conor: *Babe, you really fucking shouldn't have to learn a code to go and see your dad. And that's me. ME saying that. I was more likely to walk in on Da torturing someone than fucking someone, but he still didn't let me walk in on that shit. He did it in places where his kids couldn't witness him be that way until he wanted us in the life.*

Star: *That's the first time you've called me 'babe.'*

Conor: *Nah.*

Star: *I think it is.*

Conor: *How do you feel about it?*

Star: *I don't loathe it.*

Conor: *Lol. Good?*

Star: *Do I have to develop a name for you? Connywon?*

Conor: *LMAO. Um. NOoooPpe. *pukes**

Star: *:P*

Conor: *You could, you know, call me babe back. Or sweetheart.*

Star: *We'll see.*

Five minutes later

Conor: *Star, I'm sorry you had to go through that shit. I'm sorry he let you down.*

Star: *People let you down, Conor. That's what they do. I learned from the best.*

Conor: *Not all people. I won't let you down.*

Star: *You know what's crazy?*

Conor: *What?*

Star: *I actually believe you.*

14

CONOR

STRANGE - THE FEELING

I DIDN'T KNOW why but I left Aoife and Finn's place with a heavy heart.

While I was filled with purpose and that should have brought some comfort, I mostly felt burdened by something intangible that I couldn't evade—a belief that that might be the last time I'd be leaving their home.

The gloomy thought followed me onto the sidewalk where one of our town cars was waiting for me.

I'd already been chided by Finn for traveling to his place via cab *sans* guard—Eoghan was a fucking snitch—so I settled back in the seat and watched the city float by in stages as we got locked in by traffic.

Twenty minutes into the journey, my cell buzzed.

Half expecting it to be one of my brothers and more than ready to ignore it, instead, I found myself looking at an unknown number.

As my finger hovered over the disconnect button, the temptation was strong to cut the call.

Who knew who the fuck it might be?

But in my line of work, staying abreast of the situation was the only way to keep ahead, so even though I definitely didn't want to answer, I hit connect.

"What?"

"Conor O'Donnelly, I believe?"

The accent was strong, impossible not to recognize. *Russian.*

"Who's speaking?" I demanded.

"My name is Misha Babanin."

I recognized the name. "You like cutting up people."

A soft laugh drifted in my ear. "The knife is not my weapon of choice. Regardless, you consider a rapist a person?"

"The Stepanov boy was a rapist?"

"*Da.* Had my Pakhan not dealt with the situation, I'm certain that your sister-in-law would have suffered his attention too."

My jaw worked at that. "Why are you calling me? I'm not a liaison with the Bratva."

"I don't need a liaison. I have information for *you.*"

"From?"

"My Pakhan."

"Why didn't he call himself?"

"Because he's indisposed."

"Indisposed how?"

"Injured."

"Lyanov's in the hospital?" That was news to me.

"You may have read about a bomb that went off in Moskva's Petrovsky Park recently… He was caught up in the blast."

My brows lifted in surprise. "Why the hell was he involved in that?"

"I didn't say he was involved. I said he was caught in the blast. He has been unconscious ever since but when he woke up, he wished for me to tell you something."

This made no sense, but that he didn't just come out with what he was supposed to tell me clued me into a sorry truth. "It comes at a price?"

"Doesn't everything?"

I had to laugh. "Lyanov shouldn't mess around with the Five Points."

"My Pakhan told me to give you this information. I'm the one who is putting a price on it."

"That isn't your place. I'd heard the New York Bratva bred mutiny better than rabies spreads around a pack of dogs, but now I've got proof of it."

A growl, rather fitting considering my metaphor, rumbled in my ear. "I do not betray my brother. I ask for help on his behalf."

That had me frowning. "What kind of help does he need?"

"His… loyalty to the Bratva has been called into question. The *Krestniy Otets* has deemed him unfit to lead us here. We are evacuating him from Moskva as we speak."

"And?"

"And Moskva will learn that we do not always answer when it calls."

I blinked. "You're separating from them?"

"Maxim is the best leader we have ever had. In under a year, he's done more to protect us and serve us than Vasov did in twenty-six years.

"The men know this. They have made their decision."

"So what do you want me to do about it?"

"Power comes in many forms in the city."

"It does."

"Maxim's leadership has to be recognized by the other factions."

I pursed my lips. "Tell me what he wants me to know. The Five Points recognize Maxim as the leader of the Russians. We don't give a fuck if the name of your gang changes."

"Your brothers feel the same?"

My brothers didn't give a fuck about the Russians.

"Your infighting means nothing to us," I dismissed.

There was a pause. "Maxim wished for you to know that he attended a ball at Petrovsky Palace with Star Sullivan. She danced with a man called Anton Kuznetsov and he took her into his office.

"That was the last he saw of her."

My brow puckered as I repeated, "Anton Kuznetsov?"

"*Da.*"

"Have you heard of this man?"

"Most of Russia knows of the Kuznetsovs but they are not a name you speak out loud."

"Why not?"

"Because people who speak it tend to find their tongues cut out the next day."

"Intense."

He grunted. "Very. Maxim attempted to recover Sullivan."

Now *that* stunned the crap out of me. "He tried to rescue her?!"

"He did. Maxim is an honorable man." His voice had turned gruff. "Even if it means he doesn't watch his own ass in the process.

"The rescue mission failed."

"And that's why the Bratva have rejected his leadership?"

"*Da.* One does not go against the Kuznetsovs. Especially if you are Bratva."

My mouth tightened at that news but... "For no other reason than that he attempted to rescue Star Sullivan, you can tell Maxim that he has the full support of the Five Points *and,* when the next Summit is held, he will be backed by my family."

Silence filled the air for a moment. Then, Misha rumbled, "I appreciate this, and thank you on my brother's behalf."

He ended the call before I could say another word.

Pressing the corner of the cell phone to my bottom lip, I tried to figure out my next move.

I had my confirmation that Star was in Moscow, but she hadn't been behind the bombing as I'd thought.

Maxim Lyanov was the one who'd been caught in it, not her.

Nevertheless, that didn't mean she wasn't in danger.

This Kuznetsov appeared to be the last person who had seen her alive...

A man whose name stirred fear into the heart of a Bratva foot soldier who felt no fear in chopping up an enemy's son into parts and presenting it at his feet—I'd heard the stories from Aidan and Brennan. Even *they* had been surprised by how Lyanov had handled that situation.

Contemplating what I'd just learned, I decided the best way to deal with this was to send out a group message.

Me: *Just a heads-up—Maxim Lyanov has been deposed as the Bratva Pakhan by Moscow itself.*

Eoghan: *How the hell do you know that?*

Me: *Does it matter?*

Brennan: *Yes. It matters. What's going on, Kid?*

Me: *Got a call from Lyanov's man, that Misha guy.*

Aidan: *Why did he contact you and not me?*

Declan: *Don't throw a tantrum, Aidan. Just because you're trying to set yourself as the big boss of everything, lol, it don't make you president.*

Eoghan: *Hahahaha.*

Aidan: *Fuck off, Declan.*

Declan: *Just calling it how I see it. ;)*

Eoghan: *I agree. We gotta keep your head from exploding, Aidan.*

Aidan: *Savannah does that just fine.*

Finn: *Before this takes us down a rabbit hole none of us want to explore, what happened, Conor? What did Misha have to say?*

Me: *Lodestar has gone missing. As a result of his rescue attempt, the head of the Moscow Bratva deemed Lyanov's judgment to be unsound. His men on the ground here are retrieving him from Moscow and are bringing him home to lead, no matter what the Bratva mothership wants.*

Me: *Misha asked that we support Lyanov's claim to leadership and because of what he tried to do for Star, I said we would.*

Brennan: *You had no right to decide that. Not without speaking to us first.*

Me: *Like you'd consult us if anything jeopardized Camille's safety. She's my woman, Brennan.*

Brennan: *You've never met her. You could hate her the minute you set eyes on her. What if she's catfishing you, for fuck's sake? I know she ran out on you; doesn't that tell you she ain't good people?*

Aidan: *Brennan, watch it.*

Finn: *Yeah, you're out of line.*

Brennan: *Someone has to think realistically here. I get how you can fall for someone out of nowhere. Jesus Christ, do I understand that. But I'm looking out for us all. Conor too. She's no good, Kid. She wouldn't have taken off and run if she gave a shit about you.*

Me: *You're entitled to your opinion. I'll allow her to change it when I bring her home.*

Aidan: *YOU'RE going? As in, leaving the country?*

Me: *She needs me.*

Brennan: *You hate flying.*

Me: *I don't.*

Eoghan: *You're a shit flyer.*

Me: *So? I'll have a couple of whiskeys to take off the edge. It would help if aerodynamicists could decide how planes actually stay in the air.*

Declan: *You read too much, Conor. That's always been your problem. Sometimes, you just have to appreciate technology. You don't have to understand it.*

Finn: *At the risk of this developing into an argument about aerodynamic lift and how Declan can't talk when he can wax lyrical for hours about why Mondrian liked squares, WHO is behind Lodestar's disappearance?*

Me: *According to Maxim, a guy called Anton Kuznetsov. They attended a party together. She went into the guy's office and never came back.*

Brennan: *That sounds really loyal. Attending parties with a guy from the Bratva and going into some fucker's office AT said party?*

Declan: *Shut up. Lodestar's different. She's ex-CIA and she's on a mission to annihilate the Sparrows. This ain't like Camille deciding to swan off at some gala with the Dragon Head of the Triads.*

Aidan: *If the local Bratva isn't on Lyanov's side, then we have no way of helping you get to her, Kid.*

Me: *I'll figure it out.*

Declan: *You're not on your own in this.*

Eoghan: *If you need me to fly over, just tell me.*

Brennan: *FFS, same.*

Aidan: *I'm not fit to fight. My knee's a thousand times better but I'd just slow you down. I can send men though.*

Me: *Stop. I don't need any help yet. First, I need to get on the ground. Then, if I need backup, I'll call them in, okay?*

Declan: *We're here for you, Kid. Always. Brennan's just being his usual grouchy-ass self.*

Me: *I get it. You all baby me. But I'm not a child even if that's my nickname. Maxim Lyanov did me a solid. The least we can do is back him if he has the support of the foot soldiers here. Which we know he does.*

Brennan: *He's been a solid leader so far. One of Camille's cousins told her that the mid-to-lower ranks love him. It's upper 'management' who have a problem with him.*

Aidan: *Why?*

Brennan: *He believes in playing fair.*

Declan: *Meaning he spreads the cash around so the upper ranks get less of a cut?*

Brennan: *Sounds like it.*

Eoghan: *Kid, I've heard of that Kuznetsov guy.*

Me: *You have? I haven't. Misha indicated that the Kuznetsov family holds a lot of power in Russia.*

Eoghan: *Yeah. I remember now. I had to take a specialist class and there was this real-life situation that was being used as an example of how NOT to do shit.*

Eoghan: *This guy was driving along with his wife and kid in, fuck, Ohio? I think it was anyway. They had diplomatic plates. Someone took them out.*

Brennan: *What kind of teaching moment was that?*

Aidan: *What kind of class were you taking?*

Finn: *How to be G.I. Joe, lol.*

Declan: *101 :P*

Eoghan: *Fuck off.*

Me: *Go on, Eoghan. What happened?*

Eoghan: *It was supposed to appear like an accident. They tampered with the brake lines but in the crash, no one died. An opera-*

tive had to take them out by hand. The girl got away though. Ran into traffic if memory serves. It was a big stink that had to be hushed up quickly.

Brennan: *This was a cheerful story time, Eoghan. Remind me if I have kids not to get you to read them bedtime stories.*

Finn: *Yeah, I'm never letting you tuck Jake in lol.*

Me: *What does this have to do with anything, Eoghan?*

Eoghan: *The diplomat's name was Kuznetsov.*

Brennan: *Probably just a coincidence.*

Me: *Yeah, probably, but I'll dig deeper, Eoghan. Thanks, bud.*

Eoghan: *There'll be nothing to look into, Kid. I'm telling you it was cleaned up. That's how I know it's not a coincidence. The level of bleach that was required to sweep this under the rug was insane.*

Me: *Interesting.*

Aidan: *What happened to the kid? The girl?*

Eoghan: *If I remember right, oncoming traffic knocked her down. I have a feeling she died in the hospital but I don't remember more than the bare bones.*

Declan: *Your job sucked. I thought working for Da was bad. At least we didn't have to kill kids.*

Eoghan: *Why do you think I tried to get out? At least working for Da came with a penthouse. All Uncle Sam got me was PTSD and into deeper shit than anything my mobster father could cook up.*

Me: *:/*

Me: *Aidan, you'll back Lyanov, won't you?*

Aidan: *I don't see why not. Lyanov might not have kept Moscow happy but he's maintained order in New York, and that's all that matters to me.*

Me: *I think you should check in with Padraig, Declan.*

Declan: *He hates being called Padraig. His road name with the Sinners is Sin.*

Brennan: *So original.*

Declan: *Don't think he gives a flying fuck what you think of his road name lol. What do you want me to tell him, Kid?*

Me: *Star's a Sinner. Whether she remembers that or not. Just loop him in so that he knows I'm working on bringing her home.*

Declan: *You want him to know about this?*

Me: *Of course. Katina is Star's daughter. If you update him, then Katina's sister can at least reassure her that I'm hunting Star down.*

Aidan: *Surprised you thought of that.*

Me: *She's the one who told me Star was gone.*

Aidan: *Really? So, she's a good mom then? From what Savannah told me of Star, I wouldn't have thought she was the type.*

Me: *She's definitely the type.*

Brennan: *What did she leave her for then?*

Eoghan: *Don't worry, Con. I'll kick his ass on your behalf when I see him next.*

Me: *Appreciate that, Eoghan. (You're a jerk off, Bren.)*

Brennan: *I own it.*

Finn: *Kid, remember, if you need help, we're here.*

Me: *I appreciate that, deartháirs.*

Declan: *Let us know when you land.*

Me: *Being a dad has turned you into a real mother hen lol.*

Declan: *I'm not ashamed of it. ;)*

Lips curving, I switched screens and went to reserve a flight.

I had a name, and I had a location.

That was more than I'd had when I woke up this morning, and I'd accomplished plenty with a lot less.

"Star," I muttered under my breath. "I'm coming to get you."

15

CONOR

Conor O'Donnelly

IT WAS with actual relief that I boarded the commercial jet.

My tickets had been accepted at check-in, my permission to fly hadn't been revoked, TSA hadn't gotten a hard-on for me, and once I was settled in my seat, I had to reason that this was it—I was allowed to leave the States.

The CIA hadn't figured out that I'd had a hand in storing their director in a shipping container in the Catskills, or if they had, then they weren't going to hold a grudge against me.

Preliminary scans on several servers prior to departing for the airport had let me know I wasn't about to get my ass arrested, and my penthouse was untouched when I arrived, my security measures still in place—both of the high- and the low-tech varieties—and the door hadn't been knocked down either, but you never knew sometimes.

That whole shit at Langley had come as a complete surprise to me, so no source was perfect.

At the moment, I figured it was best to take everything with a grain of salt until I had more of an idea of what was going on.

Once I was buckled in, I stared over the concourse, not even turning my head when someone took a seat beside me.

I was probably the only person in my family who didn't hate flying commercial. The rest of my bougie-ass brothers would have taken a private jet, but statistically, this was safer.

I'd done the math.

I'd also bought out the rest of first class apart from my neighbor's seat which had been scooped up while I was busy reserving the others, so I'd be traveling pretty much alone anyway.

Refusing to admit that I was nervous, I checked my phone when it buzzed.

Goldstein: McClure's got a sex slave.

Goldstein: Wait for it.

Goldstein: In the basement. Of his HOUSE.

Me: The arrogant asshole. These goddamn senators just think they can do whatever the fuck they want.

Me: Leave it with me.

Goldstein: Leave WHAT with you? I'll collate the evidence and start putting together records for an Interpol investigation.

My eyes narrowed.

Me: Sure. Thanks for keeping me updated.

He replied, but I ignored his text channel and, instead, hit up Dead To Me.

Me: Senator John McClure.

Dead To Me: Doesn't believe women have rights to their uteruses, thinks we should be stuck in a kitchen, and was pivotal in that deal that fucked Alaskan reservations up the ass and is going to turn it into oil soup...

Dead To Me: That the Senator John McClure
we're thinking of?

Me: Sure is.

Me: He needs to be gone.

Dead To Me: Any reason other than the
above.

Me: Goldstein says he has a sex slave in his
house. It would be wise to monitor his
property.

Me: McClure has a wife. See if she's in the
know.

Dead To Me: If she is, she's a goner too. Just
warning you. I'll do her for free.

Me: Don't coordinate with Goldstein. He isn't
in the know about our sideline.

Dead To Me: He knows of me.

Me: How?

Dead To Me: Fucked him.

Me: Ah, shit. When? In fact, never mind. Did
he make you?

Dead To Me: He knows what I'm capable of.

I rubbed my temples—this was an unexpected complication, but if they never came into contact, then there wouldn't be an issue.

"O'Donnelly."

That had my head whipping to the side.

I knew I'd be sharing the cabin with one other person but... fuck.

My eyes flared wide as I took in the weirdly angelic features of Temperance goddamn Black.

"What are you doing here?" I snarled, her mere presence triggering an earthquake in my mind.

She was worse than nails on a fucking chalkboard or one of those bastards who couldn't chew pizza without keeping their mouths closed.

She studied her nails. "I'm keeping you company."

"I don't want your company."

Her sniff told me that she really cared about my 'wants.' "I'm under orders."

My throat tightened. "Whose orders?"

She arched a brow.

The United Brotherhood.

Great. Just great.

"You owe them."

Anger flooded me. "I owe them dick. You're the one who got me involved in this shit."

"You're the one who'd be dead if I didn't."

True.

Crap.

I narrowed my eyes at her. "What do they want?"

"You to take a trip on a plane."

"Managed that without their input."

"They decided you needed an escort."

I frowned. "Why?"

"You'd have been heading to the wrong place," was her simple reply.

Reaching up, I rubbed at my nape. "What's going on, Agent Black?"

"Temper, please. We've already been introduced."

I knew madness. I knew insanity. I'd seen it light up both of my parents' eyes at some point in my life—Temperance Black hit differently.

Very differently.

She put me on edge in a way that few people ever had, and that set uncomfortably in my bones.

It was, I thought, her righteousness.

I'd seen that in Da's gaze too many times to count. An inherent belief that what he was doing was right even when he was very, very wrong.

Temperance was worse, somehow.

Which, trust me, was saying fucking something.

She was a zealot, and I didn't believe that was based solely on her being a 'patriot.'

When Star had tried to describe her to me, I hadn't picked up on that. Maybe it was a trait you had to uncover in the flesh.

At my prolonged silence, she huffed. "You want to find Star, don't you?"

"I do."

"That's where I'm taking you. To her."

"You know where she is?"

She preened. "I was recently let in on that secret."

Secret?

"Why is it a secret?"

"Only top Brothers know."

"Why?"

"She's important to the Union."

My nostrils flared at that. "She didn't even know they existed until recently."

"That doesn't mean they didn't know *she* existed."

Eyes narrowing, I demanded, "She doesn't know that you're a Brother, does she?"

"Of course not," Temper scoffed. "No one knows outside of the Union. And you, of course. You know now."

"If that's a threat—"

"It isn't. Yet." She slipped that final word in like a knife through my lung.

My jaw clenched before I released it to bite off, "You betrayed her."

"I did not," Temper hissed, ducking back when the flight attendant came around with a glass of champagne for both of us, a hot towel, and some nuts. Only when we'd been served and were alone again did Temper lean over the armrest to rasp, "I have never betrayed Star."

"You are now, aren't you? Something's clearly going on with her. She hasn't spoken to her foster daughter in weeks and that would only happen if she *physically* couldn't because Star wouldn't let Katina down like that.

"For whatever reason, she's incapacitated, and you're in cahoots with the goddamn people who are holding her."

Temper eyed me over the glass of bubbly. "This is a far deeper game than you know."

"Doesn't take a fucking genius to figure that one out." I pinched the bridge of my nose. "Is she safe?"

"Of course. We're not Sparrows."

"You're a secret society that functions outside the bounds of the law."

"We *protect* the law."

I hooted. "I'm sure Director Reinier agrees."

Temper squinted at me. "Are you trying to tell me that you feel sorry for him? After what he put Star through? After how he betrayed her? How he betrayed our country? He should have been taken out sooner. I'm lucky that I got to be the one to bring him down."

My brow puckered.

Lucky?

That right there told me a whole helluva lot about Temperance fucking Black and her goddamn Brotherhood.

Needing the fizz to overtake her poison, I sank back the champagne and let it hit my bloodstream. Then, I turned away to look out of the window again.

Finn said the United Brotherhood had been white hats back when they'd approached him, but he was dead-on when he said he didn't know if they were now.

I didn't live in a black-and-white world. I lived very squarely in the gray, and somehow, Temperance Black was the worst *gray* I'd ever come across in my almost four decades on this godforsaken planet.

Taking out the trash, human or otherwise, was one thing; feeling *lucky* to get that chore was just plain weird.

"Just make sure he stays alive for Star," I warned, hands on the armrests, digging my fingers into the soft leather.

Around me, the plane readied itself for takeoff. The champagne glass was retrieved by a flight attendant and a bottle of water was put in its place. The doors were closed, and, for whatever reason, Temper left me alone as I kept my attention averted from her.

Only then did I reply to Dead To Me:

> Me: If Goldstein contacts you, just do what you have to do.

> Dead To Me: He's a stickler but I don't want to kill him.

> Me: That's on you. I don't think he'd turn you in. Just be careful. It's more than likely that you'll never meet.

> Dead To Me: Got it.

That didn't allay my tension any, but at least that bastard McClure would be dead.

Though I should have conferred with Aidan, there was no way in fuck I could let that poor woman exist in the basement of some senator's house, just waiting for the ax to fall. Which was exactly what'd happen if McClure thought his dirty little secret was about to see the light of day.

The woman would die to cover his sins up and…

Fuck.

It smacked too much of Star. Of the precariousness of her situation once upon a time.

Just thinking of what I'd learned about her, of what they'd put her through, was enough to make me want to kill someone.

While vengeance had always been my da's preference and not mine, I understood his mentality at that moment.

Reinier was going to die in a shipping container, whether it was at Star's hand or of starvation and dehydration and only God knew what else. When I thought about what he'd put Star through, I hoped he went full-throttle *28 Days Later* on himself.

An hour into the flight, when I felt as if I'd managed to draw on a strong enough mask, I turned to her and, creepily enough, found her watching me.

It was like being studied by a scorpion. One wrong move and she'd sting me. The only difference was, on the outside, she was beautiful: golden-blonde hair, bright-as-a-button blue eyes, flawless skin, a neat figure that was destroyed by a bland, boxy, off-the-rack suit. If Barbie had developed a CIA agent doll, it would have looked like Temperance.

"Is your first cousin a Brother?"

"No," she derided. Her head angled to the side. "Why?"

So, Dead To Me was a solid ally. I figured as much, to be fair.

"Why did you say 'no' like that?"

"Because my cousin has a side gig that wouldn't wash in the Union."

"Meaning?"

"Meaning that only the best are inducted into the Brotherhood."

The best?

She was a psycho who had an in with a society of fucking nutcases.

Coming up with the 'leave the asswipe to rot in a shipping container' plan was something even Da wouldn't have rolled with.

Didn't mean I wasn't glad about it.

I'd once watched a horror movie where a serial killer left his victims to rot like Reinier would and, back then, it had freaked me out. Enough that Aidan had gotten sick of me waking him up with my nightmares and he'd told my very young twelve-year-old ass to research what would happen to a person left like that because, in his words, *to know was to control.*

Looking back, it wasn't a standard way to deal with nightmares, but what in my family was standard?

He'd probably amplified a toxic trait of never being able to leave any stone unturned, which had undoubtedly put me in my current position, but hey, every step I'd taken down this path had led me to Star.

That was something I could never regret.

"Is someone going to check in on Reinier? Make sure he doesn't die?" I questioned. "I can't imagine Star would be okay with him wasting away before she can get her hands on him."

I intended on bringing her home sooner than it would take Reinier to die, but I wanted to keep our bases covered.

She nodded. "He'll be monitored. Star would want to be involved —you reminded me of that back at Langley. I shouldn't have acted as impulsively as I did."

I studied her. "*Was* it impulsive? You said I should be glad you were there because it stopped me from getting my ass killed, but were you there for me? Or for Reinier?"

A smile danced on her lips. "Couldn't I have been there for both?" I watched as she accepted a drink order I hadn't heard her make, and only when the flight attendant had left did she continue, "Reinier had the entire building evacuated. Triggered a whole protocol as if we'd had some kind of accidental spillage in one of the labs just to make sure you and the coders were on your own there."

"Was Riggs in on it?" I rasped.

"No."

"Why was she there?"

That smile I detested made another reappearance. "She was your handler."

"Was?" Fuck. "Meaning *you* are now?"

"That hasn't been decided by my higher-ups yet."

I grabbed my water bottle and nearly ripped off the cap in my haste to drink some. Mind racing as I gulped it down, I emptied it before I realized it. "Why are you telling me this?"

"I've been told that I can answer any questions you ask of me."

"By whom?"

"People with far more authority than the director of the CIA."

"Who?"

"Leaders of the Union."

As annoying as she was, this was good.

I could get answers and that would help Star.

"What is the Union?"

"A group older than the Freemasons who serve the people."

I wanted to scoff, but I didn't. Her eyes lit up like a Christmas tree with how ardently she believed that BS.

"How do they serve the people?"

"They bring neutrality and non-bias where politics does the opposite."

"People vote for politicians," I pointed out, to which she snickered.

"It's cute that you believe that. Politicians get into power through super PACs which are funded by companies that don't give a damn about anything other than the policies that will keep their businesses intact and running on low taxes.

"You think our current method works when the so-called popular vote means nothing if the electoral colleges don't sync up? The population and its wants are irrelevant. Elections are fodder for the masses.

"The Union makes sure that people *are* protected."

"It functions only in the US?"

"No. It's a global endeavor, one that I'm proud to be a member of."

I could smell her pride from over here. She was practically creaming in her panties over each goddamn word.

"Star was CIA. Why wasn't she invited to be a Brother?"

"Star bent the rules. The Union doesn't allow such people to be a member."

"And you don't bend the rules? Aren't you as dirty as she is?"

In less than a second, she'd knocked the stand of the champagne flute in her hand against the armrest. The sparkling wine arced in a neat spray over the aisle before the jagged tip of the stem was pressed into my carotid.

"I am *not* dirty. I serve the people. I act for the people. I *protect* the people," she spat. "Do you understand?"

"I'm one of the people," I retorted calmly. "You're trying to stick a piece of glass in my throat." I reacted as she placed more pressure on the stem, and with one hand on her wrist, the other on the flute, I jerked it from her grasp and pressed the broken stem into her palm and sliced downward. "You're not the only one who can fight dirty."

Her mouth tightened. "You're a mobster."

"So that means I deserve to bleed out in first class?" I mocked, digging deeper into her palm.

Her lack of suffering at what had to hurt told me she'd been reared as I had. Whichever side of the path she believed herself to be on, we both knew pain.

"It means that you can't possibly understand what the Union does."

Because I was used to death threats and dealing with insane people, I retracted the stem and, as I handed it to her, drawled, "I'm certain your leaders wouldn't appreciate it if you killed me seeing as I'm so important for this next phase of whatever plan you've concocted."

She sniffed. "You are correct."

"When Star asked you to help her, who were you serving?"

From her hesitation, I had my answer without her having to utter a word.

"So, it *was* betrayal."

"No. Her purpose aligns with mine."

"The United Brotherhood wants the Sparrows taken down?"

She dipped her chin. "They do, and they're willing to help her if she'll accept their aid."

16

TEXT CHAT

PAST

CONOR: *Are you a patriot?*

Star: *I used to be. You?*

Conor: *Yeah. I guess.*

Conor: *Did you change after Afghanistan?*

Star: *No. It was before then. I saw a lot of corruption in the sand-box. We were supposed to be there to bring freedom to those people, but it was just about oil, power, and leverage over both.*

Conor: *Isn't it always about that?*

Star: *Why do you think I'm not a patriot anymore lol?*

Star: *But I love my country. I love what we used to stand for. I just don't love it how it is now, and with everything that comes out about the Sparrows, it confirms that we've never been further away from what our founding fathers wanted for us.*

Star: *Sorry, I didn't mean to get deep. Why do you ask?*

Conor: *I'm infinitely curious about you.*

Conor: *Haven't you figured that out yet?*

Star: *Lol. Weirdo. My turn at twenty questions then.*

Conor: *Hit me with it.*

Star: *What's something you're afraid of?*

Conor: *Living in a world without my brothers in it.*

Star: *Really?*

Conor: *Really. Nearly everything I do is to keep them safe. It's one of the only reasons I always answer to Da when he comes calling.*

Star: *Why?*

Conor: *He's paranoid about being betrayed.*

Star: *He thinks THEY would betray them?*

Conor: *Yeah. The older he gets, it's a fear that, I guess, niggles at him. I think he knows it's irrational. At least, I hope he does.*

Star: *Is that why you developed that bug?*

Conor: *Yeah. I listen to about one percent of all the recorded conversations and have the software weed out keywords for me to check, but I have everything on file so that I can always prove they're innocent of whatever BS he accuses them of. It hasn't happened yet, but I can't see that being the case forever.*

Star: *He didn't ask you to do that?*

Conor: *You know from personal experience that people don't know what we're capable of.*

Star: *Meaning he wanted you to do something but he didn't know what. Just wanted to make sure his boys weren't traitors.*

Conor: *Yup. So I came up with the bug. It keeps him happy.*

Conor: *What scares you?*

Star: *Dying alone.*

Conor: *Even though you, in your own words, push everyone away?*

Star: *It's not an irrational fear then, is it?*

Conor: *Not like mine. There will come a day when my brothers die. We might evade taxes, but death is something we can't avoid forever. Whether I'm the last one standing or another is, it'll happen at some point.*

Star: *Uh huh.*

Star: *This is a cheerful conversation.*

Star: *How did we get onto this subject anyway lol?*

Conor: *You're the one who brought up fears.*

Star: *I was listening to a podcast.*

Conor: *YOU? You listen to podcasts? What kind?*

Star: *Nvm.*

Conor: *Ohhh, no. You can't go quiet now. We're sharing.*

Star: *Goddamn sharing.*

Conor: *You're the one who started it.*

Star: *It's your fault.*

Conor: *It can be.*

Star: *Where's my Christmas gift?*

Conor: *I'm still developing it.*

Star: *Jesus. I'll be old and gray by the time it's ready.*

Conor: *It'll be worth it.*

Star: *Says you.*

Conor: *Which podcast?*

Star: *It doesn't matter. I'll tell you the title of the episode though.*

Conor: *Deal.*

Star: *"How to maintain long-distance relationships."*

Conor: *…*

Conor: *…*

Star: *Fuck off.*

Star: *Okay, don't. I mean. You don't have to fuck off.*

Conor: *…*

Conor: *This is me being speechless.*

Star: *Don't make me regret telling you.*

Star: *Oh, wait, I already do. Jesus. Let's go play* Halo, *yeah? We haven't played this week.*

Conor: *Oh, noooo. You're not getting out of this. "How to maintain long-distance relationships"? I'm assuming this is about us, or are you talking to someone else like we talk?*

Star: *Conor, if you think I have the patience to talk about the shit we talk about with someone else, you're insane.*

Star: *But of course, I speak with other people. Don't you?*

Conor: *Yeah, but I don't tell them that I'm scared of living in a world without my brothers in it. ^^*

Star: *Exactly. We have a thing.*

Conor: *A thing.*

Star: *Yes. A thing.*

Conor: *An LDR?*

Star: *Well, if you want to label it.*

Conor: *Oh, no, honey. You're the one labeling it lol. I'm just watching you dig your own grave.*

Star: *I'm going to play* Mario Kart *with Kat. She doesn't give me shit.*

Conor: *Lies. Plus, it's three AM. Lol. Doesn't she have school tomorrow?*

Star: *No. School's out for the summer. Duh.*

Conor: *Oh, yeah.*

Star: *Really observant. It's hotter than hell outside.*

Conor: *Don't leave my apartment much. Air conditioning FTW.*

Star: *Yeah, I hate going out too.*

Conor: *We have so much in common lol.*

Star: *Yeah, we vibe over AC. :P*

Conor: *We could vibe over other stuff...*

Star: *What stuff? I already told you I won't watch cartoons with you anymore. You'll have to stick with Jake for that.*

Conor: *If I send you something, would you use it?*

Star: *Sure.*

Conor: *Would you let me watch you use it?*

Star: *Oh.*

Conor: *Oh.*

Star: *You mean a literal vibe, don't you?*

Conor: *Yes.*

Star: *TBH, I thought that was what my Christmas present was supposed to be.*

Conor: *It is. But I can't get it to stop glitching.*

Star: *Is it supposed to glitch? How much code can you pack into a vibrator?*

Conor: *What kind of question is that? Rude.*

Star: *LOL. Does it talk?*

Conor: *No. That's what I'm for.*

Star: *Oh.*

Conor: *I don't want to send you something that will electrocute you.*

Star: *I appreciate that lol. You're all heart.*

Conor: *I know. :P So... if I send you something, will you use it? And let me watch?*

Star: *I'll let you listen.*

Conor: *Thank you.*

Star: *Can I listen to you too?*

Conor: *In full surround sound.*

Star: *I share my place lol. I don't need Link knowing what I get up to. He's kinky enough without me giving him ideas.*

Conor: *That's fine with me... I don't want your housemates to know what you sound like. That belongs to me.*

Star: *I belong to myself.*

Conor: *Never said you don't. But if you're getting off on a toy that I sent you and listening to me talk dirty to you, then that orgasm is mine. I earned it. Agreed?*

Star: *By that logic, if you're getting off to listening to me get off then your orgasm is mine too.*

Conor: *Without a shadow of a doubt. Haven't you figured it out yet, Star?*

Star: *I don't think I have. What's to figure out, Conor?*

Conor: *That I'm all in.*

Star: *Oh.*

Conor: *Yeah, oh.*

17

CONOR

AS WE CROSSED over the most southernly tip of Finland, I felt a change in the airplane.

We still hadn't edged into Baltic territory but we were descending as if we were.

Frowning, I stared at the blanket of clouds below us as if I could figure out what was happening by sight alone before I turned to Temper, who'd been watching me throughout the flight like I was more interesting than the onboard entertainment.

I wasn't altogether unaccustomed to being watched.

People tended to do that when I was hacking. It was easier to study my face for expressions than to read my code, so I didn't gripe at her about it.

Not when she was clearly unhinged.

"We're losing altitude," I informed her.

She blinked at me. "It's in hand."

My mouth tightened. "We were supposed to be going to Moscow."

"And I told you her location had changed."

"So we're being rerouted?"

She dipped her chin. "Why would you go to Moscow when she isn't there?"

"I told Riggs where I'd be heading."

"And she informed the people who need to know that you are, in fact, stopping in Finland."

"Why?"

"Star said you were clever." She huffed impatiently, her fingers toying with the bandage the flight attendant had applied to her palm. "We're going to wherever Star is."

"Why Finland?"

"Why not Finland? You'll find out when you get there."

I frowned at her. "I thought you were supposed to answer my questions."

She glowered at me. "Her relocation was necessary because there was an attempt to rescue her.

"Star, however, isn't in danger." She sniffed. "She's with the Union. She's safe."

"You sound like James Garfield."

"That fits. He was a Brother too."

My eyes flared wide at that. "Fuck off."

Her smirk was smug. "See? You don't know everything, O'Donnelly. The Old World Sparrows took him out. Bastards."

I turned in my seat to better look at her. "You're being serious."

It wasn't a question.

"Of course I am. I told you we were older than the Freemasons."

"So, what, you're benevolent overlords?"

She scowled at me. "You put a negative spin on everything, don't you?"

"I'm sorry if I don't like the fact that Boatman Jim was a part of some secret society!"

"O'Donnelly, secret doesn't mean corrupt."

"You're living proof of *that*, I suppose."

"There are ten different ways to kill you in this cabin and each one involves me not breaking into a sweat—"

"That doesn't confirm what I just said, does it?" Before we could start bickering, I demanded, "When did your indoctrination start?"

Her nostrils flared. "I wasn't indoctrinated. In Afghanistan, I reported my CO for misconduct unbecoming, but I was the one who was punished. I was approached then. For my *candor* and honesty.

"Whatever you choose to think about me, I believe in my country, in its freedoms, and its inherent desire to provide its people with a safe haven."

I'd bet my rig that Star didn't feel free and in a haven at this goddamn moment.

She didn't see my glower, too busy preaching, "I pledged my life to protect the United States, not knowing that its enemies weren't just overseas but in our government and its Armed Forces.

"The United Brotherhood fights to correct that imbalance."

I stared at her like the lunatic I believed her to be, but something in her words hit me on the raw.

The New World Sparrows *had* infiltrated every aspect of government in our nation.

Our enemies weren't just overseas but inside the corridors of power that few traversed.

Their names were hidden and protected, their identities in the shadows.

Weren't my brothers and I working to uncover the identities of Sparrows in office?

Hadn't we already erased a couple of senators and a congressman?

Didn't a Sparrow almost sit in the vice president's chair?

And, worse than all that, hadn't a Sparrow been seated in the Supreme Court? Not just any judge but the chief justice, and not just any Sparrow, but the *head* of them all.

Unable to school my expression, I turned away from her.

She might have believed she served a higher power, but that didn't mean I did. Especially now that Da was dead.

Yet there was no denying the singular truth that our nation *was* imbalanced.

I never claimed to wear a white hat, but at that moment, I'd never wanted to right those wrongs more than I did now.

18

CONOR

PRAY - SAM SMITH

Conor O'Donnelly

THE SO-CALLED emergency landing had us disembarking at Helsinki Airport.

An hour later, we were guided onto a private jet where we set off on the next leg of a journey that I was completely in the dark about. Our final destination was still a mystery even after we landed.

We were still in Eastern Europe—the weather alone told me that. Never mind the guttural language Black uttered as she spoke to the driver of a limo that was idling on the concourse, its engine surrounded by dancing eddies of steam as the heat tangled with the frigid air.

I wasn't sure if I was about to be hit over the head and dragged into the trunk, but no, the door was held open for me and my carry-ons were handled with care and deposited where I'd imagined I'd be sitting for the next part of our journey.

It was only when we were on the road that I worked out our eventual destination—Dubrovnik.

"She's in Croatia?" I sputtered.

Black sighed. "Not much gets past you, does it?"

"I'm getting pretty fucking sick and tired of your sarcasm."

"Ditto." She sniffed. "Luckily for you, I'll be leaving shortly. My job was to deliver you where you need to go. My task is almost complete."

"Probably for the best. When Star realizes you double-crossed her," I taunted, "you'll need to be on the other side of the world."

For the first time, I knew I'd said something that scared her.

Her throat bobbed.

That was it.

A bare whisper of a micro-gesture.

But it was enough.

Satisfaction filled me, enough that I sank back into the leather seats and just settled in for the ride once I'd updated my brothers who were clucking over my messages like mother hens.

> Me: Change of plans. Flight rerouted and am going to be staying in Croatia. Will be in touch when I know more. DO NOT blow up my messages because I won't answer.

A half-hour later, the sun barely peeking over the mountains as we climbed up a hill, I realized we were approaching a massive building that sat on the edge of the coast.

While it was modern in design, it was built like a fortress. There was no taking away from that.

Upon our approach, like a light switch being turned off, it was dark, and in the distance, a lighthouse flashed. Close enough that I knew there had to be islands dotted nearby.

Large gates opened for us as we passed by them, and we were taken down a long driveway that had us circling the property to reach the front where an entrance could be seen.

Two water displays decorated the facade on either side of the doors, and because of the temperatures, steam drifted on the air around them, making me wonder if this was how the Pevensies had felt as they tumbled through a closet into Narnia.

"This is where I leave you," was Black's stony retort.

"I won't say 'miss you,'" I mocked, relieved to be away from her, to be honest.

Even though her explanations had further cemented my opinion that she was a headcase, sometimes, those who weren't in their right mind had a way of speaking the truth as no one else could.

By this point, I had no idea what I was expecting.

A talking lion would make sense in the grand scheme of things. I hadn't been restrained, my personal effects hadn't been taken away from me, and my cell phone was still in my jacket pocket.

While my flight had been ambushed, according to Black, I was being taken to Star—my sole intention in the first place—and I hadn't been threatened or hurt.

Maybe the talking lion could clarify my situation because nothing was going as planned.

The door was opened for me and I stepped out without a farewell. The driver carried my bags over to the sheltered portico where a butler in a sharp suit hovered, immediately greeting me with a warm smile.

"Welcome to Uvala Lapad." His accent was sharper than the King of England's.

"Thank you, I guess," I replied, returning the smile though this fucker could be my smartly-attired, cut-glass British jailor for all I knew.

But I'd always aspired to the adage that you should treat others how you wished to be treated yourself. For the most part, anyway. Michael Byrne, the last person who'd crossed my family and had found himself on the end of one of my 'devices,' didn't count.

The butler's arm swept out to guide me inside. "My name's Edgar, sir. I'm on hand twenty-four hours a day if you require my assistance." Though my brows lifted at the offer, he continued, "Mr. Kuznetsov has asked me to pass along his request that you treat Uvala Lapad as if it were a second home."

My ears pricked at that. "Mr. Kuznetsov? He owns this place?"

"He does." Edgar beamed at me. "He has instructed me to guide you to your suite and, when you're adequately refreshed, I will lead you to his office."

Black hadn't lied.

According to Lyanov, Kuznetsov was the last person to see Star, and here I was, at his private fortress in Croatia.

"I'd appreciate it if I could speak with him now, Edgar."

"But you've been traveling for over fifteen hours, sir!" was the immediate protest.

"I'm well aware of that," I drawled. "And I appreciate the offer, but I have urgent business to discuss with him."

Edgar's disapproval was clear, but he muttered, "Very well, sir. Please step this way."

He guided me along a wide corridor that opened up onto what could only be described as a stateroom. A massive chandelier hung overhead, shooting light to all four corners of the massive space. Two fires flickered in hearths on opposite ends of the room, and a desk stood in the center of it all, overlooking a wall of windows that I knew, in the full light of day, would reveal an unencumbered view of the ocean.

There, behind the desk, was Kuznetsov. His head was bowed as he read a printout. A pair of glasses was perched on his nose and a lowball glass, filled with what I assumed was vodka, dangled in his hand.

At our steps, which echoed in the cavernous space, he didn't look up.

Edgar hovered, accustomed to being made to wait, but I wasn't, so I cleared my throat. Kuznetsov immediately peered at me over his glasses. He studied me, his head still bowed, then he rumbled something that sounded Russian, but I didn't understand it.

A dialect, maybe?

Whatever he said, it prompted Edgar to fade into the background with the supernatural skill of a highly-trained servant.

Kuznetsov chose that moment to raise his head, giving me my first glimpse of his face.

Recognition was immediate.

The unknown fourth man who'd met with Prince Ludwig, Prince Edward, and Ke Jintao of the CCP.

The photograph Star had shown me months ago.

Kuznetsov angled his head to the side. "You have seen me before?"

I gritted my teeth. "In a picture."

"Unusual. I am in very few pictures."

"I don't believe you knew you were being captured on camera," I admitted, stepping nearer to the desk.

For the first time in a long while, my confusion and uncertainty faded.

With a name to the face, I suddenly understood.

The clarity was so blinding that it hit my brain like a dose of Adderall, immediately dispersing the fog that had been stalking me for months.

"She came to question you."

"You mean she came to question *and* kill me." A smile danced around the other man's lips. "As you can see, she failed."

"She rarely fails."

"I couldn't allow her to succeed. That is why you're here."

I frowned at that, and while it could put me at the center of some unseen crosshairs, with clarity came the desire to do what few ever had for Star—to back her to the hilt even if it meant dying for it.

Hell, I'd flown for her. What was dying after that?

"I'm on Star's side," I rumbled.

"Of this, I'm aware, Mr. O'Donnelly." Kuznetsov got to his feet and stepped around the desk, arm outstretched. I realized he wanted me to shake his hand. Hesitantly, I accepted it but he continued, "Allow me to introduce myself properly. I am Anton Kuznetsov. I believe we should do away with the formalities, Conor. It will simplify things and, in this maze of contradictions, that will serve us both."

Nodding, I murmured, "That sounds good to me, Anton. Why the hell am I here? Why is Star in Dubrovnik?"

"I have traveled to many places in this world, Conor, but this is one of my favorite homes. You'll understand why when the sun rises."

"That didn't answer my question. Why would you bring someone who wanted to kill you to your favorite home?"

"Because my would-be murderer, Conor, is also my grand-daughter."

Okay, so maybe I needed another dose of Adderall.

For a second, I could only gape at him. Mouth working like a goldfish, I tried to make sense out of the nonsensical.

"That's not possible," I rasped eventually.

Amusement trickled into his eyes. "I'm quite pleased to say that you're wrong. It's very possible. Isn't she magnificent?"

"Magnificent?" I repeated blankly.

"I've been watching her for years from afar," Anton agreed. "In the flesh, she packs even more of a punch, doesn't she?"

"I've never met her."

Anton's head tipped to the side. "I don't understand."

I scratched my jaw. "We're in a long-distance relationship."

"But you've never met?"

"No. We meet online."

"Online," he repeated. "Why?"

"Why what?"

"Why have you not met her?"

"Because as *magnificent* as Star is, she's also pricklier than a hedgehog. The nearest I've managed to pin her down for a meeting is when she broke into my penthouse to hack into my computer.

"We have an atypical relationship."

"Apparently." He retreated a step and took one of the seats in front of his desk, offering me the other with a waft of his hand. "And yet, you've flown across the world for her."

"She's mine."

"As simple as that, hmm?"

"Nothing about us is simple," I said gruffly, retreating to the seat with a weary sigh.

"It would seem so." He continued to study me; for what purpose, I didn't know. Then, he blew my world apart. "She's in this house, Conor."

That had my blunt fingernails digging into the palms of my hand as I balled them into fists.

"Is she safe?" I bit off.

"She's furious but safe."

I frowned at him. "What do you mean?"

"She believes herself imprisoned. It is down to you to explain the situation to her. I can't have someone wandering around my halls and trying to kill me, Conor. Be reasonable," he quipped, but his amusement wasn't feigned.

While another person might be offended at being the target of an ex-CIA agent, evidently Anton was *not.*

"This is crazy." It was all I could think to say.

"Many things are in this life," he agreed as he made a bridge with his hands and rested his chin on them. "I am not Star's enemy. I never have been."

"She doesn't agree or she wouldn't have wanted to kill you."

"She doesn't know who I am. She has tarred me with the same brush as the Sparrows." For the first time, he made his distaste known. "I'd be offended, but my people make it their mission to keep me anonymous. For a reason." He stared at me. "I am the head of the United Brotherhood, Conor. I explained this to my granddaughter, and she immediately slotted me into the same pigeonhole as those damn birds.

"I am the Union. I am law. I am order. I stand for these things. And you must explain this to my errant grandchild before she tries to kill the only person who can give her what she wants."

Bemused, I stared at him. "And what, Anton, do you think that is?"

"The complete and utter annihilation of the New World Sparrows."

19

———————

TEXT CHAT

PAST

CONOR: *Do you think about what will happen once you're done?*
  Star: *I don't think I'll ever be done.*
  Conor: *Because you don't think you'll get to them?*

Ten minutes later

Conor: *Star? It's okay. You know you can talk to me?*
  Star: *I'm David in this fight, Conor. They're Goliath. I know what I'm up against and I know God definitely isn't on my side. I will accomplish what I can and I will die trying. That's all I can do.*
  Conor: *That's 'doing' a hell of a lot.*
  Star: *It'll never be enough.*
  Star: *I think, this past year, I've come to accept that.*
  Conor: *You knew they were big but not as big as they are.*
  Star: *Correct.*
  Conor: *Star, you're allowed a life.*
  Star: *They almost took mine.*

Conor: *Almost, Star. Almost. But they didn't. You got out. You fought your way out. You deserve to live.*

Star: *I AM living. I'm doing what I was put on this earth to do. I'm giving voices to the women who weren't as privileged as me.*

Conor: *I think you can do all that and be happy too.*

Star: *You make me happy.*

Conor: *Me?*

Star: *Yes.*

Conor: *I didn't expect you to say that.*

Star: *No. But I realized I've never told you how much I appreciate you, Conor. I wanted to before it was too late.*

Conor: *Too late for what?*

Star: *I don't know. Before I fuck this up.*

Conor: *You got a game plan I don't know about?*

Star: *I exist in chaos. You know that.*

Conor: *Luckily for you, chaos is my jam.*

Star: *:P*

Conor: *I like that you can always surprise me. It keeps me on my toes.*

Star: *You get bored easily.*

Conor: *God, I do.*

Conor: *You never bore me. ^^*

Conor: *It's one of the better features of being close to you.*

Star: *Better than my tits?*

Conor: *You've never shown them to me. Lol. My imagination is good though. So I'll say they're almost on par, but I'll reserve judgment until you show them to me in the flesh.*

Star: *I wish I were normal.*

Conor: *I don't. I like you as you are. Perfectly difficult. Normal's overrated.*

Star: *You don't mean that.*

Conor: *I don't?*

Conor: *Do I wish you hadn't suffered? That you hadn't been hurt? Of course. Do I wish you didn't have to fight this fight? Yes. But never underestimate how much I enjoy you for you, Star.*

Conor: *It's okay to not be perfect. God knows I'm not. But I think we're well suited. And, one day, just like I managed to convince you that you're not in this fight alone, I can convince you that you're allowed to sit back, enjoy the fruits of your labor, and LIVE.*

Conor: *But... that's for the future. As for now, did Katina tell you what she wanted to wear as her trick-or-treat costume yet?*

TEN MINUTES LATER

CONOR: *Star?*

20

STAR

Star Sullivan

WITH A SCREAM, I hurled the chair at the window.

"Not a fucking dent," I snarled, retrieving the chair again and slamming the feet into the glass, but it made no impression.

The bulletproof glass was next level in this godforsaken house.

In the room I'd stayed in prior to this one, a room I'd been trapped in for almost three weeks after pistol-whipping the guard with his own gun, I'd tried to shoot my way out through the window, but though most of the bullets had lodged in the specialist glass, one had ricocheted off the fucking pane and had almost hit me in the shoulder.

It was one of the prettiest prisons I'd been in, with a view of the sea that was insane even if it was winter and the sky was bleak and the ocean, as a result, was moody, but it was exactly that—a fucking prison.

I let loose another scream as I tried to slam the chair into the window again, but the force of the hit made the joint securing the front legs in place weaken and tumble under the pressure.

"FUCK!"

Outraged, I stopped trying to break the window and just smashed the chair into the floor because, having looked at the clock on the wall, the only thing I *hadn't* destroyed, I knew, yet again, I'd missed calling Kat before bedtime.

With a scream, I continued pounding the chair until I was an exhausted mass of sweat and heaving skin.

Once upon a time, I used to watch my dad destroy everything on stage—he'd slam his Fender against the ground and scream through one of *noxxious's* most famous hits—"Community Grinds."

The crowd hadn't known that for that song, the last on the line-up, the shit he wrecked were stage props and that he switched guitars so the new one in his hands got trashed and not his beloved 'Casey.'

The memory stirred something in me.

Something unbidden.

Unwanted.

It gathered in my throat.

Lodging there.

I breathed in quickly. Released the breath.

No.

I couldn't—

The tears burned. Hot and searing. Appearing like a flash flood, devastation their intent.

I ground my teeth together, trying to hold them back, but the memory was too real. Too raw.

Casey.

My mom.

Allegedly.

Her lies gave me purpose.

They let me take back my emotions.

With the remnants of the chair, I reined myself in.

"I." *Smash.* "Will." *Smash.* "Not." *Smash.* "Break." *Smash.*

That was when the door opened.

I didn't hear it, didn't even register it at first. I was too busy losing control and trying to haul myself back from the edge to notice.

"You bastards want to break me?" I screamed at the ceiling where I knew there were cameras. "It'll never happen."

Heavy, panting breaths had my chest rattling until I realized I was no longer alone.

Head whipping to the side, I saw the door was open.

Standing in the entryway was…

I blinked.

No.

Mirages didn't happen outside of deserts.

Some light phenomena occurred on the water, but I wasn't looking at the fucking ocean, and this wasn't a trick of the light.

It was a person.

A fucking person.

Someone I wanted.

Someone I craved.

Someone I betrayed.

My brow puckered with confusion, then I saw that he wasn't cuffed.

He stood there without restraints.

The ramifications of that hit home before anything else.

Traitor.

I picked up the chair again.

And I charged.

PART 2

Some women are more moth than butterfly, unveiling their painted wings in the moonlight where only someone who isn't afraid to enter the darkness is worthy to adore them.

- Amanda Celek

21

STAR

Star Sullivan

BEFORE THE CHAIR collided with him, his hands were up, fingers swiping the battered frame from my grip with an ease that took me aback.

Conor was a desk jockey.

I'd seen the pictures on those few occasions he'd starred in an article on *Page Six* and had seen his upper half during video calls, so I knew he wasn't doughy, but this was different.

He was strong.

As he snagged the chair and threw it across the room, I gaped at him.

He just arched a brow at me. "Lodestar."

My throat bobbed at that.

Lodestar.

Not Star.

He was mad at me.

The pain that overwhelmed me crushed my chest. I shook my head as I keened the words, "You're a traitor."

He sniffed. "I'm not the one who ran away."

"So you turned against me? You're one of them!" I shrieked, confusion tearing me to shreds because a part of me just wanted to hurl myself at him and another part wanted to kick him between the legs and crack those fucking nuts of his.

"No. I came here to find you," he corrected, folding his arms across his chest. "*You* are the one who embroiled me in a million conspiracies and then cut and goddamn ran."

A million conspiracies?

The ache in my head doubled down, making my temples feel like they were pounding as blood rushed to the sensitive skin. "Are you really here?" That was wishful thinking.

If he wasn't here, he hadn't betrayed me.

Not Conor. No. *He couldn't be a Brother.* He couldn't be a member of the United Brotherhood.

Completely in the dark as to where my mind had taken me, my question had him scowling, then he stunned me by stepping closer, his hand moving toward me. I jolted in surprise, turning to the side to avoid his touch. He only tutted his irritation, ignoring how I'd twisted away from him so he could press the backs of his fingers to my forehead.

"You're running a fever."

"I'm not sick," I argued, pulling back when I just wanted to sink into him.

My body was confused. *This was my Conor.* I'd dreamed about him, for God's sake. I'd shared things with him I'd shared with no one. And he was here. But... his presence was problematic. His presence had to mean—

"It'd explain why you think you're hallucinating," he pointed out.

"No."

"No?"

"No. I'm not hallucinating. I don't want you to be here if it means you're a Brother. You can't do this to me. And I was—"

"Breaking shit?"

"Yeah. That's why I'm running hot." I released a breath. This wasn't some lucid dream. It was random, but... "You *are* here."

"I am."

"That means you're a Brother."

"No, it doesn't," he scoffed. "It means the Brothers want me to help you."

My mouth rounded as I darted away from him, growling, "So you *are* on their side!"

"I haven't betrayed you, Star," he grumbled. "Temperance has. I met her, by the way. She makes *you* look sane."

"Temper? You met Temper?" If I sounded bewildered, then that was because I *was*.

"Sadly, yes. I've made her acquaintance."

"She's not a traitor," I dismissed.

"She is."

"I've known her for years."

"Longer than you've known me so you trust her more than me?"

"You're standing here. She isn't." When he grunted, I stepped forward, peering at him as if he could disappear at any minute. "For a traitor, you're hot. I'll give you that."

Conor straightened. "Jesus, you must be sick. I barely got you to accept that you like me via text chat, never mind in real life. And I'm *not* a traitor. You know me well enough by now to recognize that I'm not good with authority figures, Lodestar."

He had a point.

Conor was like a teen rebel. He enjoyed hacking into shit because he *could*. Locks meant nothing to him. They were only an enticement because it meant something juicy was on the other side and if it was being hidden, then he was curious about it.

I didn't say that aloud, just muttered, "I'm not sick." I didn't think I was. My head hurt, sure. But that was normal in these high-pressure situations.

"When was the last time you ate?"

"I-I don't know. Yesterday?" Unable to stop myself, I moved nearer. My hand reached out to gently touch his arm. He tensed at the stroke of my fingers but didn't pull back.

"We were supposed to be a team," he gritted out.

Seven words.

Somehow, amid the many arguments I'd had in my life, those seven hurt the most.

"I'm sorry."

What stunned me was that I meant it.

Traitor or not, I meant it.

He didn't accept my apology though. I could see it in his eyes. He didn't push my hand away so I didn't move it, just stared down at how my fingers, speckled with dots of blood from where splinters had dug into them, rested against the black sleeve of his turtlenecked sweater.

I wasn't the kind of woman to go gooey over men. I knew the depravities to which they'd sink better than anyone, after all. But there was something that always got to me about this one—his eyes.

They were soft.

Not in a bad way. Nor a weak one.

Just gentle.

I wasn't used to that.

His voice was the same.

Even if he was annoyed with me, he never failed to make me feel guilty because he always sounded disappointed in me rather than angry.

I just didn't know why I reacted to him like that.

The headache triggered some nausea, and I had to reason that was why I blurted, "You're not one of them?"

Hope filled me.

He sniffed, the tension rippling through his arm again. "They're insane."

Was that an answer?

"You told me once that runs in your blood." I stared at him, trying to read his expression and find the truth in those eyes that enchanted me like he was a snake charmer and I was a python.

My inquiry had him tipping his head to the side, and he stunned me by smiling. "If it does, we're both fucked. Me with Da, and you with… well, Kuznetsov seems to think you're his granddaughter, so insanity is in both our lines."

My mouth tightened. "My mother was a liar."

"Mothers tend to lie."

"I don't lie to Katina."

He hitched a shoulder. "You're weird."

"No." My brow puckered as I reiterated, "Moms aren't supposed to lie."

"In my experience, they do. Little white lies. Santa exists. The tooth fairy pays for dead bits of collagen and calcium. '*I'll call every other day…*' All lies."

That stung.

That fucking stung.

He knew I'd made that promise to Katina, but how?

"There's a big difference between telling a kid that Santa's real and —" My throat felt tight. "Katina's worried about me." It wasn't a question. *Of course, she was worried.* I'd broken so many goddamn promises to her that she'd probably never trust me again.

Who the hell could blame her?

I'd let her down when I'd sworn I never would.

"She is. I met her. She ran away to the city to find me."

Startled, I whispered, "Why?"

"Seemed to think I'd be the one who'd bring you back."

My knees felt weak at that.

My kid was worried about me and he'd comforted her.

Self-control shot to hell, I squeezed his hand. "That's why you're here?"

"It's one of the reasons." His arm dropped away, breaking the bridge we'd made with our fingers. "I'm pissed at you."

"I deserve that."

"You do. The first time I saw you, I was supposed to hug you and kiss you. I wasn't supposed to be attacked by a chair and then have to defend my goddamn honor." He huffed.

"Everyone betrays me, Conor. I don't inspire loyalty in people."

He snorted, but before his disregard could sting, he waved a hand at me. "Yeah, because I'm *not* standing here. I got a fucking concussion from Maverick because he thought I stole Kat—" That same wafting hand motioned at his forehead where the smudge from a bruise was still apparent as well as a goose egg. "—and I got on a plane for you, Lodestar. A plane. I don't do that for many people."

Confused, I asked, "You're afraid of flying?"

"No."

"No?"

"I like my feet on terra firma."

"You live in a penthouse."

"So. It's more *firma* than a plane," he grouched. "Then I had to deal with that bitch Temper for the whole flight, and *then* I had to get into a private jet to land here! Private jets crash, Lodestar."

"Not often. Planes are safer than cars."

"I rarely drive."

Though our conversation was bizarre and I was still standing in a jail cell, I rolled my eyes. "But you do it."

"If I didn't have to, I wouldn't. It was a lot easier when my parents lived closer to the city." He pointed a finger at me. "None of that takes into account the fact that I got my ass involved with a CIA/United Brotherhood-sanctioned hit on—"

"I didn't ask you to," I snarled, not letting him finish.

"You didn't have to!"

More confused than ever, I questioned, "Wait a minute. Who was the sanctioned hit on?"

"Sheridan Reinier."

I gaped at him. "The director of the CIA?"

"Yes," he hissed. "It's one thing killing and hiding the body. It's another job to shit on the CIA's doorstep and not expect them to stand in it. He's alive and kicking in a container, just waiting for you to—"

"Let me get this straight," I interrupted before he could go down a tangent. "You had the chance to kill Reinier but didn't?"

"You want to kill him. Who am I to accomplish one of your goals for you?" He sniffed.

There were bigger fish to fry than this, but... "Where is he?"

"Somewhere in the Catskills. You'll have to ask Temperance for exact coordinates." He grimaced. "That container has been there for a while. Probably not the first time it's been used as a jail cell."

"It'll be a black site."

"And people say that mafia factions are dirty."

"Your brothers would cry over the shit I've done in the name of serving the United States," I said rawly, but I'd admit, the bizarre conversation was putting me at ease. Enough that I stepped nearer to him. Enough that, even though the door behind him was open, I didn't try to knee him in the balls to make my escape. "Will they let me go?"

At my whisper, he stared deep into my eyes. "So long as you don't try to kill your grandfather."

"Don't call him that," I spat, rearing back in disgust. "He's—"

"Your only chance at eviscerating the Sparrows, Lodestar."

The words were uttered flatly.

But it was his repeated use of my handle that hurt.

Which was stupid.

He wasn't calling me 'cunt' or 'American slut.' I'd been called far worse things in my time by men, but never by Conor.

Hell, even when I'd first bombarded my way into his alarm system with Hunter Lachlan, the new Don of the Camorra, at my side, he hadn't talked down to me.

Confused, I drew away and headed toward the back corner of the room.

The door was wide open.

I could leave.

Conor was here. Not in the US.

This was real.

I slumped down into the wall, not stopping until my heels met my ass as I stared up at him.

"Star? Are you feeling okay?"

Star.

I shuddered at the sound of my name on his lips. It wasn't the first time I'd heard him say it, but it was the first time I saw his lips in the flesh as they formed the word. When they were within biting distance.

I almost growled under my breath at the thought.

Concerned, he stepped closer and squatted in front of me, one hand dropping down between his thighs to prop him up. He smelled clean. Fresh. His aftershave wasn't musky, but light.

Peering at him, I meant to speak, but the words froze in my throat.

He was so much better in real life.

That was all I could think.

His hair was longer than when I'd last seen him and it flopped onto his face. A thousand shades of brown glinted in the overhead light, making his skin more golden than it should be in the winter. His jaw was leaner than before, tougher. His mouth was a flat line like he was pressing down hard on his lips to stem the flow of words he wanted to spill.

But it was his eyes that got to me—they held his fucking heart.

More than that, they bore the burden of his soul.

I almost couldn't stand looking into them, but they drew me in like little else ever had.

The truth was on my tongue as a result when I rasped, "My mom lied to me, Conor."

Though I was definitely changing the subject, he knew what I was talking about. I had no idea what his relationship was with Kuznetsov, but my words came as no surprise to him.

"Maybe she had a good reason for it," he reasoned.

"She wasn't American. She was a spy."

Conor grimaced. "You're a spy."

"She was a double agent."

"She was loyal to someone."

My brow puckered. "Stop making excuses for her. The only reason I'm even here is because of her. I needed to avenge her but what if she deserved to die?"

"What if she didn't?" he asked simply. "Do you understand the reasons behind her death?"

"No."

"I'd assume your grandfather knows. If you ask him, perhaps he'll tell you. But he can't tell you anything if you kill him first."

That had me pouting. "His guards keep stopping me."

"They must be damn good if they can get the drop on you."

I tried very hard not to preen at that. "I'm outnumbered." His flattery wasn't just verbal. It was in his eyes. The sight had me sucking in a breath and whispering, "Conor?"

"Yes?"

"You're here."

"You're here too."

Swallowing, I pressed my hand to his shoulder so I could prod him. "Are you sure you're not a Brother?"

"Do you remember what I told you?"

"You told me a lot."

He hummed. "I told you I'm all in, Star. I didn't say that lightly."

"I ghosted you."

"You helped murder my father."

I bit my lip. "I got you involved in a conspiracy."

"Plural."

"Plural," I admitted, wincing.

"You left me. You said that I'd leave you." He slowly shook his head. "I didn't go anywhere, Star. *You* did."

My throat felt thick so it made it difficult to croak, "I needed to draw Dagda into the open. And it helped that the First Lady was a traitorous cunt." My chin tipped up as, suddenly, it was easy to get the next admission out. "Your da used you, Conor. You were a tool to him. You deserved to be free of him."

A single muscle flicked in his cheek. "By that logic, you should kill my brothers too."

"No! It wasn't like that."

He shrugged. "Each of us serves a purpose in my family. Love binds us together, but we're generals for an army we never chose to enlist in. We're all doing shit we don't want to do, Star."

The lack of anger in his voice surprised me. As did his: "You didn't kill Dagda."

"No," I said with a grimace. *I'd missed his heart.*

Dead To Me had been ribbing me about that ever since.

Well, before I'd gotten my ass imprisoned, that is.

"You *did* get the First Lady though. Via him, of course."

"I don't regret it."

"No, and I think that includes Da's death too." His nostrils flared. "You knew I loved him."

I closed my eyes. Nodded.

"You did it anyway."

My head fell back against the wall as exhaustion plagued me. "Are you here for vengeance, Conor?"

He studied me. "I'm here because I don't walk away when I make a commitment. The O'Donnellys might be fucked up, but there's one thing we do that's right…"

"What is it?"

"We atone, and you can't do that if you're stuck in Dubrovnik."

Something, a weird emotion, sharp yet soft at the same time, flickered into being inside me. "It's not that simple—"

"Don't you think that's for me to decide?"

My mouth rounded but I didn't have anything to say—there were no words.

He surged to his feet and held out his hand for me once he was standing. "You can stay in here and rot or you can stop trying to kill the man who'd like to help you. I think you should take option two."

"I only wanted to kill him once he…" I sighed. "I didn't target him to kill him."

"You didn't?"

I stared at my feet. "No. The others, maybe. Him, no."

We fell silent.

He cleared his throat. "You were going to seduce him?"

I let my chin drop.

"That'd have been awkward."

"Just a little," I croaked.

"Probably a good thing he knew who you were to him, no?"

"Yes."

"Your list of things to atone for is getting bigger."

I almost gave myself whiplash when I tipped my head up to look at him. Hope *lacerated* me. Tore me to shreds. Ripped me to fucking pieces.

Hope was futile, but he handed it to me on a plate with an arched brow and a, "Sex is a weapon for you, Star." *Star*. Not Lodestar. He wasn't angry. More… sad? *God*. The guilt burned like hydrochloric acid through the sinews of my heart. "We need to unteach you that lesson." That same brow furrowed. "This feral vibe you've got going on is hot. We may need to unteach me that lesson too."

Gaping at him, I rasped, "What the hell are you talking about?"

He sniffed. "I grew up on comic books, Star. You think I don't like a woman who could kill me?"

I had no idea where it bubbled from, but a laugh burst out of me before I could control it.

The second it did, he shot me a dopey grin and flexed his fingers in a silent prompt. I stared at him like the digits were rattlers waiting to bite me but, cautiously, I reached out.

Just as cautiously, he tugged me upward.

No part of me touched him aside from where our hands connected. I stared down as he untangled his grip on me.

"One day at a time, Star."

"I'm a horrible person," I confessed.

"Then I have shitty taste in women."

"I kill people."

He grimaced. "Can you stop killing my family?"

"You can't have forgiven me for that."

"No. I told you. That's what atonement is for."

"Does atonement involve sex?"

His grimace morphed into a scowl. "No, of course not. Don't be ridiculous. Would you forgive me for killing your mother with a quick fuck?"

That *did* sound ridiculous. Especially considering the lengths I'd gone to to avenge her memory.

The thought sent splinters of pain through me.

How would I ever atone for the things I'd done to him and his family?

Just because I'd thought his father was a sadistic asshole didn't mean Aidan Sr. wasn't beloved. I'd known Conor loved him and had still gone through with my plans.

Feeling wretched, I heaved a despondent sigh. "I told you before, Conor, I'm toxic."

"Maybe I don't think you are. Maybe I think you hide behind what you consider your toxicity—"

"Do you want to fix me? Is that it?"

"Only women think they can fix their partners." He had a point. "You can't change a person, and I don't see why you'd want to. Why be with them if you think they should change?" His shoulder hitched up into a soft shrug. "So, what, you're a fucking minefield. Nobody has ever kept up with me apart from you, Star. Nobody. Do you know how goddamn lonely that is?"

It took me longer than it should to whisper, "I do."

He shot me a knowing look. "Because you've been just as lonely as me. Because no one has ever challenged you. No one can understand you and how your brain works and what you're capable of. No one—" He pointed a finger at himself. "—but me.

"So, I'll forgive you eventually because you'll work for my forgiveness and we'll deal with this because, where you and I are concerned, we're all in and there's no going back. It was already too late the moment you crashed through my code like a bull on a rampage."

As I stared at him, his words ramming home as nothing else could, and with more of that venomous hope filtering through my bloodstream, a single thought ricocheted around my mind.

He was right.

22

CONOR

SHE WAS EXACTLY how I knew she'd be.

Cautious.

Wary.

Feral.

Beautiful, even in sweats.

Cat-like in her movements.

Strong.

Powerful.

Furious.

Fuck, I hadn't been messing around when I said my inner kid who'd been raised on comic books loved that about her.

She was a live wire, flaring and hissing, and me being a moron, I was just begging to be burned.

But maybe that was how we'd work—I didn't need to dull that spark.

Who better to stand by her side than a man who loved playing with electricity?

"If you were trying to seduce him, then why did you try to kill him?"

Okay, it was hard saying that out loud, even if I understood why. *I was possessive.* That was a trait that had been bred into every O'Donnelly in our family tree. I couldn't share her. Not in that way.

The thought made me grit my teeth.

Would she do that in the future? Try to use her body to get information?

No. I wouldn't let it get that far. If she needed information, I'd crack the fucking Pentagon to get it so she never had to put herself in danger again.

I breathed easier at that game plan.

Being proactive was better than nothing.

She peered at me from beneath long lashes. "Because he pissed me off."

I had to laugh. "That's enough to kill someone?"

"He told me that it was my past that made me deadlier than my mother."

My eyes bugged. "Well, damn, that was just asking for it."

She made a gesture with her hand. "Who was I to disagree with him?"

I pondered her situation for a moment. "Temper is a Brother. Honestly. Whether you believe anything else I've said, believe that. She's a fucking bitch too."

Her nostrils flared. "I'll deal with her later."

That shouldn't have filled me with satisfaction but it totally did.

"I told her that she'd regret betraying you." My smile turned smug. "It was the only thing that shut her the hell up."

She huffed. "She does like the sound of her own voice."

"Affirmative," I groused. "She said something, though, that made me question shit."

"What?"

"It's something Kuznetsov said later too. They stand for law and order. Or, at least, they believe they do."

"Then why is there so much injustice?" she grumbled with a pout.

I didn't have an answer and, to be honest, I was more focused on not touching her than anything else.

That pout.

I shoved my hands into my pockets.

Since the moment I'd walked through the goddamn door, I'd been fighting those urges.

Being attacked with a chair should not have led to an erection, but fuck if I could tell my cock that she wasn't play-fighting.

Still, she looked at me expectantly.

"I never said that I don't think they're insane."

She choked out a laugh but her amusement slowly faded as she mused, "He wants me on their side."

"Are you sure?"

"Why else would I be here?"

"I don't know. Temper said that Dead To Me wasn't a Brother—" Her shoulders sagged in apparent relief at that. As someone who'd been betrayed by more friends and family in the past few years than was healthy, I got it. "—because of her side gig. So, and I hate to break it to you, Star, but you're not squeaky clean, are you? Why would they want you but not her?"

"Because I'm his heir, aren't I? And because you can believe you're a good person but if you want to make a difference, blood always has to be spilled.

"No wars are won without soldiers."

I knew she was right.

As depressing as that was.

"Maybe he doesn't want a soldier."

"He said he made my mom do whatever he wanted. She went where he sent her. She was cannon fodder."

I pursed my lips. "He's old now. It changes things."

"I doubt it. I guarantee that everything he wants comes at a price."

I thought about my conversation with Misha. "Sometimes that price is worth paying."

Though she arched a brow at me, she tipped her chin down in agreement.

"Imagine if he could follow through on his promise. If he could take down the Sparrows... Temper said that James Garfield was a Brother—"

"The president?" She scoffed, "And you believed her?"

"I don't know to be honest. I don't know what the hell I believe. I just know that we were standing in the CIA HQ at Langley with Reinier pissing himself because she'd tasered him in his boardroom and, out of nowhere, a team of soldiers appeared, further incapacitated him, then took him from the building and plunked him on a helipad."

"The Sparrows have that power," she remarked.

"The Sparrows are scum, granddaughter. I have told you this many times since our initial meeting; you just choose not to listen."

Star immediately tensed at the old man's voice, but when we whipped around to stare at the room, we were still alone.

I studied the ceiling, on the hunt for a speaker, and only relaxed when I found it and two others. A tiny glass-like bead told me we were being watched too—unsurprising that they'd been surveilling her.

He'd caged a tiger in one of his bedrooms…

What else did he expect other than carnage?

Star stared at the ceiling, right where I'd been looking, telling me she'd done her homework despite her outrage. "I doubt the Sparrows would classify themselves as scum. Does anyone really think they're evil? Doesn't every one of us have justifications for why we do what we do?"

Kuznetsov hummed under his breath. "How can I prove to you that we cannot be tarred with the same brush?"

"I don't think you can," I answered, silently shooting her a glance that asked her to confirm or deny my belief.

Her gaze was locked on mine as she said, "If you can take down the Sparrows, why haven't you already?"

"A very good question, granddaughter."

Her nostrils flared.

"I wouldn't call her that yet."

I made the choice not to call him by his name, even if it would further the conversation. It could indicate a relationship between us that would sow the seeds of distrust between Star and me.

She was all that mattered here.

Not whatever purpose Kuznetsov had for her.

"Yet? You mean never," she muttered under her breath.

If she'd been a cat, she'd have been spitting and hissing.

It made me want to stroke her. Soothe her. I could appreciate her strength and could even be fascinated by it, but her many facets were what repeatedly drew me in.

For the first time in my life, I understood why Declan could study a portrait for hours on end and not get bored.

Code had been my raison d'être for so long, and that was an art form in and of itself, but there was nothing on this earth that I found more magnetizing than Star Sullivan.

Kuznetsov clipped, "We can discuss this like rational human beings if you'd like, Star. You must be hungry."

I nudged her in the side with my arm. "I haven't eaten in hours."

"Hours? You weren't made for action, Conor, were you?"

I grinned at her. "I was. Just not the kind of action you're talking about."

Her mouth rounded at my blasé tone. Not that I could blame her. I'd gone from spitting fire at her to joking around, but that was how I rolled. Quick to temper, quick to calm. Quicker still to react accordingly and to adapt. She was still bristling. If we were going to get anywhere, I needed to help bring her down from this high-stress plateau she was subsisting on.

That chair she'd been slamming into the ground wasn't a forty-buck special from IKEA. It was a goddamn antique. Mahogany. Velvet horsehair cushion. *Heavy.* I'd tossed it across the room with half of its weight missing. She'd been throwing it around like she'd been taking the same supplements the Hulk did.

No, she needed gentling.

I was prepared to be mauled to allow that to happen.

Da might have taught the shittiest life lessons, but how he'd been with Ma was rich with wisdom.

A man burned so his woman didn't have to, and pissed at her or not, she was that—mine.

We were standing in the same room, breathing the same oxygen. At last. She was *there*. Anything else in the long list of troubles we shared could be fixed at a later date.

I just had to ensure there *was* a later date.

"Are you really hungry?" she grouched.

I shrugged. "Temperance pissed me off. I barely ate on the plane over here."

She ran a finger down her nose—it wasn't the middle finger. "Fine." To the ceiling, she growled, "If you drug my food, we're back to square one."

God, did she know how exhausted she sounded?

"I haven't drugged your food at any point, Star," Anton said with a sigh. "I'm not going to start now. I've gone to a lot of effort to bring Mr. O'Donnelly over here to help you. You needn't persist in seeing me as the enemy."

She pursed her lips. "So I can just walk out of this room, huh?"

"Yes."

"No guards?"

"None. Unless you attempt to take my life again."

"They'll probably kill me before they kill you."

Her eyes widened at my quip. "What?"

"I'm expendable here," I said easily, watching as that news settled in her bones and rattled her.

Well, that was a relief.

She *did* care.

"I'd better behave then." Something flickered in her eyes, something that warned me I needed to get better at interpreting those looks. Her face, after all, was blank. Utterly expressionless. Even when she grated out, "Or protect you before they can get to you."

"I'm willing to be saved," I teased.

The tiniest of smiles curved her lips—I'd take that as a win. "Why am I surprised you're like this?"

"I don't know. What am I like?"

"A joker."

I was with the people I trusted. She hadn't earned that admission yet, even if it was the truth, so I just said, "I'm the middle child. We have to stand apart from the crowd."

Though she snorted as I intended, I saw her unease start to drift back into her expression. I half-hoped she'd share her concerns with me, but whatever progress I'd made over months and months of text chats had been stalled by our time apart.

The irony was, of course, that if anyone should be pissed here, it was me.

Her chin angled up and she inhaled briskly through her nose as if coming to a decision she didn't let me in on, one that had nothing to do with purple soup... "If he feeds us borscht, I expect you to eat it."

"I'm not Katina," I retorted.

"I'm only breaking bread with the man because you're hungry, so if he serves beet soup, you'd better start eating."

I hid a smile of my own. "You eat it; I'll eat it."

Though she sniffed, her hand reached out. I stared at it, unsure of what she was doing, then her fingers curled in on themselves before she could make contact with me.

Fuck, I wished she *had* touched me.

"I'm sorry Maverick hurt you."

Ah, the bruises.

"Don't be." I meant it too. Everyone needed a support system like the Sinners' MC. "It means Katina is in safe hands."

Her eyes tangled with mine. Just when I thought I could drown in them, she told me, "I wouldn't have left if I didn't think she was safe."

At first, I thought she was being antagonistic for the sake of it, but then I realized she *wanted* me to believe her.

I gave her a nod. "She's with family but she wants her mom."

Agony flooded her eyes, but she didn't answer, just straightened her shoulders and started toward the door.

How she edged around the corner let me know she was on red alert.

I guessed, as miserable as it sounded, I'd grown used to Eoghan behaving similarly—ever prepared. Ready to face anything—a bullet to the face or to the heart, whichever struck first.

I didn't realize that it would destroy something in me to see her share the same mannerisms.

Because I thought Kuznetsov was telling the truth, even if that truth was another person's insanity, I didn't fear for my life as I stepped into the hallway.

I was, however, surprised to find that she'd waited for me, but I noticed that the hand closest to me was balled into a fist and I wondered if she wanted me to take it. To slide my fingers around hers as I'd done in her pretty, battered prison.

She was in fight mode—I didn't think Lodestar had a flight mode to be fair—so it didn't make sense for her to want tenderness from me. Support, yes. Gentleness? Affection? No.

If anyone understood that she had to play harder, faster, and stronger than a man in this situation, it was me. I had no desire to undermine her. So instead, I moved alongside and, very carefully, let my pinkie connect with her knuckles.

Though we were both staring straight ahead, I heard her quick inhalation. Then, I hid another smile when she bounced pinkies with me too.

My fingers flexed with the desire to reach out but I kept myself under control, fortuitous considering a man appeared at the end of the corridor.

Her tension was immediate, and I knew she expected him to be a guard, but I thought it was a servant. Something the stranger confirmed by nodding at us, his arms fixed at his side, his back to us as he descended the same staircase I'd used to get up here.

The edifice itself was constructed like a fortress, but inside, it was more of a five-star hotel than anything else. It was strange that Kuznetsov had used his home as a prison, but everyone had a different way of dealing with family, I guessed.

Her gaze darted around as we traversed different hallways, and I knew she was marking exits. Much as I permitted Eoghan to do the same thing wherever we were, like I'd let him sit with his back to the wall so he was looking out onto any given room, I stayed quiet as she found her bearings.

When we reached a large set of doors that opened up into a dining room, that was where we discovered her grandfather. Standing at the head of the table, one that ran the length of the thirty feet-long room, he remained behind his chair, clearly waiting for us.

The man was old. His skin was more papery than Da's had been. But his back was straight, his shoulders weren't hunched, and he appeared to be as sharp as ever from the intensity of his study during our walk over to him.

The state of the room she'd been kept in was proof enough of what her grandfather had said—she'd been like a caged wild animal. But it was the number of guards in the dining room that confirmed what I already knew—how deadly she was.

Nine of them.

Nine fucking guards all hovering in place around Kuznetsov because of *one* woman.

Upon our approach, I braced for Star to hurl herself at him, for her to pick up a spoon from the table and to use it to stab him. I knew the guards who were standing nearby did the same, but she didn't mistreat the silver cutlery. No, she retained her composure, casting me a knowing glance as she calmly sank into the chair the servant held out for her.

Kuznetsov and I withdrew our own seats and took our places, sandwiching her between us.

Her spine would make a ruler seem curved. Her shoulders weren't high, but her tension was so fierce that she was practically vibrating.

It was only at that moment that I really got a chance to study her.

Sure, I'd been looking at her before, but in the silence that settled among us, I took in the almond eyes that missed nothing, the gentle lines of a mouth that had a tendency to angle downwards at the corners —her inherent discontent visible in the flesh.

Fuck, I wanted to change that.

I also wanted to kiss her more than I wanted my heart to take its next beat because her upper lip was full, the bottom fuller. I just knew kissing her would feel like heaven.

Her nose was strong, and there was the tiniest of breaks at the bridge. Her brows were arched and they led to the faintest of widow's peaks that sank into rich brown hair that was just a couple of shades lighter than mine.

Her body was strong. Compact. A weapon.

I didn't want that to turn me on, but it did.

She was more than a weapon. She was a woman. She needed to be respected as such because, until now, that had been her worth—her ability to kill.

My body didn't understand the nuance even if my mind did.

Three servants appeared out of the woodwork to disturb the awkward silence. They brought soup, but I thanked God that it wasn't purple. Even starving, beet soup wasn't my jam despite my Russian sisters-in-law trying to tempt us with it.

Give me a goddamn steak any day of the week.

Star tensed at the sight. What had offended her about cheesy soup, I didn't know, but her fingers bled white around the spoon in her hand.

"French onion soup was her favorite dish," Kuznetsov said demurely.

"You turned your daughter into a weapon," was her flat response. "Don't think I'm impressed that you remember her favorite foods."

"I never asked for you to be impressed," he countered, but his voice contained no ire.

From the corner of my eye, I studied them both, well aware that Star was still vibrating like I'd hooked her up to that prototype toy I was building for her and that Kuznetsov eyed her warily, as if she were about to strike.

His guards remained on red alert which also spoke louder than words…

But she stayed quiet.

Her spoon dipped into the gooey mass of bread and cheese and she placed it between her lips with a grace that came as a surprise.

Not that I figured she'd eat like a Viking or anything but there was a demureness about her actions that took me aback.

A quick glance at her lap showed me how her legs were pressed together, the toes of one foot neatly tucked behind the other ankle.

This wasn't a brat who'd been raised on tour buses. This was—

"Did you attend a boarding school?"

Star arched a brow at the astonishment in my tone. "Why would that come as a surprise considering how rich my father was and how fucked up everything was after Mother died?"

Mother. Not Mom.

I winced for her hurt but still questioned, "Where?"

"Switzerland, of course. Only the best for Gerry Sullivan's daughter who needed *'structure'* to overcome her mother's death." Her sneer told me what she thought about that 'structure' before it morphed into a smug grin. "I got expelled before I could graduate though." It was almost a relief to hear her sounding more like the woman I knew —cocky.

I'd take that over bitter.

"How long were you there?" Kuznetsov asked politely, but I got the feeling he already knew the answer.

"Four months."

"What got you expelled?" I quipped.

Soup forgotten, I turned into her, my curiosity so absolute that it was easy to forget we were in the middle of a conspiracy with a previously unknown grandfather who was currently existing on tenterhooks just in case she tried to attack him again.

"I hacked into their database." She winked at me, knowing full well I'd enjoy this story. Hackers loved sharing their wins with people they trusted, people who understood and appreciated their skills. "Found the good shit on the girls and sent it to a gossip rag in London."

My mouth rounded. "They pinned it on you?"

She chuckled. "I made sure they knew it was me behind the job."

"Jesus."

"Got myself established with some dollars and began the emancipation process from my dad."

If I'd been gaping before, that was nothing to now. "What?! You divorced Gerry Sullivan?"

She snorted. "You know it's weird when you do that, don't you? He wasn't Gerry Sullivan to me." Her gaze dropped to her soup. "I was his daughter, and I was trying to shake some sense into him by being a rebellious brat."

Guilt hit me. "Sorry, Star. You know I—" I grimaced. There was no excuse, not when she was hurting. "What happened?"

"The record company swept it under the rug. It never got pushed through."

"So you didn't get emancipated?"

"No. I'm glad now that I didn't, but back then I was furious."

"I'd gather he was too?"

"No. I think he knew I was attention-seeking. I'm pretty sure that's why Savannah's Mom has a problem with me still."

I frowned. "She had to recognize that you wouldn't do something so drastic unless there were… issues."

Her gaze found mine and, beneath my fascinated study, a blush bloomed to life on the arcs of those high cheekbones I really wanted to press my lips to. "Not everyone has as much faith in me as you do, and not everyone believes all sins can be atoned for."

"It's the Catholic in me," I teased her softly, sensing that my words had meant a lot to her.

I was glad they had but I was also confused. I didn't understand how anyone could be around her, never mind watch her grow into the woman standing here today, and not understand how she worked.

Star was loyal.

It just wasn't a loyalty that most were accustomed to.

She made the tough decisions, the hard ones that would leave her being hated, but that would protect those she considered her family.

As someone who'd been impacted by that negatively, if her MO registered with me, I didn't understand why it wouldn't with people who'd known her for decades.

I'd met Savannah's parents a couple times, and I found it hard to reconcile this with those meetings. It was evident to me that family meant everything to them, so how could they have let Star down so badly?

In the aftermath of that short conversation, she returned her focus to the soup and continued eating. While my mind ping-ponged around with this new knowledge, I shot Kuznetsov a glance he interpreted correctly—*don't disturb her when she's eating.*

His gaze drifted over her pallor, and he nodded his agreement.

Now that the color of exertion and then embarrassment had faded, she looked pale, but the soup appeared to help.

We all needed fuel, but Star probably burned through calories like a Mack truck sucked up gas.

When she'd finished her appetizer, I asked, "Do you feel better?"

She reached for her napkin, picked it up, and gently prodded the corners of her mouth.

With a smile that fooled me, she half-turned toward me.

It was misdirection at its simplest.

In those moments, while her focus seemed to be directed at me, that was when she snagged the fork beside her glass of water, reached over, and stabbed the hand Kuznetsov had rested on the table as he ate.

Guards poured toward us as Anton screamed in pain, but Star merely sat back in her seat and drawled, "Now, we can talk."

Men roughly grabbed her and dragged her arms behind her back, needing two for a one-man job because this was Star, and I watched as they cuffed her.

"Do you go out of your way to be difficult?" I grumbled, but when she made a slight moue as they jerked her shoulder and locked her in place, I snarled, "You're hurting her."

That was when I saw the guard's temple was discolored...

Using his distraction against him, I seized his hand and rolled it backward, not stopping until the bone in his wrist snapped and he was yowling.

"You learned Krav Maga," Star stated, her eyes wide in surprise and...

Now wasn't the time to enjoy her appreciation.

Ignoring her, I grated out at the other guard, "You do not hurt her." Then, to Kuznetsov, I demanded, "Get them to back the fuck down."

Though he was breathing hard through the pain, Kuznetsov *did* groan something at them in that dialect he'd used with Edgar, which was when the guard cradling his wrist traipsed off with a glower at me, while the other loosened her cuffs and she relaxed some.

Now that she was free, I shot her a disapproving glance. "He's old, Star. That'll take ages to heal."

Her sniff could only be described as dismissive. "He locked me in a bedroom like I was thirteen, Conor—"

"You *were* trying to kill him," I countered.

"I've stopped trying. I won't kill you," she shouted over her grandfather's wails as he cupped his bleeding hand to his chest. "But you turned my mother, the only person who never betrayed me, into a liar. That required punishment."

Kuznetsov spat something at her in that dialect I couldn't understand again, but Star surprised me by retorting, "If you thought I wouldn't try anything, you're an idiot and that means you're too much of a moron to be able to help me as you promised Conor."

At her words, Kuznetsov sagged into his chair, and, out of nowhere, a medic rushed in, an old-fashioned doctor's bag in her hand.

Used to chaos around the table, I carried on finishing my soup, watching as a couple men popped up from out of nowhere, bringing what appeared to be a type of mobile scanner of some variation.

Within a few moments, the healer was peering at Star with surprise then down at her boss. "She missed every joint, artery, and nerve."

Star's smirk was cocky enough that I rolled my eyes. "Only you," I muttered under my breath.

Kuznetsov hissed at the doctor who, right at the dinner table, sewed him up, cleaned the wounds, then bandaged his hand. She dosed him with what I assumed were pain pills and antibiotics, then the medical team darted away as swiftly as they'd rushed in.

"Granddaughter, you are a fool," Kuznetsov snarled. His anger fired him up but he remained slouched and slumped over in his chair.

"You can't expect deadly weapons not to fulfill their purpose," I defended, using his own words against him. "Star usually doesn't say anything she doesn't mean. She won't attack you again."

"You expect me to believe that? I brought you here to calm her down—"

"Hey," I argued. "I'm many things but I'm not human Valium. Star is Star. You don't like what she turned into, well, hell, I figure you could have helped out along the way instead of living in your own bat cave on the Adriatic."

Kuznetsov spat in that dialect again, but Star hitched a shoulder. "He's right."

"I helped where I could," he grated out.

"Sounds like you were really helping her when she sought emancipation from a father who was fully jacked up on heroin for days at a time and put her in unsafe situations," I sniped.

Still cradling his now-bandaged hand, Kuznetsov growled something at the guard stationed behind Star and, a moment later, she was released from her cuffs.

She curled her fingers inward, stretching her wrists back and forth and rubbing the flesh where the restraints had been too tight and had bitten into her skin.

Annoyed at the sight, I grumbled, "Fine way to treat your granddaughter."

Before he could answer, she reached up and rubbed the balls of her shoulders, rotating them carefully as she mocked, "I'm not a granddaughter to him. I'm a tool."

"That's not true," was Kuznetsov's retort.

"No?" Star cocked a brow at him. "I don't doubt you will require payment for bringing down the Sparrows. No matter what bullshit you fed Conor."

"Payment is a harsh word."

She smirked. "You don't deny it."

"You don't," I pointed out with a scowl.

Kuznetsov's jaw worked a moment before he hissed something at his men—I was definitely going to have to learn that dialect.

As I wondered how Star had picked it up and where it came from, I watched as his men drifted away from the edges of the room and disappeared through the doors I assumed led to the kitchen as that was the exit the servers had used earlier.

When we were alone, Lodestar pinned her grandfather with another look. "I don't like being manipulated. You want something from me, you tell me. We can come to some arrangement.

"The moment Conor opened that damn door, I knew something had to be going on. At first, I thought he had to be a Brother, but then, Conor told me Temperance Black was a part of your little Illuminati crew and it hit me.

"*She* was the one who told you about Conor and me working together, and you reunited us not because he could talk me down from killing you—that was a bonus. You brought two of the most powerful hackers in the world together. That wasn't out of the kindness of your black heart.

"So," she drawled on. "Let's cut to the chase. What is it you actually want from us?"

Kuznetsov reached for his wine glass with his good hand. Eyes locked on his granddaughter as much as hers was on him, he took an unhurried sip.

As if they were playing an invisible game of chess, he eventually said, "It was unexpected, you teaming up with Conor O'Donnelly."

"An advantage?"

He nodded. "How could it not be? The great aCooooig and Lodestar, working as a unit, making history together..." His smile was too cheerful for the conversation we were having. "You've made a lot of friends along the way, haven't you, child?"

"Some are better than others." She stunned me by gently pressing the backs of her fingers to my knee under the table. "If you know who has earned that label from me, you'll also know the lengths I'll go to to protect them. So, tread carefully, old man. I'm not afraid to bite."

Star Sullivan

"WHAT I OFFER, child, is everything you've been working toward since you escaped your prison."

I studied him, reading between his lines in an attempt to come up with the raw bones of a deal that'd make him my version of a fairy godmother.

But Conor wasn't naive and, like he'd said, he was one of the few, if not the *only* person who could keep up with me. That meant Kuznetsov had used his feelings for me to manipulate him and that Kuznetsov would do that, would use feelings that too few people had felt for me in this godforsaken life I'd been leading, annoyed the ever-living shit out of me.

"If something sounds as if it's too good to be true," I countered in response, "then it usually is."

Kuznetsov grimaced as he tucked his hand closer to his chest in a subconscious act. "So distrusting."

"I wonder why," I mocked, not an ounce of guilt plaguing me for stabbing him in the hand.

I didn't give a shit if he was ninety or nine. Conor was right—you fucked with my people, you fucked with me.

And, already, he'd fucked with Conor.

He'd brought him *here* when I'd taken myself away from him on purpose.

I was many things but not a hypocrite.

I was fucking with my people, so I needed to be punished.

Maybe Conor and I were more alike than I realized.

He called it atonement. I called it retribution.

Conor gently pushed his bowl away, leaned his elbows on the table, and started playing with his hands as he reasoned, "It must be a massive task if your idea of remuneration is bringing down the Sparrows."

Kuznetsov angled the glass at Conor. "The task is not gargantuan but it is specialized."

"If you think only Conor and I can do it, that's an understatement."

"It requires more than just the two of you."

I frowned. "You need a team of hackers?"

"You can use the *Pauks* for assistance—"

"They work for you," I clipped. "If you think I'd trust them—"

"You can use BDSec if you prefer," Kuznetsov slipped in quickly. "I don't care so long as the job is done."

As my brow furrowed, Conor rasped, "BDSec? Why would we work with them? We're not affiliated—"

"I was one of the founding members," I admitted, cringing.

His nostrils flared. "You didn't think to share that with me?"

"I'm not a member anymore," I retorted. "I stepped back—" Before I could give Kuznetsov insight into why I'd done that, I broke off, muttering, "I'll tell you later if you really want to know."

"BDSec is one of Europe's biggest hacktivist groups," he snapped. "Of course, I want to know the backstory of how you came to be one of its founding members."

"It was years ago!"

"Are you still friends with them?"

I glowered at Kuznetsov's interruption. "Yes."

"They would be amenable to helping you?"

Minerva and Ovianar *would* help if I went crawling on my knees to them.

I didn't say that though. "If the justification *and* the payment are big enough."

Slowly, he nodded. "Good."

"What is the job?"

"It's actually twofold." Kuznetsov paused to take another sip of his drink.

From how heavy his eyelids were, I got the feeling he shouldn't be mixing his pain meds with alcohol.

"Start at the beginning," I prompted.

"I have another granddaughter. Her name is Lyra."

"I have a sister?" I shrieked, jerking to my feet so quickly that my chair toppled back and onto the floor.

Conor immediately snatched at my fingers and held me in place. The feel of his hand around mine was surprisingly calming and, in this situation, I needed all the help I could get.

Behind me, he dragged my chair upright, then he ordered, "Sit down, Star. Let's not make this situation even worse."

My calm disintegrated into dust. "He's saying I have a sister and I didn't know about her—"

"I did not say that, child," Kuznetsov growled. "I said that I have a granddaughter. She is your cousin."

This news was as bad as the time I'd been stabbed in the abdomen.

"My mother had siblings."

What else had she kept from me?

"I had a son." Kuznetsov stared into his glass as he swirled the red wine around the base. Soon, his head was moving with the motion. "His name was Aleks."

"Was?" Conor asked quietly, his fingers still locked around mine.

Kuznetsov shot him a glance. "Yes, he's dead."

Out of nowhere, Conor straightened up so fast he nearly bounced on his seat. "It wasn't—"

The old man sniffed. "No. Your band of Irish hooligans didn't kill him."

"Oh. I just figured that might be why I was here."

"Who did?" I slipped in.

Kuznetsov hitched a shoulder. "I have no idea."

"I thought you were—"

"All-seeing and all-knowing?" Kuznetsov snorted at Conor. "Black is one of our more zealous believers."

"I'd never have guessed," Conor mumbled.

Anger shot through my veins, as if they were filled with gas at the mention of her goddamn name.

Temperance fucking Black was next on my shit list.

She was going to regret sharing my secrets with this old bastard, and Dead To Me would too if she knew her cousin was involved with these secret society numbnuts.

"Where did he die?" Conor queried.

"The US."

"I don't understand how this, as sad as it is," Conor said politely, "has anything to do with helping bring down the Sparrows."

Kuznetsov focused on me, his blurry eyes seeming lucid as he rumbled, "I want you to find my granddaughter and bring her home to me, and I want you to find who killed my son and seek vengeance on his behalf."

Conor sniffed. "I knew this Brotherhood was as corrupt as the Sparrows."

Kuznetsov's attention snapped away from me so he could glower at him. "We are not. As the Union, we are beyond reproach, but I'm an old man. I have lost all my family. God only knows how much time I have left, and if I can spend those years with children who are my blood, then I will."

I frowned at him. "I don't want to spend time with you."

"You might like me if you were open to the idea."

"I doubt it."

Kuznetsov's top lip curled into a snarl. "Then how about this? Your task is now threefold. You will avenge my son's death, you will find my other granddaughter, and you will spend time with me before I die if you ever want the Sparrows to be taken down."

"You could live until you're a hundred," I bitched.

"Then you're about to be very well acquainted with Dubrovnik, aren't you?" he sniped.

Conor cleared his throat. "Before you two trigger World War Four over empty soup bowls, I have to ask how you believe you can eradicate the Sparrows? I assume you wouldn't offer your granddaughter hope without being able to follow through with it…"

"A good point," Kuznetsov agreed. "Originally, the Sparrows used chat windows on online video games to communicate, but over the past year, we have uncovered another method they use—a private app that is available for sale on the biggest app markets.

"They shield their app behind a shadow operating system. We've been working on using this platform as a means of mass-identifying their numbers and targeting them that way."

"As easy as that?"

"Trust me, child, it is not easy. I've had the *Pauks* working on this for eighteen months. It's only recently we discovered how they communicate and that was through intense, shall we say, *study*."

His admission had me pursing my lips. "How would you deal with the individuals identified as Sparrows?"

He shot a pointed look at Conor. "It would be an entirely different method to the one the O'Donnellys have cooked up."

"What's he talking about?" I demanded.

"Some, we've been killing," he admitted unapologetically, running a hand through his hair. "Others are more complicated. We're starting to plant law enforcement agents in the offices of known Sparrows and they're taking them in that way."

I twisted in my seat to better study him. "How do you decide who dies and who gets arrested?"

"Declan conferred with Rex on the matter."

Rex—the Prez of the Satan's Sinners' MC.

But that didn't make any sense.

Unless…

"If Hawk's Old Lady," I stated, not wanting to name Amara, "identified them, then they die?" At his nod, I mused, "A solid decision process."

Thanks to an unusual condition, Amara had never forgotten a face she'd seen. As a Sparrow sex slave, that meant she recognized either victims or fuckers in need of having their dicks cut off and their throats slashed.

Kuznetsov released a sharp bark of laughter. "And this, granddaughter, is why I never recruited you into the Brotherhood. It would have made my life a hell of a lot easier, I assure you, if I'd been able to have you on my team from the beginning, but how could I when your morals are beyond dubious?"

"Product of my environment, old man."

He narrowed his eyes at my disrespectful tone, but whatever he threw at me, I'd dish back.

I wasn't scared of him.

"If you don't intend on utilizing our methods, then how will you do this?" Conor persisted, ignoring the mutinous glares Kuznetsov and I shared.

"Interpol."

"Interpol?"

"You've heard of them, I presume?" he bit off sarcastically.

"Why them?"

"I trust the leadership."

"Meaning they're Brothers," I complained.

"Not all of them, and Sparrows have systematically been weeded from their ranks."

My mouth tightened. "What would you do?"

"Develop a special task force to deal with the Sparrows themselves. Who knows which names will crop up during this investigation? It's not something that can be swept under the carpet, nor is it possible to murder every individual who pledged themselves to their cause." At my sniff, he argued, "There are millions of them around the globe, Star. Their deaths, whether you like it or not, will trigger questions. And this is not 1930s Russia!"

"He's right," Conor muttered.

Mouth tight, I nodded. "I know he is." That didn't mean I had to like it.

"The body may be frail but the mind is not weak," Kuznetsov rumbled, sinking back the final dregs in his wine glass. "This plan has been underway for a long time. Ever since you became involved with them, to be precise.

"You can judge me as you want, granddaughter, but I pushed back retirement from my position to ensure that you see justice for what happened to you."

Discomfort tunneled its way inside me. His words would mean something if I trusted him, but how could I?

He could tell me anything and make it fit a narrative that would get me on his side.

There was one undeniable truth that he couldn't run away from— he hadn't come to me. I'd had to find him. The concerned 'grandfather' role, until he put weight behind it, was just an act.

Thus, I dismissed him and his help. "I could handle this on my own."

"No, you couldn't. This is power beyond anything you've come across. We're not just talking about some dirty cops in the NYPD. They've infiltrated the most powerful offices in the US. And that's not accounting for the European and Asian bodies—"

"If you're so worried *now*, where were you when I was being passed around as a cum dump?"

He flinched, his muscles locking up.

Good.

The truth fucking hurt.

When it didn't look like he was going to reply, Conor frowned at him. "If this Brotherhood of yours is so all-fired powerful, and if you've existed for so damn long, then why did you let them come to be in the first place?"

"The Union protects, but we do not intercede unless necessary. My predecessors were staunch believers in that ideology.

"The Old World Sparrows came to exist because they were Brothers who were annoyed at our isolationist ideals. They believed we didn't involve ourselves enough with active government so they created a body of power where they could fulfill their own goals.

"As with everything, it usually starts from a good place and quickly spirals out of control. *This* is why we stay back and monitor the global stage. Involving oneself too much can lead to corruption and manipulation of the society we strive to protect.

"It was only after the Sparrows came to be that we began to evolve our own methods. We pushed Brothers into office and we passed laws to protect a nation's core values to stop them—"

"Why didn't you keep gangs from forming? Why does the mafia even exist?" I butted in. "How is crime still a thing—"

He interrupted me right back, "Because we police laws, not people."

"That's bullshit," I scoffed. "You've been doing a shitty job in the US recently then, haven't you? Not so observant lately."

Kuznetsov scowled at me, but Conor mused, "That makes sense."

I gaped at him. "It does *not*."

"It does. People die. Laws don't." He folded his arms across his chest. "Star's correct, though. Those addendums to the Clean Water Act that just got passed were riddled with loopholes. Never mind all the other bullshit laws that get through every fucking day."

"Loopholes that only exist because of dirty money flowing into political parties that is used to elect corrupt officials," I grumbled, interrupting him.

Kuznetsov shrugged. "Would that act have even been voted in if it weren't for our support?"

"Of course, it would—who'd be against clean water?"

Conor stilled. "He has a point, Star."

I scowled at him. "Dammit, you're supposed to be on my side, not his."

"I *am* on your side. Why would I be here otherwise?"

"Does it look like I don't have a mouth?"

He studied my lips, long enough for it to get awkward. "I know you do. I also know that you're not afraid to use it."

"Then keep your nose out," I griped.

"I'm just saying... I can see where he's coming from."

I huffed. "We'll discuss this later."

"Yes, *dear*," he mocked, which had me scowling harder at him than ever and pinching his thigh.

Into our staring match, Kuznetsov tiredly rumbled, "Do we have a deal?"

Gracing him with my attention, I noticed he appeared as exhausted as he sounded. Blood loss probably hadn't helped.

"You want revenge for your son. Did you seek revenge for my mother?"

Kuznetsov paled even further. "I will not speak of her more than is necessary."

Huh.

That was interesting.

"How did she betray you?" When his lips pursed into a mutinous line, I knew I wouldn't get an answer. "Why did she give birth to me? Why did she marry Gerry Sullivan? What about any of that role was important to the United Brotherhood?"

Kuznetsov turned his face away.

"She traveled all over the world, Star. Didn't you tell me once that *noxxious* played at the weddings of foreign royal families?"

My gaze was measured as I studied my grandfather. "Is Conor right?"

"As I said, I will not speak of her."

"Seems like I'm not the only one she betrayed." His good hand clenched into a fist, his tension evident. Knowing that I'd have to hunt down my answers the hard way, as fucking usual, I changed the subject. "What do you constitute as eradication?"

His relief was palpable as he asked, "Percentage-wise, you mean?" At my nod, he mused, "Seventy-five percent under arrest. Sixty percent incarceration rate."

That was both higher than I expected and lower than I'd like. "If you want me on board then I want help with a side project too."

"What kind of side project?"

My throat felt thick as I rasped, "I want to make sure everyone they hurt gets back home."

His already tired eyes seemed to droop at my admission. "Not all of them will be able to return home, child. They don't exactly register the deaths of their victims."

I bobbed my head. "I know, but I have to try."

He sighed. "The Union will help."

I let my left hand drift over my plate. He eyed it warily, his other hand moving to his chest in case I went for another piece of cutlery, but I just let it hover there, waiting for him to shake it.

Only then, as his papery skin slid against mine, did I state, "Then, we have ourselves a deal."

24

CONOR

Conor O'Donnelly

FRESH FROM MY SHOWER, I grabbed the bag of treats from my suitcase and headed for the door.

Dinner had been over for about an hour now, and I'd finally seen the room where I'd be staying—the best part? Star was just next door.

Hefting the candy in my hand, I left and made my way to her quarters.

Our suites were so large and grand that I had to walk a good eighty feet before I even reached her door. Once there, I knocked.

"One minute," she called, the words muffled.

With nothing else to do, I tipped my head back to stare at the ceiling, trying to uncover the location of any speakers or cameras.

On this occasion, I only found one 'bubble' above the door. Smaller than a fingernail and transparent, it was hidden damn well.

Star opened the door and found me mid-study of the ceiling.

"There are two inside the living room, but none in the bedroom," she greeted.

Rocking forward, I studied her and tried oh, so fucking hard not to get a boner.

She was wet.

Wrapped in a towel.

Shoulders gleaming.

Hair curled around her throat.

Eyes sleepy.

Mouth relaxed.

Fuck.

I was literally looking at my living, breathing, *walking* fantasy.

"Just the one in mine. They must trust me more than they do you."

At my joke, she huffed. "Apparently."

"That's what you get when you don't stab your host in the hand."

"I think I'd have had two even if I'd have curtseyed when I met him," she grumbled, but she retreated a step. "Come in."

I hadn't actually intended on sticking around but I wasn't going to argue about how easy that had been.

Then, she startled me.

Star grabbed my arm, leaned into me, and for a moment, I thought her lips hovered over mine. My heart raced, my dick stood to attention, and I breathed her in. Disappointment struck when she tilted her head then whispered in my ear, "Did you bring your toy?"

My toy?

The little brain in my cock had no understanding of what she was talking about.

Unless she meant… "Your Christmas present?"

She reared back. "No! Dammit. The *toy*. The one that—" She moved into my personal space again. "—cuts out footage and blocks transmissions," she finished on a hiss.

Oh.

"I didn't."

Her scowl was immediate. "Why not?"

"I was tired! I barely remembered to pack boxer briefs!"

Her eyes flared wide, then her gaze drifted down my length.

Double fuck.

I leaned into her, my hand lifting to tuck a stray lock of hair away from her cheek and—

She jerked away.

Triple fucking fuck.

I cleared my throat. "Brought something for you."

Her brows lifted when she saw the bag in my hand, immediately snatching it from my grip and tearing it open. "Fuck, nothing tastes as good as American candy."

I sniffed to hide my discomfort when she moaned around the treat. "We can agree to disagree on that."

"Hey, I like that you hate the candy I love," she countered before chomping on a couple candy hearts. "That means I don't have to share."

"You make a good argument," I concurred, shifting my hands behind my back as I looked at her and tried not to make it creepy.

Maybe I was asking for too much. It had already been impossible to keep my eyes off her throughout dinner, especially once Kuznetsov had left partway through the entrée course.

Now, it was even more of a task because she was naked apart from a towel—I didn't have a snowball's chance in hell, did I?

Deciding that it was safer to escape while she was still in G.I. Jane mode, I muttered. "Anyway, you probably need to get some rest. I just thought you'd appreciate the candy."

As I stepped back and away, she caught my eye. Brow puckered, she said, "You were mad at me."

"When? Earlier?"

"No, when you came for me, and you still brought me candy?"

"I'm a glutton for punishment," I derided, turning on my heel before we could get into this. "You get some rest. We'll reconvene tomorrow and figure out our next steps."

"Are you mad at me for stabbing Kuznetsov?"

I paused. "I would be if they hadn't put me in that nice suite and had me in a dungeon underneath this building. But..." I tried to get my thoughts together. Jet lag wasn't helping me any. Nor was the scent of her. Flowers. G.I. Star wasn't supposed to smell of flowers. *Concentrate, Conor.* "I think I knew he'd let you get away with it so I wasn't worried."

"What made you think that?"

"How he looked at you."

She stopped chewing the candy. "How did he look at me?"

"Like you were his granddaughter."

"He was manipulating you—"

"Yes, he was. You were right to push him like that at dinner. He did twist my arm to get me to help you to talk to him, but that doesn't take away from the truth—he wants you in his life. This other granddaughter too."

Her shoulders sagged. "I don't have room in my life for family."

"I think you know that's a lie," I said carefully, trying not to show how much her words hurt. "Katina's family. What are the Sinners if not family too?"

Brow furrowing, she retreated a couple steps, backpedaling until she could plunk down on a comfortable couch.

As modern in style as this place was, as luxurious, comfort was the keyword. That meant everything was squashy—from the couches to the chairs to the beds. Amid the modern, Scandinavian styles, there were antique pieces that were more befitting the tastes of a man Kuznetsov's age.

It made for an eclectic but homey mix. One that enabled Star to sink back into the cloud of cushions and actually look comfortable for once.

She'd sat with her spine straight all dinner, and it was only now that I saw her slouching that I remembered how infrequently I'd seen her like this and never so stiff.

She'd been hyperaware at dinner—on red alert.

Now, she wasn't.

Something she confirmed when she breathed, "I'm tired, Conor."

"I told you—we can reconvene tomorrow. I'm seriously jet-lagged, so—"

"No, you don't understand. I'm *tired*. I have been tired for years." There was a weariness in her usually blank expression that backed up her words. "It feels like even if I sleep, it never eases up my exhaustion."

I was a confident man in most things, but I had to admit, Star made me more hesitant than I was used to being.

It was pretty annoying, to be honest.

If she hadn't had the past she did, I'd have grabbed her and dragged her to bed. I'd have tucked her in and—

I sucked in a breath.

I could still do that.

I wasn't taking this anywhere, not yet.

She needed sleep.

I wanted to take care of her.

I just needed not to earn a broken wrist in the process.

Striding toward her, I gently grasped a hold of her elbows and tugged her onto her feet.

"What are you doing?" she grumbled as I snagged the bag of candy, tossed it on the coffee table, then urged her toward the bedroom.

"No more sugar for you. We're going to rest tonight and then, tomorrow, we'll talk about game plans and what needs to be done," I repeated as I walked her backward.

Her gaze tracked mine as I maneuvered her around the suite, and, with every step I took, she stunned me by mimicking me.

When we were standing in her bedroom, I asked, "Do you need a shirt?"

The idea of her wearing my clothes was going to make sleep hell.

And heaven.

Was her being naked better or worse for the wet dreams I was about to have as if I were a teenager again?

Her mouth opened. Closed. "It's okay. I can go to sleep in the robe in the bathroom."

My T-shirt was the best option.

"Would that be comfortable?" I countered, trying some reverse psychology on her.

Slowly, she shook her head.

"Wait here," I warned her. "Don't. Move."

Her brow furrowed as she watched me back away.

Less than five minutes later, whistling beneath my breath, I returned with a T-shirt for her.

Her hands were fisted at her sides and she was scowling with annoyance. "I don't like being bossed around."

"Do you boss Katina around when she won't go to bed and she's tired?"

"Yes."

"Well then," I pointed out. "This is precisely like that."

"It is not," she argued. "I'm not ten."

"I'm not going to do anything or take this anywhere, Star. You're safe with me.

"I'm going to put you to bed and you're going to sleep in here and I'm going to return to my room and sleep in there.

"But, before then, I need to make you comfortable. So, arms up."

Her mouth rounded but, like the good little soldier she could sometimes be, her arms slipped upwards.

A second later, the soft cotton was swooping along the length of her biceps and puddling around her neck. Carefully, I angled her head through the opening then dragged the mass of fabric over the towel she'd tucked under her arm.

"I'm not going to look," I promised her, my gaze locked on hers as I fiddled with the knot that kept the towel in place.

My hand clapped against her belly to hold it up as I pulled the sides of the tee down so she was covered.

Only then did I move my hand. Gravity did the rest.

When she was dressed in my tee, the hem sitting high on her thighs but low enough for decency's sake, with the towel puddled around her feet, I gently cupped her elbow.

"You ready for bed now?"

"My hair's wet."

I grabbed the towel, moved around her, and started patting it dry. It wasn't much drier than it had been before I started, but it was better than nothing.

Without waiting for her to complain about my hairdressing skills, I gently tossed the towel at the bathroom door and started shuffling her toward the bed.

When I dragged down the sheet, I ordered, "Get in, Star." I waited for her grouchy compliance then tucked her in. "Sleep," I encouraged. "Tomorrow's problems are exactly that—for tomorrow."

Her eyelids drifted lazily up and down. "Your tee smells of you."

My lips twitched. "It smells of detergent."

Softly, she shook her head. "No. You smell of oranges."

"I don't even eat oranges," I muttered under my breath when I saw she'd closed her eyes.

I routinely ate fruit that could be put in a pie and that was it.

I drew back and headed for the living room, tugging my shirt away from my body and taking a surreptitious sniff down it—where the fuck did she get oranges from?

It was when I entered that space that the strangest urge hit me—I didn't want to leave her. Not even to go to my room next door.

I scraped a hand over my head as I fought an internal battle.

Call me crazy, but I trusted that her grandfather had no desire to hurt her. Maybe that was because he thought she'd already been hurt enough, or he truly believed she and I were the only people who could find his other granddaughter.

Whatever the reason, physically, I believed she was safe.

But Eoghan… I knew he had terrible nightmares. I'd heard them myself. I'd also eavesdropped on Inessa telling Camille about them, and how she was worried when he froze up in the night and went to work it out in the gym for hours on end.

Star had been perennially alone for decades.

It felt important that I prove to her that she wasn't anymore.

That, in the depths of the night, if her memories came back to haunt her, I was here.

It was dumb, but it was an urge I couldn't fight.

So, I stopped trying.

Switching off the lights in the living room, I pulled out my cell phone to guide my path to the couch, then I unfastened my belt buckle, dropped my jeans to the ground, yanked my tee overhead, and, in my boxer briefs, flopped onto the cushions.

There was a throw over the back of the couch, so I covered myself with it then sighed at finally being able to lie flat after such a long time awake.

Having shoved my exhaustion aside for hours by this point, it was no wonder that it was starting to rear its ugly head again and with a vengeance.

The screen of my cell popped on though, illuminating the darkness in a way that made my eyes ache.

With a huff, I reached for it and saw I had about three million texts from my brothers.

Feeling bad about not texting sooner, I shot off a simple message:

> Me: Alive, well, on the ground.

I hit send before I thought about what to tell them re Star.

Deciding that the truth was easier to maintain than a lie when things were about to get complicated, I continued:

> Me: I've got her. But we have some work to finish off together here in Croatia. (Don't fucking ask.) I'm gonna crash. Been on the move since I set off for JFK. I'll speak to you in the morning, dearthairs.

'*Dearthair,*' whether we admitted it out loud or not, was our code word.

We rarely shared that we loved one another, but Gaelic was our poison of choice whenever we did the deed.

Not wanting to see their replies because I'd have to answer them, I flipped my phone screen side up after I'd set it on silent, then I closed my eyes.

I had no idea how long I slept for. My eyelashes felt like they were rimmed with salt and my eyes were dry and crusty, but something had made me stir.

That was when I felt it.

Felt *her*.

For a moment, I just thought I was dreaming.

Star couldn't be here. Not on the couch.

With me.

But she was.

Her face was nuzzled into my armpit of all places which totally made me freak out about whether I'd used enough deodorant after my shower last night, and her hand was on my chest.

What the hell was she doing on the couch with me?

And had I dragged the roll-on twice over each armpit like I usually did or was I too tired and only did it the once?

My eyes drifted down before I had answers to those questions. My head tilted to the side and my lips gently brushed the crown of her still-damp hair.

Then, I fell asleep again.

Not knowing what magic had brought her here, I just hoped I'd wake up and it wouldn't be a dream…

25

———

STAR

Star Sullivan

CONOR WAS HOT.

I wasn't just talking appearance-wise which, being an O'Donnelly, was a given. I meant he was like a furnace. He gave off more heat than a radiator, and my feet, always cold, were toasty warm thanks to how I'd tucked them between his calves.

My face was pushed into his side, his arm was around me, and our legs were a tangled knot.

The couch was too small for us, the cushions not wide enough for two people to lie flat, and yet, I hadn't slept so well in years.

The only reason I'd woken up in the first place was because I knew he was texting someone. His arm was flexing slightly and a soft laugh rumbled from him that made his chest vibrate against my cheek.

For a moment, I just enjoyed myself. His citrusy scent filled my senses, he was warm and comfortable, and he felt so fucking good beneath me that I knew I'd made the right move last night when I'd found him on the couch.

While I could have rested a lot longer, quality usurped quantity with this man.

"Who are you talking to?" I rasped drowsily, nuzzling my nose into his ribs.

"My brothers."

He answered so easily that I blinked.

Was everything so simple with him?

He'd make a shit spy.

"What are they saying?"

"Declan said Shay got drunk for the first time last night at a party and puked all over the girl he's got a crush on."

My lips curved. "Fuck. He'll be mortified."

"That's more of a punishment than what Aela's got him doing for getting drunk at sixteen…

"Through his dad, Shay's apparently begging me to eradicate all online footage of it happening from Instagram."

"That's extreme."

"I don't think he wants Inessa and Camille to know who his crush is."

Frowning, I asked, "What do your sisters-in-law have to do with anything?"

"Their baby sister is his crush."

I hooted at that, then something occurred to me. "Don't they use Snapchat now?"

"Who?"

"Kids?"

"Apparently not. He's the one who pointed me to Instagram."

I hummed.

"I'll check." His arm flexed some more as he continued typing. "He wants Snapchat erased too."

I smirked. "The whole site?"

"I don't think he'd be averse to it crashing forever, no," he teased.

"What'll it cost him? You worked out a fee?" I joked.

"When he's president, he's got to let me visit NASA. I'm not allowed anywhere near it."

Taking note of the pout in his voice, it was his words that gave me pause. "*When* he's president?" I took a moment to let my mind filter through those loaded sentences. "Wait, you're not allowed to visit their museum?"

He huffed. "Why would I visit their museum? I'm talking about Ground Control."

"You're a space nerd," I accused.

"Of course I am," he scoffed. Then, he admitted, "Didn't expect to wake up with you on the couch."

Another woman would have felt awkward.

I was me.

I shrugged. "When you didn't leave the room last night, I figured you wouldn't mind the company."

"I didn't like leaving you unprotected," he said apologetically. "I should have asked."

"You didn't encroach upon my personal space, Conor. I did. *I* should have asked you if it was okay to join you."

I should also have just offered the other side of the king-sized bed like I'd wanted last night.

Stupid nerves.

He cleared his throat. "You have an open invitation to always join me where I'm sleeping."

I tipped my chin up. "Really?"

"Really."

"Even though I haven't worked on atonement?"

"Even though you haven't worked on atonement."

"Do you know what I need to do before you'll forgive me?"

"I have a semblance of an idea." Yet again, he changed the subject. "I asked Aidan not to tell Savannah that I'd found you."

I pondered his words. "She can know."

"She's upset that you stopped answering her messages."

"I upset a lot of people."

"You did. You should work on that."

I probably should.

"Did you sleep well?" he asked when I didn't reply to his comment.

"I did. You're like a heating pad."

"I run hot." His shrug jostled me. "Didn't think I'd spend the night like this."

"That bad or good?"

"You looking for compliments?"

"Maybe."

"You know it's not bad."

"Is it good though?" I queried wistfully.

"Do you want it to be?"

"I'm not like a regular woman, Conor."

"No, you're an alien. Aren't you glad I'm a space nerd now?"

My lips twitched. "Shut up."

He chuckled. "No, you shut up. Not like a regular woman? What's that supposed to mean? You have nuances, Star. If someone gives enough of a fuck about you, then that someone will learn them.

"You think I don't have nuances of my own? There's a reason I topped Manhattan's most eligible bachelor list for so long."

"What reason?"

His arm tightened around me. "I don't like people in my space."

I should probably have cringed considering I'd eaten over half the room on the couch and was making his personal space my own, but I didn't even bother fidgeting at his words.

I knew that I'd disturbed him. When I'd settled at his side, I'd felt his lips brush the crown of my head, so he could have told me to get back into bed if he'd wanted.

Now, I felt his arm around me.

He was making damn sure that I knew, to him, I wasn't people.

"Where *do* you like people?"

"Wherever I'm not. Apart from family. Family, I'm more... hell, shall we say, permissive with?"

"Why?"

"Because you have to let someone in. Plus, I didn't have a choice. I grew up with them. They were already in. It was nice to get them out when we all moved into our own places, but it's a habit. Like Katina and Savannah are with you."

Slowly, I nodded. "I get that."

"Shay and Jake are different though."

"You don't like hanging around them?"

"Nah, I love it. I wasn't sure if I would because kids aren't something I've ever had much experience with. But Shay's wicked smart and he has so much potential."

"Jake's already got an attitude and he's a toddler. I'm more scared he'll break than Shay though."

"Toddlers are resilient."

"He wails the fucking house down if he bangs his head on something," he pointed out.

"Wouldn't you?"

"I swear."

"He can't, can he?" I retorted, tone droll. "You swear; he wails."

"True. But, anyway, I choose my people carefully and it's hard to become one of them."

I knew he said that on purpose.

"I don't deserve to be in your inner circle."

"I get to decide that. Not you. Anyway, it's not like you're arguing. You came to me last night."

I had.

I didn't immediately reply, just let his words percolate.

"Where did you pick up on that dialect?"

"The one Anton speaks?" At his hum, I looked down at his forearms. What was it about men's forearms that were so sexy? Letting my eyes flutter to a close, I answered, "My nanny spoke it. I learned it from her. Have to think Mom picked her for a reason now."

"What's the dialect?"

"Chechen."

"So, the Kuznetsovs don't originate from Central Russia then. Interesting."

I sniffed. "It's an endangered dialect. He could have learned it just because so few people speak it."

"Maybe." He cleared his throat. "That wasn't the answer I expected."

"Thought the CIA programmed it into my brain?"

"That'd have fewer familial repercussions if it were the truth."

"There's no denying that," I admitted. "Do you believe in kismet?"

His hand and arm had started flexing again so, even with my eyes closed, I knew he was texting his family.

"Umm, not really."

"Why not?"

"Because my brain's too logical."

"It's not totally logical."

"It is."

"Is not."

"It is!"

"It so isn't. Otherwise, you'd never have let your da control you," I grumbled.

He stilled a touch. "That made sense, and you know why."

"I know it was to keep your brothers safe, but that's also not logical. They're grown men. They can care for themselves."

"No, they think they can. They've never had to do shit without me around and that makes all the difference."

"Love isn't logical," I reasoned. "You love them."

"More than life itself," he agreed.

"That's not logical," I repeated.

"No. But that's why I hesitated. Smart ass. I UMMED. Remember?"

My lips quirked. "Explain, Mr. Logic."

"Remind me why I got on a plane for you again?" His huff told me he was teasing, but I couldn't have misinterpreted his words anyway. Not when my feet shuffled around and he clamped his calves around them to keep them in place. "I didn't believe in things like kismet *before*. I don't wholly now, but—"

"What changed?"

"I think you already know the answer to that."

His voice had darkened, deepened. I gently nipped my bottom lip, bobbing my teeth around the soft flesh I'd trapped.

Me.

He was talking about me.

And I was talking about him.

"When this is over, I want you to meet my family."

His words didn't just ram their way home, they slipped under my skin, sank into my muscles, and dispersed through my bloodstream.

"They'll hate me."

"They'll be wary around you until they see why I like you."

"I'm not even sure why you do," I said calmly. "I don't know if I would like me if I were standing in your shoes. It's one thing to say that we challenge each other, but—"

"But what? Don't you think that's the basis of a friendship?"

"I guess."

"And don't you think that the basis of a friendship should be at the heart of every relationship?"

"Maybe." I rolled onto my side and propped myself up so I could look down at him. His words sent hope flaring inside me and that was the deadliest, most addictive drug alive. There were many things I could have said or done, many apologies I could have made and offered. Instead, I stuck with a truth I knew would resonate with him. "I promise I won't run again."

His hand reached for mine. "That's my favorite kind of promise."

26

CONOR

Conor O'Donnelly

"OKAY, HIT ME WITH IT."

She stared down at her decaf coffee. "There isn't that much to hit you with."

"Lies," I rumbled, but I saw the despondency in her expression and the slight slump to her shoulders.

The day hadn't started how I'd imagined. Not only because she'd still been there when I'd woken up and it *hadn't* been a dream, but also because it had been five PM when we'd finally dragged our asses off the couch.

She'd headed to her shower, I'd gone to mine, then we'd met up in her suite because it had a bigger living area.

By the time I'd finished showering—and checking my products for oranges of which there was *zero* citrus scent in any of them—two types of coffee, croissants, some preserves, and a spread of ham and cheese had arrived at her suite.

One cheese and ham croissant in and I was grilling her about BDSec.

"I should have known you had something to do with that hacktivist group when they started calling themselves Pussy Patrol."

Her nose crinkled. "It was a 'fuck you' to the patriarchy."

"No," I drawled. "I'd never have guessed."

She squinted at me. "Why do you even care?"

"Because if I'd been a *Pauk* or had been with Anonymous, wouldn't you have wanted to know?"

"No," she grumbled.

"Lies again! No coffee for you." I made to snatch her mug but she literally hissed at me and held it between her tits. Amused, I rasped, "I knew you were part cat."

"Better than being part dog." She sniffed.

"Meaning?"

"Meaning you are."

"How did you figure that out?"

"You're loyal and you obey orders."

"You were a soldier."

"Yeah, and when I stopped obeying, they tossed me in Club Pervert because I'm a cat."

"What kind of cat?"

She smirked. "Siamese."

"Does that mean you yowl if I tug on your tail?"

Her eyes flared. "Um, no."

I almost started snickering, but I saw I'd shocked her.

Damn, she was edgy. And I loved it. There was no relaxing around her when she was in a mood, which was clearly our current issue.

"What dog am I?"

"Maybe an Australian Shepherd."

Shoving a hand through my hair, I chuckled. "Random."

"Nah. I grew up with one. They're the best. Smartest breed around, hear anything, keep a watch on everything, playful, pretty... What about that isn't you?"

I pondered the description. "I think I'll take that. Also, you thought about it," I teased. "I'm touched."

She glowered at her coffee. "Katina asked me once."

"Katina did. Right."

"She did! She's at that age where she asks stupid shit. We're almost past that point." She crossed her fingers. "I preferred it when she wanted to know why Link and Lily 'slept' so much—"

"Because they were in bed all the time?" I shot her a mocking wink. "That's what *Old* Men and *Old* Ladies do?"

She scrunched up her nose at my play on words. "I'm honest but I'm not that honest. I wasn't going to tell her that they were fucking like rabbits. It was easier to say they're very sleepy." Her gaze drifted to my temple. "The bruise is better."

"Almost gone. Spent the night in the hospital for that one. As for the other, I was out for the count for almost a whole day."

"Wow, Maverick really decked you, huh?"

Deciding not to incite more ire for Temper Black after hearing a soliloquy about that already this evening, I merely grumbled, "He did."

"I'm kind of glad. I know she's in safe hands."

"Yeah, so safe that she managed to run away from them!"

Star shrugged. "Don't get me wrong, I'm furious and I'll make him regret the day his mother gave birth to him, but she's a smart kid. You can't keep her somewhere she doesn't want to stay. She needed to talk to you, so she made it happen, and look, you didn't let her down, did you?"

Well, there was no arguing with that. "I guess I didn't."

Returning the mug to the table, she started dosing a croissant with jam. I watched her move the pastry to her mouth, trying not to be enchanted by the sight of her licking her lips when some of the preserve collected at the corner, definitely trying not to groan when she sighed with appreciation.

"You still haven't told me about BDSec," I complained because it was either that or kiss her, and I didn't think she was ready for that.

Yet.

Please, fuck, let there be an expiration date on when I couldn't press my mouth to hers—

"I started it with two other hackers after I got away from the Sparrows. I needed to find someone, and they helped me."

"*They* helped *you*?"

"With the amount of time I was out of action, I was slow," she admitted. "I needed some help getting back into the swing of things. You know how quickly our world moves, and if you're slow, you lose."

"Who did you need to find?"

"A man helped me when I was in Lebanon. He almost got killed for his troubles." She shoved more of the croissant between her lips. "You probably know him. His name's Hunter Lachlan."

"The Camorran Don. Met him at his niece's christening."

Her brows rose. "Niece?"

"He's married to Aurora Valentini now."

A smile danced on her lips. "So, the old bastard made it happen."

"Who's the old bastard?"

She wafted a hand. "It doesn't matter. I'm glad for Hunter though. He's been pining for Aurora since they were kids. What did you talk about with him?"

"You, of course. I wanted to know if he'd heard from you."

Her nose crinkled. "I burned that bridge."

"Why?"

"To save him."

I shook my head. "You're the most complicated woman alive, Lodestar."

"Do you know you call me Lodestar when you're being pissy with me?"

"You answer to both, don't you?"

"I do."

"So what's the problem then?"

"Nothing. I'm just onto you, that's all."

I rolled my eyes. "Okay, so Lachlan was the reason you needed help back then."

"I had to know if he survived. It... I used to think about that time and it would give me nightmares." She cleared her throat and tossed the croissant back on the table.

"You don't have to tell me what happened."

"I don't think I could," she said rawly, her gaze low. "Minerva and Ovianar are the other leaders of BDSec."

The memory had to be bad if she was getting back on track. "Not sure I've heard of Ovianar," I admitted.

"That's exactly how she likes it," she mocked.

"Minerva—didn't she hack the Senate's power grid when they were going to vote to let oil companies drill in Alaska?"

"She did. Didn't stop them from letting that law pass though." Her brow puckered. "How can Kuznetsov sit there, so high and mighty, when all this shit is happening in our society and he could help but doesn't?"

"Maybe they're not as powerful as they want us to think. We only have it on their word that they are."

She shook her head. "No. I know they're powerful. It's why I targeted them in the first place. But I guess there's power and there's *power.*"

Because I didn't want to think about her seducing Kuznetsov, I changed the subject. "Aren't you friendly with Minerva and Ovianar anymore?"

"What makes you ask that?"

"You seem sad when you talk about them."

"We couldn't agree on how to take the group forward. I dumped BDSec on their laps and we haven't really spoken since."

"Do you think we'll need their help?"

"Don't know. We'll need Dead To Me though."

A knock sounded at the door. Before she could, I headed over to it, pulled it open, asking, "Yes?" before I saw that it was Edgar.

"Good evening, sir. I have Madam Sullivan's personal effects."

Star jerked up at the news —she was wearing the robe from the bathroom.

That wasn't distracting.

At all.

Neither was the fact that she'd slept beside me with only my tee and a pair of panties on.

Dead. I was so fucking dead.

"Where did you get all this?" Star cried as Edgar appeared with a few other servers, each loaded down with bags.

Edgar cleared his throat. "I'm not certain if Mr. Kuznetsov would appreciate it if I answered that question, ma'am."

"Meaning he raided your Airbnb or hotel room," I drawled, tone cynical even as my heart seemed to twang in my chest as I watched her eyes light up when she uncovered her case and found her phone tucked neatly in one of the pockets.

Edgar shot me a disapproving look, which was fucking hilarious seeing as he didn't know me and I didn't know him, but I hid my smile and just watched as the staff faded into the woodwork as they had a habit of doing around here.

I'd think they were half-ghost or they were just terrified of being caught lingering by—

"Stop thinking about *Downton Abbey*."

Peeved, I folded my arms across my chest. "Who said I was thinking about *Downton Abbey*?"

"I can guarantee it," was her smug retort as the staff bustled around in her bedroom, swiftly unpacking her two mid-sized cases. "You were thinking about Mr. Carson—"

With a sniff, I countered, "*Actually,* I was thinking about Mrs. Hughes."

Her grin was mostly hidden by the cascade of hair that fell over her face as she ducked around, plugging her computer and cellphone in to charge, apparently uncaring that people were touching her stuff.

Although, with her past, maybe she'd grown up being cared for like that.

Da hadn't believed in any of that bullshit. Ma had run our home and we'd had to keep our rooms neat; the only deference to his status was that he had maids come in and keep everything tidy every other day.

Even then, he hadn't liked having people rummaging around his stuff.

The memory made my lips curve. Especially when I thought back to the time he'd accused one of the maids of stealing his underwear when it was Eoghan who had taken to using them as flags for the fortress he'd built in our backyard…

What the hell he thought a maid would want with his boxers, I didn't know.

"Do you need anything, sir?"

Torn from the past, I turned to Dubrovnik's version of Mr. Carson and requested, "More coffee if possible."

"Of course, sir. Mr. Kuznetsov had to leave unexpectedly but he asked me to extend the invitation to treat this house as your own." Then, his attention aimed at Star, he stated, "In his words, this is a family retreat."

Star snorted but didn't reply.

When Edgar's shoulders hunched at the non-verbal rebuke, I slapped him on the back. "Don't take it personally. She's just grouchy."

Though he nodded, his gaze was plaintive as he continued gazing at Star. "What time will you be requiring dinner, sir?"

I shrugged. "If Kuznetsov's not here, then we're not tied down to formal dining hours?"

"That is correct, sir."

"We'll ring if we're hungry. That okay?"

"Of course, sir. If not I, then Grimaud, the footman, will gladly attend to you."

"Great."

Once he'd left, Star peered at me. "You're totally getting a boner for all this servant shit, aren't you?"

"You can't deny that it's cool."

"It's cool if you're not a servant."

"You're used to it."

"I'm Gerry Sullivan's daughter," she said with a laugh. "Do you think he picked his dirty towels off the floor or cleaned his own toilet?"

My nose crinkled at the imagery. *Never meet your heroes,* I thought before tacking on, *Or their daughters.*

With the last of the staff having disappeared, I asked, "Do you think they were trained by British royals?"

"Yeah. I can just imagine the royal family getting down and dirty with the staff and teaching them how to deal with guests who beat the shit out of security guards."

"You know I meant the royal *household*." My lips quirked up. "But that would totally be worthy of a Netflix show."

"If they wanted an audience of one. *You.*"

Delighted with her argumentativeness, I sighed.

"What?" she demanded, mid-click of her mouse, clearly seeing that I was studying her and unafraid to call me out on it.

"Nothing. Just…" I smirked. "You haven't changed."

"I'll get dressed after I set my computer up. Fuck knows what he did to it to track my—"

"I wasn't talking about clothes, Lodestar," I grouched. "I meant *you*. You haven't changed."

She frowned. "Why would I have?"

"People change when you meet them in real life. Plus, there's some stuff you just can't predict."

"Like the fact you smell of oranges?"

"I checked every toiletry I brought with me and there isn't a single citrus top note in any of them."

"You smell of oranges."

I rolled my eyes.

"I'm glad. I like oranges," she grumbled. "But I know what you mean. You could have smelled of oud and then I'd have had to go puke."

"Oud isn't that bad," I retorted, thinking about an aftershave I really loved that used oud in its composition.

"It is. It's horrible. It makes me sneeze."

There went the two-thousand-dollar-an-ounce bottle into the trash.

I huffed on my way over to her, but I was careful not to block her in place or to trap her between myself and the table. She grew tense at my proximity yet allowed me to gently collect her hair into a soft ponytail.

As I moved closer to her, she turned more and more rigid, but when I pressed my nose to her nape, a soft sigh drifted from her lips.

"What are you doing?"

"Finding out what you smell of," I whispered.

"You slept with me."

"Technically, *you* slept with *me*, and my nose was too far away."

She snorted, which I took as silent assent for my ministrations to continue, then shivered when I ran the tip of my nose along the line of her neck. I pressed a kiss to the top vertebra of her spine, enjoying the soft, surprised breath she released, then let my forehead rest against the back of her head.

"What do I smell of?" she whispered as my free hand moved to her stomach where I spread my fingers wide to hold her in place.

I closed my eyes.

Mine.

But I didn't have a death wish.

"Cinnamon."

It wasn't a total lie.

The spicy notes were there, making my senses burn in response.

I breathed her in, trying to make myself register that she was actually here. That I could—

Translating thought and desire into action, I reached for her with my other hand and let my finger run down the side of her throat. At first, her tension amped up again, but then she released a shuddery breath that I felt in my bones.

"If you taste of it too, I'm fucked."

"I doubt I taste like a cinnamon roll, unless I eat one first," she rasped.

"I could ask Edgar to make us some. The guy seems to enjoy doing stuff for us."

I felt her soft chuckle as if it came from my own chest. "I'm not sure if he 'enjoys' it. It's his job, Conor."

"Hmm. Better than killing people for a living. It can't all be bad. Want a cinnamon roll?"

She paused. Gave it far more thought than junk food—aka Mother Nature's treasure—required, then she whispered, "Yeah."

This time, I let my tongue trace down the central line of her nape. "I'll tell him when he brings coffee."

A broken, keening sound escaped her that went straight to my dick. "G-Great," she stuttered, watching her hands flatten on either side of her laptop, the fingers spreading wide. "I-I guess I should get changed."

I was more than okay with her staying in her current outfit, but I didn't say that, just stepped back, knowing that she needed the space. Well aware that I'd taken this further than I'd intended.

Giving her room to breathe, I asked, "We'll hash out a game plan once you've changed?"

"Yeah," she agreed shakily. "Sounds good to me."

As she stepped away, her gaze lingered on mine for a handful of seconds.

Neither of us were ingenues. Nor were we virgins. But we both knew what it felt like to have our consent stripped away from us— maybe that was why we were dancing around each other?

When you found a hundred-carat diamond in the earth, after all, you didn't excavate it with a mallet from Lowes.

Some things took time.

Some things were worth waiting for.

Some things required cultivation.

It was as if she read my mind because she graced me with a soft nod before heading off to the bedroom.

When the door closed behind her, I cracked my knuckles, trying to get myself under some semblance of control.

Nothing about the last twenty-four hours had gone according to plan; nothing had gone down how I'd imagined it. She was here with me, though, and that was all that mattered.

Only if we were together could we bring the world to its knees, and for Star Sullivan, I'd do more than that—I'd bring civilization itself to a halt if that was what she needed to be liberated from the burden of her past.

27

Star Sullivan

THE MOMENT the bedroom door closed behind me, I pressed my back to it and covered my face with my hands.

I could still feel his breath against my nape. The tender trail of his finger down my neck. The way he kissed the top of my spine. How his tongue tip had traced the sensitive skin.

The tiny hairs on my nape were still standing at attention from the sensory memory alone. Never mind the violent reactions in my core— Mount Vesuvius probably hadn't been as active before she'd devastated Pompeii with her wrath.

On edge, I whispered a solid truth that I needed to hear out loud: "That was Conor."

Conor.

The man I'd been growing closer to for almost two years now had been the one to make me feel these things. To make me shudder with want. To make me wet with need.

The idea shouldn't have been nerve-wracking, but it was.

Tiredly, I rubbed my eyes before I let my hands drop to my sides then strode over to the cases the servants had unpacked for me while I'd been dealing with my rig.

Because I traveled light, I didn't have that many wardrobe options, but I dragged on a pair of skinny jeans and a cotton tank that came with built-in tit support.

After I'd used the restroom, I stared at myself in the mirror over the vanity, hands wet as I splashed cold water onto my face.

With no artifice to hide behind, the water stripping me bare, I sighed.

It was me.

No change there.

I forced myself to glance at the reflection of my eyes. There were shadows beneath them, but as always, it was the shadows *in* them that concerned me.

Did I look as dead inside as I felt?

The thought had me glancing away.

I finished washing up, left the bathroom, and returned to the living room which was where I found Conor with his legs cocked on the table, his own computer on his lap, a phone in each hand, a tablet to the side, a smaller laptop next to it. Within easy reach, there were two external mice and a spare keyboard that glowed like a rainbow.

My lips quirked at the sight. "Of course you'd go for the rainbow setting."

His gaze drifted from his monitor to me. As he spoke, he scanned me, and I swore I felt the path he took as if he'd touched me with his hand. "I like rainbows," he admitted.

"I've seen your office. It's space age, not hippy."

"I take my rainbows where I can find them. It's the Irish in me." He winked. "I've always been on the hunt for that pot of gold." How he eyed me up and down told me that *I* was the pot of gold. And I wasn't averse to that imagery. "Anyway, at least I don't like holo."

"That's for Kat," I joked.

"We can't all appreciate navy blue and brown," he chastised, pointing at the leather cases and slip-on pouches from which I'd unpacked my gear.

"I like demure colors," I retorted.

"Nah, you're too used to fading into the background for your own good." He tipped his head to the side as if he were envisioning me in another color. The woman in me wondered which color he'd prefer. The spy didn't give a fuck—she preferred her 'fade into the background' uniform.

"Your phone keeps buzzing," he informed me, lips twitching as if he knew what I was thinking.

I blinked at the change of subject. Though I was accustomed to that in our chats, it still jolted me when he did it in person. "Probably missed call notifications," I dismissed.

Walking over to my cell phone, I saw it had gotten enough charge to have switched itself on, then I grimaced when it registered how many times Katina had called.

"Conor…?"

"Call her now," he ordered softly. "I'm working on some other shit. Take your time."

I sent him a grateful look and tapped on her name.

She answered within seconds. "STAR!" she screamed before immediately bursting into tears.

The sound tore me to fucking shreds and I regretted falling asleep last night without ringing her beforehand. She should have been my first port of call after I'd finished eating with that fucker who called himself my grandfather.

Not much made me cry anymore. When you'd gone to hell and back, you just adapted to the misery of this existence. But hearing her sob tore at my heartstrings like nothing else could.

"Baby, I'm sorry I missed your calls. I'm sorry. So sorry," I whispered, not even realizing I was saying it over and over again until she started sniffling in my ear. "I'm sorry, Kat, sweetheart. So—"

"Promise you won't do that again!" she sobbed.

I had no idea why I did it—but I looked at Conor. He shot me a gentle smile then surprised me by dumping his laptop on the table and striding over to me.

As he slipped his arm around my waist and drew me toward the couch, I told my kid, "I swear I'll never break another promise."

She hiccupped in my ear. "That's not what I asked for!"

"Kat, Star didn't mean to cut contact with you. Sometimes, life just has a habit of breaking promises for us."

More sniffling sounded, then she whispered, "Conor?"

"Yeah, it's me."

The next moment, I received a video call request, and I accepted it so she could see us.

"I knew you'd find her," she cried, joy and relief making her blood-shot eyes bright as she swiped at her cheeks with her knuckles. "I knew it!"

Thickly, I swallowed, rasping, "You sent the right person to find me, baby."

"I-I thought long and hard about it and knew he'd come and get you. Maverick's sick again so I knew I couldn't ask him, but..." She hunched her shoulders. "Don't let Alessa tell you that I ran away."

I arched a brow. "Don't 'let' her tell me? Did that happen or not?"

That sparkle I was used to seeing in her eyes was back with a vengeance. "In a sense, yes."

"'In a sense.' Have you been watching *The West Wing* again?"

Conor chuckled as he pulled us back into the couch. My shoulders were still hunched into him, but the position encouraged me to relax.

"I haven't *not* been watching it."

"This isn't a courtroom, Kat," I grumbled.

"You should treat life like it is, Star," came the reprimand from my preteen kid. "Then if people take ligitious action—"

"Litigious," I corrected.

"—then you're prepared."

"You don't have to be prepared. You're ten."

"Nearly eleven."

"In ten months. So ancient."

"I know," Kat said smoothly. "My wisdom knows no bounds."

I slapped a hand against my forehead. "I don't need Alessa to tell me that you ran away to Manhattan to find Conor. I need to tell *her* to change the pin code on the TV!"

Her nose crinkled. "Don't do that. I learn loads."

Like how to be more precocious...

My grin made an appearance because the last thing I wanted was for her to change. "You know you did wrong."

"You're not supposed to smile when you tell kids off," Conor whispered in my ear.

"Says who?"

"Speak up, Conor," my kid groused. "It's rude to whisper."

Conor laughed. "It doesn't matter, Katina."

"That means it does," she said with a pout.

Knowing I had to make a point, I brought us back to the subject at hand. "What happened after Conor took you home?"

Katina ducked her head. "Maverick punched him and he hit his head on the ground. But I didn't know that was going to happen! Maverick's the bad one. Why didn't his mom tell him you're not supposed to hit people like you told me?"

Fuck. I nearly choked on my laughter as I managed to get out, "Our actions have consequences, Kat."

"Conor found you though."

"He did." *She had me there.*

"He wouldn't have found you if I hadn't asked him to go looking. You would still be lost."

Conor cleared his throat. "I'd been searching for her for a while, Katina. I know you wanted to speak to me because you were scared, but it scared *me* to think that you ran away from Jersey and came into the city alone.

"New York isn't safe for little girls."

"New York isn't safe for big girls," I retorted.

He winced. "Star's right."

Kat crinkled her nose. "I won't do it again. I'm really sorry Maverick smacked you, Conor. Alessa made him sleep on the couch because of it after she stopped crying when she saw I was back." Knowing what was incoming, I waited for the drum roll... "Star, why is sleeping on the couch a punishment? I like sleeping on the couch."

"You like watching TV before bed," I quipped. "You don't like the couch. Plus, you're little."

"I'm not that little!"

"You're littler than Maverick, aren't you?" I argued.

She pouted. "Not by much."

"By two and a half feet," I drawled.

"That's not much."

"It makes all the difference on a couch," Conor teased, which considering how we'd spent the night, had me turning to him with a laugh.

Kat flicked a glance between us, then slowly, she asked, "When are you coming home? I miss your PB&J sandwiches."

"I've found a way to get to the people who hurt me, Kat," I admitted. "It won't be for a while. But I will have more time to call you now. I—" The word 'promise' was on the tip of my tongue.

Conor squeezed my arm. "I'm here now, Kat. You know she's safe because we're always safe when we're with family."

Jesus, his words made me want to cry as much as her tears had.

Confusion bled into her expression. "You're not family though," she answered him, her tone careful.

Gruffly, he corrected, "Family can be chosen."

"Star chose me," Katina agreed.

"And I choose you both," was his light reply.

With an imperious glare, she stared down her nose at him. "Will you look after her?"

"I will."

"You said you'd bring her home to me."

There was no hiding the accusation there. "And I will. Just when the time's right."

Now, she started squinting at him, her nose scrunched up, but she began to nod. Then, she broke me some more—her bottom lip trembled. "I missed you, Star."

"I missed you too, baby." Being away from her hurt more than I'd expected. She was my kid. I didn't give a fuck who'd given birth to her. Didn't care whose DNA she shared and whose blood ran through her veins. She was *mine*. I kept my possessive thoughts to myself and, with a warning note, queried, "Are you going to be good for Alessa and Maverick?"

"I'm always good."

"Well, we know that's a lie," I mocked.

My kid wafted a hand. "I had to fix things."

"It's *my* job to fix stuff," I corrected before something occurred to me. "Are you covering your eyes when people kiss on TV?"

She giggled. "Yes."

That meant no.

"If you don't, I really will tell Alessa to change the pin code."

"I'll change it back." She tipped her nose up. "I'm a strong, independent woman, Star." She spoiled that by crying, "Girl Power," then cascading into even more giggles.

I smiled at the sight of her rolling around like a lunatic and, shaking my head, drawled, "I'll call you later on before bedtime. Tell Maverick I want to talk to him?"

"You'll call before bedtime?"

"I will. Don't forget to tell Maverick?" At her excited nod, I winked at her. "Be good."

"I'll try. Love you."

"Love you too."

I let her cut the call then I turned my face into Conor's throat, not even bothering to ask why that was so easy to do, and I let the impossible happen—I allowed the dam to burst.

He embraced me through it. Silently. Didn't say a damn thing. Just let me loop my arms around his waist and clutch at him.

The tears burned like a corrosive as they coursed down my cheeks and he held me together as I fell apart.

I'd let her down so badly.

"She's okay, Star."

I clenched my eyes closed. "More by luck than anything else."

"She snuck out when Maverick had a hospital appointment." His hand smoothed over my hair. "It was an aberration, and now that they know she has mad skills like her mom, they'll be watching out for her more.

"But there won't be any need for that, will there? She's a good kid. As long as you call her, she'll stick fast to her home until you're back."

"When I think what could have happened—"

"No point in thinking of what 'could have' happened," he interrupted firmly, "It didn't. She's fine. Safe. Happy to have heard from you and even happier that you're calling her tonight."

"You're right," I whispered, inwardly sighing when he started to pull away from me.

Before disappointment could take over, his hand dipped into his pocket and he withdrew a packet of Sour Patch Kids.

Biting my lip at the sight, I accepted the treat with a soft snicker. As I opened the bag, the first piece of candy I removed, I placed against his lips, chuckling when he took my offering then nipped my finger.

Taking a piece for myself, I asked, "You really meant that, didn't you?"

He knew exactly what my mind had focused on. "About choosing you both?"

Awkwardly, I nodded.

"You know I have."

"I think you're crazy to pick me, but I won't argue."

"Like I said yesterday—" He winked. "—insanity runs in the family."

"That works out to my benefit then."

"It does," he agreed, eyes twinkling.

His expression was so much brighter than I'd have thought. *He* was brighter. That came across on the chats, but this was different.

This was real.

He was the bubbles in a bottle of champagne and I hadn't anticipated how badly I needed that effervescence in my life.

Like always, when hope rose, it immediately sank.

Turning my face away from him and dropping the bag of candy on the coffee table, I muttered, "Everyone leaves me, Conor."

His hand grabbed mine and his fingers slipped against my knuckles, forming a bridge between us as he stated, "*Everyone* doesn't matter. Only you. Only me. And only Katina."

That had me nipping the inside of my cheek between my molars. "Don't give me promises you can't keep."

He sat up, his hand coming to cup my chin. "That wasn't a promise."

"What was it?"

"A statement of intent."

"Do you watch *The West Wing* too?"

His chuckle eased some of the tightness in my chest. "I watched it when it first aired but not since then. My tastes have evolved."

"Into *Downton Abbey* and *Bridgerton*?" I inquired politely.

He smirked at me, his thumb running down the line of my jaw. "I don't have them on a constant loop."

"Good to know because I'd have to break the TV if you did," I joked, trying not to close my eyes when his thumb reached the underside of my chin where a sensitive patch of skin had me squirming in my seat.

"You going to rip Maverick a new asshole?"

"What do you think?"

"I think he did his best, and you can't keep someone sneaky inside when they want out."

"You're defending him?"

"Not particularly. I just don't think there was a snowball's chance in hell of keeping Katina away from me when she believed I was the only one who'd bring you back."

My shoulders sagged at his words because I heard the truth in them.

When the couch jostled slightly, I realized I had closed my eyes. They popped open, only to find that Conor's face was a lot closer than before. I could see the striations in his irises. The outer rim was umber. Mossy green notes merged with amber before becoming a rich caramel in the tight confines where a fully dilated pupil took up most of the space.

His proximity overloaded the air with his citrus scent, and I breathed it in, watching as he moved ever nearer. So close. Too close. My heart stuttered.

"Can I?"

Trying to find an answer, a verbal one, was impossible. I swallowed. Nodded. Stiffened some more. Then I relaxed when his lips gently brushed mine.

A groan whispered from me.

It was unexpected.

Everything about him was.

That was what I should have expected.

He was a wild card.

The Joker.

I shuddered as his pointer finger propped my chin up, angling my head back so he could press his mouth more firmly against mine.

I wasn't a passive person. Not by nature. But at that moment, I was.

I let him kiss me.

I allowed him to explore my lips because I had no desire to stop this.

I wanted his kiss.

But it was too—

I swallowed.

Too everything.

Feeling hurt because I'd locked everything down, grown accustomed to pain, but not of this type.

So, after being in the deep freeze for so long, sensations plucked at my nerve endings, transforming pleasure into bittersweet agony.

The heat puddling in my core was alien.

My nipples actually ached with the need to be caressed.

My hands craved the feel of his hair against my palms because that would ground me.

My lungs burned because I needed air.

But… he gave it to me.

With each deepening exploration, my lips parted more until I had to whimper when his tongue brushed along the inner curve of the flesh inside.

That was when the ice in my veins began to melt, warmth puddling in its place, and I jerked in reaction as something pulled at me, twisting and writhing.

Out of nowhere, as, internally, he brought me back to life, other things came to my attention.

Those citrus notes were clean and tangy, clearing my head and replacing it with awareness of him.

His jaw prickled with stubble that scratched my skin, but it high-lighted his tenderness.

Then, there were the ragged sounds of his breathing—they hit my ear drums. Each groan bled with his want. For me. *Me*. The one-time American cum dump. No one else.

And, there was his taste. Coffee and… *jam*? Sweet and syrupy, yet earthy too.

My mouth trembled against his and I pulled back with a jolt. His eyes were closed now, too, but he didn't move. Just carried on breathing my air as I breathed his.

His confidence was new.

Not unwanted or unwarranted.

Just new.

In our chats, he was always careful. Not wanting to push me too far. I hadn't expected *this*. Not so soon. Yet it felt right. I didn't want to be pushed, but I needed the reminder that I wasn't supposed to have ice at the heart of me.

I wasn't just a soldier.

I was maybe made for love too.

When I remained where I was, he let his head tip forward and our foreheads rested against one another. I didn't want to move. I wanted to stay here forever. We had people to save, but not even a tornado warning would have made me pull away from him.

He was warm.

He smelled good.

I liked him.

What had made me pull back again?

Confused, I tried to make sense of the nonsensical.

Then, it hit me.

With his eyes closed, it made it easier to answer the question he hadn't asked: "I haven't kissed anyone in a long time. Sorry if it sucked," I whispered. Did that sound apologetic? Sure, I'd said the word, but I wasn't even certain if I meant it.

Why had I said it again?

Oh, embarrassment.

I probably *did* suck, but he soothed my ridiculous nerves by rocking his forehead to the side, inadvertently massaging mine as he did so. "I've wanted to do that for over a year now."

Relief struck.

"Me too," I whispered.

And I had.

So why was I nervous again?

Or was I nervous?

What the fuck was even going on with me?

This was Conor.

He'd heard me come over the phone.

We'd talked about anything and everything.

He knew I liked *Halo* when that was more top secret than Area 51's real purpose. I knew he had a weird obsession with rom-coms that he let me tease him about.

No, nerves had no place here. Ghosts of the past didn't either.

"Can I?" I whispered.

"Always."

So, I angled my chin up and let my mouth press against his this time.

For a moment, neither of us did anything. We just stayed like that. Then I laved my tongue over his bottom lip, tasting remnants of the sour sweetness from the candy I'd rested there, and he groaned again.

That sound was hardwired into my senses.

It was a catalyst—one my body responded to. One that had my hands reaching for his shoulders and gripping them. Not to push away but to pull closer.

His lips parted and I thrust my tongue in deep. No hesitation. No thinking. Just feeling. And it felt better than good, and he tasted better than good too.

I sighed as he let me play, let me take charge this time. His tongue slid against mine, going slow where I was starting to speed up. The sensations began to build. Cravings stirring to life that I didn't think I'd ever experienced before.

As I slid into the bizarre realization that was *wanting* him, I released a whimper as I tilted my head so I could get closer.

Fuck, even that wasn't enough.

I could feel the fire in my veins starting to flicker everywhere, making my heart race and my skin flush.

My hands reached up to cup his face. Without knowing I was doing it, I dragged my fingers through his hair and he immediately jerked back.

For a second, we were both frozen.

Then I remembered.

He didn't like anyone gripping his hair.

We stared at each other.

Eyes wide open.

And something whispered into my mind:

I will not bend.

I will not break.

That was my mantra.

The truth was—I'd already been broken. I'd already had to bend. That was why I repeated that to myself so often—because it would never happen again. I wouldn't let it.

But I wasn't alone.

We were in this together.

We knew what the worst of humanity could do and we were survivors.

Somehow, that laid all our cards on the table. In one fell swoop, we were fully dressed yet totally naked in front of each other.

His nostrils flared as I pushed him back against the couch. Eyes locked on his, I moved slowly, straddling him, giving him time to say no but not stopping until my knees pinned him in place and my pussy found a home above his dick which was hard, despite having pushed one of his triggers.

As we'd done earlier, I rested my forehead on his. "I won't touch your hair again."

His hands settled at my hips, the fingers angling downwards so they splayed over my ass cheeks. He didn't answer me, just instigated another collision of our mouths.

This time, he took charge. Lips locked, tongue drawing mine out to play, his hands tugged down on me to urge me into moving.

Slowly, I began grinding my hips, but a sharp cry escaped me the second the friction centered itself at the top of my sex, and that blast of pleasure had me seeking more.

God, how could I have forgotten that it wasn't always about pain and misery?

There was *this*.

Joy and need and craving and desire.

There was Conor.

He encompassed it all.

He growled into my mouth as his own pleasure made itself known. I knew it was good because he started to rock back into me until we were humping on the couch like teenagers.

"Can I?" he rumbled against my lips, nipping me there, plucking the tender flesh.

Blindly, I nodded, even though I didn't know what his next move was going to be, and in response, his hands slid up my sides, tracing the curves of my breasts before one planted between my shoulders and he used that to keep us together as he twisted us over.

Tension hit me for a split second before I was crying out as the new position let him grind harder into me, the thick notches of our denim flies adding an extra pressure that had me ripping my mouth from his to sob at the sheer fucking ecstasy that tore through me.

Even as I cried out, he didn't stop moving. His hips continued rocking as he ducked down, lips finding my throat as he sucked along my jawline, testing the skin's resilience as he nipped there, biting and suckling, sending pinpricks of sensation tumbling along my nerve endings.

Head rocking from side to side, I dropped my hands to his ass and gave as much as I got before I started keening out my pleasure, stunned by the intensity, mind blown by the power of the sensations he triggered in my core.

When his lips returned to mine, he consumed me in a fire that was perfumed with the scent of oranges and cinnamon.

I could feel it—waiting for me in the wings.

There.

Right there.

God, so close.

But, not close enough.

I moaned against his mouth as I squirmed harder, trying to find something that had always been so easy before, something that I'd taken for granted in the past.

My heart started pounding, my skin felt flushed, and the specter of ecstasy was excruciating.

My body began to ache both from exertion and need. It was there. So close. Yet so far. His fingers dug into me, encouraging me, *guiding* me, and all along, he kissed me as if there were no tomorrow.

Just as I feared it wasn't going to happen, it bombarded me when he did this thing with his hips, moving them in a circle that hit *right*.

When I screamed out my orgasm, ecstasy shooting through my extremities, I felt his movements turn frantic until he choked out a groan that merely augmented my enjoyment.

His rocking switched from smooth to jerky, and then that groan turned guttural, the vibrations making my lips tingle as he continued to kiss me, ravishing my mouth as he took me further than some guys had when I was fully naked and being fucked.

And even as we came down from that, he continued kissing me.

Softer, this time. Not as hungry. But still needy. His mouth clung to mine and mine to his. We ate from each other, finding warmth and comfort and, God help me, *love* in the eternal tangle of our tongue, teeth, and lips.

When he started to pull back, I gripped his shoulders and held him to me, my legs slipping around him to clutch at him tighter.

His soft, contented chuckle had my eyes popping open, but I didn't chide him for laughing at my expense. Just watched those pupils of his return to normal as he turned us over so we were lying much as we'd done earlier—me curled into him like I'd known him for decades, as if I'd trusted him since the beginning of time itself.

I felt good. Better than I had in… *years?*

The thought made me realize it had been that long since another had granted me release, and when I did it on my own, it was like a sneeze in comparison to the Niagara Falls effect Conor had just had on my weary body.

"Remember when you asked me if I believed in kismet?"

The question was unexpected, and still faintly dazed by the aftermath of his ministrations, it took me longer than it should to figure out what he was talking about.

"Vaguely," I settled on, lying because I didn't remember at all, face burrowing into his side so he wouldn't know I was out for the count.

He pressed a kiss to my temple. "That just proved it's real."

28

CONOR

Conor O'Donnelly

I USED her shower instead of going back to my room.

I didn't know if it was an invasion of privacy, but by the time it occurred to me that it might have been, I was already soaping up with her shower gel.

So, I got myself clean, pulled on my jeans without my now-wet boxer briefs, dragged on my tee, and strode out after I selected one of three girly deodorants she had on her vanity—who needed so many?—and aimed a double pump of the spray at my pits.

As I walked into the living room and spied her chewing one of the candies I'd given her earlier, I declared, *"Now,* I smell of fruit."

I figured she'd be distant, the stirrings of dissociation coming to life, but as I'd intended, my statement disarmed her. "What changed?"

"Your deodorant."

"You used my deodorant?"

I smirked at her. "It's a spray. No cross-hygiene issues. Does it matter?"

"No. But it doesn't smell of fruit. What the hell's wrong with your nose?"

I wrinkled said appendage. "Nothing. It said 'lychee' on it."

"It also says white blossom." She hid a smile. "Come here." Not about to argue, I obeyed for once, and she yanked my arm down then, surprising the fuck out of me, shoved her nose under my arm. "Oranges."

"You're doing it on purpose," I accused. "I don't smell of oranges."

"I'm not saying you smell of shit," she countered as I raised my forearm and smelled the skin. I could only scent soap. *Her* soap, at that. "Maybe if you scratch it, it'll be like a 'scratch and sniff' sticker."

Huffing, I flung myself on a seat beside her. "What are you doing?"

"Edgar came with a tray of cinnamon rolls and a package." She pointed to the tray that I hadn't spotted and I leaned over to grab a bun. "We should have waited. I'd have tasted like cinnamon for real."

"If we waited much longer, my dick would have exploded."

"I thought it did," she said smugly.

"We're talking annihilation." I made a motion with my hands. "Boom."

"Melodramatic."

I heaved a melancholic sigh. "You just don't care."

She snorted then snagged the bun from my hand and took a massive bite out of it. I groused under my breath, but I was quietly content with how at ease she was around me, especially after antici-pating the opposite.

As I reached for another one and began eating, she stated, "The package Kuznetsov sent was a phone."

"Interesting. Whose?"

"A Sparrow's."

"Fuck, these taste good," I mumbled once I finished chewing.

She nodded her agreement as I reached for the cell she tossed at me and flicked it on. "And I do care, by the way. I have a definite interest in your controlled explosions now."

I laughed and almost choked on a pecan nut that decorated the top of the sweet treat.

"Jesus, you're worse than Katina. Walking disaster area much?" she complained, slapping me on the back with more force than was necessary.

"I think you gave me a hernia," I clipped, voice hoarse from choking.

"You can't give someone one of those."

"You can. Don't talk about controlled explosions if you don't want a response. *Or*, talk about them as much as you want, just expect to be a part of the blast."

A small smile kicked up the corners of her lips, but she didn't reply, just motioned at the phone.

"What am I looking for?"

"The calculator app, apparently," she reasoned, picking up a letter that Kuznetsov had written her. A quick scan from afar told me it included the basics he knew about his son, Aleks' death, in a car crash, and his granddaughter, Lyra, who disappeared in the same accident, as well as pertinent details about the app. "He says it's a shadow app. You tap in a code and there's a login page."

As my mind focused on the fact her uncle had died in a wreck and her cousin had disappeared, I tapped the appropriate numbers—it really did lead to a login page.

The screen was black apart from the two white windows where the username and password could be entered.

"And he doesn't have any login details?"

"No. While the *Pauks* managed to break the code to the app, they've failed to get any further. That's probably why we're here." Absently, she sucked her fingertip to clear away a remnant of icing. At least, I assumed that was why she sucked on her finger and that it had nothing to do with trying to torture me. She appeared to be totally unaware that I was fascinated by the move. "So, the game plan I had in mind has shifted," she prompted briskly. "I'm surprised he passed this along to us. Figured he'd make us wait until we gave him some answers."

As I stared at the app, trying to see if it had any recognizable features amid the black soup of the login page, I drawled, "I think he wants you to like him."

"*I* think it'll happen when hell freezes over."

"Never say never. You don't have much family left," I pointed out softly.

"You were the one who said we can choose our families."

"And you can, but what if he's a nice guy and you and he could have had a great friendship? You don't have to treat him like a grandfather to get to know him better."

Her lips formed a moue. "I suppose."

"Look, he could be an asswipe. But you stabbed him in the hand with a fork and he took that on the chin, didn't he? That's got to mean something."

"You call that caterwauling taking it on the chin?"

Shaking my head, I laughed at her disgust.

"He also locked me in a bedroom—"

"Literally a *bedroom*. With antiques. That you destroyed. All when you were trying to kill him. You said it yourself, the United Brotherhood is powerful. I'm sure there are plenty of places where he could have locked you up and tossed away the key."

Like a shipping container in the Catskills.

She huffed. "Back to the game plan. Where do we start?"

"I think we actually start with a phone call to my brother." I scratched my jaw. "Not a Brother. No capital 'B.'"

"I can tell the difference," she quipped. "Which one and why?"

"Eoghan."

"How come?"

"I mentioned the name Kuznetsov to him before my flight and he had a story to tell."

"About?"

My gaze darted from the notes Kuznetsov had left for us to her. "A car crash." I lifted a hand to stall the incoming questions as I reached for Anton's letter to her.

Star,

Here is a phone we procured from a now-dead Sparrow.

We believe the calculator is a shadow app. My Pauks have been working on this for months since the phone came into our possession, but they have uncovered very little other than the access code for the app that leads to a login page.

It's all very complicated, but the Pauks warn that there's some kind of threat to the hardware. Too many failed login attempts will damage the phone itself so be careful.

Please find their notes included in this envelope.
Your loving grandfather,
Anton

Though he was laying it on thick with that 'loving grandfather' bullshit, I read it, scanned the *Pauks'* findings to make sure I hadn't missed anything, then woke up my computer and logged in. A few seconds later, FaceTime had loaded and I was waiting for Eoghan to answer.

"Kid? You okay?"

Faintly, I smiled, just relieved he'd picked up. "I'm good. You?"

"Be better if you were in New York. When are you coming home again?"

"Dunno. You might be able to help with that."

Eoghan, obviously fresh from the shower as he'd been dragging a towel over his head, paused. "You need me overseas?"

"No." I grabbed the back of Star's chair and hauled it nearer to my side so she was sitting within the webcam's frame. "Star's here. Star, this is Eoghan. Eoghan, meet Star."

My baby bro narrowed his eyes at her. "You gonna keep giving Conor the runaround?"

"Maybe I like the runaround," I retorted. "And be nice. I was nice to Inessa."

"Inessa didn't take off to Russia and ghost me."

"He has a point, Conor," Star said softly, then, to Eoghan, who was somehow the baby of the bunch and yet the deadliest of us all, promised, "I'm going to try not to repeat the runaround."

My hand slipped up to her shoulder and I squeezed her gently. "We're working together now."

"Doing what? Bringing the Sparrows down?" he inquired, his curiosity tripped.

"That's part of it. Remember I told you about Kuznetsov?"

"The guy who you said kidnapped Star?"

"Well, it was less kidnapping and more 'holding in custody' until she decided to stop trying to murder him."

Eoghan shot Star a sympathetic look. "Don't you just hate it when that happens?"

Her lips quirked into a smile. "Yeah. It sucks."

Darting a glance between them, I noticed the embers of camaraderie stirring into being.

Intrigued, I wondered if they might actually be able to help one another if they became friendly—Eoghan's PTSD was getting worse and Star's headspace couldn't be considered 'healthy.'

Trying not to get my hopes up when both made rattlesnakes appear cuddly, I said, "It's too small a world for you two not to have come across one another at some point."

"Is there a question in there?" was Eoghan's cool retort.

"Have you met before?"

Star peered at me like I was crazy. "Of course."

"Were you friends?"

Eoghan snorted. "No. We're *nodding* acquaintances."

"What does that mean?"

"Exactly what it sounds like," Star quipped. "He was in the class before me at sniper school. I followed his career trajectory, even after I was recruited by the CIA. Saw him crash and burn his position there with that dishonorable discharge."

"Which I still don't regret."

"Why would you? Not like it hurt your career if you were enlisted overseas."

"Oh, yeah, that was a real promotion," he mocked before he muttered, "I should have just stayed out of things."

Then, a thought occurred to me. "Wait a goddamn minute. *You knew of him?*"

Star frowned. "Yeah."

"Then why did you hack into his apartment on his freakin' wedding day—"

"Jesus, yeah. Why the fuck did you do that?"

Her shoulder hitched up in a half-shrug. "Because I could."

Seeing as that was the most 'Star' answer in the universe, I just rolled my eyes, but Eoghan snapped, "You had that fucking woman waiting on my sofa with no clothes on, and Inessa and I—" He froze. Blinked. Rubbed his chin. "Huh."

"Huh?" I questioned, unsurprised by his anger because I'd been pissed as fuck that day too.

A smile danced on his lips. "Nothing."

Star and I shared a look—clearly she'd been waiting for the explosion to hit too. "I mean, it wasn't just about being smug. I needed to rile 'aCooooig' too. Get his feathers bristling."

I had to laugh. "It worked." Glad that had lightened the mood some, I got the subject back on track. "Anyway, Eoghan, Kuznetsov's actually Star's grandfather."

"How'd that happen?"

"When a mommy and a daddy decide they really love one another—"

"Kid," Eoghan grouched, his exasperation explosive. "I know how *that* happened. I meant which parent is related to him?"

"Her mom."

"Okay, interesting. She worked for the CIA too, no?"

Star cleared her throat. "She was a plant and she worked as a double agent."

"Taking her age into account... for the KGB?"

"No, for the United Brotherhood," I answered him.

"Finn mentioned them." My brothers were worse than the gossiping witches in the Old Wives' Club—widows of dead mobsters that congregated for coffee. "I thought they were a bank too." His brows lifted. "They infiltrated the CIA?"

I thought about my recent experiences with that agency. "You bet they did."

"This is massive—"

"Tell me about it. Anyway, that's not why I called. Kuznetsov's doing us a deal. We help him; he helps bring down the Sparrows. *Legitimately.*"

"How would he do that?"

"Interpol."

Eoghan's eyes widened. "Jesus, when he says legitimately, he means it."

I nodded. "According to him, he'd start a specialized department there because the leaders are 'people' he can trust." I included the air quotes because the whole thing was ridiculous but, bizarrely, believable.

That was when you knew you were living in a conspiracy, I thought, hiding a wry smile.

"You believe he can do it?"

"In my research on the United Brotherhood, I don't think it's outside of the realms of possibility," Star mused. "They're much bigger than the Sparrows—"

Disconcerted, I ran a hand over my hair. "Really?"

She shot me a look. "Four times larger."

"What?!" Eoghan and I yelled at the same time.

"Are you shitting me?" I muttered, quieter now.

"I wish I were." She grimaced. "I stumbled upon their existence and that led to hunting down Kuznetsov. Every step I took, I realized just how large their operation is."

I studied her as a thought occurred to me. "Who were Princes Ludwig and Edward and Ke Jintao to your grandfather?"

"His, I guess you'd call them, crew."

"You've been learning how the Irish Mob works. Cute," I teased.

She smirked. "I pick up shit along the way."

"If you're going to start flirting, I'm outta here."

"Oh, fuck off, Misery." I flipped Eoghan the bird.

Curiosity still piqued despite his disapproval over our flirting, he inquired, "I read about their deaths… You were the one who killed the princes and that Chinese politician?"

She shrugged.

He arched a brow.

No.

Was he…?

Yes, *he was.*

Eoghan was impressed.

Studying that raised eyebrow, I tried not to get excited about the two of them playing nice and maybe becoming friends one day.

Instead of being hella obvious, I prompted him, "Tell Star what you told me when I mentioned Kuznetsov's name on the ride to the airport."

"About the car crash?"

Star glanced at me. Nodding at her, I prompted Eoghan with a, "Yeah."

Cell in his hand, Eoghan headed into the kitchen. The sound of the fridge door opening and closing rustled in the background, and it was followed by the popping of a can. After he took a sip of what appeared to be an energy drink, he stated, "Why?"

Dickwad.

Friendly. As. A. Cougar.

And Riggs said *I* used to act like a robot.

"Because he has a price."

Eoghan rolled his eyes. "Only to be expected. What is it?"

"He said that someone murdered his son—" Eoghan's gaze sharpened at that. "—and he believes his granddaughter is alive."

"The little girl," he mumbled under his breath. "They said she died though."

Aggravated, Star straightened in her seat, snapping, "Can we start at the beginning?"

Eoghan, in an eerie tone, recited, "I'd just been approached by MI6 and they sent me to this specialist training corp in Scotland of all places. Lockerbie. There's a POW camp up there, Hallmuir, and it was used as a base. Anyway," he muttered, rubbing his brow. "Long story short, it was a waste of time. I could have taught them shit *but* they had this interesting segment on how jobs had gone wrong in the past and how they wanted them handled in the future."

"That's a weird way of making sure mistakes don't happen again," Star pointed out. "Classified info being released unnecessarily—"

"The only way I'm getting out of MI6, Star, is with a bullet in my brain," Eoghan said simply. "And they don't have to fear me spreading the word of anything I've picked up because they'll kill Inessa, Victoria, my brothers, their wives, and my mother if I even attempted to defect *or* to share classified intel."

Star's brow puckered. "That's intense."

"It's an unusual division," he dismissed. "I only shared this with my brothers because we're a closed circuit. Or we used to be."

Holding up a hand, Star promised, "I've been where you are. I won't say dick. Anything you can share with me, I appreciate more than you know."

He studied her then rumbled, "Just don't hurt him."

"I'm here, you know?"

Ignoring me, she bit her bottom lip. "I hurt everyone."

Eoghan sighed. "Been there, done that. You can break the cycle, Star. You just need the right person."

"Did you find your person?" she asked wistfully, and that wistfulness spread to her gaze. I saw it because she looked at me, a worrisome cocktail of hope and need, desire and love, buried deep within that glance.

It did things to me that I couldn't even begin to describe. Mostly, I wanted to hug her. Other, less romantic parts just wanted to slide inside her and find my way home at long last.

"I did. My person came when I least expected it, at an age that still freaks me out, and she sure as hell isn't what I'd have imagined for myself, but she accepts me," he admitted. "Conor's a good man. He'll accept you. Flaws and all. If you let him."

I flickered a look between them, well aware that Eoghan was probably doing more on my behalf in this one conversation than I'd managed in months of chatting with her.

Her head bowed in understanding, which prompted me to clear my throat. "She won't say anything, Eoghan. This is too big."

"You're telling me. All our asses are on the line, Conor, if news spreads."

Uneasily, I asked, "What if the agent who took out Kuznetsov's son is killed as a result of this conversation?"

Eoghan pursed his lips. "Doubt it would be an issue. Everyone's expendable."

Star scoffed. "True dat."

"I really hate that the government is supposed to be the good guys," I muttered, pinching the bridge of my nose.

Eoghan took another sip of his drink then, seeming to have come to a decision, sighed. "Okay, the story is that this Kuznetsov was some kind of emissary for Russia. He was driving from Ohio to New York, allegedly, but before he could even leave the state, the brake lines the agent cut failed as planned, but the location of the crash was badly calculated.

"There was a collision but they limped away from it by the skin of their teeth. I'm thinking Kuznetsov thought it was sabotage, so he ordered the driver to put distance between them and the crash site, to reconvene somewhere safer.

"The agent behind the job had to go in and manually end them."

"Meaning?" Star questioned.

"Chased them down a hill until they'd picked up speed and crashed again. This time, it caused a pile-up. The driver was killed, as was Kuznetsov. His wife was strangled, and the kid ran off into traffic. That's where her story ends. My division looked for her in the hospitals and in social services, but they didn't find anyone fitting her name or description."

"That's weird," I pointed out.

Star was frowning. "She must have turned up somewhere."

"Apparently not. She never showed up in a morgue or with injuries at the local hospitals. CPS never placed her in the system."

"That makes no sense."

Eoghan shrugged at Star's confusion. "I know. But that's all I was told, and it was a 'make sure that you don't let this happen or else' kind of example."

"What happened to the agent behind the botched job?"

"I don't imagine he or she is sipping piña coladas in Cancun, Conor. So I doubt Kuznetsov will get his revenge."

"You think they're dead?"

"Yeah, I do."

Star grimaced. "I can't imagine Kuznetsov was in the dark about any of this. Why waste our time and resources on finding the agent when we could just be focusing on the girl if he didn't think the agent was alive?"

"True." I focused on my brother. "Do you have anything we can use to pin this pile-up down, Eoghan? A date or a place?" I knew we could ask Kuznetsov but, in his letter, he mentioned neither, which kept us pretty much in the dark.

It wasn't like we had the man on speed dial to pepper him with questions.

"I told you, they wiped the records clean."

"You can't bleach a pile-up away. Not a British spy agency in the US, at any rate."

"Don't be naive, Conor. My division makes the CIA look like kids playing tag around the globe," was his flat retort. "If you don't think they have leverage on key members of staff in the right places who can do as they say, you're an idiot."

I grumbled, "Nice."

"Just telling you to keep your hopes low—"

Star choked out, "Operation: Jorgmundgander."

Eoghan's tension was immediate. I cast a glance between them. "I'm assuming this has nothing to do with the MCU?" It was my turn to sound wistful.

"I thought it was an urban legend," she breathed, staring at him with wide eyes.

Jesus, it was her turn to fan girl.

"I wish it fucking were," Eoghan intoned grimly.

"Jorgmundgander is the world serpent in Norse mythology," Star explained to me.

"Yeah, I know, babe," I drawled, amused that she'd think I wouldn't know my mythology. "He grew so large that he surrounded the earth and grasped his own tail in his mouth."

"When he lets go of his tail, that's when Ragnarök is supposed to start," was Eoghan's glum response.

"I'm assuming that Operation: Jorgmundgander's purpose is to make sure he never lets go of his tail? Metaphorically speaking."

Eoghan took another deep sip of his drink which, I figured, gave me my answer.

Sensing that I wouldn't get much else out of him, I rubbed my bottom lip with the edge of my thumb. "Thanks, Eoghan. Appreciate you sharing that with the class."

Eoghan hitched a shoulder. "Start in Cincinnati."

"Thanks, bro." A thought occurred to me. "*Is* Inessa pregnant by the way?"

"No."

He cut the line before I could reply, but I didn't need to continue talking to him to know what he wasn't saying out loud.

"Don't have to worry about a long goodbye with him, do we?"

I shook my head. "Eoghan's always been a man of few words."

"He didn't seem happy at the end. Did he want her to be pregnant?"

"I'd say unhappy is Eoghan's standard state of being. But no, I agree. Knowing him, he's relieved about her not being pregnant but also pissed that she isn't."

"And they say women are contrary."

"They do. I think you, better than me, can understand why he'd be relieved and pissed. Especially after what he said."

Her lips pursed. "A kid is another person to keep alive. To worry about being killed. *But,* that's another person to accept you from the ground up and who'll love you unconditionally if you don't make a mess of everything."

I nudged her in the side with my elbow. "You're too hard on yourself."

"You're not hard enough on me."

"Is that a complaint about what happened on the couch?"

Humor made her eyes light up. "No." She shoved my shoulder. "Jerk."

I just winked, glad to see her smile again. My tone turned more serious, however, when I asked, "You've heard of the team Eoghan works for?"

Her scowl was dark. "Heard of and dismissed as BS. There are always whispers, but the agents on that team might as well exist under smoke and mirrors.

"I'd be impressed that your brother is a part of it if it weren't crazy that they exist at all."

"I guess it means we have a basic idea of how Aleks Kuznetsov died, though. And we know that whoever wanted him dead worked for a secret team in British intelligence."

Nodding, she mumbled tiredly, "I wonder why they shared details about a mission that went wrong. It's one thing to give an outline, but it's another to name names."

She had a point.

Frowning, I wondered out loud, "Unless Eoghan's division plants itself firmly against the Brotherhood?"

"Could be against Sparrows."

"Nah. Eoghan would have said. He wouldn't keep something like that from us."

"He might not know he is."

"True." I rubbed my chin. "Question."

"Answer."

"Question colon. Not... Never mind." I sighed. "If your mother was murdered, and we know she was a Brother, was she killed because she was a double agent or because she was a spy?"

"And whatever motive there was for her death, was Dagda a Sparrow or anti-Brotherhood?"

"He wasn't a Sparrow. He hates them."

"You say that like you know him."

I hitched a shoulder. "I've spoken to him."

Star froze. "He murdered my mom."

"He murdered my da," I said flatly. "Plus, I thought your mom was just a walking uterus now that you know she was a double agent?"

Her chair scraped back as she shoved away from the table. I half expected her to leave the room, but she didn't. She moved over to the window. Then, she did the saddest fucking thing... The windows looked onto the ocean—the view was pristine even with the moody sky overhead—and she closed the blinds, tipping them so she could peer through them, then stood to the side as if evading a bullet.

God, what we did to our soldiers blew my mind.

Eoghan and she were so alike it was unreal.

I rubbed my eyes at the thought, but I refused to apologize for what I'd said. The truth stung. Our truths more than most.

Dagda should have been sent up for the murder of the First Lady *and* my da. He was walking around free and clear because my brothers and I had framed a traitor in the Five Points to spare him. Did I tell her that? Did I tell her we'd done that to force him into stepping down from the IRA-adjacent group, the *Éire le chéile go deo*, so Aidan could take his place at the top of the tree?

Rather than feed the silence, I fed myself. Picking up another cinnamon bun, I chowed down as she stared out at nothing, evading bullets I knew wouldn't be coming.

A couple emails came in and I dealt with them while she sulked. Then, God only knew how long later, she muttered, "Why didn't he want us to avenge her?"

Her question had me blinking, but the only answer I was capable of was: "Huh." Turning it over in my head, I eventually reasoned, "Either because the shooter is already dead and Dagda *wasn't* behind the killing or because he doesn't think she needs to be avenged."

"Meaning she betrayed him too?"

"Perhaps."

"Wouldn't he lay the guilt on me?"

"Not unless he's religious," I grumbled. "'Sins of the fathers' and all that crap."

Reaching up, she rubbed her temple. "Why does everything have to be so complicated?"

"That's what you get for playing with spies, I guess."

She snorted. "I *was* a spy."

My lips quirked but I just asked, "I've gone digging for pile-up crashes in Cincinnati in the last ten years. There's a lot to wade through, but maybe something will be of interest to us if we look for diplomatic plates."

"Eoghan never mentioned diplomatic plates."

"He did in the message he sent me." I thought back to the conversation we'd just had. "He said they were an emissary for the Russian government."

"Diplomatic immunity," she breathed, something flicking to life in her expression that I couldn't read.

"Star?" When she didn't reply, I repeated, louder this time, "Star!"

She jolted. "What?"

"Why did that ring a bell?"

"N-No reason."

"Bullshit."

"It's really nothing," she argued, sounding more annoyed this time.

"That clearly triggered some kind of memory."

"A stupidly minute memory."

"Stop being pedantic."

"I'm not being pedantic. It's impossible. Her father's name was Bogdan Belyaev. *Not* Kuznetsov."

"Tell me where your mind's at. And whose father?" I asked, confused.

She plucked at her bottom lip. Just when I was about to prod her, she demanded, "When I first took Katina in, she used to draw a lot. More than she does now—"

"Traumatic response, I guess. Shay does that to deal with the stuff he's gone through."

"Yeah, maybe. I don't know. I knew her father died in a car crash —" Her mumbled admission had me straightening in my seat. "But her mom…"

"What's making you think of Kat, Star?"

"When I first got her, she had horrific nightmares. Used to wet the bed a couple times a night. The social worker suggested a therapist, but it didn't really do anything for her. She just used to draw in the sessions, and she'd draw afterward, then she'd come home and the nightmares would be worse than ever. In the end, I said that it was doing her more harm than good and we stopped seeing the shrink.

"She got better. Hunter Lachlan, you remember him?" At my nod, she continued, "He came to stay for a short while, and he's great with kids, so that took her out of her thoughts. She started doing normal stuff, and I let her go wild which she loved and, eventually, she stopped wetting the bed *but* the drawing continued until…" She frowned. "… six months or so before I attacked your security system that first time."

"Okay, but what about the drawings?"

"Hell, it could mean nothing, Conor. Just a tiny, minute, bit of nothing on a kid's drawing. Trust me, she's no Picasso either. I love that kid but fuck, she massacres crayons with her art."

"You're trying to convince yourself," was my flat retort.

She glowered at me but carried on, "Kat used to draw the crash scene I assumed her dad died in. You'd see the trunk of the vehicle she sketched, but the front was smashed to fuck. Always, *always*, on the license plate, she'd write the license number." She plucked at her bottom lip now. "And it would always have this red strip along the top of it."

My eyes flared wide. "Diplomatic plates?"

"Yeah," she whispered. "But it's not related. He was Bogdan Belyaev."

"Names can be changed. Lies can be covered up." I peered at her. "Out of curiosity, can you remember that license plate?"

She shook her head. "No. At least, not without thinking about it. It's been too long since I saw it."

"How did you find Katina again?"

"Remember I told you about that shipping manifesto a while back?"

"Yeah."

"Her mom was one of the women whose journey I followed. By the time I found her, Kat was already in the foster care system."

"How long had she been in it?"

"I got her when she was five. She'd been in there for two years."

"And she just turned ten, right?"

"Yes."

"So the crash her father was in would have been seven years ago."

"There was nothing in her records about *her* being involved in a crash though, Conor. Just her father. Her mom died before the accident that killed her father. It doesn't add up." She shook her head. "I should never have said anything. It's dumb."

"Dumb, but do you want to leave it at that? Don't you want to look into it?" I prodded. "You've just come across your long-lost grandfather, a man you didn't even know was long or lost… Who knows what forces put you together?"

"Kismet between me and you is one thing. This is different." Before I could counter-argue, she hunched her shoulders. "I used a fake ID to foster her."

"Knowing you, it would have been as authentic as a real one."

"Yeah, but…" She released a breath. "I don't know why my mind fixated on those drawings of hers."

"We have a story that's conjecture from Eoghan. Sure, it was used as a cautionary tale, but isn't that like a game of telephone? The agent Eoghan thinks isn't sipping piña coladas in Cancun could have told their CO anything they fucking wanted to make sure that they didn't get their ass killed—" My mind was racing a mile a minute. Too fast. But shit was starting to come together. "—and you said the front end of the car was smashed up in her drawings. Not the back."

"Yeah."

"What if she was *viewing* the crash from the car behind her parents'?"

"Why would that make a difference?"

"Because it might mean that her parents were in the car in front and she was in the back. Whoever was driving *her* could have squirreled her away, which kept her off the system until they put her into it."

"Eoghan clearly mentioned the wife was strangled. That's a key—"

"It could have been a girlfriend. Didn't have to be the child's mom."

"This is stretching the truth," she argued, her unease clear.

"Maybe," I mumbled, scraping a hand over my head. "I'm going to look into it though. Just to knock it off the realms of possibility."

She shoved her hands in her pockets. "I guess that's smart."

Another thought occurred to me. Without waiting to ask her, my fingers raced over my laptop as I drew up the server we used to communicate on.

"What is it?" she muttered, stepping over to me as I went to work on finding keywords in our many, *many* conversations. She grabbed my shoulder when I didn't answer. "Hey, you dragged that nonsense out of me, Conor. Your turn to pay the piper."

"Don't you remember?! The manifesto!!"

"Yeah, what about it?"

"You bought something else from that vendor. The login details that led nowhere," I rasped, watching her eyes flare in astonishment.

"Oh my God, you're right! It's a long shot but we have to try." She plunked her ass down beside me, watching as I flicked through the many mentions we'd had of the word 'manifesto' in our online conversations. "Wait," she blurted. "I sent you those login details via email. Not on the chat."

"Shit! You did." Fuck, my brain needed to slow down if I was misremembering crap like that.

She woke up her computer and both of us were suddenly racing to uncover that information.

Moving over to the folder where I stored any and everything

Lodestar had sent me, I rushed through the files and whooped when I came across it.

Opening it up, I grinned as I grabbed the phone Kuznetsov had left with us. When the screen switched off, I realized that it automatically kicked you out of the calculator after a set amount of time.

Tapping in the code once again, I found myself on the login page and I carefully input the username and the eighteen-digit passcode that was on my computer.

I jolted when Star's hand seized my leg. Her nails dug in as she loomed over me, watching as the 'loading' circle went around and around, her breathing as ragged as mine as we waited what felt like a lifetime for *anything* to happen.

That was when the screen glowed white.

And a welcome message made an appearance on the screen.

'Welcome, Justin DeLaCroix.'

29

STAR

Star Sullivan

IT SEEMED IMPOSSIBLE. Improbable. Unlikely…

Yet, it was happening.

It was actually fucking happening.

I stared at the name on the screen as the rawest emotions whipped their way inside me, drawing me to my feet and prompting me to rush to the bathroom where I purged the cinnamon roll and croissants and candy I'd eaten.

My stomach wouldn't let anything stay inside it as years of fighting, of striving, of struggling were, suddenly, out of nowhere, on the brink of coming to fruition.

Then, a hand was at my back, one gathering my hair as I spewed up the little I'd eaten, which was when I registered a solid truth.

My body recognized Conor O'Donnelly.

If it hadn't, I'd have slammed the fucker touching me in the throat with my fist and would have drenched him in puke as a finale.

Instead, I sagged onto my knees when my body let up and rolled flat onto my back so that my spine was touching the cold tiles of the bathroom floor.

He immediately let go of my hair but maneuvered me into a seated position. That was when a toothbrush and toothpaste were shoved at me. Because my mouth tasted like sewage, I quickly washed up then spat out the excess into the toilet bowl. Once that was done, I blindly handed the items back to him and then spaced out.

The noise from the toilet flushing filled the room, and I figured that he was just as fucked in the head as I was because, after he'd returned my toiletries to the vanity, he flopped down at my side so that both of us were now staring at the spotlit ceiling.

In the silence that flowed between us, my racing mind calmed. It wasn't the first time it occurred to me, but it was the first time I let the sensation envelop me—that of belonging.

Of safety.

Of not being alone in this.

Of sharing the load.

Of being able to admit to a mistake and not having to be perfect…

"I can't believe I forgot about that login information," I whispered.

"I'm just glad you shared it with me," he muttered.

I swallowed as his comment hit home. "God, yes." I'd been so smart trusting him before. "We could have wasted a lot of time trying to crack through that app. I-I genuinely forgot about it."

Conor grunted. "With everything you've had going on for the last decade, Star, it's no wonder."

It seemed so insane to me that something that had bewildered me for a while, an unanswered question that I kept prodding at like a sore tooth had escaped my attention when faced with a need for random login info that was Sparrows-related.

Sure, it might not have worked, but to just forget about it?

What else was I forgetting?

That license plate in Kat's drawings was one thing I definitely couldn't remember…

"What else am I forgetting if I forgot that?"

He snorted. "You're not a computer, Star. You don't have a hundred terabytes of storage in your brain for random bits of information."

"I know but—"

"No, no 'buts.' Stop being hard on yourself. Instead, applaud your-self, for God's sake. You didn't—" He blew out a breath like the ramifications of what had happened were starting to sink in. "You bought that on a whim, Star. A fucking whim. And those login details weren't just anyone's, they belonged to Justin DeLaCroix, the head of the Sparrows himself! The chief justice himself. Can you even imagine what's stored on that app? Can you—"

Abruptly, he fell silent, seeming to choke on his words. *I got it.* I rocked my head to the side to look at him and almost smiled. His eyes were wide, his mouth wider, and it was opening and closing like words were forming but he couldn't get them out. It was definitely goldfish-esque but a lot more elegant than puking up yesterday's and today's meager meals.

He clearly could *not* imagine what was stored on that app.

Neither could I.

I slipped my hand into his. "Conor?"

"Y-Yeah?" he croaked out.

"We've done it, haven't we?"

He turned and pressed our foreheads together. "I can't answer that until we look deeper into the app, but we're going somewhere instead of nowhere, and that was our end destination this morning."

His rationale stung, but I appreciated that he didn't sell me false hope. Nodding at him, I agreed, "Somewhere is definitely better than nowhere."

He kissed my temple. "Whatever's on that app—we'll tear the bastards to shreds, Star."

For the first time today, I felt more like myself as I spat, "We sure as hell will."

30

DEAD TO ME

IT WAS in a sniper's nature to prefer long-distance shots.

The farther away, the better. Less chance of getting caught was preferable to the high risks associated with kills over a short distance. But that meant I was pouting at having to go as close as the neighbor's yard to Senator John McClure's mansion in Kentucky.

His neighbors had kindly constructed a treehouse for their child and because they were ridiculously rich, it was better appointed than my loft in Manhattan.

I peered out of Cooper's scope and watched the senator and his wife as they ate their meal together, much as they'd done for each of the two nights I'd been staking out their home.

Dinner at eight PM.

A glass of wine for her and a brandy for him in front of the fire as they both read the day's papers at a quarter to nine until ten PM.

Then she'd toddle off to bed and he'd veer toward the porch where he'd smoke a cigar from ten until ten-thirty.

The audacity of men never ceased to boggle my mind, and when I thought of what he kept beneath his property, it became more than just audacious. It was proof of how untouchable the asswipe thought he was.

Tucked below the thousands of square feet of marble that had been funded by a great-great-great granddaddy who didn't believe in the abolition of slavery was a basement.

A basement I'd seen him sneak down to once during my time here.

Security roamed the land, and armed cops manned the gates to his mansion, but the man had a sex slave in his basement.

Yes, *audacious* was one word for a man like that.

But those types of people were the very best marks.

It was always satisfying to cut someone down whose arrogance made them think they were above reproach.

No one was above the reproach of my bullet.

I smiled at the thought then sighed when, deep in my ears, Siri started playing a voice note to me.

"Lucinda, I think Star might be in danger."

Inwardly grumbling at the sound of my irritating cousin's voice, I replied: "Star's always in danger. It's what she does best."

She answered: "More than usual."

I huffed under my breath, still pissed at Star for getting me involved with that shitshow back in Russia.

One thing I had to say about Maxim Lyanov was he had a surprising ability to plan a siege.

Sure, that siege had gone badly awry, but he'd orchestrated it with more talent than some of the COs I'd worked with who sported four stars on their shoulders.

It wasn't his fault that the blueprints for Petrovsky Palace were wrong, not when those blueprints had been fudged to ensure that a siege would never be successful. Whoever owned the palace believed they were above the law, that was for sure.

Still, as mad as I was at her, I couldn't leave my girl in a lurch if she really was up shit creek without a paddle.

Not willing to mess around with voice messages, I called Temper and greeted, "Star is usually good at getting herself out of trouble."

"This is different."

"Why?"

"Muñoz's sniffing around."

"That jackass." I snorted. "He couldn't shoot himself in the foot, never mind get the run on Star." *Wherever Star was.*

I still hadn't managed to work out if she'd gone deep undercover and that was why she was radio silent *or* if she *had* been taken as Lyanov claimed.

'Taken' had many connotations for people in our line of work.

A mobster had a more one-track mind—taken, to him, meant being held under duress.

To us, it could mean absorption into the ranks of a faction you were trying to infiltrate.

"I'm telling you this time it's different," Temperance repeated, breaking into my thoughts.

"You keep saying that and it's tedious if you can't tell me why."

"Why are you whispering?" She hesitated. "In fact, don't answer that."

I smirked at nothing as I watched Senator McClure eat his final meal.

"Where is she?" I grumbled.

"Croatia."

"Croatia? What the fuck is she doing there?"

"How am I supposed to know?"

"Don't you know everything, Temperance?" I asked sweetly, knowing it would grind her gears.

"Are you going to help her or not?"

"I need more to go on than a country. It's a pretty big place."

"Dubrovnik. I can send you a trace on Muñoz's phone if that'll help?"

"Of course, it will." I rolled my eyes. "I should be done here tonight. I'll be able to head out in a few days." Once I'd collected payment from the O'Donnellys, I was free and clear to do whatever I wanted for a short time. "Since when are you worried about Star, anyway?"

"Since she got me involved in this Sparrows' shit show then—" She cleared her throat. "—went quiet."

I narrowed my eyes at that odd pause. "Do you know where she is? Is Muñoz holding her hostage? Is that what's going on?"

"I-I don't know."

That soft hesitation had me asking, "That bad?"

"Yes."

"I'll head out ASAP."

"Let me know when you've dealt with the situation?"

"As if I wouldn't keep you in the loop, cousin dear," I drawled before I cut the call.

Temperance was one of those people who kept her hands clean by assigning the dirty jobs to others. Her self-righteousness irked me like little else could.

Huffing and puffing my annoyance at her stopped me from fretting about Star and Temper's odd belief that she was in danger as I observed the McClures' evening entertainments.

The clock ticked slower than ever as I watched them like they were a TV show until, finally, Mrs. McClure—who didn't appear to be in the know about her husband's dungeon—kissed the senator's cheek and made her way to bed.

If she knew, I'd assume that she'd never kiss that scrawny cheek without being under the threat of death.

I smiled as, like clockwork, McClure checked to make sure she'd gone upstairs then sneaked over to the bookshelf that housed a secret compartment. From it, he withdrew a Cuban—*tut tut for the contraband* —clipped the cap, tucked the waste into his pocket then, after packing the items away, locked the compartment. He pulled a lighter from another drawer and then retreated outside where he tossed the cap into the yard.

With a deep sigh, he started puffing on the cigar. When his head was bowed over, the gleaming flame lighting up his face in my scope, I smiled.

Stroked the trigger.

And gently squeezed.

Blood blossomed on his shirt as his body jerked in response to the high-velocity round.

Within seconds, he was slumped on the ground, the cigar no longer in his hand but tossed aside as the hollow bullet I'd chosen to cause him maximum damage, and hopefully the most agony before he died, got to work.

A puddle appeared beneath him as he bled out, and all the while, I packed up Coop and retreated.

Senator McClure was officially Dead To Me.

31

TEXT CHAT

CONOR: *Hey, random. But you thought the United Brotherhood was a bank, right?*

Eoghan: *I did.*

Conor: *Before Finn brought it up?*

Eoghan: *Yup.*

Conor: *Where did you come across the name?*

Eoghan: *Fuck, Conor, I don't know. The amount of intel I have to wade through on the regular is ridiculous.*

Conor: *So, it was MI6-related?*

Eoghan: *All my problems are either O'Donnelly or MI6-related.*

Conor: *That doesn't narrow things down for me.*

Eoghan: *Boohoo, buttercup.*

Conor: *Fuck off.*

Eoghan: *YOU messaged ME.*

Conor: *I just wondered what you might have known about them, that's all.*

An hour later

Eoghan: *Ran a search on the thread with my handler.*

Conor: *It shouldn't be cool that you have a handler.*

Eoghan: *I can confirm it ISN'T cool.*

Conor: *I know that. But the lifelong James Bond fan in me doesn't agree.*

Conor: *I also know that if I was looking at you right now, you'd be frowning at me.*

Eoghan: *You'd be right.*

Conor: *It's hard being me.*

Eoghan: *Harder being your brother.*

Conor: *Yeah, yeah, yeah. What did the handler say?*

Eoghan: *He told me there were links between the Pauks (I assume you know they're Russian hacktivists) and the United Brotherhood. I figured The United Brotherhood funded them.*

Conor: *Shame you don't have more info than that.*

Eoghan: *You know me, Kid. I live to be your font of information.*

Conor: *Jesus Christ, Eoghan. Go for a run or something. You need the dopamine.*

Eoghan: *I already ran fifteen miles.*

Conor: *Go and have sex then. The oxytocin will do you a world of good.*

Eoghan: *Was I right?*

Conor: *About the Brotherhood funding the Pauks? Yeah.*

Eoghan: *Hmm. Did you think they approached me to be a member?*

Conor: *No. I just wondered how you knew about them. Anyway, say hi to Inessa for me.*

Eoghan: *Will do. Keep in touch or I'll get on a flight to Dubrovnik.*

Conor: *Family reunion. Baltic-style.*

Eoghan: *Uh-huh. Stay alive, dearthár.*

32

CONOR

Conor O'Donnelly

"HOW THE FUCK could you let her run away, Maverick?"

Rubbing a finger down the bridge of my nose, I watched as Star's temper hit peaks and troughs throughout the conversation with the biker, where I found myself both amused at seeing the momma bear in action and turned on by the defense of her kid.

How couldn't a man like myself react to that spike in temper?

The child in me, who'd been failed, loved to see her fight for Katina. Even as she'd defended Maverick's inability to corral her kid in the face of her fear for Star, it didn't stop her from ripping him a new asshole.

"Look, Star—"

"No, I won't fucking *look*. I left her with you," she snarled. "You know what that means? She was your mission. You failed, Maverick. You fucking failed her, and you failed me."

"I know. I'm sorry—"

"Sorry wouldn't have saved her from some pedophile creep who could have taken advantage of her!"

"This could have ended a thousand times worse than it did and that fucking kills me, but I can't cuff her to a chair—"

"I'm not asking you to cuff her to a chair! Just, you know, for her not to head to Manhattan while your back is turned. Mission. Goddamn. Failure."

"I know! I'm really fucking sorry, Star. It won't happen again."

"How do you know that? How can I trust that?"

"I've set protocol in place. She got out by sneaking into one of the housekeeper's vehicles. The guards know to check—"

"Why weren't they already?"

"It was an oversight. One *we* both missed. Link too." That gave her pause because she stopped sniping at him as he continued, "The threat of her going MIA is low now that she knows where you are." Maverick sighed. "I hate to say it, Star, because I know I screwed up, but the change in her when you stopped calling was immense."

"I was taken captive, Maverick," she said wearily, some of her ire having diminished, but it didn't stop her from countering, "What would you have preferred for me to do? Tell my jailor that he was ignoring the Geneva Conventions? Maybe I should have thrown my lot in with Amnesty International. Do you think they'd have helped? Oh, wait, I didn't have access to them either.

"I left her with family. With people who love her. Who want to keep her safe. More than that, I left her with *you*. You had my back in the sandbox. You knew what it meant when I left the only thing that matters to me in your care.

"Yes, I fucked up. Yes, I'm sorry about that. You've no idea how much it hurts me to know that I scared her. She's lost so much already and I never intended on letting her down—

"You're a mom now. That changes everything. You can't just head out like you did in the past. That's not how it works."

"Fuck. You. You know what I'm working toward. I'm trying to stop women like *your* Old Lady," she spat even though his tone hadn't been argumentative, "from ever being hurt again. I'm stopping these bastards from ever getting their hands on women they think will slip between the cracks and using and abusing them.

"You think you had it rough, Maverick? I know you've been to hell and back, but you have no idea what Alessa, Amara, and myself have gone through. Never mind the fuck knows how many women the

Sparrows have trafficked over the years. *Those* women are who I'm fighting for. Kat's goddamn mother was among that unknown number.

"I didn't fuck off to Mexico for some winter sun and a spa treatment. I went to change the world so that it's a better place for my kid."

By the end of that speech, she was breathing heavily and Maverick was silent.

I didn't need to fight Star's battles for her, but I approached her with caution and gently slid my hands up her arms when she didn't shove me aside.

As I reached her biceps, I drew her against me, letting her rest her forehead on my chest instead of leaving her to stare blankly at the wall of windows beyond. Her shudder as she burrowed into me made me gladder for thinking to comfort her.

She was so strong that it was easy to think she didn't need that. But things were different with me, weren't they?

Miserably, Maverick stated, "I'm sorry, Star. I'm so fucking sorry."

"I don't need you to say sorry," she whispered. "I need you to make sure my daughter is safe."

The breath he released was audible. "Star, she *is*. She knows where you are now.

"You're raising a kid who isn't afraid to wade into the fray for the people she loves. *You* are the person she loves. Sure, she cares for Alessa and me, but *you are her mom*. You're raising a little lioness and those kinds of people don't back down.

"Can you tell me, if the roles were reversed and you were Kati and you thought that O'Donnelly guy would help bring your mom home, that you wouldn't sneak out too?"

She was quiet for so long that I knew she was trying to figure out how to say no without actually saying the word. Then, she gave up trying and huffed. "No."

As my lips curved, Maverick diplomatically reasoned, "Don't be surprised when she pulls these stunts. She might come across like an elephant-footed fairy, stomping on people's toes and accidentally kicking them as she does a cartwheel, but she's a smart kid who isn't afraid to do what needs to be done—in this instance, that was bringing you home.

"We did figure out how she left, and I plugged in the gap in our security. Even if she tried, it won't happen again, but I'm telling you, the reason for her leaving is done with so she's safe and you don't need to worry.

"Now, with that being said, that doesn't mean *I'm* not worrying. What the fuck went down? Who held you captive?"

I rubbed a hand down her back, surprised that she let me comfort her, yet also *not*. Star was starved of affection and I didn't think she even knew it. She was so hemmed in that it was a wonder she could breathe freely.

As she gave Maverick a surprisingly in-depth rundown of what had happened and the deal she'd struck with Kuznetsov, I listened and just held her.

Supporting without interfering.

My brothers would have yanked the phone away from their wives, would have wanted to fight her war for her, but that wasn't what Star needed. Me running roughshod over her life was the last thing she required of me. But I'd never met anyone more in need of someone to have her back, and I'd be that for her until the day I fucking died.

When Maverick cut the call, she released a heavy breath and sagged into me as if that had drained her dry of every ounce of energy she possessed.

"We should eat," I said, gently stroking my hand over her hair.

"I think I'd prefer a bottle of tequila."

"That can be arranged," I teased.

Her nose crinkled as she pulled back to look at me. "We can't afford to have hangovers. We need to get started."

"Technically, we *have* started."

"You and I both know that's the tip of the iceberg." She bit her lip. "Do you think he's right?"

"To blame you?" I shook my head. "You were both in an untenable situation. And, to be frank, if you didn't need to be here, I don't think you would be. I think you'd be with her."

"Of course, I would," she whispered. "When I first started this, I did it for myself. I needed vengeance. I needed payback. But with every woman I uncovered who was forced into that way of life, it became about more than just me." For the first time, she stepped away from me. Reaching up to rub her forehead, she mumbled, "So much suffering, Conor. I don't want to sacrifice a moment away from my kid, but I have to because there are women out there who are still where I was.

"I got out but they weren't so lucky, and I can't handle that. The weight on my conscience is too much for me to bear."

"We'll bear the load together," I told her simply. "We deal with this, we bring them down, and then, and only then, will we grab a bottle of tequila each and get hammered."

Her lips quirked. "I can't imagine you drunk."

"I've been told I'm a happy drunk."

"Why does that not surprise me? You're always happy."

I shook my head. "I'm not. You just bring it out in me."

She sucked her bottom lip between her teeth. "Thank you for being here."

"You don't have to keep on thanking me."

"I do." Her eyes narrowed. "Got it?"

"Got it," I drawled, amused.

"I *will* eat but only because I need to get my strength back up. I didn't trust that the food I was being served wasn't poisoned."

"Want breakfast for dinner?"

"Considering it's dinner time here, sure. Why not? Let's rebel," she joked.

So, we ordered the works and a half-hour later, Edgar delivered the feast to the suite.

As we sank around the table again, I watched her stuff bacon between two slices of bread. "We forgot to ask for lettuce, tomato, and mayo."

"Nah. I don't need it." At my look of surprise, she shrugged. "I spent a lot of time in London. They have bacon on its own with brown sauce. It's like A1 sauce."

"I'll have to try it."

"It's the best."

She finished stacking pieces of bacon into the sandwich, drizzled ketchup over it, then took a bite. Her sigh of repletion went straight to my cock, but I ignored it.

Being aroused around her was the standard now.

I'd have to control it at some point.

"How come you spent a lot of time in London?"

"BDSec is based there."

"Really? I thought it was Berlin."

"Nah. They have it routed from there as a double-blind." She chomped on the sandwich. "You heard of the Four Horsemen?"

I riffled through my memory banks. "Four cousins who pretty much run London, correct?

"Yeah, all thirty-two boroughs of the city are under their control." She reached for her coffee. "I came across their 'head of IT,' and we became friendly. That was CIA-related."

Snorting, I started to pick at the toast I'd buttered a few moments ago. "Head of IT as a job title for a criminal enterprise?"

"Right? Talk about understating someone's role in the business. Anyway, she was... I don't even know why, but after I escaped my owner, she was who I ran to."

"Why do you think you did?"

"I was in Cologne at the time and I wanted to get across the English Channel. Putting an ocean between—" She cleared her throat. "Anyway, distance felt like a good idea.

"When I arrived in Dover, I had nowhere to go, and though I had cash, I knew I needed help. Because of her ties to the Four Horsemen, she was the first person I could think of.

"She and her partner, Minerva, took me under their wings and helped me get myself together. I was a wreck back then. The autonomy he'd stolen from me, Conor, was insane. It took me a month to stop asking to use the restroom and another couple of months to stop asking for permission to eat."

Defiantly, she took a large bite of her sandwich and closed her eyes as if remembering the times when she didn't have the freedom to do that.

Her words robbed me of speech, mostly because I couldn't imagine anyone doing that to her. She was Star Sullivan. A force to be reckoned with. A powerhouse that would make the earth quake beneath her feet by the time she was done with her mission.

"What happened?" I asked, my voice raw.

"We started working together to bring down the Sparrows." She tipped her head to the side as she studied me. "What happened with Temper, Conor?"

My nose crinkled at the obvious change of subject. "She only fucking tasered Director Reinier in this massive boardroom at Langley."

"And you managed to leave the building without handcuffs?"

"She called in Brothers who helped us get out. She said they were going to kill me."

"What were you even there for?"

My brow puckered as a thought occurred to me. "I can't believe I didn't put two and two together, to be honest. I'm not a part of this Jorgmundgander BS, but the US clearly has its own program. *I'm* in it. That's why I didn't go to jail for all the shit I did as a kid.

"And, when I got to Langley, I met a bunch of coders who were working on this top-secret messaging platform for the Secret Service."

"Under the same restrictions as you?"

"Indentured servants for the state, yeah," I grumbled.

"I don't know how you kept any of this from your family," she muttered.

"I never left the US anyway. It isn't like we get to vacation often, Star. Plus, the government facilitated the secrecy of it all. I don't think they wanted my family to know either."

"Why?"

"Because I could have been viewed as a traitor and everyone knew what Da's reaction would have been to that. So, it was either protect me and keep me alive or throw me to the wolves and let me be eaten."

Her brow puckered. "I hate that you were in danger."

"You think I don't feel the same way about you?"

Her gaze dropped to her half-eaten sandwich. "True. They wanted to see if you could crack the platform?"

"Yeah. It was so fucking easy. I swear, working with you has streamlined my work. I tore it to shreds without your worm—"

"Maverick's worm," she corrected.

"—and did it in record time. According to Temper, however, the plan was for me *not* to crack it then for me to be killed to keep it under wraps."

"Sounds like a plan the Sparrows would concoct."

"Well, Reinier *is* a Sparrow. So it's on brand for him."

She snickered. "Fair. Wonder if the other coders were under threat, too."

I shrugged. "Maybe. Apparently, they wanted another coder to take my place."

"Why?"

"Temperance didn't say."

"How did you leave Langley?"

"By helicopter. I don't think I'm cut out for espionage."

"That's not a bad thing. It's a fucking awful line of work."

"Why get into it then?"

"You know why. Mom."

"Why follow in her footsteps when it killed her?"

"Do you know the story of how my parents met?"

"Of course." I rolled my eyes. "It's like you choose not to understand how dedicated I was to the band. Anyway, *noxxious* was in Madrid, weren't they? For a festival, right?" At her faintly amused nod, I continued, "The band got into a fight and were arrested. Because they were VIPs, the US ambassador green-lit them out of jail and took them to the embassy so they were 'on US soil.'"

"Biggest load of bull crap going. The injustice was unreal. Marc broke someone's jaw," she grumbled. "And he didn't even get arrested for aggravated assault or anything."

While she was dissing one of the greatest drummers alive, I continued, "When they were in the embassy, your mom was there."

She sniffed. "One look and he had to have her. Luckily for him, the feeling was mutual, but we know that his infatuation was genuine. Hers… not so much."

"Did he know she was CIA?"

"Nope. He just thought she worked for the embassy. She perpetuated that belief."

"What made the truth come out?"

"Tequila," she said with a snort as she raised her coffee cup to me in a mocking toast. "When I found out, I was fascinated. Then, after she died, it consumed me. The injustice of it."

I cupped her hand. "You've always fought for injustice."

"You make it sound like I was being courageous. As with most things me-related, it was forged in anger and bitterness."

"You can change that, Star. It doesn't have to be like that forever."

She bit her lip. "How do you teach an old dog new tricks?"

"Firstly, you're not an 'old dog.' Secondly, these aren't new tricks. If you want a better life, if you want to stop feeling so bitter about the past, that's something you can change. If *you* are ready for that."

I allowed the notion to linger as I finished up my breakfast. Maybe it'd help, maybe she'd ignore it, but I had to try.

She *was* angry.

She *was* bitter.

And did she but know it, her letting go of both would be a solid step on the path to earning my forgiveness for her involvement in Da's murder.

Only when she let go of the past would she open up to working as a pair and not on her own, only then would she really be free to be with me, and that was something I'd never stop fighting for.

Star Sullivan

I HAD no right to intrude upon his privacy.

No right whatsoever.

But I slipped into his room with a silence that came from practice, and I moved over to the bathroom where I could hear the shower running.

He'd left with the intention of washing up and catching some Zs, but the second he closed the door behind him, the empty room, a generously proportioned space, had started to close in on me.

Sleeping on the couch hadn't been on tonight's agenda, but I'd take it over being alone.

When I walked into the bathroom, I heard him humming one of my dad's songs.

It figured that the man I was falling for would love the music I'd come to hate. Though, earlier, I *had* noticed his use of the past tense in regard to his dedication to them.

It made me feel weird, like I was yucking his yum. It wasn't his fault I knew truths that would break his fanboying heart. So I guessed I'd need to work on that too.

noxxious the band and *noxxious* the artists were not one and the same. Dad had been a great father before Mom's death; after, he'd just been trying to get through the days without her.

As an adult, I registered that. Especially one who had crazy feelings for a certain someone who was currently showering in another room. As a kid, I'd been hurting too and I'd missed him just as much as I had Mom.

That was something for me to think about another day, though. Now, I just wanted to reconnect with Conor so I stripped down to nothing and headed into the shower stall.

With his face being blasted by the pounding water as he soaped up, he didn't register my presence until my front was pressing against his back. When he jolted, I smiled and slid my hands around his abs.

The strength of his muscles astonished me because he was lean and compact, a little like myself. Built to fight, not to weight train, which was the confusing part because Conor was *not* a fighter.

His brothers, sure, but not him.

"Star?"

"It had better be me."

He snickered. "Is it okay to turn around?"

"Think I'm afraid of your cock?" I countered.

"I don't know. Are you?"

It was a valid question, but this was different. This was… *I felt in control.*

Not answering, I slowly reached for his dick, *showing* him I wasn't scared rather than telling him, waiting him out to see if he'd want me to stop.

He didn't stop me and he was hard.

"Are you all right with me touching you like this?" I whispered.

He rested his forehead on the wall and groaned.

It was nice to know that I had such a dramatic effect on him, and I gave him a slow stroke in thanks before I pumped him faster, tightening my fingers around the tip with every pass.

With my other hand, I turned the water on low, and that enabled me to hear the curse he ground out. His own hands slapped against the tiles in front of him as I systematically tore down his walls just like he did with me.

His hips started to rock, jerking forward to follow the path of my fist, fucking me back, taking the pleasure I was offering and enjoying it —well, if his moans were anything to go by, he was definitely loving what I was doing to him.

My lips curved against the smooth skin of his shoulder as he spat, "What you fucking do to me, Star." His tone was angry but the words weren't.

I could tell the difference.

"I want to please you, Conor," I crooned, my confidence brimming at an all-time high. Feeling myself getting wet, I whispered, "Do you like that?"

"You know I do," he groaned, his head tipping back. "Nobody else I'd let touch me like this."

Pleased with his answer, I sped up, clamping around him while I reached down and grabbed his balls.

Rolling them in my fist, I encouraged him to climax. I milked his shaft when he hissed out a curse as his cum pelted the wall, washed away by the gentle spray.

Shocks jolted through his body, making him jerk in my hold, and I finished off with a soft kiss to the center of his back.

A rumbling sound escaped him, one of purring satisfaction that had my pussy clamping down around nothing.

That was when he shifted the narrative.

When he made it so that I was no longer in control.

The water abruptly shut off a second before he twisted around so that our fronts were plastered together.

As I dealt with the fallout from that collision, one where his fading erection bobbed against my belly, where my tits pressed into his muscled chest, he took advantage of my dazedness and stalked forward, gently but inexorably pushing me along until I reached the back wall.

Eyes wide, I stared at him, recognized the replete satisfaction in his expression, and sighed when he gently tugged me down until I landed on the bench there.

When his eyes lit up with a smile that soothed my soul, he dropped to his knees and I watched as he slid both his palms along the outer length of my thighs.

"Are you going to let me taste you, Star?"

I licked my lips. "That wasn't what this was about." I didn't entirely know what it was about, in all fairness, but I hadn't expected anything in return.

His smile morphed, turned sharp. "No? Don't you want to feel my lips on your pussy, Star?"

Gulping, I let my eyes lower to that sinful, wicked mouth that was quirking into a deeper grin at my prolonged study of it.

"I-I think we should catch some rest. We have a busy day tomorrow."

"I'm never too busy for this," he chided, gently parting my feet and shuffling forward so his knees could settle between them. My inner thighs clamped down so they didn't spread, and he arched a brow at the sight. "Don't you want to go to sleep on a high?"

My nostrils flared at the question.

Yes. Yes, I fucking did.

"No fingers," I rasped.

His eyes narrowed at the request, but he nodded. "Can I spread your legs with my hands?"

"Yes, just…" I swallowed, knowing it didn't make sense, but stuff didn't need to make sense for it to be a trigger.

"I won't finger fuck you," he promised, seeming to sense that was the source of my unease.

"O-Okay, then," I agreed.

"Just pleasure, Star, no pain."

I licked my lips again, repeating, "Just pleasure. No pain."

His smile was back to being warm, *comforting,* as he stroked my calves, shifting higher to my knees where he gently began to pry them apart. Pry—because my muscles weren't obeying.

I blew out a breath as the past and present blurred into a morass of memories I struggled to evade.

This was my time.

My moment.

As he'd said—just pleasure. No pain.

I looked at him, really goddamn looked at him, and thought to myself, *This is Conor. He'll never hurt you. He'll never, ever find pleasure in making you scared of him, in making you suffer, in exchanging sex for food.*

It helped me to let him spread my thighs.

His gaze dropped to my sex, and I knew I was wet and that the slick from my arousal had nothing to do with the water from the shower.

What he saw had him groaning.

His hands moved to my feet and he angled my knees to the side, parting me farther until I was clenching my eyes closed because every inch of me was exposed.

Exposure was something I'd had to adapt to. Nudity was a way of life, but revealing this much of myself without force wasn't.

He pressed his lips to my knee, trailing them along my inner thigh until he fluttered his tongue in the small, triangular divot where my leg met my groin. His nose ruffled over my mons, the tip trickling along the sparse hair there before he let his mouth meet my pussy.

I jolted like he'd hit me with electricity. Soft sparks buzzed through my veins, leaving me squirming as the soft flesh of lips I'd only kissed for the first time today explored the most intimate part of me with a gentleness I should have expected from him.

He seduced my pussy.

That was the only way I could describe it.

Conor didn't dive right in; he didn't ravage me.

He teased me, sure. But it was a slow, charming seduction that saw him nibbling on my pussy lips, that had him circling my clit with his tongue, that made him use the flat of it for maximum surface coverage over my most sensitive area.

He stroked and sucked and licked and kissed until my only fear was suffocating him between my thighs because I wanted to hold him closer, not push him away.

Conor seemed to sense the moment the rightness of this clicked in my head. His wet lips suckled my clit, harder than before. Still soft in comparison to things that had been done to me in the past, but with an intent that was unmistakable—he wanted my pleasure.

The flat of his tongue went to work again, stroking down the sensitive channel to my slit where he thrust inside me, gently circling it so that the nerve-laden entrance quivered at his caress.

"Oh, God, Conor!" I cried hoarsely as his flickering licks drove me up the wall.

When he chuckled, the vibrations shot through me, making my back arch and my ass almost fall off the bench. He grabbed me then but was quick to only get me comfortable before he moved his hands away.

The memories didn't have time to take over. His mouth returned to my clit and he doubled down on his efforts. The noises he made were a soundtrack that lit me up from the inside out.

He reveled in this.

It wasn't something he did to get me wet so he could fuck me with ease.

The sounds he released were of a man feasting and enjoying the banquet spread out before him.

With each groan of satisfaction he made, I could feel my body temperature spiking. My hips rocked until I was fucking his face and that was when he growled, "Yes, Star. Yes. Take your pleasure. It's yours."

The next second, his lips were back on my clit.

Ecstasy was within reach but too far away from touching—like a wall I needed to breach. I tried to throw myself over it, but it was too high. Then he shaped the small nub with his tongue. Figuratively, I got up and tried to scale the wall again.

I failed.

My breathing grew so fast that I turned lightheaded.

Every time I approached that motherfucking wall, I failed to climb over it.

But Conor never lost patience with me.

His lips had to be numb, but God, the way he feasted, how he *savored*, it made my heart skip beats it couldn't afford to skip.

His nose nudged my clit as he retreated to my slit again. When he thrust his tongue into me and I literally was rocking against his face, covering his jaw in my juices, he mumbled, "You taste like mine, Star Sullivan. *This* tastes like mine. Your pleasure is mine; your cum is mine. I want it. I want it all. Don't you want to give it to me?" Each sentence was punctuated with a thrust of his tongue or a circle of it, a nudge of my clit, a nip of my pussy lips. And the vibrations from his words had me staring blindly ahead, shivering and quaking, deep judders that quaked through my muscles.

Suddenly, the wall didn't seem so high.

This time, when I hurled myself at it, I managed to hook my leg over the top.

The next moment, as I free-fell down the other side, I screamed as the ecstasy rattled through me. It made me feel delirious. Overheated and boneless, yet also tense and taken to my limits.

I continued riding his face, and he carried on anointing soft kisses to skin that wept for him.

When I sagged back against the bench, I knew I'd been devoured and I was happy to be his feast.

There really was no better way to end the day than *that*.

Star Sullivan

"I'M TELLING NYX."

He arched a brow at the mention of the Sinner whose hobby was hunting pedophiles. "What's to tell? I thought you said he wasn't doing this anymore."

"Priest took his place."

"Priest? Oh, the kid. The one that Da…" His nose crinkled. "Never mind."

"He's an adult," I corrected. "He isn't underage. I'm not about to let this continue."

Maybe it was fate that the first email that cropped up which stopped the protocol Conor was running was this one.

A *'thank you'* for a satisfactory purchase.

I wanted to throw shit at the wall. *Needed* to break stuff. Wrecking things felt good when I was beyond frustrated with this shit show of a world, so tired of the depravity which I waded through trying to bring justice to these pieces of shit who didn't deserve to breathe the same air as me.

To many, I was a monster. I killed without compunction. I had very little conscience. But I was a fucking saint by comparison to the animals I'd come across in my dealings with the Sparrows.

Conor didn't stop me when I picked up my cell phone and tapped out a message.

Only…

I thought about Nyx, Giulia, and their son, Samael. Then the Newfoundlander and Chihuahua that followed the family around like they were Bo Peep and the dogs were sheep.

Nyx had found something I'd been seeking for over a decade—peace.

I couldn't rupture that, not when Samael's future was at stake.

Priest was seeking peace of his own thanks to the rape and murder of his baby sister by an animal who Nyx had put down, but I knew I couldn't approach him directly.

Conor, peering over my shoulder, said, "The Five Points will help. Da was on a crusade once he found out about, you know, everything."

"You sure?"

"Positive."

Deleting my message, I switched out the contact and texted:

> Me: Nyx isn't in the game anymore, is he?

> Rex: Never knew he whored himself out.

> Me: Har. Har. Har.

> Rex: We talking about hunting?

> Me: Yes.

> Rex: No, he's out of that. He'll help though.

> Me: Do we really want to tempt him?

> Rex: Probably not. I'm guessing you have someone who needs to die?

> Me: Yes. Excruciatingly. He needs to hurt, Rex.

Rex: Where are you?

Me: Can't say.

Rex: More like WON'T say.

Rex: Heard you tore Maverick a new one.

Rex: When, IMO, you were both at fault. What the hell were you thinking, just going silent like that?

Me: I didn't message you for a lecture. I know I fucked up. It won't happen again.

Rex: He wouldn't give me any details…

Me: I was taken captive so the circumstances were less than ideal.

Rex: You're safe now?

Me: I am.

Rex: How did you find this piece of shit if you're out of the country?

Me: My source is solid.

Rex: They always are.

Rex: Priest isn't ready to deal with this on his own.

Me: Can someone help him?

Rex: Amara?

Me: LOL.

Rex: Yeah, sorry. Bad joke. I just figure she'd probably get a kick out of it.

Me: She would.

Rex: Shame she doesn't know how to keep a crime scene clean.

Rex: I can think about it. How urgent is the
situation?

Me: Urgent.

Rex: Shit. At the risk of sounding like a
fucking pussy, I don't want to know the
details.

Me: Trust me, you're not a pussy.

Me: You know Conor O'Donnelly?

Rex: Know of him. Know Declan better.

Rex: Why?

Me: He says the Five Points will help.

Rex: Okay. With what in particular? Has shit
changed with their father's death?

"Making sure no arrests stick," Conor answered, reading the message thread over my shoulder.

Me: Keeping you guys out of jail.

Rex: Sounds good. Send me the details.
We'll get Priest out there ASAP.

Me: Needs to be more than ASAP.

Rex: We're on it.

Conor cupped my shoulder but neither of us said anything.

What was there to say?

This was just one more victim in an ocean of them and we were fighting for them.

I closed my eyes. "Thank you for doing this with me."

His hand slipped down to tangle with mine. "We're in this together."

A shuddery breath of relief whooshed from my lungs.

35

TEXT CHAT

CONOR: *Rex from the Sinners will be in touch.*

Declan: *Re?*

Conor: *A pedophile in upstate New York.*

Declan: *Jesus.*

Conor: *Da was on a crusade after he found out what happened to me.*

Declan: *Yeah, I know. I got a letter from him in the will about it. Did you get one?*

Conor: *I did.*

Declan: *What did yours say?*

Conor: *Lots of random stuff, rambling mostly. He said the Five Points needed to take affirmative action against these pedophile bastards and I was to coordinate that. Nothing about what happened to me, though.*

Declan: *I'm supposed to 'facilitate' when the Sinners go on a hunt.*

Conor: *There are too many of these fucking bastards, Declan.*

Declan: *I know, Kid. I know. It makes me terrified for Cameron.*

Conor: *We'll protect him.*

Declan: *Our father was a man who struck terror into the heart of monsters... But it still happened to you. I ain't Da, Con.*

Conor: *Thank fuck you're not.*

Conor: *He got to me because he pretended to care, Declan. Then, he shamed me into silence because I didn't know if Da would blame me, and the idea of that was as terrifying as what he did to me.*

Declan: *I'm so fucking sorry, Conor.*

Conor: *You don't have to be. There was nothing you could have done.*

Conor: *I don't say that to make you feel bad, Declan. You're my younger brother. I'm supposed to look out for YOU, not the other way around.*

Conor: *You need to make sure that Cameron knows he always has a safe place with you. Make sure he knows that you will never blame him or shame him for whatever life throws his way.*

Conor: *And never, EVER, minimize what he's going through. If he comes to you with something, it's because it matters to him and it should be important to you.*

Conor: *THAT is what you can do.*

Declan: *Yeah.*

Declan: *I can do that.*

Declan: *You're right. Aela's good at that stuff too.*

Declan: *She'll make sure to slap me upside the head if I fuck up. Shay's open about his feelings and things.*

Conor: *LOL. I figured that out when, over roasted chicken, he told Da that it was wrong to shame you for liking art.*

Declan: *Proudest day of my fucking life when he did that.*

Conor: *I get it. Da did a number on us all, didn't he?*

Declan: *Yeah. It's as if we're decompressing now that he's gone. Is it weird I miss him?*

Conor: *No. I miss him too. Stockholm Syndrome.*

Declan: *Lol. I'm glad I'm not alone. Brennan seems to be the most okay with it.*

Conor: *Understandable. Da treated Brennan like shit after what happened to Ma.*

Declan: *I don't know how he could blame him for any of that.*

Conor: *He was only a kid. He shouldn't have even been guarding Ma in the first place.*

Declan: *Da seemed to forget that we were children once we were Pointers.*

Conor: *I agree.*

Declan: *I'm not going to raise my kids how Da did.*

Conor: *Good.*

Declan: *It makes me glad that Aidan's got it into his head that Shay's going to be president. I can't see it happening myself, but I think he'll get into politics. Either way, he has to stay squeaky clean and I'm here for that.*

Conor: *Never say never.*

Conor: *Give us two decades, Dec, and we can make miracles happen.*

Declan: *True, lol.*

Declan: *Do you want kids, Conor?*

Conor: *It's not something I think about. Star has a daughter. I'll adopt her if Star will let me.*

Declan: *Really?*

Conor: *Why does that come as a surprise?*

Declan: *It doesn't, I guess, if I think about it. I just didn't realize you were ready for that move. It's soon, you know?*

Conor: *Not soon enough. Star's mine, Declan.*

Declan: *I know. It's killing Bren, lol.*

Conor: *Why's he got such a fucking hard-on for her?*

Declan: *He says he doesn't trust her.*

Conor: *He's got forty years to come around.*

Declan: *LMAO.*

Declan: *Okay, so I'll listen out for a call from Sin.*

Conor: *Nah. It'll be Rex.*

Conor: *Just try to keep their asses out of jail.*

Declan: *Will do.*

Declan: *You happy, Con?*

Conor: *This world is fucked, and I'm dealing with shit that makes my skin crawl, but I'm with her. So yeah.*

Declan: *I get you. Glad for you, Kid.*

Conor: *Same goes. Give Cameron a hug from me and tell Shay I deleted that video on Snapchat and IG.*

Declan: *LOL. He'll love you forever.*

Conor: *He won't when he realizes I'm the reason both will be offline for a couple days. :P*

36

CONOR

WARRIOR'S DANCE - THE PRODIGY

Conor O'Donnelly

THE FOLLOWING DAY

WHEN MY PHONE lit up with a message, I stared at the link with a frown.

Reaching for one of my earbuds, I slotted it in then pressed play.

As a rock fan, "Warrior's Dance" by The Prodigy wasn't exactly my thing, but I listened to it with a smirk, head rocking to the synth loop.

"Knew you'd like it," Star called out from the bedroom.

"You don't know I liked it."

"Sure I do. You listened to the whole track."

"How do you know?"

"You hummed the last melody."

"Sneaky. You shouldn't have been listening."

"That's our anthem. We're the warriors."

We.

Liking the inclusion, I got to my feet and stretched while I began the short walk to where she was lying down.

Burrowed among ten or so cushions that Edgar had happily provided upon her request, the duvet covering her almost entirely, she had her laptop on her knee. Beneath the duvet, she had a mouse she used to control her computer.

"It's not that cold," I remarked with a soft smile.

"It is."

"Are you coming down with something?"

"No. I just get cold sometimes." She studied me. "Well?"

My brow crinkled. "The song or my findings?"

"Both."

"I like the song even though my rock-loving heart is crying on the inside."

"So dramatic," she quipped.

"As for my findings, well, we've got less than I'd like but more than I could have hoped for."

"Details."

"It's a standard email app. Contacts aren't automatically collated. They have to be added. A set number of messages are retained in storage unless you search for keywords which will bring up older emails."

"Meaning we have to scour through individual emails to build up a contact list *and* to gain as much intel as we can from the app?"

"Yes. I'm just relieved it didn't depend on local storage."

"Shit, you're right. That would have screwed us over."

"It would. Unless the cops have DeLaCroix's actual phone, of course."

"I'm sure they have one in evidence but that doesn't mean it's the right phone."

"Yup. So, we've got plenty to work with is the good news and I can bring in some bots to start the collation process.

"You're more integrated with their methods, so do you want to draw up a list of trigger words to feed the bots so they can get to trawling?"

"Sure. I'm just trying to find any information I can on Kuznetsov's son. So far, no dice. But I'll get the keyword list to you by tonight."

"Speaking of tonight..."

She arched a brow at me. "Yes?"

"It'll take a couple of hours for the protocol I'm running to complete."

"And?"

"I wondered if you'd like to go on a date with me."

She sat upright. "You want to go on a date with me."

"Was there a question in there?"

"No," was her wary response.

"I didn't ask you to come on a murder spree with me, Star. Just wanted to know if you felt like eating pizza in Dubrovnik! Although," I continued with a huff, "knowing you, you'd prefer the murder spree."

Her grin was immediate. "You'd be right."

"Thought as much. I don't have anyone who needs to die yet so you're shit out of luck."

The twinkle was back in her eye though. That gave me some satisfaction. She'd been quiet since yesterday evening, going through the motions in a sense once she knew of the girl. We both could imagine what was being done to her, and though we were working to rescue her, it didn't exactly put either of us in a good mood.

Only after she'd called Kat before bedtime in the US did she switch focus from the girl to working on this case. Around an hour later, I'd fallen asleep on the couch, my own computer humming away on my lap while she worked at the table. Earlier today, after a restful sleep, I'd woken up with her curled at my side again, my rig on the coffee table. Single-handedly, she'd graced me with the two best wakeups I'd ever had—I included Christmas Day among those memories.

Santa Claus had nothing on Star Sullivan.

"What would we do on a date?" was her next wary question.

"Eat." I paused. "Drink, if you want."

"Water or alcohol?"

"I can afford both. But if you're worried about my net worth, by all means," I mocked, "order still water."

Her grin peeped out again. "Sassy. What would we discuss?"

"Life? *Game of Thrones*? *Halo*? Whatever the hell you want."

"If we stayed here, we could talk about the case."

"All the more reason to head out. We're letting our code do the work for us, Star, so we can go and play. It's for one night. I think you deserve to let your hair down."

She frowned. "I don't even know what that looks like."

"Then we need to work on that. Remember when I asked you what you'd do once this was over?"

Her gulp was audible. "Yeah."

"That time is approaching, Star. *I can feel it.*" I stepped closer to the bed, and though I still had shit to do and so did she now, I lifted the duvet and burrowed beneath the blanket and pillow fort she'd made for herself.

I was surprised when she leaned over and put her laptop and mouse on the floor next to the bed for safekeeping. At first, I thought she was going to leave because I'd climbed in, then she was turning on her side to face me and her hand was reaching out to gently trace the furrow between my brows.

"Have you ever let your work define you to the point that you don't have anything else in your life?"

I blinked. "You do know who you're talking to, don't you?"

Her snicker warmed my heart. "You're funnier in real life."

"I have an active audience."

"True," she teased, eyes gleaming.

"And, to answer your question, of course. I didn't have anything in my life aside from work and family for too long. Now you're in the mix as well and let me tell you, you're more trouble than both of them put together. Which, considering I've got five brothers who also happen to run a mob empire, is saying something."

She cackled. "I'll keep you on your toes then."

"I imagine you will, yes." Shuffling closer, I let my hand fall on her bicep. "How about it? Pizza. Still water. I'll even spring for some gelato."

"Pistachio?"

I hummed. "Two scoops. Let's go wild."

With a snort, she wriggled closer to me until her front was pressed to mine. Eyes at the same level, she whispered, "I'll share my ice cream with you."

"Didn't think you'd find that hygienic."

"Hygiene, smygiene. I've shared spit with you. I think I can deal with you eating my gelato."

"I was thinking you'd be eating *my* gelato."

"I'm the guest."

"True. Still, I'd get to watch you sucking ice cream off a cone. That sounds like spank bank material right there."

Her eyes widened. "Spank bank?"

Unashamed, I admitted, "Yes."

"You jerk off—"

"To thoughts of you?" I smiled. "Often."

Her cheeks glowed cherry red. Every time that happened, it was the strangest fucking thing. I had a serial killer in my bed. A serial killer who didn't give a shit about the lives she took or how she did it. Didn't care who got hurt in her pursuit of the truth. Yet she could blush when I talked about this stuff.

It was a dichotomy I didn't particularly want to change, mostly because I knew she blushed because it was *me*.

Sex didn't make her nervous.

I did.

And not for negative reasons, either. Just because she wanted me as much as I wanted her, and Star wasn't used to wanting. She'd said it herself—she used. But she couldn't use me. There was nothing to gain from sex with me other than pleasure, and her pleasure was my priority anyway.

"What do you think of when… You know?" she whispered like we were discussing state secrets.

"We added to the spank bank yesterday. Seeing you get off was better than *listening* to it."

She swallowed. "Did you like hearing me come?"

I let my finger trickle down her throat and settle between her collarbones. "Yes."

Her knee shifted and pressed against mine. I parted them so she could slot hers between my legs. When she angled closer, she whispered, "I should get to work on those keywords."

"They'll be there in an hour."

"An hour?" she queried, clearly intrigued by the prospect of how I could fill up a whole sixty minutes while horizontal on a mattress.

I didn't answer. Instead, I let my fingers do the talking. I traced over the line of her collarbones, smoothing them along her chest, watching as goosebumps popped into being. Through the tank she wore, her nipples were visible, and I let my hand come to a halt above one.

"Can I?"

Her throat bobbed as she nodded, prompting me to circle the taut flesh. She shivered, her knee pressing against my thighs, muscles contracting and releasing in response.

Her moan as I gently tugged at her nipple had me hiding a smile.

"Your moan is spank bank material," I informed her. "That little hitch is perfection. I love knowing that I make you feel good."

She exhaled. "W-Why?"

I continued on my journey, letting my fingers trail along the crotch of the boxer briefs she wore—mine. She'd stolen them and I'd never been so happy to have a thief in my bed than I was right now.

Trickling the digits along the seam, I rubbed her very gently, watching her eyelids turn heavy.

"Because a woman like you deserves pleasure."

Her gaze turned watchful.

"Because a man like me knows when he's lucky and isn't dumb enough to throw it away."

"You're not lucky," she rasped. "I'm a minefield."

"I like playing with things that could burn me," I teased, content when her lips quirked. Just when she relaxed, I found the top of her pussy and gave her some pressure. "Does that feel good?"

A shaky breath was my answer.

"Words, Star. I need to know you're all in or I'll stop."

"Y-You don't need to stop."

"Yeah, I do. I'm not willing to push your boundaries. Not until you're more comfortable being in bed with me."

She moaned when I rubbed her clit through the boxer briefs and her hips tipped back. "What if I'm never comfortable around you?"

"We're already a thousand steps ahead of where we were yesterday." *Understatement.* Even though we'd known each other for years, I hadn't put a deadline on getting into her panties. If she needed time, I had nothing but that for her. Playing with the buttons on the briefs, I heard her breathing hitch in response and asked, "Can I?"

"Y-Yes."

My fingers tucked into the gap and my nostrils flared when her knee shifted higher so it put pressure against my dick. Simultaneously, my fingers found the hot silk between her thighs. She mewled when bare skin met bare skin, and her hand reached over to cup my wrist, holding me in place as she rocked her hips, creating her own friction.

I'd thought to give her pleasure, but she took it and I'd never seen anything fucking hotter than her using my hand to get off.

Her shoulders arched as her body rippled, hips writhing from side to side as she found the place where she needed more attention.

"Eyes on me, Star," I whispered softly, happy when they popped open and clashed with mine.

Dazed, I watched the dilation of her pupils as they bloated, contracting fully as her brow puckered, soft cries escaping her as she neared—

Like it had never been there in the first place, she sagged.

For a moment, we both froze.

I thought she'd start again, but she didn't. If anything, she seemed to shrink in front of me. Shame curdled into mortification.

Surprised, I rasped, "Take it slow. There's no rush."

She wriggled her leg from between mine, jerked at my wrist to move it away, then flopped onto her back. She didn't jump out of bed though, just lay there, panting as she stared up at the ceiling.

Unsure of what had happened, I moved nearer. "What went wrong?"

"I-I don't know."

I knew she'd been into it. "Did your mind drift?"

She swallowed. "Maybe."

Definitely.

"What can we do to stop that from happening again?"

Her head rocked to the side. "How about I kill every man that touched me?"

"That's a solution, I guess."

With a huff, she muttered, "A shitty solution." Reaching up, she rubbed her eyes. "It's like conceding defeat."

"What is?"

"They used to force me to fight, Conor. My getting off wasn't fun for them, but—" She sighed. "The guy who bought me, the one I killed, he used to like doing stuff to get me off. Then he'd say it wasn't rape. He'd tell me that he loved me and he'd make me tell him…" Her brow furrowed. "I lost myself. I lost everything."

"That piece of shit," I growled.

"Why do you think I snapped his neck?" she muttered, her arm moving to cover her face so she could hide her eyes from me. "It wasn't just for the family silver."

"What happened?"

"He got me pregnant."

My mouth rounded in astonishment. "Y-You had a baby with him?"

"No." Her throat bobbed. "When I found out, he was happy." Her top lip curved into a sneer. "I'd already intended on killing him, but like I said, I got… lost. That sped things along fast."

Lost—I couldn't imagine Star ever being that way. She was such a force to be reckoned with. I couldn't imagine wanting her to be anything other than what she was—living, breathing mayhem.

"What things?"

"He wasn't my husband at the time."

"The pregnancy made it happen?"

"Yes. It worked in my favor. He said he loved me, and I knew what would happen if I got pregnant—"

"Did you make it happen on purpose?" I questioned softly.

She snorted. "No. I didn't have a say in anything. I had to ask to use the bathroom, Conor. You think he gave me a choice about getting pregnant? Hell, he could have brought in a football team and ordered me to fuck them and I'd have to or I'd end up—"

"What?" I prompted when she stilled.

"It doesn't matter," she said with a sigh. "He had a way of making me do whatever he wanted.

"I knew that with a kid and his warped ideas of love, he'd make sure he provided for us. I killed him a week after he'd been to visit his attorney to change his will.

"I broke into his medicine cabinet, drugged his whiskey, then got him ready for the end. When he started to stir, I strung him up and watched *him* dance for *me*." A ghost of a smile drifted onto her lips and I knew point blank that that bastard had made her do that—dance for him. The smile barely had a chance to exist before it was immediately quenched. "I was going to get an abortion but God proved he exists because he smiled down on me and I miscarried."

"What happened?"

"Helped Hans hang himself. He kicked me while he was swinging. I fell."

She uttered the words in such a facile tone that I knew those were the bare bones of what had undoubtedly been one of many trauma-tizing days in her life.

Her hesitation was palpable as she mumbled, "You're Catholic."

"Your body, your choice," was my immediate reply. "And I'm not really Catholic."

She grunted. "I know that, just wasn't sure if you did and if I'd have to kick you around a bit until you understood that even if I *hadn't* miscarried, I wasn't going to let—"

I pressed a finger to her lips. "Your body. Your choice. Anyway, what is it with you and fighting? Or is it just a self-defense thing?"

"Got a black belt in Ju-Jitsu at fourteen. What do you think?"

"Wow."

Another grunt.

"If you ever want to fight me... I'm not a black belt, but Brennan makes us train."

"He *makes* you train? You aren't ten and have anger issues."

"That's why you got your black belt so young?"

"Yeah."

"I had authority issues but Da let me burn that off by hacking into government agencies." Her snicker soothed the agitation her anecdote had stirred.

"That was a Krav Maga move you pulled on the guard at the dinner table."

I shrugged. "Brennan is the kind of guy who gets straight to the point."

"Why teach something unless it'll decimate an attacker?"

"That's him in a nutshell," I said with a chuckle. "Why waste time punching someone in the face when you can snap their fingers, rupture a testicle, and puncture a lung?"

She whistled. "I like his style."

"Thought you might," I quipped. "He's always taught us to be light on our feet, but I only got back into fighting and training because of Shay."

"Explain."

"Bossy."

Her nose crinkled. "Get on with it."

"Brennan got into boxing when he was a teenager; he was the one with anger problems."

"In your family, jeez, what a surprise."

"Right? Stunned us all." I smirked. "But he's always been the fists of the fam so it's fitting. Anyway, Seamus got bullied at school and I told Brennan he needed to train him. Shay needed moral support, so I got into the swing of things.

"All the sisters-in-law train with him now too."

"Self-defense?"

"Yeah."

"That's awesome. Brennan sounds like good people."

"You're only saying that because he's the fists."

Her laughter burned away some of the truths she'd spilled. "True. You know I love me some bloodshed, but I couldn't deal with my partner being like me."

Her head had rocked to the side so she could look at me as she uttered those words.

Our eyes locked on one another's, I rasped, "No?"

"No. A partnership can only sustain a certain amount of crazy. We both know I tip the balance of that set of scales."

Unsure if she'd let me touch her, I moved even closer so that we were back to where we'd been earlier—she made no move to stop me.

"Do you judge me for thinking about getting an abortion?"

"That man bought you, Star. He owned your body; I don't think he had the right to own that much of your future too."

"His name was Hans," she confessed, disgust making her lips twist. "I think that's why, when I found Katina, I had to bring her home with me. I never thought I'd do something like that. All the shit I've done in my life, all the people I've killed, you wouldn't think that'd matter, would you? But it did." Her eyes closed again. "I cried when it happened."

I pressed a kiss to her forehead. "He was a man who frequented a place that dealt in trafficked women. He bought you. He raped you. He forced you to get pregnant… I'll never judge you, Star. Never."

She swallowed. "Why not?"

I understood where her question came from, but I didn't really know how to answer. Not because I didn't have the words, but because… "I know who you are, Star," I reasoned eventually. "I've known for a while. I know you're cocky and arrogant. I know you have weird morals and a skewed system of loyalty. I know that you're brilliant and have mad skills, but I also know that we fit together. We make sense.

"So, I won't judge you because I'd also be judging myself, and people in glass houses should *not* throw stones. I've done shit that's horrific too. I've given my father and brothers evidence that led to them torturing people and I've seen things that would make the average man cry.

"If I judged you, I'd be implying that I'm perfect and I'm not. Neither of us is and I wouldn't want us to be because your crazy and my crazy work together, and I wouldn't have it any other way."

I watched her work her bottom lip between her teeth. "I didn't expect you to be patient."

"What? Nearly two years of online chatting when we live barely an hour away from each other didn't give you a hint?"

She smirked. "No. But there's a difference."

"I don't see that there's any rush."

"So, this date…?"

"What about it?"

"I'll go if I can have three scoops of gelato."

"You drive a hard bargain," I teased.

"It's one of my best assets."

"Nah, that's your ass."

She snorted. "Don't be such a guy."

"I can't help it." I winked at her then, with a slow smile, asked, "Star, will you go on an ice cream date with me?"

"Don't forget the pizza."

"I didn't."

"Ask again then. But do it properly."

"Star, will you go on a pizza and ice cream date with me?"

"Yes, Conor, I will."

"Good. And… will you let me help you?"

Her chin jerked up at that, and her legs jolted as if she wanted to raise them to her chest in a fetal position.

She knew exactly what I was talking about.

After licking her lips, she rasped, "I don't think I can." She gritted her teeth. "The bitch of it is if you try to fight me, I'd probably be fine. It's because it's… tender. I'm not used to that."

Well, wasn't that as painful as a bullet to the chest?

I was speechless, literally had no words again, then I asked the only thing that made sense to me: "Would you let me try? I think you deserve pleasure, Star. Guilt-free, shame-free, no strings attached, pain-free pleasure. Don't you?"

She studied me for so long that I didn't think she'd say yes, then she whispered, "Only if you get off too."

"That's not no strings," was all I said, not sure if an erection was even possible after that admission of hers.

"It is for us. Mutual pleasure or no dice."

Slowly, I nodded, then I pressed my lips to her forehead. "The moment you feel yourself drift away, you tell me and we stop. Got it?"

"O—" She exhaled. "—kay."

My hand drifted over the sleep tank she wore, gently cupping her breast. "Are you okay with me talking to you?"

"I-I think I'd like that. Your voice…" Another exhalation. "It grounds me."

"I'm glad it does." I squeezed her tit again. "We'll get there, Star. This isn't a race."

Though she nodded, she stunned me by sitting up and dragging her tank off. My eyes were instantly glued to the soft curves.

Once she took a deep breath, she muttered, "I don't have much sensitivity in them anymore."

Put a Sparrow in front of me at that moment and I swore I'd have killed them. Bare hands. No weapon. And with *glee*.

I rolled a nipple between my pointer and middle finger.

"Are you sure you don't want to fight?" she blurted out. "You said Brennan trained you—"

"You didn't need to fight yesterday," I said blandly, keeping my motions non-threatening.

"I didn't overthink it yesterday. You distracted me."

"Why are you overthinking it now?"

Her nostrils flared. "Because I'd like you to fuck me."

"You're not ready for that."

"No, and that's why I'm annoyed. The one goddamn man I've wanted in years and my head is taking charge. If we let my body take over—"

"No. That's not how it's going to be between us. You've given me a hand job, Star. Do you know how big a deal that was for me?" Her eyes rounded. "And I want you to put your hands in my hair when I go down on you and I want you to nearly tear it from the roots because I'm eating you out so fucking good." Her soft moan made my cock ache. "One day, we're going to be everything to each other. But you're too impatient. We have to build toward that. So, let me concentrate on what we'll have in the future, okay? Because you suck at it."

A snort of laughter escaped her then. Her wicked smile made my heart pound before it gentled and she nodded. "I'll let you be the builder, Conor."

I just hummed before I pressed my mouth to hers and kissed her slowly. I ran my tongue around her Cupid's bow, dipping it in to tease her and darting away before she could reciprocate. Soft pecks landed on the tip of her nose, on her cheeks, and on her brows. All the while, my hand continued plying her nipple.

"I've dreamed of this for years," I rasped against her lips, tugging the bottom one between my teeth. "You taste so much fucking better than I imagined."

She growled when I finally slipped inside her mouth, and her promise to be patient faded as she turned the kiss aggressive. I pulled back whenever she did, sampling her kisses, teasing and tasting, reveling in the freedom to explore her body that she handed me.

Unfortunately for her, I was waiting for something and I wouldn't stop until she gave it to me.

When I angled over her, her legs spread to cup my hips, and though her feet dug into my ass and she tried to grind into me, I stayed a heavy weight, not letting her manipulate my body. My tongue thrust against hers, gradually increasing in speed then—

Finally.

She whimpered.

The softest of sounds but I heard it.

Right at the back of her throat.

"Are you wet for me, Star?"

Her eyelashes fluttered as she moaned, "Y-Yes, Conor."

"Do I make you feel good?"

"God, yes," was her thick retort.

"You make me so hard, Star. Everything about you. I was put on this planet to make sure you know what pleasure is, do you hear me?" I ran my nose down her cheek, then, tugging at her earlobe, I repeated, "Do you hear me?"

She swallowed. "I-I hear you."

Satisfied, my lips returned to hers as I slid my hand down her side and angled her thighs higher around me. It was easier on the bed because we had more space.

With better leverage, I started to grind my hips, rocking into her. Immediately, her hands went to my shoulders, nails digging into the flesh there. I wasn't surprised when she dragged them along my spine, clawing at me as she fought my kiss, trying to make me move faster, but I wouldn't be swayed.

She cried out when I rocked my full length along her covered slit, then moaned into my mouth as I repeated the move. Harder, I ground into her, making sure I found her clit with every thrust.

Her skin clung to mine by the time she was edging ever nearer, and that was when I moved faster because her sounds had gone from high-pitched mewls to guttural groans as if I were tearing them from her.

"Take your pleasure, Star. Own it," I rumbled against her mouth. "It's yours. You earned it."

A hoarse sob escaped her, not soft like before but deep, from the soul, and she rode me back, nearly lifting us both off the damn bed in her desire to reciprocate the move.

She wriggled and writhed, seeking an orgasm, and just when I thought she'd give up, her body bowed beneath me.

It quivered like a bow that had been sprung.

She hovered in place until she gave a husky shout that saw her collapsing into the bed.

"You are so fucking beautiful," I grated out.

She shuddered beneath me, and when I thought she'd pull away to catch her breath, even though she had to be tired, she carried on until I found my release too. Both of us arched into one another, dry humping like teenagers who were scared to take it all the way. But fuck, it was perfect.

She was perfect.

Shouting out my climax while she held me in her embrace so

tightly that I knew she didn't want to let go of me, I came for the second time in as many days in my pants. If this was all we had together for the rest of my days on this planet, I'd take it because being with her like this was better than a thousand throw-away fucks which was what my sex life had amounted to in the past.

When I sank onto her, panting, the pleasure so goddamn intense that it was exhausting, I twisted us onto our sides again, one leg hooked over the other to stay tangled between the sheets.

I relaxed into the soft down and so did she, knowing that sleep was coming and embracing the newly budded trust that had formed between us.

Then, when I was an inch away from sleep, she whispered, "If I throw you out of bed, don't be offended."

The ramifications of 'why' made my eyes pop open, but around a yawn, I muttered, "It's worth being tossed out of bed to fall asleep with you in it."

Her arms clung to me, tightening as she nodded against my chest.

Shit would never get boring with Star around.

37

STAR

Star Sullivan

CONOR'S HAND remained glued to mine from the second we left the car to the moment we entered the old town of Dubrovnik. I knew why —he thought I might run off.

It was cute, really. And I wasn't a woman built for cute. But Conor had a way of worming through my defenses. Earlier on had proven that. He was slippery and sly and just that perfect amount of charming to make me putty for him.

So, I let him hold my hand. Let him tug me close. He'd already given me more than he knew, so that was the least I could offer back.

Having visited the city before, its beauty didn't come as much of a surprise to me, but Conor gaped at the slim streets, peering around corners while trying to hide the fact that he was seeking out *Game of Thrones* filming locations from me.

My lips twitched every time he decided he just 'needed' a selfie at some random place.

A quick panoramic picture of what I knew from his awed mutterings were Blackwater Bay and the harbor at Kings Landing, followed up by a shot of the Jesuit staircase when we wandered deeper into the heart of the city.

When he tried not to pose outside The Rector's Palace, AKA, Qarth, I told him, "You'd make a terrible spy."

He arched a brow at me. "Do you know how often I get to leave the US?"

His little problem with the NSA made his journey to find me even more… God help me, romantic.

Disgusted by the notion that I was turning *flowery*, I quipped, "Rarely by the looks of it. You're being a total tourist. It's bad for my rep."

It didn't stop me from letting him lead me around because he got a kick out of it, though, and his smile was hot enough to make up for the frigid temperatures.

A small street market sold preserved orange peel, which was both bitter and sweet on my tongue, and figgy bars that were impossible to chew but tasted damn good.

As we meandered through the labyrinthine streets, it actually hit me that this was the first time I was in a city, somewhere in Europe, without a mission on my mind.

It was fitting, I guessed, that not even today I'd be spared bloodshed.

We picked up pizza from one of the many take-out joints and chowed down on that as we continued Conor's exploration. I put my foot down about walking around the old town walls, mostly because I didn't feel like making myself a target—just because I wasn't on a mission didn't mean people wouldn't recognize me and mistake my purpose in being here—and he stopped arguing when I pointed that out.

He blinked at me. Slowly. Then shook his head.

That was his reaction.

It was… visceral.

At first, I thought he was disappointed, but then I saw his tense jaw and mistook it for anger. It wasn't my job to soothe his temper so I ignored him for a while and carried on eating the slice of pizza in my hand, then it registered.

Conor wasn't normal.

Just like I wasn't.

Moving closer to him, I whispered, "Are you turned on?"

His brow puckered. "Of course I am. We're in the middle of a spy game. How couldn't I be?"

"There is no game," I retorted. "Plus, even if I *were* on a mission, we could die."

His eyes gleamed. "But fuck, we'd have lived."

"You've been stuck in your penthouse for too long," I grumbled. "If my grandfather's as all-fired powerful as he claims, then you should talk to him about forcing the NSA to let you travel. Spread your wings. You've got cabin fever of the brain."

A crowd of people shifted toward us, evidently on one of the many tours around the old town, and he pushed up against me to avoid the mass of humanity.

That was when I felt his dick nudging my ass.

Rolling my lips inward to hide my smile, I muttered, "I don't know what you're doing with that."

"Me either." His free hand slipped around my waist and he pressed down against my stomach. "Do you know what's hot?"

"What?" I asked, amused.

"That you don't *know* how hot you are."

I snorted. "Thanks. I think."

He tutted. "By the time I'm done with you, you'll know."

My brows rose. "When do you think you'll be done with me?"

"When I'm ninety-nine."

"Oh." I hadn't expected that answer. Hadn't expected it at all. I cleared my throat. "You can't say that to people."

"You're not people," he pointed out, snagging my languishing piece of pie before it tumbled to the ground thanks to my lax grip.

"I'm not?"

"Nah. You're not."

Was that heartburn?

It spread throughout my chest.

It was warm.

It burned.

Yeah, I thought uncomfortably. *Heartburn.*

I cleared my throat again and watched as he ate the remainder of my pizza. "You owe me another slice."

"I also owe you gelato."

"I forgot it was winter." My nose crinkled. "I'm already cold enough."

"How about hot chocolate? There has to be somewhere around here—"

A small popping sound pinged to life to my right. The stone wall beside me exploded where the projectile hit, leaving a mid-sized hole behind and sending debris over my winter coat.

Heart pounding as I realized I'd just been shot at, I grabbed Conor's hand and dragged him down an alley. That was the best part of the city—lots of hidey holes.

As I maneuvered us down the small lanes, I muttered, "You just had to wish it upon us, didn't you?"

"Hey, I didn't ask for you to be shot at."

"Has your boner gone at least?" I grumbled.

He huffed. "My dick doesn't react to bullets like it does to the sight of your tits."

"Good to know," was my mocking retort.

By the time we were away from the small market square where I'd been targeted, we were at the other end of the old town.

Once there, I sucked in a breath, dug my phone out of my vest, and just as my screen opened, I got in an incoming call.

"D!" I greeted.

"Who's D?"

"Dead To Me," I whispered to him.

"Ah."

"If you're going to go AWOL on me, Star, then you could at least have the decency to call me to tell me you're not missing anymore."

She sounded pissed.

I grunted. "Sorry, D. I got caught up in some shit."

"I can see that. The mad hacker's finally caught up with you."

"He isn't—" I paused. Well, okay, he was. "Yeah, but wait! How did you know we're together?"

"Got you in my scope." A red dot appeared beside us, making Conor jerk in surprise then drag me from the wall and into a nook a few feet away. D snorted in my ear. "Tell him to stop being so jumpy."

My lips twitched. "She isn't going to shoot us, Conor."

"That's her?!"

"Yeah. She was showing me her location." The red light gleamed again, and this time, I twisted around and used it to find her nest on the old town walls. I pointed to her then retorted, "Told you it was a good idea not to go up there. We'd have been running around the damn perimeter trying to escape a shooter."

"Nothing to escape now. Dude's dead."

My brows rose at her sly comment. "Already?"

"Yup. Temper told me to get my ass over here ASAP so I did. Only just fucking landed and she buzzed me again to tell me you were heading into the city." She groused, "I'm hurt that my psycho cousin knows your location better than I do, Star."

"Don't talk to me about your cousin, Cin. I swear to fuck, the next time I see her, I'll shoot first and ask questions later."

"What did she do this time? That good girl act is what really gives me the creeps."

"Me too," I agreed, mock-shuddering, knowing she'd be doing the same thing as well. "She's a part of the United Brotherhood."

There was a pause on the other end of the line. "Temper's in that secret society Bear uncovered?"

"Yeah. Apparently, you and I are too naughty to be chosen," I scoffed.

"Good. If they accept members like my cousin, that's not a group I want to be a part of!"

"Actually, you're right. They're going to help me though."

"With the Sparrows?"

"Yeah. Like, hardcore." I rubbed my nose. "I have a lot to tell you, Cin. Sorry I didn't call to catch up. The last two days have been insane. I only got let out yesterday—"

"Let out? So you *were* being imprisoned. I got a text message from Maxim Lyanov telling me you were being kept in the dungeons of Petrovsky Palace. We blew the fucking place up only to learn there aren't any dungeons there! Talk about a shit show. I'm nothing without your hacking skills, Star. Don't ever leave me like that again."

I had to laugh. "What got caught in the blast?"

"A couple of people, unfortunately. No deaths though. Just scrapes. We burned down a few trees in the neighboring park, but that couldn't be helped. Oh, and they won't be cooking out of that kitchen for a while."

"I'm surprised Lyanov got in touch with you."

"No more than I was. He got knocked out by the blast—"

Conor, having heard most of the conversation secondhand, chimed in, "The Moscow Bratva has dethroned him as Pakhan because of that rescue attempt. His brothers in New York said they were going to evacuate him and take him back to the city. I don't know if they managed it or not."

"They did," Cin answered. "He's recuperating in Bellevue Hospital. He doesn't lead the Bratva anymore. They're calling themselves The Forgotten Boys. I think it's like Peter Pan but turbocharged and with knives."

Guilt speared me. "Shit. I promised to cement his ties with the leadership, not destroy them."

"Don't worry, he'll have more power this way and he won't have to answer to Russia," Conor reassured me. "The moment his brother told me he tried to rescue you, I said we backed him to the hilt. He doesn't need Moscow anymore."

I stared at him, feeling that weird heartburn start to flare up again.

Why did he have to keep saying shit like that?

Absentmindedly, I patted his shoulder in gratitude then rubbed my chest where the ache was getting stronger.

That was all I needed—to have a fucking heart attack in Dubrovnik!

"Okay, so who tried to kill me?"

"Remember Muñoz?"

"I'm assuming we're not talking about the NFL player," Conor said dryly.

"No," I said with a snort. "He's a merc."

"A dead one now."

"Aww, thanks, Cin. What did I do this time?"

"He was acting on his own."

I lifted a brow. "Jesus, he must have been really pissed about Piraeus."

"What happened in Piraeus?" Conor whispered.

"I shot him in the ass."

He snorted. "Only you."

"It was a good shot!"

"It was also ten years ago," Cin drawled. "That man knew how to hold a grudge. Anyway, I've got jet lag. Do you think you can manage not to get captured, shot, or arrested within the next six hours so I can catch up on some Zs?"

My lips twitched. "What would I do without you, D?"

"I don't fucking know. And tell Conor that I dealt with the senator in Arkansas."

"He can hear. Which senator?"

"Sparrow. Kept a slave in his basement."

"Bastard," I hissed.

"Dead bastard now. I'll deal with the corpse." She grunted. "Muñoz, I mean. Then I'm going to sleep."

"Okay. I'll text you with my coordinates so you can come and stay with us. You're shit with a computer, but you can help us out."

"Charming," she huffed.

With dead air in my ear, I turned to him. "So, that's how you're whittling down the ones who deserve to die? You hired Dead To Me?"

He grimaced. "Some are special cases. McClure, in this instance, is popular with his constituents. I wasn't about to let him, or the others, get away with serving a week in jail only to get miraculously let out."

"They wouldn't—"

"Davidson's campaigning for re-election and both parties are making the outed Sparrows integral to their campaign. They're offering massive promises they can't keep, but who knows what'll happen in the next couple months? It could be all hot air and turds."

"That's one way of phrasing it." I pursed my lips as I looked up at him. *He was so fucking gorgeous.* Especially when he started talking about murdering my enemies. "How's your dick?"

"You don't want to know."

I cleared my throat. "Wouldn't have asked if I didn't want to know."

He stilled. "Aching. Hard."

"For me? Or the adrenaline?"

"You, Star. Fuck. Always you."

The heartburn made yet another reappearance.

I stared up at him, feeling myself getting lost in the darkening shadows as the sun began to set.

That was when I came to a decision—I pushed us deeper into those shadows, away from where D's dancing red dot had enabled me to find her nest, and I pinned my hands on either side of his head.

"How do you feel about oral?" I growled, my mouth hovering above his.

"Giving or receiving?"

"Receiving."

"I'd be very amenable to it," he choked out.

I let my tongue swipe across the seam of his lips, finding myself feeling more comfortable in the position of the aggressor. "Here?"

"Fuck. Don't tease me," he snarled, and the bite to his tone did things to my insides that made the heartburn look healthy.

My core lit up because that was for *me*. Not the set of holes that I'd represented to some men, but because *I* made him crave *me*. The past that was complicated and toxic intrigued him. It got him hard because his inner nerd was geeking out over being with a real-life spy. *He wanted me.*

I rested my hand over his cock, feeling his hardness, feeling the heat emanating from him.

"You once told me you don't like hand jobs," I breathed against his mouth.

"Before the shower, I didn't." His hips jerked forward. "It's different with you," he choked out.

There was a rough emphasis on the word 'you.'

As in, nobody else.

Just me.

My core didn't just light up. I turned radioactive. It was a wonder I didn't start glowing.

Me.

Nobody had ever made me feel special before. Not even my ex, Maverick, who, I knew, had loved me at one point. Not as a friend, but as a partner. But what Conor could do with a few croaky words took me to a place I hadn't known existed, one that probably hadn't until I met him because he was carving it out as his own.

To thank him for his words, I pressed my lips to his. Then I nuzzled my nose against his jawline and gently suckled a spot on his throat. As my tongue palpated the tender skin, he rocked his head back against the stone wall and let me tease the sensitive area until I knew I'd left a mark.

I wanted to see that tomorrow morning.

I wanted to remember this moment.

I didn't want to forget tonight.

With soft motions of my fingers, I shaped him through his jeans. I didn't want to trigger him, only wanted him to adjust to the movement. Like he was trying to make sex special for me, I wanted the same in reverse.

Slowly, I dropped down, my nails running along the length of his torso as I settled on my knees. The cobblestones beneath me were cold and damp, and I'd ache later, but this was now, and now was all that mattered.

I let my lips drag over his still-covered dick, then I found the zipper with my teeth. I'd learned so many techniques during my time at Club Pervert, unwillingly, but the idea of putting it to good use, of bringing a man who cared about me pleasure, somehow seemed like the biggest revenge of all.

I tugged on the zipper and pulled it down. When he cursed under his breath as his cock appeared in the gap, I hummed and let my tongue run over it.

"No boxer briefs this time," I murmured as I traced the thick vein that throbbed beneath my tongue.

"You keep making me come in them," he bit off.

Fuck, that sent a zap of pleasure straight to my pussy.

Me. Again. He gave me ownership of that even though he did most of the work. *I* gave him release. *I* made him come in his pants.

My thoughts had me panting but I forced myself to focus as I concentrated on getting his cock wet.

"Oh, fuck," he growled. "Can I touch your hair?"

His consideration filled me with gratitude, and when I moaned my assent, his fingers speared through my loose locks, the tips dragging against my scalp, not to force, just to urge me close.

When I delved inside his fly, he hissed as his dick flopped out. He was thick and hard and long. My pussy clenched at the thought of taking him. I knew he'd split me wide open, and those inches would pack a punch if he took me roughly.

I didn't even think about it, just reacted—I rubbed my fingers between my legs, feeling the heat from my center start to filter through the denim.

Not forcing it, just exploring myself, with my other hand, I held the base of him before I started urging spit to gather around his shaft.

Following each vein with the tip of my tongue, I got him nice and wet then started sucking on the mushroom tip. He snarled under his breath, his fingers tightening around my hair for a split second before releasing me with what had to be a conscious effort.

As I familiarized myself with the flared tip, I started to rock back and forth against the tiny weeping slit there, already tasting his pre-cum and craving more of it.

"Fuck, Star, please," he growled. "Stop fucking tormenting me."

My lips curved at the plea, but the words lit me up inside. Gave me strength. I rubbed the area above my clit just for some friction, then I slowly started to take him inside my mouth.

With training came a loss of my gag reflex, something I intended to lose again seeing as it had been a long ass time since I'd sucked any prick's dick. It satisfied me to work toward giving him that. To let him take advantage of a skill I'd never wanted to learn and had been forced to adjust to.

And how he bit off curses, groaning and grunting with every inch I managed to acclimate to, made it even more worthwhile, and my over-achieving self was ever eager to please him.

With how wet he was, I slid all the way down in increments. When my nose rubbed his pubis, he was making garbled noises as if he'd forgotten the English language.

That was when I swallowed around him.

"Holy fucking shit," he rasped, the words thick and dense, dropping to the floor as if they had weight to them. "This is… your mouth. Oh, Jesus. Thank you, baby. You're so fucking good to me. Taking all of me. My bad girl. So fucking bad—"

I'd inadvertently frozen when he'd started that sentence with 'my.'

Good girl.

That was what I thought he'd say.

Those were words I did *not* want to hear.

But of course, he was Conor. And even when he was on cloud nine, when he was staring paradise in the face, he knew how to say the right thing.

That heartburn was back.

"My naughty girl. So fucking naughty," he rasped again, making my fingers speed up above my clit. "That beautifully filthy mouth of yours. So perfect."

I rumbled nonsense words around him just to hear him choke out a moan. Then I started to rock my head. His fingers clamped in my hair but he didn't force the pace.

As I fucked him with my throat, I began to move faster, then, with my free hand, I dragged at his pants to create more space so I could reach into his fly and rub his balls together.

There wasn't enough room, but the compression had him hoarsely groaning with the ecstasy that *I* gave him and made his hips snap forward.

And somehow, that gave my pleasure wings.

I came.

It was a bit like a sneeze in comparison to what he could give me, but it was better than a slap in the face.

What made it better was how I'd done it myself, how there'd been no wall to scale, but the real cherry on the sundae was when he whispered his thanks as I swallowed every drop he had to give me.

Praising me and worshiping me as if I were the first person to ever give him a blow job—

No.

My mind froze.

It tripped over the thought.

And I pushed it aside.

I stayed where I was, continuing to swallow his cum until he was done and his hands were urging me to release my hold on him.

When his dick was free, he lowered to his knees in front of me, and with his fingers still in my hair, he speared me with an unexpected kiss.

He had to have tasted himself but he didn't seem to care, didn't even care that his dick was going to freeze off if he didn't pack it away. He just thrust his tongue against mine, rocking into me, thanking me with his mouth for *my* mouth.

I didn't even know I needed that 'thank you' until it came via Conor's lips.

When I smiled, he rasped, "I need to taste this kiss."

"You are," I mumbled, angling my head, wanting more. Wanting everything.

The crazy thing was that, for the first time in my life, *everything* didn't seem that far out of reach.

38

DEAD TO ME

STARING down at Dubrovnik from the vantage point of the city walls, I smirked at a job well done as I dismantled Coop and tucked it inside a custom-created briefcase that, from the outside, screamed 'socialite chic' not 'hitman basic wear.'

Making sure my beanie still covered most of my brow line, I rearranged my gaiter so that it was covering the bottom half of my face again. The only part of me that was visible was my eyes. With the temperatures hovering above freezing, I didn't look out of place and my ID was as safe as houses.

With that complete, I hiked the strap over my shoulder and adjusted my stance to balance Cooper's heavy load, then I headed toward the exit where a man was anxiously checking his watch.

A massive tourist hotspot, the attraction had closed an hour ago, and while I'd already paid him off for letting me pass by unchecked, I tossed him some more Croatian *kuna,* enough to make his wife a very happy woman, gave him my thanks, then jogged down the steps that took me toward the center of the old town.

I wasn't bullshitting Star about being tired—my jet lag was unreal —but when my cunt-faced, twatwaffle cousin had contacted me and said that Muñoz was on the loose, I knew I couldn't leave my girl out in the cold.

Sticking to the shadows so I could yawn, I forced myself to focus and then slipped through the alleyways. Though I wanted nothing more than to dive face-first into the mattress back at my hotel room, instead, I made my way to Muñoz's nest.

The fucker liked to think he was a top-tier sniper, but the proof of his uselessness was in the fact that he'd *stayed* alive this long. Only the very best like The Whistler, Eagle Eyes, Dagda, (unfortunately), and I had survived the hunt that was currently going down.

Governments around the world had been pitching us against each other, killing too many of my brethren in exchange for cold, hard cash.

Star had gotten on Muñoz's bad side years ago—he'd just been waiting for an excuse to erase her—but not on my watch.

From twenty feet away, I found his corpse perched on a set of stairs. Slumped over his weapon, his arms tumbling slackly over the edge, and with what was left of his face burrowing against the traditional stone, I peered at him with no guilt, mostly irritation.

Using the shadows again to shield my movements, I drifted toward his position and clambered up the stairs.

A few tourists staggered past, ridiculously drunk for so early in the evening, and I dove into the wall, pressing my hands to the craggy stone, forehead brushing it, as I monitored their path via their rowdy laughs, grateful when they eventually got the hell away from my murder scene.

Ducking out of sight, I started to pat Muñoz down with my gloved hands.

Rigor had nothing to do with the stiffness of his body; it was just that fucking cold.

Retrieving his cell phone and a keycard, I slipped the latter into my pocket and then twisted his face to the side. Half of it was missing which *could* present a problem with the Face ID scanner...

Yay!

When it unlocked, I grinned happily then moved into the settings to switch off his security preferences, using his face a couple more times to facilitate the process.

With his cell and keycard in my possession, I left the fucker alone and slipped away as silently as I'd approached.

When my phone buzzed, I grimaced as I saw Temper's name on my Caller ID.

In my mind, Temper was proof that you couldn't choose your family, just your friends. I had more familial sentiments for Star than I did my pain-in-the-ass cousin.

Knowing what I did now, I answered the call. "Saving her ass hasn't made her forgive you."

She hissed in my ear. "Shit. She told you?"

Moron. "Of course she did. What the fuck were you thinking?"

"I didn't betray her," she argued. "I was acting in her best interests."

"The only person whose interests you care about is you," I retorted.

"Not true. I think of America's best interests all the time."

Groaning, I muttered, "The shit you say, Temper, is like you think people can hear you and you dare not be anything other than patriotic."

"You never know who's listening in, Cin."

I pinched the bridge of my nose as I sought patience. "What do you want?"

"Just needed to know she made it out all right. Whatever you think, I do care."

"If you say so."

She huffed. "I do."

"Well, okay, then. I'm going to go. I'm exhausted."

"Uncle Gene asked about you today."

"Why's my dad asking *you* about *me*?"

"Probably because you never answer his calls?"

"Probably because he's an asshole who tried to set me up with Jimmy McCabe."

"That was twenty years ago, Lucinda."

"You think he won't try again?"

"No. He did mention that Morris Newton was newly divorced."

"Maybe he was trying to marry you off."

"Mom would never let him."

I grumbled, "Aren't you lucky that your mom doesn't care more about appearances than your well-being?"

"They just want what's best for you."

"I think I'd know that better than they do." Though… "When was the last time you went home?"

"Two weeks ago."

"Is Creed McCabe still on that island on the Puget Sound?"

"Yes. At least, I think so. Your father said that Jimmy's unhappy that he's having to deal with the farm on his own while Creed is overseas, so I think he's deployed. Anyway, why do you care?"

Overseas.

Like he was on vacation when he was fighting for his freakin' country?

Creed had more courage in his pinkie than Jimmy possessed in his whole being.

"I don't. I'm just curious. He was best friends with Oliver," I said blandly, not close enough to my cousin to share that I'd banged Creed for a couple of months during a tour of duty.

"Oh. I forgot about that. You heard from Ollie?"

"Yeah, he's living it up in Cabo with his husband."

Temper snorted.

"Why do you think Gene's all up my ass about getting married?" I muttered as if her snort were a statement in itself.

"Haven't they come around yet?"

"What? To Ollie preferring cock to pussy? Nope." I sniffed as I finally approached my hotel. "I almost wish I were gay just to spite them."

"That's not a nice thing to say, Cin," she chided.

"I wonder what on earth made you think I was ever a *nice* person, Temper. I'd prefer to be interesting rather than nice." I scowled at the very prospect.

"I bet Creed would like it if you were *nice*."

Her sly comment made me regret mentioning the man's name.

"You want him, you can have him," I ground out, despite the fact that I'd prefer to stick pins in my eyes than for her to even *air* kiss Creed's cheeks, never mind that mouth that was capable of wicked, wicked things.

"I might just try. I'm due to visit Mom again next weekend."

"Knock yourself out," was my bland retort before I asked, "Is she sick again?"

"She is."

"Send her my love," I stated before I cut the line.

Ignoring the receptionist, I made my way up to the hotel room and during one long, continuous groan, I locked up behind me, reinforced the door with some home-made security extras, then stripped off, dumped Muñoz's crap on the dresser, and face-planted into the duvet.

For a few minutes, I just lay there, ass bared to the overheated room. Then, as always, my mind started jerking from subject to subject and I knew point blank that I'd never get any sleep.

With a grunt, I clambered off the bed, reached for my cell, and texted my brother:

> Me: Can you stop dicking Alistair down long
> enough to give me Creed McCabe's cell
> number?

That sent, and feeling utterly ridiculous, I turned to Muñoz's phone and, out of cursory interest, switched through his currently used apps.

Frowning when I saw a calculator app that wasn't native to the device, I flipped away from it and started scrolling through his emails for any info on who'd given him the job. Unfortunately, it was mostly spam.

Studying the keycard, I pulled up the address of the hotel stamped on the plastic and decided I'd visit tomorrow.

When I received a message alert, I picked up my phone.

> Ollie: Why? What's he done?

> Me: I'm saving him from Temperance. I want
> to warn him.

Ollie: I could warn him.

Me: Just give me his damn number.

Ollie: Anyone ever tell you you're grumpy, Cin? Anyway, why is Temperance sniffing around him?

Me: Because she thinks I have a crush on him.

Ollie: Do you?

Me: No.

Ollie: So what's the problem?

Me: What's his number, you pain in the ass?

Ollie: Charming.

When he gave it to me, I saved it to my contacts then replied:

Me: Thank you. How's Alistair?

Ollie: Wonderful as always.

Me: Any jobs for me?

Ollie: Nope. Your calendar is pretty quiet for the moment.

Me: Might not be a bad thing. I'm out of the country.

Ollie: Where are you?

Me: Croatia.

Ollie: Why? AND why am I only hearing this now?

Me: Long story. I'll tell you all about it when I come to visit.

Ollie: You'd better. Keep your ass alive, Cin,
or I will be pissed.

Me: Love you too, dick.

Ollie: Bye, bitch.

Lips curving, I tossed my cell down on the bed and picked Muñoz's up again. Spying an unread message from a contact with no name, only a number, I read the text with interest.

Need you in London tomorrow. Will provide address when…

The message preview cut the text off at that point. When I tapped on it, oddly enough, it opened that non-native calculator app again.

Bizarre.

But that was a dead end and I couldn't see anything in the message inbox either.

Yawning, I checked my cell, saw Star had sent me an address in someplace called Uvala Lapad, and I replied to her with a thumbs-up, then found Goldstein had messaged me too.

God, Interpol agents were always such a drag, but he was the worst.

Goldstein: McClure's dead?!

Me: What did you think was going to happen
when you reported he had a sex slave in his
fucking basement?

Goldstein: The whole point of me infiltrating
his office was to gather evidence, for fuck's
sake.

Me: Interpol's fine with sex slaves suffering
while their agents dick around looking for
evidence?

> Goldstein: I don't dick around. Shit like this is
> sensitive. It takes fucking time.

Me: She might not have had time,
goddammit. I'm not going to argue with you. I
wasn't the only one who okayed the hit. I'll
assume you think it's easier to get in my face
than the Five Points'?

Me: I hate to tell you this but they'll just kill
you. I'll bite your face off.

> Goldstein: You're a cannibal?!

Ah, my reputation had spread farther than anticipated. I *did* enjoy scaring grown men.

Lips twitching, I tapped out:

Me: I don't particularly appreciate seared
'Goldstein face' for my supper, but I'm handy
with a knife and I know a dog who'd
appreciate those sweet cheeks of yours.

Me: Back the fuck off and if you've got any
complaints (I'd recommend that you don't
btw) then take them to Conor. He's your
liaison, isn't he?

> Goldstein: This is a career killer. He promised
> me a fucking promotion out of this.

Me: I don't think he's the kind of guy who
doesn't follow through with his promises if
that's any consolation.

> Goldstein: I got a US senator killed so I'm
> game for conspiracy... That'll help me get to
> sleep without Lorazepam.

Me: I like chamomile. Very soothing. Try it
with Manuka honey.

Unsurprisingly, he didn't reply to that. Chuckling around another yawn, I turned off the lights and did something foolish.

I sent Creed McCabe a text.

> Me: You probably don't remember me,
> Creed, but I'm Ollie's sister. Cin? The chick
> you fucked in Ghurmach. Nili. Oh, and
> Chora…

> Me: Just wanted to give you a heads-up. My
> cousin Temper is going to be in town this
> weekend. If I were you, I'd stay in the
> sandbox until she stops trying to date you. If
> you think I'm bad, she's worse.

Because a strange sensation settled in my stomach, something that seemed, oddly enough, to be nerves, I put the phone on the nightstand and forced myself to rest my eyes.

I didn't think about Creed on the football field after he and the school team won the state championship.

Nor did I think about the time I'd seen him climbing out of our pool after Ollie had dragged off his shorts in a prank that had gone very, very right.

Nope, Creed was just someone I wanted to spare from my horrendous cousin.

Just because I was a hitman didn't mean I couldn't be a good Samaritan too.

39

TEXT CHAT

BRENNAN: *You still alive?*

Conor: *I can feel how much you care all the way from across the ocean.*

Brennan: *You were supposed to check in with us.*

Brennan: *You didn't.*

Brennan: *Remind me to smack you for that when you're back.*

Conor: *Why the hell would I remind you to smack me?*

Brennan: *I'll just set a reminder on my phone.*

Conor: *Having memory problems? It comes to us all, dearthái.*

Brennan: *Fuck off. Do you know how much shit I juggle on a daily basis?*

Conor: *Isn't it easier now that Aidan's back in full form?*

Brennan: *Sure, but there's still a fuck ton to manage. Da, believe it or not, was a hard worker.*

Conor: *He worked long hours. Didn't think he did much though.*

Brennan: *Me neither, but he did. Aidan's picked up Da's shit, but I've had to pick up Aidan's.*

Conor: *If you've got a lot on your plate, get Declan involved.*

Brennan: *I have, but there's still a lot going on right now. Plus, did Aidan tell you those fucking Valentinis called a Summit?*

Conor: *No. He didn't tell me. When?*

Brennan: *He said their new Consigliere has been pestering him since Christmas.*

Conor: *Why's he listening now?*

Brennan: *Dunno. It's tomorrow.*

Conor: *Shit. So soon?*

Brennan: *Yup.*

Conor: *Your first time stepping up. How you feeling?*

Brennan: *You gonna make fun of me if I tell you?*

Conor: *Nah.*

Brennan: *I'm nervous.*

Conor: *Thought you would be.*

Brennan: *Why?*

Conor: *Da's life's work was to perpetuate the belief that nothing you did would ever be enough to make up for what went down with Ma.*

Conor: *It served him to keep you under his thumb. Gave you a great work ethic, of course, but it doesn't help in situations like these.*

Conor: *He was wrong though, Bren. Not only do you have nothing to make up for, but you're a better man than Da could ever be.*

Brennan: *What's with you today?*

Conor: *Feeling introspective, I guess.*

Brennan: *Has that woman been running you ragged? Because you don't fucking deserve it, Conor. Do you hear me?*

Conor: *I appreciate the big brother act, Bren, but it isn't Star. You know what's funny?*

Brennan: *What?*

Conor: *I bet you two'll get along great when you meet.*

Brennan: *When, not if?*

Conor: *Definitely. I told you she's the one.*

Brennan: *I didn't know you were a romantic until recently.*

Conor: *I'm not. This isn't about romance. This is about knowing.*

Brennan: *Yeah, right. That'll be the day.*

Brennan: *But thanks, Con. You know, about Da…*

Conor: *I meant it.*

Brennan: *We gave him a lot of power over us.*

Conor: *We did. I think we're only just breaking free of those shackles.*

Brennan: *You were cut up when he died.*

Conor: *I was.*

Brennan: *Aren't you anymore?*

Conor: *I dunno what I am. A part of me is still reeling. But another part knows that we're free now and I think we've been chained in place for long enough.*

Brennan: *I agree. It's rough atm. So much going on. I'd still take this over having him second-guessing everything I fucking do.*

Conor: *Agreed.*

Conor: *How's Ma?*

Brennan: *Loopy. Going on about 'Our Lady' not being happy about this and that. Thought she was fucking around at first, then Camille said she was talking to Our Lady's picture in the kitchen when she was cooking.*

Conor: *Jesus.*

Brennan: *No, Mary. ;) I think she's fine though. Talking to yourself is the only way to get some goddamn sense sometimes.*

Brennan: *She was pissed you weren't at dinner on Sunday. Fuck knows what she'll be like when you ain't here this week either.*

Conor: *Paddy ate with you?*

Brennan: *Yeah.*

Conor: *How are they getting along?*

Brennan: *Are you matchmaking? Because that's fucked up. Ain't it illegal for a man to marry his brother's widow?*

Conor: *Maybe if this were 1922 lol. But I'm not matchmaking.*

Conor: *I just think that Paddy got out from under Da's thumb a long time ago. Ma's been under it since she was a fucking teenager. If anyone could help her reacclimatize, it's Paddy. Not Our Lady. Although, maybe she'd help. Lol.*

Brennan: *Fair point.*

Conor: *Plus, if she did fall for him, it wouldn't be the end of the world, would it?*

Brennan: *I dunno.*

Brennan: *It's weird around here without you, Kid. I'll feel better when you're back in the city.*
Conor: *Say it... You miss me. :P*
Brennan: *Fuck off.*
Conor: *And after I was so nice to you as well. Sheesh.*
Brennan: *Fine.*
Brennan: *I miss you. Fucker.*
Conor: *:P I won't be away for long.*
Brennan: *I'll hold you to that.*
Conor: *I'll let ya.*

40

TEXT CHAT
DON'T LEAVE - MØ

LODESTAR: *Who are you talking to?*
Conor: *Brennan*
Lodestar: *What's he want?*
Conor: *To know if I'm dead.*
Lodestar: *What did you tell him?*
Conor: *Lol.*
Lodestar: *:P*
Conor: *Got a song for you.*
Lodestar: *Hmm?*
Conor: *"Don't Leave" - MØ.*
Five minutes later
Lodestar: *There a message in those lyrics?*
Conor: *That's why we're sending each other songs, no?*
Lodestar: *Maybe.*
Conor: *Definitely.*
Lodestar: *I'm not going to leave.*
Conor: *You said that before.*
Lodestar: *I did. But I have to make up for shit now. Atonement. Remember?*
Conor: *It's only atonement if you mean it. It can't be forced.*

Lodestar: *I don't WANT to leave.*

Conor: *Well, that's good.*

Lodestar: *Just good?*

Conor: *Better than good.*

Lodestar: *You don't have to work in there…*

Conor: *Figured you might need some space.*

Lodestar: *Maybe if you weren't you.*

Conor: *I am me.*

Lodestar: *I know. That's my point.*

Conor: *Do I have special privileges?*

Lodestar: *I believe you do.*

Lodestar: *Conor?*

Conor: *Yeah. I'm coming. Just gotta finish this up.*

Lodestar: *I like that song.*

Conor: *I'm glad.*

Lodestar: *But, I think it's wrong.*

Conor: *Why?*

Lodestar: *I should have sent that to you. I'm the mess. Not you.*

Conor: *Star, we're both messes. But, somehow, when we're together, it doesn't feel so tumultuous.*

Lodestar: *It doesn't…*

Conor: *Gimme two mins and I'll be right in.*

Lodestar: *<3*

Conor: *xo*

41

CONOR

Conor O'Donnelly

"BOGDAN BELYAEV IS A FRONT," I said by way of greeting, taking note of the fact she was playing the song I'd sent her again.

After turning down the volume, Star picked up her coffee mug from the nightstand. "What?"

"Did you do a rundown on him?"

"Yes, at the time. No criminal record. He lived off a trust fund. Had a house in…" She frowned. "I want to say somewhere on the Ohio/Kentucky border."

"Yeah, and that's it. That's what I found too. No loans, no credit card debts. Not even a car was registered in his name. Just the house and money that came in from a 'trust fund.'"

"And a Russian bride," she drawled, starting to take a sip from her coffee before, eyes lighting up, she paused when I handed her a pack of Jelly Bellys.

"I couldn't even find a payment for her in his accounts. I'm telling you someone bought his ID and used it as a front."

Halfway through opening the bag of candy, she rolled her eyes. "I don't know why I was fixated on that story yesterday, but it's a waste of time."

Knowing she wanted me to drop it and seeing her abandon the treat out of nerves, I obeyed… in a sense. "After what Eoghan said about there being a total wipeout from the accident, I went digging."

"For?"

"Insurance logs."

"Interesting." Her gaze drifted to my throat where her hickey peeked back at her. "Why?"

Fuck, I loved that possessive look.

"Because people always file for insurance after a pile-up. Unless the agent killed everyone involved, which is possible, don't get me wrong, someone was bound to claim medical care."

"So you've been swiping through years' worth of health insurance claims in the Cincinnati area?" She pulled a face. "I need to start paying you."

I had to laugh. "Yeah, it's been pretty torturous."

"Sounds like it."

"I started with ambulance call-outs then narrowed it down to walk-ins to the ER department."

"Why?"

"Because the ambulance call-outs' source ran dry but also because, if this is a whack job conspiracy, maybe the person who needed an ambulance to get to a hospital could have 'died' en route."

"I felt like Eoghan was saying there was one person on the job."

"He did. But does that seem likely for a mission of this scale? Plus, he's known for being a sniper. Would you send a sniper in to start a car crash?" I hitched a shoulder. "I'm not a spy so I don't know, but I'd assume that people have talents and these kinds of divisions have teams to fulfill certain tasks."

"Logical assumption." She took a sip of coffee. "Operation: Snake may have a different method."

I laughed. "That's a less grandiose title."

She just toasted me with her mug. "Okay, so you've come to me about this while I'm assimilating keywords for a reason, I'm guessing? And not just because you want a wage increase from unpaid data analyst to paid hacker?"

Snorting, I informed her, "I want a better job title than that. And a corner office with windows."

She hid her grin behind her mug of coffee. "Technically, you have an office with a view."

I looked straight at her. "You're right. I do." When she blushed, I smirked, pleased with the reaction which I promptly ignored to reason, "Anyway, as I was saying, it took a lot of digging and my code outdid itself as I'm sure will come as no surprise." Her eye roll told me I was reaching. "But I found one patient on the twenty-fourth of February who walked into an ER in Cincinnati, complaining of a fractured wrist after being involved in a vehicular incident in New Cloverfield."

"And?"

"That vehicular incident was never recorded *anywhere*."

"So the medical insurance never paid out?"

"Nope. Remember I said my code outdid itself? I had it trawl through fucking claims all night too. Honestly, the code deserves the office with a window and not me."

"You think that's the crash in question?"

I shrugged. "Not sure. But it's funky, isn't it?"

"Not really. Lots of things could be filed under 'vehicular incident.'"

Because I'd trapped her in a corner, I smirked. "This patient went on to be remanded into a mental health facility for speaking about a massive pile-up that occurred on their main exit out of the town. She apparently went crazy at the local police station and attacked one of the cops when he told her she was losing her mind."

"What?!"

I nodded.

"The bastard was gaslighting her!"

"Seems like it. The insurance paid out *that* time. On her medical records, she states that three vehicles were involved. It's a road that people commute through to get to Cincinnati so it's busy with out-of-towners."

"How big is New Cloverfield?"

"Not big. But it's mostly a township. Clusters of houses around a lake."

"Huh. What happened to her? Can we find her to question her?"

I winced. "That's the sad part. She killed herself. Unrelated to that, I think. But who knows? Her husband died and they had a ton of medical debt. That fracture she got in the crash, there were complications. She needed surgery and you know how that can run up the costs."

"All of a sudden, you owe a hundred grand for being involved in a crash that the cops say didn't happen. I think I'd have lost my shit too."

"That's what makes New Cloverfield perfect for a cover-up like this. They're served by a small unit of cops who are overstretched. Anyone who did make a fuss, it'd be easy to kill them or to pay them off."

"More likely they'd die." She rubbed her temple. "This is a massive stretch, Conor."

"You think I don't know that? If I was certain about any of this, I'd have crowed from the rooftops. Instead, I've got a potentially unstable woman claiming she was involved in a road traffic accident that no one else says happened." My arms flopped in the air. "It's definitely a stretch, *but* isn't that what also makes it perfect?"

Star tapped her fingers against the table. "Maybe."

"Did Dead To Me call?"

"She did. She's on her way."

"What do you want her to do?"

"Be involved. She keeps me honest."

I leaned back against the table. "Stops you from lying?"

She hummed. "To myself. Plus, she's a great multitasker. Operation: Snake would definitely send her out on a task like this by herself. She makes MacGyver look un-MacGyvery."

"There's an adjective for you."

"Perfect for D, though." Sinking back into her pillow fort, she folded her arms across her chest. "We have an unknown accident taking place in a tiny township with no witnesses. How does that get us anywhere?"

"It doesn't. But I thought you could ask Kat about it."

"I'm telling you it was a brain fart," she groaned.

"You should ask," I prodded.

"Ask her about a random town she probably didn't drive through? Bring up a subject she's finally stopped having nightmares about on a whim?"

"It isn't a whim. You think I'd want to stir up old nightmares when I know how fucking horrendous they can be myself?" I pointed a finger at her. "You wouldn't have had the thought if your instincts hadn't kicked in."

"Say it is her and she's Kuznetsov's granddaughter. Don't you think that's statistically unlikely?"

"Anomalies happen for a reason."

"I just happened to move into the MC where her long-lost sister lived. That's one anomaly already. And we were lucky. Lucky because Kat needs Alessa, so I won't argue that miracles don't happen, but does lightning really strike twice?"

"You know it can happen." But I grimaced, accepting it was unlikely. Unless… "Could you have been fed the information?"

She blinked. "What?"

"You heard me. Let's say she isn't your cousin. But don't you think it fucking smells rotten as hell that you bought a manifesto on the dark web, which led to you finding her mom and then Kat? Maybe you were pushed onto that path by someone else."

"By whom?" she demanded. "The tooth fairy?"

"Whoever put her into CPS. Who was that by the way?"

She sighed. "Her records said she was brought in by a stranger who found her."

"Well, that's not suspicious. Or befitting our narrative."

"Let's say the manifesto *was* planted. How would they know I'd be the one to buy it?"

"I dunno. I'm just saying anything's possible. How did you find it? Dumb luck?"

Tugging on her bottom lip, she played with it, and I knew she was processing my argument. As wild as it was, nothing would surprise me in this throne of lies that was our basis for *everything.*

In a flurry of movement, she exploded upright to grab her cell from where she was charging it. Then, she selected a name, hit dial, and placed it on speaker. "Don't speak. They won't appreciate hearing from you."

"Why?"

"Because you have a dick."

That was the only answer I got before:

"Long time no hear."

The voice was distinctly British.

Star grunted but watched me as I leaned against the wall. "Have you missed me, Minerva?"

The other woman sniffed. "Your ego is still larger than North America."

"Seeing as yours is as big as South America, I think we're pretty even." Star narrowed her eyes at nothing. "I have a question for you."

"Why should I answer it?"

"Because we used to be friends and this is a massive deal."

Minerva sighed. "Is this about the Sparrows?"

"It's Sparrow-adjacent. Sort of." She rubbed her eyes. "Have you heard of Operation: Jorgmundgander?"

Minerva was silent a second, then she called out, "Ovianar?"

"Hmm?"

"You're still living together?" Star queried politely.

"That's irrelevant."

Star huffed. "Just trying to be friendly."

"Don't bother. We're not friends."

"Who's that, Minnie?"

"It's Lodestar."

"God, that's a blast from the past. What do you want, Lodestar?"

"She's asking about Operation: Jorgmundgander."

There were a flurry of whispers that were too soft for me to properly make out what they were sharing.

Then, there was a hissed, *"She needs to know."*

Star and I shared a look.

"...*find... come here...*"

"*Danger—*"

"*...Sparrows down...*"

One of them cleared their throat then rasped, "I think I heard about it. It's a division that brings high spec prisoners out of jail and gets them to act on their government's behalf to cut down their sentences."

"Did either of you two ever work for them?" Star inquired, her tone bland, unlike the gleam in her eyes.

She'd scented gold.

The other women were silent for so long that I didn't expect an answer. Then, Minerva, I thought it was, asked, "Why do you want to know?"

"I have a foster daughter," Star intoned. "And I want to know if the reason I do is because one of you guys led me to her."

When they cut the call without another word, I figured we had our answer.

Mouth taut, I rumbled, "Where do they live?"

She turned to me, but her eyes were unseeing. "London."

Nodding, I headed over to the intercom and waited for Edgar to answer me.

"You need to tell Kuznetsov that we're going to London for a few days."

"Mr. Kuznetsov believed you'd be remaining in Dubrovnik, sir," was the butler's cautious reply.

"I'm well aware of that. But this is about our investigation. We'll be back."

"I'll inform him, sir."

"Appreciate that, Edgar."

Turning to face Star once more, I wondered if it was a blessing or a curse to see this side of her.

She was strong. Fierce. A warrior.

She was a *killer*.

Unashamed. Unafraid. Unswerving in her dedication.

But she'd allowed me to pass behind that veil, and seeing her devastation was a gift because I was being given something no one else was permitted to see, yet that also meant I wanted to kill whoever made her look like this.

Those bitches were going to fry if I had my way.

Who the hell set someone up with a kid like that?

It didn't matter that she loved Katina as if she were her own flesh and blood—she'd been played.

By allies.

I strode over to her and cupped her shoulders. She looped her arms around my waist, tucking herself into my embrace with surprising alacrity, then held me as close as I did her.

"Do you think their intent was malicious?"

Her hoarse words had me closing my eyes as I rested my chin on the crown of her head. That was when I accepted this truly was an honor—to be this woman's strength could only ever be considered a blessing.

"We'll find out when we get there, won't we?"

She bobbed her head against my chest. "I don't understand how this is possible."

"Me neither. But when something seems impossible, it just means we haven't figured out how someone could get to us when we think our defenses are impenetrable." I gave her a little squeeze. "I think you should get Alessa to collect a sample of DNA from Kat on the down-low. Overnight a lock of hair to her and get them tested for familial markers. That's the only way to know for sure if she's related to you or not."

Again, her head bobbed, her forehead rubbing against my chest.

Her listlessness was concerning, but before I could address the issue, my cell buzzed. I dug it out of my pocket and stared at the 'Unknown' on the Caller ID.

Suspecting it was Kuznetsov, I hit accept.

"Edgar tells me you wish to leave Uvala Lapad?"

"We need to head to London for a few days."

"He said it was related to the case."

"It is. We've got ourselves a lead on your granddaughter's whereabouts."

His indrawn breath was sharp. "Already?"

"Don't get your hopes up. We're still deep into our investigation—"

"I'm surprised. I thought you'd be working on the Sparrows' app first."

"We already cracked that. We're collating information as we speak to pass onto Interpol."

"I'm in Lyon now."

"Interpol headquarters?"

"Yes. A division of this breadth requires time and many wheels to be greased prior to its formation."

"I'm sure," was my polite response, but I was grateful he was going to be following through with his promise.

I'd *hate* to have to electrocute another old man to death.

Star snatched the phone from me, hit speaker, but spun away as she rasped, "Kuznetsov, what do you intend to do with your granddaughter if we find her?"

"When, not if. I have every faith in you, child."

Her spine straightened as she repeated, "What do you intend to do with her? What if she's living with a family who cares for her? What if someone adopted her and loves her?"

"What if she isn't?"

"Say she is. Would you leave her alone?"

Silence hovered on the other line. "I'm an old man, Star. My time is short. I won't steal her away from a loving family, if that's what you're thinking. But I want to know her. I want her to be safe. I want security protocols put in place that are necessary for the grandchild of a man whose position is what mine is. I want to ascertain her education is appropriate for my grandchild, and I want to ensure that her future is set."

I placed a hand on her shoulder. "Those are wishes that anyone would want for their family, Star."

Her jaw clenched, then she repeated, "You won't steal her away?"

"No. I have no intention of causing her misery or to tear a family apart if that family is worthy of her. Not when I won't be here for her forever. But for the time I have remaining, I'd like her to know that she was not forgotten by her blood."

"Fine."

When she blindly shoved the phone at me, I accepted it, only to hear Kuznetsov say, "I will have Edgar arrange for your transportation to London."

While I knew it wasn't an offer made out of kindness but one of necessity to keep track of our whereabouts, I merely said, "Fine."

"You should probably know that we intend to spill blood, *Grandfather*," she mocked. "If your guards believe they're the good guys like you do, I'd send men who have dubious morals along with us."

Kuznetsov's sigh carried down the line, but he didn't reply, simply cut the call.

I stared at her, wondering if she knew she antagonized him much as a teenager would with an authority figure.

Did she register that that came from an inherent feeling of safety?

A belief that Kuznetsov *wouldn't* actually hurt her?

"What are you looking at, Conor?" she sniped, glowering at me.

I shot her a smile. "You're beautiful when you're angry."

My smile morphed into a grin when she let out a shriek of outrage then stormed over to the bathroom. The door slammed only after she flipped me the bird. Once inside, another growl made itself known to me, and I left her alone, knowing that would take her mind off things for a short while.

Retreating to my computer, I stared at the programs I had running. Right now, I wasn't dealing with content, but contacts. Messages were being crawled through and email addresses were being collected.

As I stared at my secondary laptop that was still flexing its muscles as it waded through a decade of rejected insurance claims, I pursed my lips. We were no closer to uncovering the truth, but it was definitely uncanny that something had cropped up—

My cell rang again.

"Yes?"

"Your plane will be ready in an hour."

Fucking flying. I mean, I knew we couldn't *walk* to the UK, but Jesus H. Christ, this sucked.

"Thank you." I nearly choked on the lie as I was *not* grateful, but then something popped into my head. Good timing seeing as I needed the distraction. "Kuznetsov, have you heard of Operation: Jorgmundgander?"

"Yes, of course. I'm surprised you have."

"Ran across it during our investigation," I said smoothly. "Are they Montagues or Capulets? Montagues being Brothers and—"

"Capulets being Sparrows, yes, yes," was his impatient retort. "I understood the analogy. They are neither. It's an interesting division. Neutral, allegedly. But Brothers are among the ranks as, I assume, are Sparrows."

"How does it work?" I asked.

"The nature of the division is to prevent calamity. It was introduced during the Cold War by NATO who acted as intermediaries between the US and the USSR. High-risk, skilled operatives who were arrested by the opposition were funneled into one of three specialized prison units in the UK.

"Now, it operates only for NATO powers. Prisoners have the chance to reduce their sentences for time served while inside."

"Was it just for field agents?"

"No."

I thought about Eoghan and the role he played in this fuckfest. "Do they just use criminals?"

"No. It's grown exponentially to include all manner of operatives. *But* it's unusual in that nationality doesn't matter. Only skills do."

That answered why an American had been drafted into this operation, I guessed.

Pursing my lips, I stated, "When we're ready to return to Dubrovnik—"

"You will be traveling with two men who, as my granddaughter suggested, have dubious morals." He sighed. "She endeavors to see the worst in me, but I never claimed that the Union was perfect. We are but humans, and humans are, at their hearts, self-serving."

There was something about this old man that got to me. He had a way of saying things that hit me hard. Maybe it was because I was used to Da who was a crackpot and who hadn't exactly sprouted words of wisdom at the dinner table, or maybe it was because Kuznetsov was *right.*

No body of power was capable of being entirely neutral. The human condition would never permit it.

At my lack of an answer, he asked, "May I ask why you're heading to London?"

"We need to speak with the heads of BDSec."

"Curious." He paused. "I appreciate your honesty."

I hummed.

"You're an ally, aren't you, Conor?"

I knew what he meant but drawled, "I'm Star's ally. That will never change. But if I can open her eyes to something that will make her life better, then I won't shy away from it."

My words seemed to require some time to be absorbed. "I do not wish to hurt her."

"I see that. She doesn't. Are you sick? Is that why this is happening now?"

"No more than a man my age has his ailments. Death could be tomorrow or in five years."

"So, why now?"

"Star set the timetable," was all he said. "She found me when she was ready to."

"You could have forced the meeting. Could have had more time with her."

"Hindsight is a wicked beast."

For some reason, my mind landed back on Da. "I know what you mean."

"Mistakes are made. Rectifying them is possible. But only if we're alive to do so."

Though he couldn't see me, I nodded. "Family means everything to me, Anton. If you truly mean her no ill will—"

"And I don't."

"We rarely believe that we do, but that doesn't stop it from happening. You've never had the chance to be a grandfather before. As you say, mistakes happen. Keep on cheering for Team Star and I'll have your back. Throw her aside and I'll make that fork to the hand look like a walk in the park."

"I should be annoyed, but my granddaughter deserves a partner who will make foolhardy threats to a man who could have him killed in an instant."

I smiled. "It's like I keep on telling her—insanity runs in the family."

PART 3

"I was never really insane except upon occasions when my heart was touched."
- Edgar Allen Poe

Star Sullivan

Me: Got eyes on Katina?

Maverick: She's watching Naruto.

Me: I fucking hate that fox.

Me: And Alessa? Is she nearby?

Maverick: She's in West Orange.

Me: You need to bring her home. Lock her
down.

Maverick: You're not talking bondage,
are you?

Me: Wish I were.

Maverick: What's going on?

Me: Bad feeling.

Maverick: Bull. What. Is. Going. On?

Me: It sounds insane.

Maverick: Already think you are. Still trust you. Talk to me.

Me: I just found out that Katina was steered in my direction.

Maverick: Huh? By a social worker or something? You fostered her, no?

Me: I did. It's a long story but to cut it short, if you remember, her mom was a Sparrow bride?

Maverick: That's what we're calling them now?

Me: Yeah. I found her details in this manifesto and when I looked into her, I found Kat.

Maverick: As easy as pie, huh?

Me: Nah. Took some wrangling. But the manifesto that I came across, I thought was just by chance. It wasn't.

Me: You need to lock them both down. Just to be on the safe side.

Maverick: You fostered her years ago.

Me: I know. But I'm rattling cages. Who knows what locks will fall open?

Maverick: True. I'll bring them in. Alessa's a homebody anyway and Kati's calmed down now that she's heard from you. I'll go to her gymnastics practice myself. Will bring Link with me for extra security.

Me: Perfect. Thanks, Mav.

Me: You heard of Operation: Jorgmundgander?

Maverick: Sounds like a video game.

Me: Wish it were.

Maverick: What is it?

Me: They take skilled prisoners and let them
work off their sentences by doing jobs for
whichever government needs them.

Maverick: Sounds like The Suicide Squad.

Me: The basic premise is the same. Without
superheroes. Or Harley Quinn.

Maverick: Course. We got our own Harley
Quinn here in West Orange.

Me: How is Giulia?

Maverick: You'd think having a kid, Nyx's kid
at that, would calm her down, but nope.

Me: Typical.

Maverick: Never heard of that group before.
They're bad news?

Me: They're not good.

Me: Mav, I might be her cousin.

Maverick: What?!

Maverick: How the hell are you related?

Me: Remember that I told you my grandfather
was the head of the United Brotherhood?

Maverick: Not something I'm likely to forget.

Me: True. When he offered to help me with
the Sparrows, he wanted me to find his
granddaughter who'd been missing since her
father's death. When I looked into it, I think
Kat could be the missing granddaughter.

Maverick: No such thing as a coincidence.

Me: My problem exactly.

Me: I'll let you know when I find out if she is
or not.

Maverick: Thanks, Star.

Me: For?

Maverick: Not keeping us in the dark.

Me: You guys have been fighting to take
down the Sparrows since you found out
about them. I can promise you, Mav, that
we're getting there.

Maverick: Good. Alessa deserves some
peace.

Maverick: Stay safe.

Me: Keep your eyes open.

Maverick: O.O

BLOWING OUT A BREATH, I stared at my reflection in the vanity.

Now that was done, and once I thought Maverick would have had enough time to speak with her, I tried Alessa's cell.

"Star? I was hoping to hear from you."

I grimaced. "Should have called sooner but it's been crazy here."

"I'll bet. I'm so glad you're safe. We were worried about you."

"I'm sorry I freaked you out," I said with a sigh. "I just…"

"I'm Kati's sister, and on her behalf, I'm pissed," Alessa declared, the sound of her Baltic roots filtering through the words. "But as someone who was a sex slave for the Sparrows, I can only hope that you're close to annihilating them."

"I am," I rasped.

"That's phenomenal news!"

"Yeah, I guess it is," I said with a soft laugh before I rubbed my temple where an ache was brewing. "Alessa, I'm the reason Maverick wants to bring you home."

"He just called—"

"Don't argue with him. Go home and lay low until I tell you otherwise."

"For how long? What's this about, Star?"

"I wish I could give you answers but I have none yet. What I do know is that Katina might be related to me."

"What?" she squawked.

Once I explained the convoluted situation to her, I requested, "Can you get some hair off her brush? I'll overnight some of mine to you so we can compare for familial markers?"

"Of course. Whatever you need."

"Mostly I just need you to both stay safe until I know which way is up. Can you do that for me, Alessa?"

"I can. Anything to keep Kati safe."

"Thanks, Alessa. Next time I call, I hope I have more answers."

"Me too, Star. Please take care of yourself. Not just for Kati, but for all of us."

There was that ache again.

It was different than the heartburn Conor gave me, but it was no less strong.

There was no time to wonder whether I was suffering from cardiac issues—Conor and I had to make our way to London, and we had to pick up a certain assassin before we headed out.

43

TEXT CHAT

CONOR: *How did it go yesterday?*

Aidan: *The Summit?*

Conor: *No, Aidan, your visit to the proctologist for a yearly physical. Fml. Of course the Summit.*

Aidan: *Jeez, you're in a bad mood.*

Conor: *Lots going on.*

Aidan: *Always. Story of our fucking lives.*

Conor: *What went down?*

Aidan: *Sicilian Consigliere figured out that we're behind the murders of those politicians.*

Conor: *Someone was bound to pick up on it eventually.*

Aidan: *She had a point—we don't know who is in whose pocket. She suggested we confer to make sure we don't lose a source.*

Conor: *I think we should put that plan on the back burner.*

Aidan: *What? Why?*

Conor: *Because I'm playing a bigger game over here, Aidan.*

Aidan: *What kind of game?*

Conor: *The Sparrows are fucked. Can't go into details but I know we're going to take them down. I want justice for Star and all those* *other victims first, then those who don't get what they deserve, we deal with them.*

Aidan: *What's going on, Conor? You were a key part of this plan.*

Conor: *I know, but by the time Star and I are done, there's a more efficient way to go about this and we don't have to get our hands unnecessarily dirty. The more dirt we accrue, the harder it is to look clean for Shay later on.*

Conor: *I need you to trust me, deartháir.*

Aidan: *I do trust you.*

Conor: *Enough to not ask questions?*

Aidan: *Fuck.*

Aidan: *You want to change our whole goddamn game plan. I'm the leader of the ECD now. I was supposed to take over the Sparrows next!*

Conor: *I know, but wouldn't it be better if they didn't exist at all? If that tower was toppled and you just needed to lead the Five Points and the ECD?*

Conor: *Brennan said shit's crazy over there as it is without adding that to your workload.*

Aidan: *It is. I'm barely spending any time with Savannah and it's driving me up the wall.*

Conor: *It makes me happy you have her, Aidan.*

Aidan: *Me too.*

Aidan: *How's shit with Star?*

Conor: *It's going well. She's not locking me out. I figured she might.*

Aidan: *Don't think many people could lock you out when you want in.*

Conor: *She's different. I won't force her to do anything she doesn't want to do. She's had enough of that in her life.*

Aidan: *You know I didn't mean it that way.*

Conor: *I'm taking this slow.*

Aidan: *How slow is slow? You've already been seeing her for, what? Almost two fucking years?*

Conor: *Time is irrelevant.*

Aidan: *If you say so, bro. Your balls are the ones on the line. Not mine.*

Conor: *My baby makers are fine.*

Aidan: *Lol.*

Conor: *Speaking of... How's Eoghan?*

Aidan: *His usual grouchy self.*

Conor: *Grouchier than usual?*

Aidan: *Maybe? Why? What made you ask?*

Conor: *He thought Inessa was pregnant.*

Aidan: *Is she?*

Conor: *No.*

Aidan: *Ah, shit. He'd make a great dad. Can you imagine the nursery? It'd give Alcatraz a run for its money.*

Conor: *LOL.*

Aidan: *You know I'm right. To be fair, he's probably not ready for kids.*

Conor: *His mind isn't in the best place right now.*

Aidan: *No. Think I should talk to him?*

Conor: *You have a lot of work going on, don't you?*

Aidan: *Yeah.*

Conor: *Maybe get him to help? Could be a way of getting his mind off things.*

Aidan: *Okay. Sure. You don't think it'll put pressure on him?*

Conor: *He's tougher than he looks and he already looks like he'd fuck up Ronan the Accuser.*

Aidan: *You and your comic books.*

Conor: *It's from a movie too, Aidan. It ain't my fault that you haven't watched Marvel movies.*

Aidan: *Yeah, yeah.*

Aidan: *I'll talk with Eoghan.*

Conor: *Good.*

Aidan: *When are you coming home?*

Conor: *Sooner than you think. But maybe longer than you think too.*

Aidan: *Informative. I didn't ask for a riddle, Kid.*

Conor: *Might be dropping by over the next couple of days but then I'm heading back out again.*

Aidan: *Why?*

Conor: *Gotta see someone.*

Aidan: *Who?*

Conor: *Doesn't matter.*

Aidan: *You're a pain in my ass, do you know that?*

Conor: *Maybe you DO need a visit to the proctologist?*

Aidan: *Nah, my problems are all brother-shaped.*

Aidan: *Stay fucking safe, do you hear me?*

Conor: *I do. Same goes.*

Aidan: *Yeah, deartháir, I know.*

44

STAR

Star Sullivan

"I ALWAYS WANTED TO COME HERE."

"London's better than New York," I told him, my gaze locked on the house in front of us and not on Conor who was being remarkably patient for someone bored shitless after sitting in the backseat of a car for the past three hours.

"That's bullshit," Cin grumbled. "New York is so much better."

"It's overpopulated," I countered, turning over the cell phone she'd given me earlier.

Fucking Muñoz—so typical that he'd be Sparrow scum.

"And London isn't?"

My lips quirked. "Only in the summer when the tourists are around."

"You got to know it well when you were here forming BDSec?" Conor inquired eagerly.

His eagerness was more about the fact I was actually talking than an interest in my answer, I thought.

Since my conversation with Ovianar and Minerva, I hadn't exactly been in the mood to 'chat.'

Dead To Me had made it easy on us by popping up outside the

gates to the fortress at Uvala Lapad just in time to hitch a ride with us, so she'd been keeping him entertained.

Mostly with tales of her tormenting that self-righteous cunt of a cousin of hers when they were kids.

"I did. Grew to love the place. It's not home, but it almost is." Subconsciously, I still thought of it as a haven.

"What I don't understand is how they managed to get you to do what they wanted," Cin complained. "I can't get you to sit still long enough to teach me how to do that thing—"

Hissing under my breath to stop her from finishing that sentence, I glowered at her. "No talk of torture in front of them." I prodded my finger at the guards up front.

"They're on your side," she grumbled, rolling her eyes.

"Torture?" Conor inquired.

"When she was deep in the CIA's good books, they used to call her The Nutcracker. No one knows what she did to make them squeal, but she had a rep for getting the hardest nuts to crack. Hence the nickname."

"I lost the ability."

"BS."

"Maybe I'm out of practice." Though it *had* worked on Donavan Lancaster, the one-time moneyman of the New World Sparrows. "Used it a few times this year and it failed twice."

Cin frowned. "Maybe your heart wasn't in it?"

Actually, that made sense. I was a different woman from the one I'd been before. But the truth was, Lancaster had earned his punishment. I'd only tortured Jintao and the two princes because I wanted Kuznetsov's name and location.

Jesus.

Had I grown a conscience?

Sickened by the prospect, I straightened in my seat. Thankfully, I didn't have to worry about that for long because two women showed up in a Mini in front of the house we were staking out.

"For traitors, they have good taste in cars."

I snorted at Conor. "Only you'd have a Mini when you're a gazillionaire."

"It's compact and I can park it. What about that sounds like a dumb move in New York?"

"How often do you even drive it?"

"Every Sunday, thank you *very* much."

"Are you two going to start making out after the bickering? I'd be down for watching that if we didn't have other shit to do first."

"Come on. Don't slam your doors."

That warning uttered, I headed out of the car then slipped across the street just as Minerva was following Ovianar down the short path to the villa that Minerva had inherited from her aunt as a child.

I'd known they'd come here. That they'd leave their place in Soho and head for Kensington because it wasn't as built up and was more residential.

Staying in an apartment might have seemed more logical, but I knew that once they got inside the house, there was a slick alarm system that would have the cops *and* O's employers outside within twenty minutes.

I knew because I'd fitted the fucking alarm.

In one seamless move, I seized Minerva from the back, slid my arm around her waist like I was hugging her, and dug the tip of a knife into her side.

"It's been so long since we last got together, Minnie," I clipped in her ear before she even had the chance to choke out a warning to Ovianar who was up ahead now, unlocking the front door for us.

Dead To Me drifted along the path as silently as I and made sure Ovianar couldn't lock us out by grabbing her in a chokehold and dragging her deeper into the house.

As I guided Minerva inside, Conor made up the rear, and he closed the front door behind us.

"You said you'd leave us alone," Minerva spat, her anger clear, but she knew not to mess with me. She stayed rigid in my arms but didn't try to escape my hold.

"By meddling with my fucking life, you literally pulled me back inside!"

Ovianar, struggling against D's strength, dropped to her knees as D knocked her out.

Minerva released a cry at the sight, but Conor shuffled ahead and, calm as you like, asked, "Where are we doing this?"

It was easy to forget sometimes that he was a son of the Five Points.

I was better acquainted with his nerdy side than the O'Donnelly in his genes.

"Kitchen. It's down the back. The garden is enclosed so no one will see and the place is soundproofed so no one will hear them scream."

Minerva released a terrified sob at that.

Jabbing her in the side, I muttered, "It doesn't have to come to that. You know I'll fuck off again if you give me the answers I need."

"You're such a cunt, Lodestar. I wish we'd never met—"

"You and me both, bitch. But you fucked with me first. I'd have stayed away but you had to have the final word, didn't you? That's always been your goddamn problem." I shoved her down the hallway toward the kitchen when I saw that D, Conor, and Ovianar were no longer sharing the space with us.

Seeing they were zip-tying her to a chair, I waited for D to snag a knife from the counter and press it to Ovianar's throat in a silent warning.

"You're going to sit down," I told Minerva, "without any fuss. If you try to fuck with me, D will slice her throat."

Minerva tensed at that but gave me a nod of assent. Conor grabbed her and zip-tied her to the seat too.

Within five minutes, both of them were under control and that settled me like little else could.

I will not bend.

I will not break.

Nostrils flaring, I spat, "Which of you were a part of Operation: Jorgmundgander?"

Minerva clenched her eyes closed. "Ovianar."

"What happened?"

She peered at the knife D was still holding to the other woman's throat then rasped, "We hacked into the Saudi embassy. Thought we got in clean, but we didn't. I was pregnant." She tipped up her chin. "Ovianar took the blame and dealt with the punishment."

"You have a kid?" I queried, surprised.

"Yeah. You fucking touch him, I'll kill you!" she spat.

I didn't bother being hurt. She knew what I was capable of. It was why she was speaking so freely without me having to force things and get nasty.

"I have no intention of hurting your family if you give me the answers I want."

Her anxiety didn't lessen. "Leave him alone."

I heard the plea. It made something ping in my chest.

"Lodestar doesn't hurt kids for fun." Conor's defense of me, so immediate, hit me on the raw. I shot him a glance, not sure if I was grateful or not.

"It doesn't have to be for fun. She's relentless," Minerva hissed.

"Ovianar was drafted into Jorgmundgander?"

"She's still in it. They just let her out of jail early for good behavior." She swallowed. "What do you want to know?"

"I told you on the phone. I have a foster daughter and somehow, you made that happen. I want to know how."

Minerva whispered, "I'm in the dark about most of the details. Some of this happened while she was away from me—"

I jumped in with: "You were running BDSec alone during that time?"

Her nod was shaky but guilt filtered into her expression. "I needed the cash."

I experienced a 'eureka' moment. "So, that's why you started being the go-to service for hitmen?"

BDSec had been formed in the aftermath of my 'ex-husband' Hans' death. We'd started the hacktivist group with the intention of using it to bring down the people who'd hurt me but, as with anything, intentions changed. *Morphed.*

The US had the Ledger—Hunter Lachlan ran that. But before he came along, Europe had BDSec's Rolodex of hitmen and they acted as escrow for the client, only paying the hired gun once proof of death of the intended target had been submitted.

"I had no choice. We were on our asses. Without Ovianar…" She bit her lip. "I broke down. It was hard for a long time and we almost lost everything, but then, when I visited her in prison, she suggested we start the service and that's when things got better."

"If I were you," D drawled. "I'd remember what you do for a living and what puts food on your table and dresses your kid when you're judging Lodestar for her actions. You're not exactly as pure as the driven snow."

Minerva's mouth tightened but she bowed her head to evade eye contact with us.

I cleared my throat at D's defense of me. I was more used to her having my back than I was with Conor because he'd never been in a position where it had been necessary before.

As I studied the pair of them in silence, a whisper of a new truth settled deep inside me.

I wasn't alone anymore.

"Your foster daughter, is she in danger?"

Minerva's question had me blinking in surprise. "What? Why would you ask that?"

She swallowed. "That's why Ovianar put her in your line of sights."

My hands balled into fists. "So you admit she set me up?"

"I admit it but not for the reasons you think. There was no malice in it. Ovianar…"

"Less than five minutes ago, you were scared that she was going to kill your son or use him for leverage, but Ovianar was fine with sending some unknown kid to her for protection?" Conor queried, his tone perplexed.

"She has more faith in her than I do," was Minerva's bitter response. "Plus, desperate times call for desperate measures."

"Explain," I bit off.

"I told you there's only so much she told me. What I do know is that she put the girl with you for her own protection. Someone was hunting her in the foster care system. I don't know who or why, just that O was worried."

Dead To Me cracked her knuckles before informing me, "She's already started stirring. It won't be long before she's awake."

Nodding, I folded my arms across my chest as I leaned against the kitchen wall. "Then we wait."

"Please don't kill us," Minerva pleaded.

"I want answers. Give them to me and we'll consider this settled."

Minerva tensed when Ovianar groaned, and a couple moments later, when her eyes fluttered open, Minerva whispered, "Just explain why you did what you did. They won't hurt B. I told her about Jorgmundgander."

Ovianar's head rocked back, then she froze when she saw D looming over her. I figured that woke her up better than ice water to the face because she started struggling until D dug the knife deeper into her throat. Deep enough to cut.

"Stop it!" Minerva snarled. "This isn't necessary. Give her what she wants. We have a family. You swore you'd protect us!"

The words appeared to penetrate Ovianar's thick skull because she stilled then, nostrils flaring, growled, "Ask your questions then get the fuck away from us."

"How?"

It was a simple question that, I knew, led to an impossible array of answers.

Ovianar swallowed. "You heard of a guy called Dagda?"

Conor stilled.

Dead To Me cast me a look.

I just drawled, "Ex-British serviceman? One of the best snipers in the world?"

"Yeah. That's him. Eamonn's his name. He's good people. They used to team us up a lot. We worked well together." She tipped her chin away from the knife. "Is this really necessary?"

Once I jerked my chin at D, she backed off.

"There was this meeting in Ohio," she continued without pause. "It was a gathering of six or so Sparrows. Six of their top brass had gathered at this hotel in Cincinnati. Two teams were sent to deal with them."

"They all died?"

"No. Two of them did. The other four…" Her mouth tightened. "I later learned it was a power grab."

"What happened?"

"Each team got a target and a time limit. We already knew something was different because we only had a handler and not an active operative on our team."

"What's the difference?"

"When we had a handler who dealt with us remotely, we knew it was a dirty job. If there was fallout, it'd be on us, not on them." Her throat worked. "We didn't know the targets would be traveling with their families. Not until it was too late."

"Were the families also targets?"

"They were," she whispered. "They wanted us to kill kids. Dagda wouldn't do it. We were in agreement. We'd handle our target then figure something out—"

"Wait. You said *kids*," Conor muttered.

She nodded. "Our target had two with him. The other team's target had just the one—a daughter."

My throat closed.

"Why did they travel with families?"

Ovianar cast a look at Conor. "A trust exercise otherwise nobody would have shown up. They brought their families along because—"

"No one thought they'd kill their wives and children," D intoned grimly.

"No honor among thieves," was all Ovianar said. "But some of the six were faces we see on the news. Politicians. I guess they figured they were safe because you know what the US is like. You can barely be a politician without a spouse at your side. Kids just pretty up the family image."

"Go on," I demanded. "What happened?"

"There were complications from the start. There were definite trust issues, especially with *our* target. He traveled in a separate car from his children so that made it easier for us.

"Dagda shot the father but he clipped the driver. They crashed into the car in front. When the secondary car took off, we knew we had to follow because if it got back to our director that we'd let the kids live, they'd add an extra year to our sentences as punishment *and* send someone out to kill them anyway.

"I was tracking the cars so Dagda managed to follow them, but the driver was good at his job. They almost got away but there was a head-on collision. The driver and one of the kids were killed. The girl, well, Dagda took her in. We had barely any time to deal with her but we knew we had to do something.

"After you took off, we didn't stop investigating the Sparrows. We'd managed to uncover some of their transactions before I got arrested. Not much, but..." She shot me a wary look. "There was a shipping manifesto. I didn't have time to think. I just acted. I doctored the manifesto, put the kid's mother on there, and set it on sale on Silk Road."

"I asked Thyme to pass you the link," Minerva admitted.

My brow puckered as the memory lifted. Conor had asked me how I'd found the manifesto among thousands of other listings and I genuinely hadn't been able to remember how. "I'm surprised she was willing to help."

"She did it for me," Minerva intoned darkly.

"Thyme as in the hacker who shut down the power grid at Svalbard?"

I nodded at Conor's question. "That's her. She's whacko. She thinks there's a portal to another planet there."

"Never meet your heroes," he muttered under his breath.

"Dagda didn't have much time but he took the girl to a church and offered the priest a donation to take her in and drop her off with social services a few days later.

"For something that we cooked up under pressure, it still stuns the shit out of me that it worked. Especially because I kept my eye on her and I knew they were hunting her in the foster care system. I'd have left her there if I thought it'd keep her anonymous, but they were sniffing around—"

"How do you know?"

"I put checks on her file in social services. The girl's records were accessed by too many people, some high-ranking officials at that. It was odd. Dagda and I agreed that we needed to put her somewhere safe.

"That was when *you* came to mind. I knew you'd protect her, knew you'd love her like she needed to be loved and would help her get over what had happened to her. I'm guessing you have, otherwise you wouldn't be here now. Is she in danger?"

My mouth tightened as I folded my arms across my chest. Ignoring her question, I stated, "She wasn't in the car alone."

"I know you're fostering her. I recognized your alias—"

"I'm asking the goddamn questions," I snarled.

Ovianar bowed her head. "Her cousin was with her. He was with Bogdan because the kid was his 'heir.' Never seen Dagda so cut up in my life when he found the dead boy. He's like a robot when he's on the job. After he'd settled the kid at the church, he came back to our motel room and he cried."

Reaching up to rub my temples, I muttered, "She's never mentioned any of this."

"Retrograde amnesia?" D queried.

"Maybe. She was fucked up when I got her. The trauma… it would explain a lot."

My poor little girl.

Misery twisted inside me, making me wish she were close by so I could give her a hug. So I could try to make this better. But, for all my concern, Kat was fine now. The nightmares still happened from time to time but there hadn't been a bed-wetting incident in years.

That didn't mean it wasn't a ticking time bomb.

"No one came for her when she was in my care."

Ovianar shrugged. "I buried her file once I knew you had her."

That made sense. Once I knew I wanted to keep her, when she'd stopped being 'my foster daughter' and had become simply *mine*, I'd done the same.

It'd probably explain why, whenever I'd peeked into the system in Ohio, the ID I'd burned on Kat's behalf hadn't been on the state's most wanted list.

Though I should thank her for that, I wasn't about to.

Conor, keeping things on track, asked, "What about the other team and their target?" He moved closer to me though, not stopping until only inches separated us.

When his pinkie brushed up against mine, I swallowed.

The need to be held by him was intense, but I fought it. I had to keep my shit together. We were drowning in filthy fucking lies and conspiracies. I needed the truth or I felt like I was going to choke on it all.

"Was the second target a guy called Kuznetsov?" D asked.

"How did you know that?" Ovianar demanded, twisting around to glower at her.

"Lucky guess," D mocked, but we shared a knowing glance.

Kat wasn't my blood.

I guessed I'd known that already but maybe a smidgen of wishful thinking had made me hope she was.

"What happened with the kid?"

"There was a pile-up. The kid—she was only a toddler—wandered into traffic. The team seemed to think she got hit."

"Do you think she was?"

Ovianar hitched a shoulder. "No. I think they said that to give her a fighting chance."

"We need to find that girl," I rasped.

"Why?"

"Because my foster daughter isn't the only one who needed to be kept safe." Kuznetsov didn't mean her any harm, but if the bastards behind that mission ever found out my cousin and Katina were alive, they were screwed. "But you and Dagda," I almost choked on the name, "were kind and put her in the path of someone who'd care for her. The other team didn't."

"I don't know anything—"

"Did they get you to wipe the accidents away?"

She pursed her lips. "Yes."

"So you know plenty. We need a date, time, and locations."

"This was years ago, Lodestar!"

"I'm sure you'll figure out a way to remember what we need to know."

Ovianar huffed. "I need to access my computer."

"Any funny business and you won't be seeing your son again," D warned.

Minerva stiffened. "Ovianar would never risk our son."

"Glad to hear it," was all D said.

"Conor, cut the zip-ties on her wrists first then tie them again in front of her."

He nodded at my order and accepted the knife I handed him without question. Ordinarily, I'd have done it myself, but getting close to her would be asking for trouble.

As he slashed through the nylon, Ovianar didn't give him any crap like she might have done with me, just let him bind her again. Then, he released her feet.

"I'll stay with Minerva in case you change your mind and stop being cooperative," D threatened.

Ovianar's mouth tightened but she nodded her understanding.

Conor returned the knife to me, and my eyes caught and held Ovianar's as I pledged, "I have no desire to hurt you."

"But you will," she said bitterly.

"Yeah. I will. If I have to."

She staggered through the door and I followed her into what had once been our HQ. There were a couple of laptops in here and two desktops. She headed for her rig and kickstarted it.

"It needs to sync up," she muttered.

"Fine."

I stared around the office, unsurprised to see it hadn't changed that much. Minerva's aunt had been a hedonist shipped from the sixties and they hadn't been that interested in interior design back in the day. The same 'groovy' wallpaper decorated the walls, big swirling loops that made me think of an acid trip I'd experienced one time with Savannah and her brother, Camden.

"You really want to help the girl?"

Jarred from my exploration, I nodded and did the unthinkable—I told the truth. "I'm related to her."

"What?!" Ovianar blurted out. "How?"

"Her father was my uncle."

"Her father was a Sparrow," was her bitter retort.

I rubbed my nape. "That's the part I don't understand."

"What's to understand? He was scum."

Tired, I leaned against the wall. I didn't think she'd pull any unsuspecting moves, mostly because she was still aghast at my revelation.

"How did you find out that it was a power grab?"

"We were told six teams were being shipped out. One team per target. But later on, those same names and faces were alive and well and on TV again."

"You remember them?"

"Of course."

"Write them down."

She cut me a look, but whatever she found during her exploration of my features had her nodding. "You're working to tear them down still, aren't you?"

"After what they put me through, bet your ass I am."

"If you need help, Minerva and I are on board."

"Doubt Minerva would agree."

"Maybe not, but the shit we've uncovered about the Sparrows is enough to make Satan puke. They deserve to be ripped to shreds."

It was my turn to study her. "Any intel you can pass my way, I'd appreciate."

"You're close?"

I'd always been a lone wolf, so it was hard being a part of a pack. Harder back then, when I'd first met these two women who'd become integral to my life, to accept that I needed help. I didn't know if it was Cin who'd shown me the way or Conor, but I couldn't deny I was different than the person Minerva and Ovianar had known.

This was, I gleaned, the chance to extend the hand of friendship.

A mutual enemy often united people...

"Finding my cousin is a part of a bigger deal I'm involved in."

"What kind of deal?"

I needed to fudge the truth here. "My grandfather on my mother's side is high up in Interpol. He says that if I find my uncle's murderer and my cousin, then he'll set up a division that will work solely on investigating and imprisoning Sparrows."

"Instead of just dealing with everything on a case-by-case basis?"

"Yes. An entire department dedicated to nothing else but these pieces of shit."

She bit her lip. "I'm assuming your grandfather doesn't know that his son was a Sparrow?"

"I think that's a smart assumption."

"You never mentioned a grandfather in the police force..."

"I only met him this week."

Her eyes flared in surprise. "Oh."

"Yeah. It's been intense."

"I-I really didn't mean any harm, Star. With the girl. I-I knew you struggled after you had that miscarriage, and while you're not a natural mother, not like Minerva—"

"I'm a natural killer," I said flatly. "Who better to keep someone safe?"

"Exactly," she whispered.

Not bothering to be offended, I nodded my understanding as she awkwardly reached out and picked up a pen and paper. She scrawled names down on the sheet, then she started to delve into her files. More information was jotted down and I watched her hit hibernate as she clambered to her feet again, the note in her hand.

"This is literally all I know about that day." Her fingers tightened around the piece of paper. "I understand that you want answers and that you'll go to any length to get them, but I know nothing else. I'm not hiding anything.

"I have a son now, Star, and you've got a daughter—I hope you realize I wouldn't put him in jeopardy over this."

I snagged the note from her grasp, shoved it in my pocket, and ignored her entreaty. "How did you get DeLaCroix's login information over to me?" At her frown, I growled, "The same account sold me an email and password combination, O. Don't pretend you don't fucking remember."

"I slept since then, Lodestar!" she shrieked, panic filtering into her voice. "Give me a second to remember." Her lashes fluttered as her mind raced, then after a good thirty seconds, she released a heavy breath. "I remember. The email and password combo. I didn't know it was... Wait, DeLaCroix? That Sparrow who was the chief justice of your SCOTUS?"

"Yes, him. We used the combo to log into an app the NWS use to communicate with one another."

"Jesus." Her eyes lit up. "I had no fucking idea it was his."

"You don't expect me to believe that, do you? After what you've admitted to orchestrating?"

"No, seriously. I knew it was something Sparrow-related. But hell, it could have been to access their account with a grocery store for all I knew. I was just padding out the account so you weren't suspicious."

"Where did you get the details from?"

"It was on our mark's person. Dagda said he had a bunch of notes on the other leaders."

"Did you put them up for sale too?"

"I did. I sold the docket too. Got a pretty penny for that intel."

"You know who bought them?"

She shrugged. "Never bothered to look. Why, is it important?"

"I hate loose ends." I grumbled under my breath, "Hold out your hands."

Licking her lips, she complied. I notched my knife between her wrists then sliced through the nylon to liberate her.

"I don't think we can ever be friends," Ovianar muttered.

"I'll settle for allies."

Her expression resolute, she nodded. "Allies."

45

CONOR

Conor O'Donnelly

"NO FUCKING WAY," I clipped as I read the names on the list.

Justin DeLaCroix.

David Foundry

Sheridan Reinier

Aleksandr Kuznetsov

Bogdan Belyaev

Garry Smythe

"We all know who DeLaCroix is—chief justice and ex-head of the Sparrows. That means this meeting was no bullshit. These really are, *were*, at the top of the tree."

Cin nodded. "They're still doing well for themselves. Foundry's the US attorney general now."

I nodded at Cin as I crossed my ankle over my knee. "And Reinier's the director of the CIA."

Though I could sense that meeting with BDSec had shaken her, Star was holding her own. But she was back to saying nothing and leaving me and Cin to do most of the talking.

For a paid hitman, Cin had a great sense of humor. Give me *her* over Temperance any day of the fucking week.

Currently holed up in the family room of Minerva and Ovianar's home, we were discussing the situation away from the Union guards who were waiting for us outside.

"Garry Smythe is a pretty commonly used name. But isn't he the White House chief of staff?"

"Yeah. At least, *a* Garry Smythe is."

"Never heard of Bogdan Belyaev, have you?"

Star and I shared a glance at Cin's question, but she just admitted, "He was Katina's father."

Cin asked, "That's all you know about him?"

"We know he looks like a front," I drawled. "No debts, no car loans, no possessions apart from a single bank account and a freakin' house. *And*," I directed at Star, "if some of Eoghan's story is true, then he was an emissary to Russia."

"Maybe they covered up his identity?" Star offered.

"Why though? What did they have to hide?"

"That he was a Sparrow?" Cin retorted with a snort before she changed the subject. "How didn't your grandfather know his kid was a Sparrow?"

"I don't know," she admitted.

I thought about the conversation I'd shared with Anton prior to heading onto the private jet. "I think he thinks your mother betrayed him."

She scowled at that. "And the son didn't?"

"He might have been a spy," I pointed out. "If Anton planted him there, then…"

"True."

"How could your mom have betrayed him? She was with the CIA until she married your dad. Then she quit, right?"

Star shrugged. "I feel like whatever she told me was a lie, so I don't know what's true and what isn't."

"Do people who work for the CIA share their careers with their families? Don't they hide it, or have I watched too many Bourne movies?"

Cin snorted. "Star and I weren't in a position to share our job titles, no. But some are. Depends on what they do. I guess they'd just say they were analysts though. Did she tell you she was in the CIA, Star?"

"Not directly. Dad did."

"So she told him?"

"Yeah, over tequila." She pinched the bridge of her nose. "When did you talk to him anyway?"

"Your grandfather called to confirm our flight when you were in the bathroom," I said easily.

"Why didn't you say anything?"

"You were too busy being beautifully angry."

Laughing, Cin elbowed me in the side. "Do I want to know?"

"Probably not," I joked, watching as Star's lips twitched into an aggrieved smile. "I asked him about Jorgmundgander. He claimed that it's run by NATO and that it's neutral."

"Bullshit," Cin scoffed. "Nothing's fucking neutral in this world."

"He meant with the Brothers and the Sparrows."

"But that goes against what Ovianar just said."

"It does if Jorgmundgander was being used in a Sparrow power grab," I concurred. "But I don't think he was lying to me. He believed what he was saying."

"What else did he say?"

"Not much."

"Sounds like his standard MO," she groused. "He's purposely keeping us in the dark."

I couldn't argue with that. "Maybe it's for a reason—fresh eyes. This happened nearly seven years ago. You can't tell me that we're the only people he's put on the case."

"No," she agreed warily. "Meaning everyone else failed."

"He's probably putting you through your paces as well. Wants to see what you're capable of," Cin stated. "You know what those fuckers are like. It's all a game."

With a begrudging grunt, Star nodded her agreement.

"Wonder which of these three is in charge now that DeLaCroix is out of the picture."

I shot Dead To Me a look. "That's a good question."

"I'm left wondering what it was about Belyaev and Kuznetsov that required eradication…" Star rubbed the back of her neck.

"We might never know."

Cin sniffed at my answer. "We have a time and a date now, some places too. What's the next move?"

"Is Troy still alive?" Star asked Cin.

"Think so. She retired though."

"My brother said you can't retire."

Cin arched a brow. "You can if you lose your twenty-twenty vision."

"She's blind?"

"Had an accident," Cin confirmed. "Nasty one. Probably karma."

"You'd better hope that doesn't exist," I pointed out.

"He's right. Or we're all fucked," was Star's gloomy rejoinder. "Where's she living?"

"Connecticut, I think." Cin's gaze turned thoughtful. "Started up a bee farm. Remember she used to go on about how we were going to die without bees?"

"I remember."

"Einstein said the same thing," I pointed out.

Star shrugged. "Our problems have always been of the more immediate variety than global warming."

I knocked her knee with mine. "Troy didn't agree." When she just hummed, I said, "We have an elephant in the room."

"By this point, Conor, I think we have a full fucking circus," Star groused.

"We do, but… Dagda was one of the Jorgmundgander operatives. What if your mom was a sanctioned hit?"

Her fists clenched at that. "We need answers."

"Where do we start?" Cin asked. "Troy? She'd probably be able to help with your cousin."

"She's also who Kuznetsov wants handed to him on a platter," she retorted. "I have to find my cousin *and* bring my uncle's murderer to him."

"And that's a problem?" I queried.

"I like Troy," she grumbled.

Cin nodded. "She's good people."

"For an assassin," I joked.

"Hey, you always want us on your side," was Cin's comment.

"Troy was damn good at what she did too. She came up with us, but left, what? 2009, Cin?"

"Yeah. Went private. Far more lucrative. I'd heard that she got arrested in Paris so that must have been when she got involved with Jorgmundgander."

"The bitch of it is, if I don't want Troy to die for her part in this, then if Dagda's hit on my mother was sanctioned, how can I blast his brains out like I've been trying to?"

"Revenge doesn't have to make sense," was all Cin said.

Star turned her gaze upon me. "I guess it doesn't."

"Forgiveness is a lot less complicated."

"Plus, do you even need vengeance if you don't like your mom anymore?"

Star huffed. "You always have to be so practical, Cin. It's tiresome."

"Well, sor-ry," she grouched.

"Okay, let's break this down. We have your uncle's murderer and the masterminds behind it.

"We don't know where your cousin is, but we have more names for the new Interpol division, and I can stop digging into health insurance providers for random conspiracy theories."

"You were right though, weren't you?"

I winked at her. "I usually am."

Belyaev's crash *had* taken place in New Cloverfield, Ohio, according to Ovianar.

Though she scoffed, she stretched out her arms and groaned. "Next move has to be Troy. She's probably the only one who can help us because Red Knight died five years ago."

"And he is truly missed. *Not.* I hated that fucker."

"What did he do to you?" Cin's curiosity was practically bubbling.

"He was a conspiracy theorist and he used to hunt evidence that would back up his claims. Basically, he was the search engine of conspiracies."

Star's lips curved. "He believed the British royal family were lizards in skin suits."

"Not one of those morons," Cin groaned.

"Yup. And trust me, having dealt with the royal family, I can tell you their blood isn't blue *and* they're definitely not reptilian." Star grinned at my grimace. "So… next move?"

Cin got up and moved over to the window so she could peer out of the blinds. "I liked flying private. Think your grandfather would pop for another flight on that jet of his?"

"To visit Troy?"

"He doesn't have to know she's his son's killer, Star."

She nodded. "You're right. We're in agreement, then? We speak to Troy?"

"Yeah, I think that's for the best," I concurred.

As always, we'd gotten some answers but had blown open a mine-field that we needed to dig through.

One thing was certain—those bottles of tequila we were going to drink when this was over had never been further from our reach.

46

TEXT CHAT

LODESTAR: *I have news.*

Maverick: *Let me bring Alessa into this chat so I don't have to relay it.*

****Alessa added to group chat****

Alessa: *Hey, Star*

Lodestar: *Hey. There's no need to run that DNA test anymore.*

Alessa: *You're not related?*

Lodestar: *No. Her father was a high-ranking Sparrow, Alessa.*

Alessa: *What?! That's impossible!*

Lodestar: *It isn't. It's the truth. He was killed in a power grab and Kat almost died as a result.*

Maverick: *Jesus Christ. Has this been confirmed?*

Lodestar: *Yes.*

Maverick: *Fuck. What's your next move?*

Lodestar: *I'm coming back to the US. On a plane now, heading to New York. Conor's going to arrange for one of his men to collect Kat. I need him to bring her to the city.*

Maverick: *Why?*

Lodestar: *I want to see her. I don't know how long I'll be stateside* *and if she finds out I've been here without visiting her, I'll never hear the end of it.*

    Maverick: *Lol.*

    Alessa: *I'll make sure she's ready. What time?*

    Lodestar: *Five okay?*

    Alessa: *Sure. You're certain she will be safe?*

    Lodestar: *Conor's men mean business.*

    Maverick: *I can have a brother ride with them.*

    Alessa: *She'd love that.*

    Lodestar: *Lol. She would. That would be great.*

    Maverick: *Sin? He liaises with the Five Points anyway.*

    Lodestar: *No. There's nothing to liaise with as of yet. Link would be fine. He doesn't have to stay once she's dropped off.*

    Maverick: *Will you send her back the same night?*

    Lodestar: *Very likely. But she'll be fine without Link. Conor would never let anyone hurt Katina.*

    Maverick: *That much faith in him?*

    Lodestar: *I love him, Jameson.*

    Maverick: *You mean business if you're bringing out my real name.*

    Lodestar: *I just wanted you to know it's serious. When things are settled down, I'm going to move in with him.*

    Alessa: *It's not far from our house to Manhattan. I know that's where the Five Points live. You won't mind if I visit often, will you?*

    Lodestar: *Of course not! Are you sure you don't mind me moving her there?*

    Alessa: *If I've learned anything from this stay, Star, it's that YOU are her mom. She needs you.*

    Lodestar: *I need her too.*

    Maverick: *Conor will look after her, won't he?*

    Lodestar: *I guess there wasn't much time for conversation when you were punching his lights out.*

    Maverick: *I stand by that decision.*

    Alessa: *I don't!*

    Lodestar: *Anyway, guys, I gtg. I need to catch some Zs before I fall down. Just wanted to get the arrangements put in place.*

Maverick: *Keep us in the loop.*

Lodestar: *I will.*

Alessa: *She never needed you to be her cousin, Star. She just needs you to be her mom.*

Lodestar: *That's all I've ever wanted to be.*

Maverick: *Stay safe, Star.*

Alessa: *Yes, take care of yourself.*

Lodestar: *I will. Stay vigilant. I don't know what the hell's going to happen. I just know that the cages I told you I was rattling, Mav, are wide open now.*

Maverick: *Understood.*

47

STAR

GOD ONLY KNOWS - BEACH BOYS

Star Sullivan

I HAD to hand it to Kuznetsov—he was accommodating.

So long as we kept the guards with us, he gave us free rein to use his jet wherever and however we wanted, which could only be considered an advantage.

It also meant that Dead To Me was in the cockpit talking to—i.e. flirting with—the two pilots, whereas I was sitting in the back with Conor, who was working on his computer, while I made arrangements for after we landed in the States.

Well, in between watching him do his thing, that is.

Maybe I noticed because I was more relaxed now that we had a lead, but his hair had flopped onto his forehead, and he kept shoving it back with a glower. That glower did things to me that made me doubly glad we were flying private and not on a commercial airline.

"I can feel you watching me."

With a smile, I mused, "You're so pretty that I have to watch you."

He snorted. "Do you have any dollar bills? I can cock my hip out and you can stick them under my belt."

"Looking is free," I argued, chuckling when he peered at me over his screen then closed it and started studying me with as much dedication as I'd been studying him.

The impasse made me laugh even harder.

He was somehow sexy as fuck with that tight ass of his and those abs that didn't quit, and never mind that goddamn hair and the face— was there ever a face made for kissing more than Conor's? I didn't think so.

Yet, for all that, he was also the funniest guy I'd ever been with, someone who didn't take himself seriously, who embraced his own quirks and celebrated mine.

It was impossible to stay where I was and not to move around the other side of the table. I plunked myself on his lap, knowing he wouldn't argue, then I hooked my arm around his shoulder and pressed my forehead against his.

I felt his brows lift in reaction, but he just gripped my hips. "You'll find that my knee is more comfortable than any chair that has ever been made."

Wiggling my ass, I hummed. "What about La-Z-Boys?"

"Do they come with the orgasm option?"

"I doubt it."

"I can get in all the nooks and crannies. It's one of my top features."

"I bet you can. But you don't vibrate, do you?"

"No, but I'm working on something that does. Seriously, I'm better engineered than any armchair on the market."

When I gave another wriggle of my hips, I felt the solid girth of his cock against my upper thigh and butt cheek. "What's that big, thick, hard ridge there?"

"I don't know. Might be a manufacturing defect."

My head tipped back as I burst out laughing. "Stop! Seriously, stop."

He smirked at me, seeming very self-satisfied at my amusement. It wasn't the first time I'd seen that particular reaction out of him and the 'why' occurred to me—he liked to make me smile.

This man.

"How are you doing?"

I shrugged. "We have a lead so I'm okay. But it was an intense day."

"It was," he agreed. "Are you going to tell Katina that she had a cousin? Hell, an aunt and uncle too—there's no reason to assume they're dead."

"She's in a good place and I don't want to wreck that. She might remember seeing his body or something." I bit my lip. "But I think I'll consult with a child therapist and get their take on things."

"How will you explain something that never officially happened?"

"Would they look into it? They just need to know the details, surely?" Nerves fluttered to life in my belly and made it more imperative that I say: "Thank you, even though you hate flying, for taking two flights in a twenty-four-hour period. But more importantly, thank you for not letting me do this alone."

His fingers squeezed me then they retreated to his pocket where he pulled something from within its confines. "I could say the same back to you—one is a hella lonely number."

I stared at the Airheads and laughed. "Where do you keep getting these from? Are you really Willy Wonka?"

His eyes twinkled as I accepted the candy. "Sugar for when the world is too bitter for your tongue."

"The implication being that your kiss isn't sweet enough…?"

He liked hearing that. His grin was a delicious mixture of dopey and sheepish and cute, making it far sweeter than anything candy could offer.

"Do you know you're very romantic?" I rasped when he remained silent, toying with the end of the wrapper.

"Nah."

"You are."

"I'm not."

"The shit you say belongs in a Valentine's Day card," I argued, unsure *why* I was arguing when I was coming to rely on the little things he did and said. "In fact, I know you're lying about not having a sideline with Hallmark."

His lips twisted. "If I do, it's only in the section that's specifically for women called Star."

I shoved his shoulder. "See?! There you go again with this romantic stuff. I'm not made for it, Conor!"

"Stop whining and take it," he teased.

Though I huffed, I admitted, "I have a song for you. But you can't listen to it with me here."

"Why not?"

"You just can't. And I'm going to go for a nap because I need to let my brain process all the crap that's happened today."

Pressing a gentle kiss to my mouth, he whispered, "Go and get some rest."

"You can join me. When you're done, I mean."

His grin was like quicksilver. "I will."

"We've still got seven hours left of the flight so there's time to sleep."

His grin died and he groaned, "Seven hours."

"I'll distract you," I promised with a soft smile, shooting him a shy look as I hustled off his lap then got to my feet.

Grabbing my cell, I sent him the link I'd prepared earlier and then moved my ass so that I didn't have to hear him listen to the sappy song.

He found it easy to say stuff to me that gave me Conor-heartburn. For me, it was much harder.

Even now, knowing he was listening to "God Only Knows" by The Beach Boys made me nervous, and I forced myself to use the bathroom then to clean my face and then to dawdle some more until I was certain the short song had finished playing.

Returning to the bedroom, I switched off the lights once I'd clambered into bed and immediately dragged the pillows around me so I was surrounded by their comforting embrace.

That was when I heard it.

Fuck.

I clenched my eyes closed as the song sounded in the background.

Growing nearer and nearer. Until it was no longer outside the bedroom but in the doorway.

The melody always tore at me. The words snuck inside and did damage to the thing in my chest that some would call a heart, but I didn't know what to make of it. It hadn't done much else apart from send blood around my arteries before Kat and Conor.

Now, it did other things too.

Odd things.

It beat funny when he was near, and I could hear it pounding in my ears if he was kissing me.

That was, I reasoned, how I knew that it belonged to him—because he made it behave out of character.

"You can't send this song to me and then disappear," he grumbled.

I gnawed on the inside of my cheek rather than answer.

His phone clattered as it dropped against the nightstand, and then the duvet was being lifted and my pillows were being rearranged so that he could be inside the fort I'd made. When his heat spread all the way down my back, I sighed as it surged into the many cold spots that infected me like a disease.

With one arm around my waist and his chin on my shoulder, we listened until the song finished.

"I never imagined you'd like The Beach Boys," he mumbled in my ear.

"Some of their tracks are nice. They used to..." I cleared my throat. "Some of their songs were my mom's favorite. Which I always found hilarious seeing as her husband was Gerry Sullivan.

"But, I guess, who the hell knew what she truly liked? Everything could have been an act."

"You're right," he said softly. "It could have been an act. Maybe a lot of it was. But I can't see all of it being one. Tell me about the last birthday you spent together."

I knew what he was doing. Humanizing a double agent. Still... "She sneaked me away from our guards and we headed to Chuck E. Cheese."

He laughed. "Really?"

"Yeah." I twisted over so I could peer at him through the dim lights. "We stuck around for about twenty minutes, grabbed the food, and left."

"You didn't do the whole kids' party thing?"

My nose crinkled. "I was a teenager. I didn't want Chuck E. Cheese."

"So why did she take you there?"

"Because I'd had a tantrum about how being Gerry Sullivan's daughter was ruining my life and that I never got to do anything normal."

"And that was her reaction?"

"Yeah. Then she took me to Target and we headed into Bed, Bath and Beyond afterward, and…" My smile was shaky. "I guess she just made us do normal stuff. I never imagined that that wouldn't have been normal for her. She fit in seamlessly, Conor. You'd never think she was Russian."

"Her job was literally to fit in, but it wasn't her job to be a good mom. Was she, Star? Was she a good mom?"

I wanted to say no but I couldn't. "She loved me."

Conor seemed to recognize that by saying those three words, I was admitting that she had been a good mother.

Fuck, she'd been the best.

For no other reason would I have gotten myself entangled with this bullshit if not to find the reason she'd been snatched from me too soon.

He reached for my hand and gently squeezed my fingers. "And your dad?"

"He was different when Mom was alive. Back then, he was a good dad. They did what they could when we were growing up in the gold-fish bowl that's life on tour and in the spotlight.

"After, he was lost. I knew he loved me, but he stopped being a 'recovering' addict and fell back into bad habits. I was too much to handle, so broken and lost, just as much as he was, and instead of us coming together, it pushed us apart."

"When you talked about him with me in the past, I never realized…"

"How strained things were between us in the end?" I grimaced. "I don't focus on those times. They make me sad and I'm sad enough. I was a daddy's girl. Even after everything went wrong, that never changed."

"If anything, it probably made you rebel more."

I hummed in agreement. Sharing him with my mom was normal. But with groupies and roadies? No. Fucking. Way.

"Conor?"

"Hmm?"

"Were your ma and da good parents?"

For the longest time, he said nothing. To the point where, when he pressed his face to my shoulder, I just thought he was going to shrug my question off and go to sleep.

My own eyes were starting to close, beginning to feel heavy with fatigue and the stress from the day by the time he muttered, "Do you know how people do what they can with the best they're given?"

"Yes?" was my drowsy retort.

"That's what Ma and Da were like. They did what they could with what they'd learned, but my grandfather was a mean son of a bitch. Da was two screws loose of a full set, but he didn't help any. Ma's family wasn't much better, and she was always irate and erratic, quick to temper because, I think, she knew Da responded well to that—"

"What do you mean?"

"The more irate she was, the more he calmed down in an argument. He didn't fear her, not by any stretch, but she was a loose cannon. We have this inside joke about her hitting him over the head with a rolling pin, you know?"

"Yeah, you told me the story."

"But she used to throw shit at him too."

"Really?"

"Yeah. Cans. One time, potatoes." A soft chuckle drifted from his lips. "Nothing hits harder than a fucking Idaho potato. That was actually hilarious. He got a black eye from it."

"That's spousal abuse, Conor," I pointed out with concern.

"It was, but I don't think we looked at it that way back then."

"Doesn't mean we shouldn't have."

"No. I agree."

"Did he hit her?"

"Never."

"Were the attacks frequent?"

"No. Only when he pushed a topic."

"Like what?"

He sighed. "Do you really want to know this?"

"Of course. You don't talk about yourself a lot, do you know that?"

"I talk plenty."

"That's an understatement," I drawled. "You definitely talk plenty, but not about where you come from."

His nose crinkled but he explained, "Da was terrified that Declan was gay—"

"Why?"

He kissed my shoulder. "Catholic."

I grunted my disapproval as I twisted around to face him.

"Trust me, I wouldn't give a fuck if he was gay, but I'm not Da. So, anyway, he found out this one year that he took art in school…"

"Well, that's normal."

"He wanted him to not be in that class, and if Da had gone down to the school and told the faculty he didn't want his son learning art, it would have soon been swiped off Declan's class schedule."

My brow furrowed at his words, and the atonement I was supposed to be attempting to achieve hit a plateau because how the fuck could I be sorry about eradicating that type of man from the earth?

"It's when you say shit like that, I wonder how I'm supposed to atone," I admitted, unable to hold my tongue. "I couldn't be Catholic."

"Most Catholics can't be either. You're just supposed to promise your priest you will repent and cross your fingers behind your back."

"That's the standard treatment?"

"Yup."

"And you won't accept the standard treatment?"

"Nope."

I blew out a breath. "Did your da think wanting to draw was contagious or something?"

"Who knew how Da's brain worked? Anyway, Ma would chide him for this stuff, but I think she was worried too. Not for the same reasons, but because it'd have been harder for Declan to find a path in the Points…"

"Homophobic asswipes."

"It's a breeding ground of toxic masculinity," he mumbled. "What else did you expect?"

Knowing my defiance shone through, I declared, "I don't care if Katina is gay."

"Good. You shouldn't care. Who the fuck cares so long as she's happy and loved?"

That encouraged me to tip more of my weight onto him as a silent reward. Not that I'd been testing him, but maybe I'd have found some potatoes and thrown them at him too if he'd come out with any of that bullshit—

Oh.

"She hit him with potatoes to get him to back down? That's where you're going with this, aren't you?"

His chuckle was low. "Yeah. He was going to the front door and about to head to the school when, out of nowhere, *boom*, straight in the shoulder. One on the head. He twisted around and she got him in the nuts. Got a couple more licks in too before he tackled the potatoes out of her reach."

"You saw all this?"

"Was sitting on the stairs listening to them argue."

"Why?"

He shrugged. "This was after the priest. I used to listen to the arguments to make sure they weren't talking about me."

That made me deflate. "Oh, Conor, you did nothing wrong."

A shaky breath escaped him. "I know. Now. Back then, not so much. Plus, Aidan and Finn had killed him and I'd drawn my godfather into this, so I was terrified they were going to get arrested… Good times," he finished weakly.

Letting my arms tighten around him, I whispered, "Did it stop him from going to the school?"

"Yes. It also led to shit I didn't want to see," he complained, but he sounded more like his normal self, thank God.

It made me tease him, "I think your da was an asshole but he was a silver fox. You'll be hot as fuck when you're his age."

"You going to stick around to see me mature like a fine wine?"

My lips curved. "You going to stick around to watch my tits sag?"

"I'll hold them up so gravity can't attack them," he vowed.

"That's dedication."

"I'm a dedicated man," he quipped.

I cupped his cheek. "I know that already." He tipped his head down and rubbed his nose against mine. "Thank you for sharing that with me, Conor."

"You don't have to thank me."

"I do." I gently, cautiously, *warily*, reached out and let my fingers stroke through his hair. He tensed at first, released a soughing breath, swallowed roughly, and then sagged into me. I knew he was forcing himself not to react, so I cut it off there and let my hand retreat to his shoulder. "I wish I'd been around when you were a kid."

"Why?"

"Because I'd have killed that priest before he even had the chance to look at you funny."

"Why do I believe that?"

I hitched a shoulder. "Because you know it's the truth."

He grabbed my hand and returned it to his head. It was very awkward, enough that if it weren't such a serious situation, I'd have snickered, but his intent was obvious.

With a care that I wasn't known for, I stroked my fingers through the sable locks that felt like silk and love and non-verbal promises against my skin.

Because I knew it helped me when he talked to me, I whispered, "I know I have to atone, Conor, and I know I'm by no stretch of the imagination America's greatest parent, but I really dislike your da."

His tension broke some at my unexpected words. "Da didn't care about being liked or disliked. He wanted your respect and your fear. Actually, I had it easier with him than the rest of my brothers."

"Why?"

"He accepted I was different and that my gifts weren't what he was used to dealing with, *but* he learned quickly that I was good for padding out a bank account."

"So he was a user." It wasn't a question.

"Yeah, but it was for the family." He shuddered when I accidentally touched his ear. It wasn't a good shudder. My hand whipped away, but he rasped, "No. I want to take this back, Star. You should—"

"I should, what?"

"*He*'s affected how I do things for too long."

"Did I give you your first blow job?" When he tensed, I whispered, "You were very grateful. You never told me that—"

"I'm not a virgin," he blurted out.

"Even if you were, it wouldn't be a problem," I replied easily.

"I'm not and I've never come that way."

"Okay."

"I've fucked but... I don't... God, I'm going to sound like such an asshole."

"I'm an asshole too. We can both be assholes together."

His laughter sounded choked. "I used to hate jerking off. Until you."

Startled, I blurted out, "Really?"

"Yeah. I have a high sex drive. I used to have a lot of one-night stands because I couldn't just tug it in the shower to burn away some of my tension, you know?"

I didn't know. But God, watching Conor doing that in the shower was definitely something I needed to see before I died.

"Yeah," I croaked out.

"But then, after I met you, I didn't want to fuck a hole. I just wanted you. So I had to get used to my hand and it worked. So I know I can do this, but it has to be you. Don't stop."

Biting my lip, I whispered, "You don't need to do this so quickly. We can build up to it."

"I've been building up to meeting you every day I've been on this planet, Star."

I clenched my eyes closed at those words. "The stuff you say, Conor. Christ. How can I… I can't say it back, not because I don't feel it, but because it's not something I'd imagine saying."

"You think it comes easy to me? You think I routinely go around squawking out lines that, what did you say earlier, belong in a Valentine's Day card? You have to open the door to it, Star, and I did that a long time ago with you."

"I-I'll try," I promised.

"That's all you can do, and that will always be enough. And, some days, if you can't find the words, then that's what songs are for."

Some of the tension abated in me.

Songs.

I could do that.

Music had always been integral to my life because of my dad, and it was fitting that Conor's love language could be found therein too but he had more tunnel vision than Dad who used to listen to everything, not just rock.

It was ridiculous then, that as I cuddled up to him, my hand still stroking over his hair, I started to hum the melody to "God Only Knows."

As he relaxed into me, gracing me with the priceless gift of consent, I had no idea why but I started to sing the lyrics.

If Dead To Me heard this, I'd never live it down, but what did it matter? He was important to me. He deserved to know I was as all in as he.

Tears burned my eyes as the meaning behind the lyrics hit home, somehow making more sense to me now that I'd experienced them on a personal level. He had to hear the emotion in my voice, but I didn't care and I didn't think he did either. Maybe that made it better. Stronger. He could *feel* what I could only say through lyrics someone else had written because they'd felt this way too.

Love—the great connector.

When I finished, he was still and I was almost embarrassed by my stupid singing, then he whispered, "You got your dad's voice," and he sank into me totally.

It took me a moment to realize that he was asleep, our legs and arms tangled together, his face pressed against my shoulder, my fingers still in his hair.

And it was perfect.

Nirvana.

Enough that I closed my eyes and allowed myself to rest too.

48

CONOR

IT WAS the knock on the door that woke me. I stirred, clambering off the bed to unlock it and peer at an amused Cin.

"Two hours until we land."

I scowled. "Couldn't you have woken us twenty minutes before?"

She shrugged. "We gotta talk strategy and she can't do that without hot chocolate."

My mouth rounded. "What?"

"Which part didn't you understand?"

"The hot chocolate part."

"She should have it instead of coffee."

"Why?"

"Because coffee makes her aggressive and hot chocolate puts her in a better mood." She tapped her nose. "My top tip is to always order for her because she never remembers."

"How do you know any of this?"

"Worked a lot of jobs together. You pick up shit about people in close quarters, and I've always liked Star. We have an unusual friendship."

I leaned an arm against the door, curious despite myself because in all our conversations, she'd never really spoken about Cin. She'd mentioned how she believed Savannah and Katina would always leave her at some point because she was toxic but…

"Why is your friendship unusual?"

"Because we accept the worst parts about each other with no judgment and always forgive one another."

"Why?"

Her smile was wicked. "Because we don't know who'll shoot first if we don't get along."

"Literally?"

"Exactly. It's the great leveler, isn't it? We may not always be in each other's pockets, and I might not have even known she'd been inducted into the Sparrows' trafficking business, just as she doesn't know where I spend most of my time, but we have each other's backs. Always."

"She needs friends like you."

She punched me in the arm. "I know."

Rubbing my bicep, I clipped, "Was that necessary? I was saying something nice!"

"Just associating that sentence with pain."

"What?!"

"Negative reinforcement. Don't ever try to tear our friendship apart or I'll hurt you." This time, her smile was sweet. "Wake her up with a smile, Conor. Do us both a favor."

Gaping at her now-retreating back, I rubbed a hand over my face before I returned to the bed and clambered onto the mattress.

Belly flopping beside her, I mumbled, "Star, two hours until landing."

She grumbled her own dissent but slowly started to wake up—soft stretches of her toes, little wriggles of her arms as if she had an ache in them.

The gentle movements intrigued me enough that I pried my eyes open and tipped my head to the side to watch her awaken.

That was when I remembered how she'd sang to me…

This woman—capable of violence and so much cruelty—had serenaded me.

And she had no idea how beautiful her voice was. No idea whatsoever. But I did now.

Yet another of this woman's secrets that I was starting to unravel.

I wouldn't stop until I knew them all.

Until she was an open book.

"What time is it?"

"Too late and too early."

"At the same time?"

I grunted.

She peeped at me with one eye. "How long until we land again?"

"Two hours," I garbled around a yawn.

"I dreamed of you."

My yawn froze like I'd been plunged into a vat of liquid nitrogen. "What did you dream about?"

A soft hum was her answer.

Fuck.

My dick reacted to that hum.

Hair trigger, much?

"Where was I?"

"The shower."

The immediacy of her answer told me she'd been stringing me along for effect. Two could play that game. "What was I doing in the shower?"

A soft smirk curved her lips. "Getting clean."

I snorted. "Is that all?"

"You were very, very, *very* thorough."

"There's a shower in the jet's bathroom," I informed her.

"Nah, you were too thorough for a five-minute cleanup."

She bit her lip and then reached over to place her hand on my abdomen. I tugged on her wrist, encouraging her to straddle me. Then, I settled my hands on her hips which was when I discovered that, at some point during our sleep, she'd dragged off her jeans and wore only the boxer briefs she kept stealing from me.

I lifted the duvet and peered beneath it to take a look at her.

"My boxers suit you better than they do me."

She snorted. "That's because you don't get to see your ass in them."

"No, I prefer this view." I let my thumbs arc downwards, mimicking the V-shape of her apex, framing it with my hands. "You going to show me this?"

A soft, surprised breath escaped her. "You want to see?"

"Does it save time to loop an algorithm instead of duplicating and ultimately having to debug malfunctioning code?"

She blinked then grinned. "DRY." *Don't repeat yourself.*

I smirked at her pun. "Nothing about you will be DRY."

"You'd prefer me to be WET?" *Write everything twice.*

My thumbs rubbed in a gentle circle. "I think you know the answer to that."

She arched up higher and wiggled her ass. "Go on then. Start moving."

With permission granted, I tugged on the waistband of the briefs and drew them over the ripe swell of her ass. She wasn't skinny; she wasn't just curvy—she was muscled. Solid. I should have stopped watching *American Gladiators* when I was a kid. It totally fucked me over in the sack because her body was my idea of *the* best time.

With the briefs trapped in the crease between hips and thighs, revealing her upper mons, I gritted my teeth as I locked my eyes on where I most wanted to be.

She didn't give me a sexy strip tease, just made me jump by bouncing once on the bed and using the momentum to stand. She kicked her leg over me, shimmied the fabric down her thighs, straddled me once they were puddled around one ankle, then seamlessly returned to my lap.

"You're harder," she growled, her hand settling on my cock.

"You just flashed your pussy at me, Star, *and* pulled ninja moves. How did you think I was going to react?"

"You're such a nerd."

Her laughter was teasing, but I ignored it to watch as she dragged off her tank and sat there utterly naked in front of me. I knew she had no body issues. I'd also picked up on the fact she wasn't uncomfortable nude—I didn't want to think about why because it would have nothing to do with body positivity.

Tongue cleaved to the roof of my mouth, I watched as she pressed a hand to her breast, fire gleaming in her eyes, lighting up her expression with sparks I felt wherever we connected.

The difference in her was electric. If she was leading things, she was at ease. It was when I was the one doing the touching that she shied away. Just thinking about her aggressive blow job made my cock weep pre-cum at how *this* could turn out.

She plucked at her nipple and tipped her head to the side. "I want to see your dick."

Not about to argue, I angled upright and dragged my tee off then tossed it on the floor. My belt came next, and then I unfastened my fly and released my cock from the crippling pressure of my jeans.

When my shaft flopped back against my stomach, her eyes lit up. The tip was already slick and white pearly dots had started to leak onto my skin.

"Who's wetter?" I rasped.

She licked her lips then reached down and spread her pussy lips.

That was me—*boom*. Cross-eyed.

"I can't see," I countered. "Show me."

She released a shaky breath as I took back some of the control, and I watched as she let her fingers rub her clit before sliding farther down to 'test' her slit.

When she retreated, the tips gleamed, and I opened my lips. "I want to taste."

She moaned as she pressed the digits to my mouth and I sucked one in deep, then the other. Her hips rolled in response and she whispered, "How do I taste?"

I nipped her pointer finger. "Like mine."

The moan morphed into a groan.

"I want to see you come, Star. In the full light of day."

Her gaze turned playful, those cat's eyes of hers peering down at me like I was the supplicant and she was the queen, and I was more than okay with that kind of goddamn roleplay.

"Only if I get to watch you too."

"You want to watch me jerk off?" I asked, using the words.

Her mouth worked before she whispered, "Yes. I want to see how you stroke your dick so that the next time you let me do it, I get it right."

"I don't think I could handle you getting it *righter*, Star."

She released a soft chuckle that made me grin at her.

Whenever she got tense, I knew humor would calm her down, and for some reason, she liked my jokes. Talk about a match made in heaven.

Then, her grin faded as the gleam in her eyes disintegrated to be replaced with something else—need. For me. It was ten times more electrifying, a thousand times more potent than a bottle of Valium.

I watched her fingers slide back down, still slightly wet from my mouth, and she touched her clit. I released a guttural sound when she did, then she angled back so her legs were farther apart and I could see every-fucking-inch of her. Goddammit, she was beautiful. So fucking beautiful.

I had to tell her.

"You are amazing," I breathed. "My sweet, sweet girl."

The need in her expression seemed to double down. "I like being your naughty girl, Conor," she rasped, her head arching back.

I clucked my tongue. "Eyes on me, Star. Always keep your eyes on me so you know who I am and you know what I am to you."

Her throat bobbed but she listened. Her gaze, now locked on mine, turned dreamy as she started to finger herself. Her whimper made my dick ache, but I groaned in return when she shifted down and drew her digits along her folds, gathering her slick and using it to move faster.

"Conor, I want to see your hand around your dick."

My smirk was honestly earned. Smug, I grabbed my cock and fisted it. She sighed in delight as I started to roll my hand up and down my shaft, and she watched me use my pre-cum as lube because it bubbled free for *her.*

"You get me so fucking hard, Star. Do you know that?"

Her next inhalation hitched in the middle. "I-I do?"

"You think I'm a two-pump chump for anyone else?"

That made her snicker. "Don't make me laugh when I'm rubbing my clit."

I winked then showed her my fingers. "My dick is leaking for *you*, Star. No one else. Just you."

She bit her lip then reached over and slipped her other hand through the mess I'd made on my stomach. "You haven't come yet," she breathed, the tips sticky with both of us now.

"Not yet. Soon. Touch your pussy with those filthy fingers, Star," I whispered, watching with satisfaction as she complied.

A keening noise escaped her and she wriggled forward until my dick and her cunt were barely inches apart. She coated her clit with more of my seed then rolled her hips as if she were really digging the feel of that.

Eyes locked on mine, she whispered, "Rub my clit with your cock."

Her hands fell against my abs as she leaned into me, and I nudged my shaft forward, letting the glans slap against her pussy. Both of us were a slick mess as I placed pressure on the tip and rubbed it around her clit.

"Fuck," she choked out. "That feels so goddamn good."

Gritting my teeth, I nodded as I started to move faster, sliding it in a circle around the sensitive nub, watching as her pink skin became dotted with more of my pre-cum.

I wanted to coat her in my release. Wanted her walking around all day with it dripping down her—

God damn it.

My head arched back against the pillow as the imagery whacked me in the face with the power of a two-by-four to the temple.

"You are so fucking perfect, Star. Do you know that?"

"M-Maybe I'm perfect for you."

I growled, "Who else matters?"

"No one," she conceded shakily. "Conor, that feels so fucking good. I-I think I'm going to—"

"That's it, baby. Give it to me," I ordered. "I want it. I want your pleasure. I want to see you shatter. You're so fucking gorgeous when you let go for me. Me. No one else. Me. This belongs to me. Just like I belong to you." I slapped my dick against her clit, watching her jolt in reaction. "My cock is yours, Star. Who owns your pussy?"

The moment I said the words, I regretted them. I half-expected them to trigger a deep freeze, but she stunned me.

Her pupils like pinpricks, she whispered, "You do, Conor. It's yours. *I'm* yours."

"Please tell me you're on birth control," I groaned.

Shit, we should have had that conversation the first time we dry-humped on Anton's sofa.

"Copper," she panted. "IUD."

Thank fuck.

I sped up then because I needed her to get off so that I could find my release too.

When she whimpered, I could feel how close she was, but something was blocking her. Maybe my words, maybe her orgasm was just out of reach, so I stayed patient. I carried on teasing her clit, but with my other hand, I played with her slit, filling her with the tip of my finger.

Then, with her bombarded with me, my scent, my touch, I whispered, "Let go, Star. You need to let go so I can see you come. So I can watch it happen. You are the most beautiful woman in the world to me, baby. But when you come, I could die a happy man at that moment knowing that *I'm* the one getting you off. That I'm the one doing this to you.

"I'm going to slide into you someday soon. I'm going to fill you with my cock. And you're going to ride me until you climax—"

She started to shatter.

Right in front of me.

Her arms tensed, her back stiffened, her head rolled on her neck, and she quivered in place, all her muscles frozen, still, her strength locked in as if that were amplifying the ecstasy.

When it cascaded from her in a choked sob, I let myself fly too.

I focused on the sensitive tip, knowing that would make me break faster, needing to share the moment with her.

Working my hand quickly, I came with a long, low groan and my cum splashed over her cunt, drenching her in the mess.

For endless moments, nothing mattered other than the sound of her choppy breathing and the ringing in my ears from just how fucking awesome that had felt. Then, her hips rocked forward and she started to rub her silken, slick folds down the underside of my dick, gently working every drop of pleasure out of us.

When I thought I'd go blind from her ministrations, I grabbed a hold of her hips to keep her in place, then I peered at her. "If you want to wake me up every day like that, you're more than welcome to."

She hid her smile by rolling her lips inward, then her hand landed on the pillow beside my head and she loomed over me, her mouth connecting with mine in a soft, gentle kiss.

"Thank you for being patient with me."

For a second, I didn't know what she meant. Then, I thought about her struggle midway to find release.

Hitching a shoulder, I told her the truth, "Whenever we're together, it won't end until you come, Star."

"I get... That's a lot of pressure."

I tutted her. "I don't mean it that way. It's not a sprint. It's a marathon. If you want to stop, we stop. But if I can feel you're close and just can't get there, then I will do everything in my power to make you find that release because there's no fun in this if we don't do it together."

"You really mean that, don't you?"

"When have you heard me say things I don't mean?" At her slow blink, I teased, "Anyway, I've come to accept I'm Starsexual."

She sniggered. "Shut up."

"I won't. It's true." I knew she saw my amusement and was waiting for the punch line. "It's my fate to only want to fuck you. That's been my problem all along. If you hadn't taken ages to find me—"

"Break into your code, you mean—"

"Exactly. My code was always there, waiting. Just like me. For you to come in and rattle things."

Her fingers traced over my jaw. "I think I'm the same."

"It's called something."

"Everything's got a label now," she sighed. "Can't we be undefined?"

"Nope. Demisexual. That's us. We connect on many different planes, not just sexually."

"That sounds... right," she agreed, her voice gruff.

"Star?"

"Yeah?"

"If it triggers you, you don't have to but... I want to think about my cum covering your pussy for a little while."

She angled her head to the side. "Fair's fair. You stay crispy; I'll stay crispy."

My nose crinkled. "Don't spoil the imagery!"

Her eyes twinkled with a light I knew that only I put there. "You want to think about me all wet and creamy for you, hmm?"

The breath choked from between my lips.

It was official.

She was going to kill me.

49

STAR

JE L'AIME A MOURIR - FRANCIS CABREL

Star Sullivan

I'D BEEN a cum dump so he probably didn't realize how fucking hard it was not to go and shower, especially when I didn't have to ask permission to go clean up. But I did it. Not because I had to, but because he'd laid it down on the table—he'd said, "If it triggers you, you don't have to."

Those were the magic words.

And if anyone deserved magic, it was Conor.

It was strange how we both dressed each other in the aftermath. He pulled up my briefs for me like I couldn't manage by myself then did the same with my jeans while I fixed his fly for him. He dragged on my tank as I patted down his shirt when it hooked under his arms.

When we were both decent-ish and had washed up in the bathroom, he slipped his hand in mine and guided me out of the bedroom. There, Dead To Me was watching something on her phone, a coffee in front of her.

Quicker than her because she was distracted, I snatched her cell and chuckled at the sight of the porn she was watching.

"Pilots?" I mocked. "Really?"

She huffed. "Don't kill my buzz. The dudes flying this plane are hotties."

"And you needed to see them fuck a flight attendant?"

"I couldn't get the real deal," she argued. "They needed to man the plane. But I figured there'd be some porn somewhere that would scratch my itch."

"Are you the flight attendant in this scenario or the pilot?"

"I'm not sure yet."

Conor peered at the pilots who were doing very bad things against the cockpit's dashboard. "They'd have crashed the plane if they were flying and fucking in that position."

Dead To Me grinned but made a 'gimme' motion with her hand and I returned the device to her just as mine vibrated. "You took a while to wake up."

I ignored her to check my messages.

Conor: "Je l'aime a mourir" - Francis Cabrel

Me: French?

Conor: Don't tell me you don't speak it…

Me: I love her so much I could die… Stop with the sweet talk. I'm going to disintegrate in front of Cin and she's not the kind of chick you disintegrate in front of.

Conor: Lol. True. :P

"You know I'm cranky when I first get up," was my easy retort as I dropped my cell on the table and picked up the hot chocolate I knew she was responsible for.

"Is that what that noise was? You getting a splinter out of your hand?"

I flipped her the bird, then I watched as Conor rested his elbow on the table separating us and muttered, "Are you two always like this?"

"Pretty much," she chirped.

He huffed then, head bowed, hid his grin in the coffee mug he was holding.

"What is it?" I asked.

"Can you imagine her and Kat locked together in an argument?"

The imagery had me cackling. "Dead To Me doesn't like kids."

"You're not offended?" Conor queried, his surprise clear.

"Nah. I don't like kids either. Just mine."

Chuckling, he shook his head. "Have you met her, Cin?"

"Nope. But she's getting to that interesting age, isn't she? She doesn't need any help eating or things like that."

"How old do you think she is?" I grumbled. "She's ten *years* old, not months."

Cin wafted a disinterested hand. "Okay, less of the kid talk." She shuddered with revulsion. "Let's come up with a game plan. You two have already wasted an hour—"

"Jesus, we were in there an hour?"

"Yeah. The noises coming out of there sounded good or I'd have barged in and told you to hurry it the fuck up."

Conor choked on his coffee, but me, I was just thinking about how long it had taken me to come.

Fuck, Conor was *patient*.

I mean, I'd known that, but a freakin' hour?

Conor, unaware of my thoughts, retorted, "What *is* the game plan?"

Sucking in a breath, I stated, "Uncover any info we can from Troy about the girl. Then, we need to figure out how to keep her safe from my grandfather."

Cin waved a hand. "I've got that under control."

"We're all ears."

"You blame it on Reinier. Oviana said the four Sparrows were behind the crash, that it was a power grab, *but* he was the one with all the connections. He was the one who'd have been able to get Jorgmundgander to cooperate."

"She's right," Conor agreed. "So we blame him?"

Liking the symmetry, I nodded. "And he's still in that shipping container in the Catskills, isn't he?"

"As far as I know—"

Cin interrupted him. "He is. I asked for confirmation from Temper.

She's requested that you don't kill her just yet, Star, because America still needs her."

"She literally said that?"

Cin arched a brow at me. "What do you think? She's nuttier than a bag of nuts."

Typical Temper. "She sold me out."

"She did," Cin agreed. "And ordinarily, I'd be all over this. She totally deserves to be waterboarded, but she's already crazy and my aunt is sick again, so if anything happens to Temper, then that'll hurt my aunt and Shelly makes the best cookies."

"What does that have to do with anything?"

Cin frowned at Conor. "You never purposely get rid of someone who's good at baking."

"Temper isn't the one who's good at baking though."

"No, but Shelly is. Do you think she's going to bake for me if I kill her kid, dude?"

Rolling my eyes at their philosophical debate, I checked the messages on my phone.

"Then you have to weigh the balances of their baking with their evilness."

"That you even had an answer for that is disturbing."

"Says the guy who electrocutes people for fun!"

"Hey, you told her!" he grumbled at me.

I hitched a shoulder. "I was impressed."

"I was as well. Here was me thinking you were this soft fucker who just plays with computers. Turns out you make your own torture equipment for fun! You totally belong in our clique, Conor."

"Is this a sorority of two?"

Chuckling, I patted his knee under the table. "Four if you want to pledge."

"Hey, who's the third?"

"Savannah, but she doesn't know she's in it yet."

"What do you think, Conor? Wanna join?" D taunted.

Conor smirked at us. "My masculinity can take the hit, just don't tell my brothers or I'll never hear the end of it."

With a grin, I picked up my hot chocolate and took a deep sip. The immediate hit of dopamine had me sighing with delight. "I won't kill her for now," I informed Cin.

"See? If I'd given her coffee, that answer would have been very different."

"No. It wouldn't—"

"Don't kid yourself," she interrupted.

Ignoring her, I continued, "—but if she fucks me over again, she's dead meat."

"Fair," Cin concurred with a bored yawn.

"Are you sure you guys are okay with us stopping in New York first?" I asked when I saw a message from Link confirming he'd be escorting Kat to Hell's Kitchen.

"Little late to ask that, Star, seeing as we're almost there." Cin sniffed.

"Did Alessa and Maverick agree to have one of our drivers collect Kat?" Conor questioned.

I nodded. "She'll be there at five."

"Great. We should make it by four-thirty."

"Do we take it as a positive or a negative that you want to meet the people you love before we take off on this Herculean trial?" Cin inquired.

Narrowing my eyes at her, I retorted, "Shut up."

"I mean, if we're about to meet our Maker," she continued, "how come I don't get to see my mom and dad?"

"Are you even talking to them?"

"No."

"What's the problem then?"

"I'd have liked to be asked."

"You'll never die, Cin. We'll face an apocalypse first and you'll be the star of the next *I Am Legend* but the BAMF version."

She preened. "I will accept this form of apology."

"It's not an apology," I countered with a sniff. "Plus, I don't think we're going to die. I just haven't seen Kat in too long and Conor needs to catch up with his brothers."

"I don't," he informed me. "They're just going to grill you."

Cin hooted. "More like *she* will grill *them*."

My lips curved as I reached for his hand and entwined my fingers in his grip. "You do know that isn't going to happen, don't you?"

Conor's eyes collided with mine. "Why do you think I want a front-row seat?"

It was beyond hot that he knew what I was capable of and it turned him on.

"I'd like to meet with The Whistler anyway." Cin interrupted our prolonged stare with a cluck of her tongue.

"How do you know him again?"

"It's a *long* story and we definitely don't have time for it right now."

A couple hours later, still none the wiser about how Dead To Me knew The Whistler well enough that she wanted to meet up—seriously, she hated everyone, and meeting people was her idea of torture—I stared at an overly large brownstone that, in this city, was ugly as fuck yet had a value of thirty million. Or maybe more.

NYC made no sense.

"When did they move into this place?" I asked Conor as he rested a hand on my back and guided me toward the door.

The last I knew, Aoife and Finn lived in one of the Acuig penthouses.

"A few weeks after Da died."

I grimaced. "Oh."

His lips twitched. "*Oh.* You always look like I've caught you with your hand in the cookie jar when I mention that."

"Atonement. Remember?"

"It'd be easier to get that in a tattoo. Instantaneous results," Cin chimed in.

"That's not the point, Cin," Conor chided.

"By the time you reach the point, Conor, you'll both be eighty. Guilt, *shame*, these aren't feelings that plague people like us. We get them burned out of our psyches during training."

"Not true," I argued.

She scoffed. "Tell me, are you at all sorry about what happened at the 'you know where' with the 'you know who?'"

"Not really."

Her lips twitched. "And would you do it again if you could?"

"Yes."

"Okay, so what about that sounds like you're sorry?"

"Well, I wouldn't want to hurt Conor—"

"Yes, but you just said you'd do it again and hindsight is a beautiful thing because you know you missed 'you know who' so it was like a pointless endeavor."

"No. That bitch is eating slugs now," I retorted, referring to our dearly departed First Lady. "That was worth it. Traitorous cunt. She hurt Conor's family, Cin. Shit like that people have to pay for."

"Wait, that's why you wanted her… *gone*?"

"There were a lot of reasons, but she was integral to your sister-in-law losing her mother, wasn't she?"

"Yeah."

"Did she deserve to, you know, be alive?"

He frowned. "And with Da, that was because…"

"He was a shit dad," I said flatly. To Cin, I grumbled, "He said that art was making his son gay."

Cin's brows lifted. "Are you bi, Conor? I'd be interested in watching—"

"Cin!"

"What? Sex is art, Star. I've told you this a million times. You know I like watching—"

"Are we having this conversation on my brother's front stoop?" Conor sighed.

"It isn't art. It's a private moment—"

"We're losing focus," Conor argued. "Back to my da."

Cin eyed him. "*His* sex life? He was hot."

"No."

"No!"

"Jesus, you need to get laid, D," I groused.

Her lips formed a moue. "You know, you might be right. I wonder if those pilots would be down for a threesome?"

"Your da used you, Conor," I interrupted her before she could start deep diving into the orgies she'd enjoyed in the past. "I told you that already."

"You did and I told you—"

Ignoring him, I queried, "Cin, do you remember that story about the Aryans?"

"The urban legend where they were suspended over a car crusher, got turned into human Spam, and now they haunt the breaker's yard?"

"Yeah. That one. Conor's Da was behind that. And get this, he had one of his sons push the button."

She pulled a face. "Dude sounds crazy. Hot, but crazy. Just how I like them. Not dad-material, though. Even I know you don't expose children to torture."

Conor rubbed his eyes. "He *was* crazy."

"So, why do you want Star to be sorry about wiping him off the face of the earth?"

"He was my da."

Cin looked unconvinced—*we were totally on the same page.*

Sharing a glance, I shrugged. "I'm sorry I hurt you."

"That has to count for something, Conor," Cin peppered. "Unless is this the Catholic in you? Do you want her to confess? Because if you do, I mean, you should be prepared for the fact she'll be in there for weeks. The list of sins... *whoo-ee.* No one's got time to listen to that. We're on a tight schedule here because I'm doing this pro bono and I'm missing out on millions—"

Conor raised a hand to stall her. "Okay, you two. I get it. But I'm the one who decides when I forgive Star for what she's done, and I'll have you know she's well on her way to earning it."

"I didn't know you were that good in bed, Star," Cin muttered.

I elbowed her in the side as Conor snapped, "It has nothing to do with sex. It's just who she is as a person. She's letting me in."

Cin pulled a face. "Is he always this mushy?"

Biting my lip to hide a smile, I reached for his hand and knotted our fingers together. "I like him. I'm keeping him." He narrowed his eyes at that, but I saw he was mostly amused *and* perplexed by this conversation, not upset.

Cin sighed. "He's making you mushy too."

"He isn't."

"How are you supposed to unalive people if you start—" She gaped at me. "That's why you didn't crack those nuts this year! He's making you have a conscience!"

She made it sound like an STI.

"He's not exactly a saint himself," I retorted. "And that wasn't why I couldn't do it."

"All this sounds like he's asking you to change." Cin sniffed. "I like her as she is."

Conor frowned. "So do I. But why would she want to be in a relationship with me if she isn't willing to bring me on board?"

Those words hit me something fierce.

He hadn't given me a working solution to earning his forgiveness, but there was no denying that he was right.

I could stay on my own. Remain independent. Maintain this unforgiving lifestyle and be *alone*.

Or I could let him in and have him.

Christ, there was no comparison.

I wanted *him*.

Always.

Forever.

"We have an audience," Cin muttered, pointing at the side window where five women were staring around the folds of a set of curtains at us.

Conor, turning to see what I was talking about, took note of his sisters-in-law and waved at them. "In a clockwise direction: Aoife, Inessa, Camille, Savannah, and Aela."

"Ooh, Aela's the one with green hair?" Cin asked.

"Yeah."

"And Aoife's the redhead?"

"She is. You'll like her, Cin," Conor enthused. "She's a great baker. She went viral last year over—"

That was D, outta there. She'd already headed to the door and was banging on it as if the brownies I knew Aoife was famous for were fresh out of the oven and waiting for her to devour them.

Me?

I was just focused on Savannah.

Her eyes were narrowed upon me, lips pursed in irritation. That glare took me back to the many times, too many to count in total honesty, where I'd forced my way into her bunk on the tour bus, sobbing my eyes out because of something my dad had done. She'd glared *for* me then. This was just *at* me.

For someone who hated being at odds with her, I did it often. The last couple years of talking shit through with Conor made me wonder if I tested her—tested everyone in my life if I were being honest— because I was just waiting for them to abandon me.

And when they did, instead of getting hurt, I could be like, 'See, I knew they wouldn't stick around.'

The glimpse into my nature made me fidget, until Conor rumbled, "Think Savannah needs to use the bathroom."

His insight had me hiding a laugh. "Think that's less to do with constipation and more with her being mad at me for ghosting her."

How was that my voice? I sounded like I'd choked on a frog.

"Ah, well. You're getting good at asking for forgiveness. Say that you're sorry and mean it and I'm sure she'll forgive you."

"You're more generous than she is."

He snorted and curved his arm around me as he guided us toward the front door. "You're my penguin. I can't be at odds with you. Where would the logic be in that?"

"We're not penguins," I pointed out. "We're very much humans. Not birds."

Rolling his eyes, he groused, "Of course, you'd be one of the freaks who never watched *Friends*. What is it with you and pop culture?"

"I saw one episode and wanted to shoot myself. That dude shout- ing, 'Pivot,' was so fucking annoying." I chuckled at his gasp of outrage. "Plus, I don't even watch the show, and I remember that blonde chick was talking about lobsters."

"Huh?"

"She did. She was talking about lobsters, which, by the way, don't mate for life so that makes even less sense because, at least, penguins do."

He scratched his chin. "I'm still calling you my penguin."

"Well, yeah, but that makes sense because they *do* mate for life." I sniffed. "Anyway, I don't hate pop culture." I smirked. "I hate *wrong* pop culture. I just avoid the rest at all costs."

"You really are the antichrist."

"Admitting to not watching *Friends* was what it took to figure that out?"

"There's just no helping some people." Pitifully, he shook his head but tapped his finger against my nose. As I swatted it away, he continued, "Savannah loves you. She won't be mad for long."

Nodding, I mumbled, "I'm used to her being pissy with me. That's how we spent most of our fourteenth year on this damn planet."

He snorted but fell silent as Aoife appeared in the doorway and finally opened it up.

Cin, ever polite, asked, "Did you make brownies?"

Because Aoife hadn't been raised in a barn, she frowned, her gaze switching between Conor, whom she knew, and the strange person she'd never met who was asking for baked goods. "Well, yes, but they're for dessert—"

"Dessert makes a great appetizer," was Cin's cheerful retort. "Can I have one, please?"

"Yeah, um, sure." Aoife frowned at Conor. "Conor, who is this?"

He shot her a happy grin that twisted my heart into a knot. That happiness was because of me. It fucked with my head that I was the source of that joy.

"This is Star," he greeted. Aoife and I shared a smile. Hers was polite but not unwelcoming, and mine was strained. "That's D—" He paused. "Cin."

"Cin?" Aoife's frown deepened. "Is it 'D' or Cin? People tend to have the same initial, Conor."

"I'm Cin. D is my nickname. But it's for people I've kicked ass with."

"Oh." The other woman blinked. "You're like Eoghan. Come in." What kind of family was I about to walk into when 'handles' were dinner table conversation and an ice breaker?

I guessed inviting spies into her house was totally an everyday occurrence for Aoife O'Grady.

As I approached her, I felt incredibly underdressed in a tank and a pair of jeans with some slimline leather boots, whereas she wore a wraparound dress in a rich green that highlighted her curves and augmented her bright red hair. She was dressed comfortably, but affluently. Whereas I was wearing mechanic chic in the form of jeans from Carhartts and a Target special wife beater—hey, in my world, people *leaked*. I couldn't exactly go around like I was dressed for a cocktail party.

Holding out a hand, I murmured, "It's a pleasure to meet you."

"Same." She darted a glance at Conor. "I know he's been waiting a long time to meet you, but I'd just like to tell you that—" Her smile was sweet as saccharine. "—if you ever hurt him, you might be some ninja spy, but there are five women in this house who will make you regret the day you were born."

"Aoife!" Conor argued. "You don't need to protect my honor!"

"Like you don't protect ours," she countered, lifting a brow at him.

Unoffended, I patted Conor's stomach and reassured him, "You deserve to be loved, Conor, and you deserve to have people at your back." To Aoife, I merely answered, "I won't hurt him any more than necessary."

"What the hell does that mean?"

"It means that life sucks," was my simple reply to her huffy demand. "And I know you know that better than anyone." As her nostrils flared with annoyance at the direct hit, I continued, "I have no desire to hurt him, but I can't control what happens around us. If there's one thing I've learned in my life—we don't control our futures."

She studied me with narrowed eyes but tipped her chin in understanding. "Welcome to my home."

"Thank you. I appreciate it. You need to watch Cin. She might look as skinny as a wraith but she can pack away a tray of brownies in under ten minutes."

Aoife's eyes widened at that news, then she threw at Conor, "Finn told me to tell you to take her to his man cave. Your brothers are waiting in there for you."

When she bustled down the hall, intent on saving her dessert from my ravenous friend, I noticed Savannah waiting at the end of it, her arms crossed against her chest as she stared me down, a stiletto-clad toe tapping against the wooden floor.

Turning to Conor, I murmured, "I'll join you after I speak with her, okay?"

"Get her to show you Finn's man cave?"

I nodded then grabbed a tighter hold of his hand when he made to separate our fingers. "Do you have any candy with you?"

Though he frowned in concern because I was confirming that life was a touch *bitter* at the moment, he reached into his pocket and pulled out a Jolly Rancher. After he passed it to me, he pressed a kiss to my temple and soothed, "She'll forgive you."

The question was, did I deserve to be forgiven? *That* was the source of my unease.

While I gave him another nod, I didn't say anything other than, "Thank you."

Deep in Conor's core was a streak of kindness that, I believed, was inherent in most things family-related. For some reason, he'd brought me into that fold and that was why, though I'd committed unforgivable acts against the O'Donnellys, he didn't hold it against me.

As for Savannah, she wasn't kind.

She was a bitch.

I loved her, but still, I knew what she was.

Just like she knew what I was—an asshole.

Out of nowhere, the theme tune from *The Good, The Bad, and The Ugly* sounded, and I grumbled, "Fuck off, Cin."

Her cackle was the last I heard of her as I unwrapped the candy and popped it between my lips.

With watermelon taking over the bitter tang on my tongue, I strolled over to the woman who was practically my sister and braced myself for the fallout of being *me*.

Her chin tipped up. "Months' worth of messages, Star Sullivan. All unanswered. Each ignored."

I stared at her. "I'm sorry."

"You're sorry," she scoffed. "Is this like the time you were sorry when you accidentally squirted Elmer's glue in my face? Or the time when you kissed Jonny Macho on my bed on the tour bus? Or when you ran away *without me*?"

My nose crinkled at the overload of memories. "Thank fuck my taste in men has improved since then."

"He was gross," she agreed. "I think you only kissed him to piss Gerry off."

"Probably. He hated him. He's in jail now, isn't he?"

"Kissing sixteen-year-olds on their father's tour buses? Yeah. He's in jail, Star." She rolled her eyes. "You're lucky I found you before anything could happen."

"I didn't particularly care if it did at that point."

Her brow furrowed. "Don't make me feel bad for you. Not yet. I've earned this anger, Star."

"I'm not saying that you haven't. Just telling you the truth. You know I wasn't in a good place back then. Hence the running away."

Dad had been at the end of his tether by then, which had led to me being indoctrinated into a boarding school in goddamn Switzerland.

I knew he'd meant well. I fully accepted I'd derailed. But shoving me on another continent, away from everyone I loved, had only made getting expelled ten times more satisfying.

Jesus, I'd been such a cunt. It was no wonder Lorelei, Savannah's Mom, had issues with me.

She bit her lip. "Well? Which is it?"

"An apology on par with the Elmer's glue incident."

"You didn't mean it that time."

"I did," I argued hotly. "I meant to get you in the face, but I didn't mean for it to go in your eye."

"Gee, thanks." She growled under her breath. "You're such a nightmare."

"Like you can talk." I scowled at the sleek pantsuit she wore. "What is it with you women anyway? It's a family dinner and you're dressed for the Oscars."

"Some of us like to have more than jeans from Dickies in our closet." She tossed her hair over her shoulder. "You'll get used to dressing up again."

"Carhartts, actually, and maybe I don't want to get used to that crap. I hated it as a kid and I fucking loathe it now."

"You won't have a choice. The family is on the campaign trail."

"What?" I sputtered. "They're putting one of the sons up for election? They'll never win—"

"No. They're building up to the time when Seamus can become a politician. That means we're going legit. Or looking like we are." She arched a brow at me. "From that display on the front stoop, I'd say Conor intends on keeping you around. God knows why."

Shoving my hands in my pockets, I muttered, "Below the belt, Vana."

"Isn't that what we do? Isn't that why you think you can just waltz out of my life and then waltz back in as if nothing happened?" She pinched her nose. "Aspen is dating a fucking Russian mobster. Paris is still trying to get me on her reality TV show because it's sinking faster than the *Titanic*, and Camden is—"

"—drinking again?"

"And gambling. Then Mom got it in her head to write her life story.

"I swear that Dad and I are the only normal ones in the bunch and I'm married to the head of the Five Points and got kidnapped last year. It'd be nice if my childhood friend, a woman who's like a sister to me, would have answered my fucking texts. They're your family too."

The words sent an ache spearing through my chest.

"Are they? Is your mom even talking to me?"

"I made her…" She sighed. "I didn't tell her what happened, but I let her know that she was wrong to judge you. I guess I opened her eyes some. And of course, they're your family. Just like you're ours."

Tipping my chin up, I said, "I had things I needed to do and I couldn't get distracted—"

"So, that's what I am? A distraction?"

I groaned at her wounded expression. "No, Vana. You might have been a few months ago. But now, I don't think so."

"Your kindness overwhelms me," she grumbled, shoving my shoulder with an expensively manicured hand.

"Did you get hurt?"

She frowned. "When?"

"When you were kidnapped?" That was my area of expertise and I hadn't been around to save her ass. *Some sister I was.* "I'm sorry I wasn't there to help."

"Conor did most of the heavy lifting. I'm fine."

"Are you sure? That's a lot to have to deal with."

"I'm fine," she repeated. "Aidan shored up his position and it—"

"It could happen again. No matter what he does to try to protect his role as leader, there are no guarantees," I warned, but I had no desire to shit on her parade just to make sure she knew that the storm wasn't over.

That it never would be.

"You say that and you're standing in my shoes now too. You love an O'Donnelly. That means you're going to love his brothers, are on the brink of becoming an 'afternoon tea with the girls' kind of woman, will eat Sunday dinner with his mother even though she talks about Our Lady more than she does her grandkids, and will be as married to the mob as I am."

Inside, I squirmed, but I just mumbled, "I know."

She squinted at me, her confusion evident. "Then what the hell happened while you were gone? Because the Star I know would rather drink strychnine than lead her life according to someone else's plan."

My mouth tightened. "I realized that I didn't have to be a lone wolf anymore. I'm part of a pack now."

"Have you been binge-watching David Attenborough documentaries again?"

I shrugged. "They help me concentrate."

Her hum was loaded with her disbelief.

Because I didn't get it either and could only assume it was because this was Conor, who accepted me warts and all so how couldn't I do the same for him, I changed the subject. "Aspen is really dating a Bratva man?"

"They're calling themselves something else now." She pursed her lips. "She's gaining weight though."

Brows lifting, I stated, "That's a positive sign."

Another hum. "Well?"

"What?"

"Where's my apology?"

"I literally told you I was sorry at the start of this conversation."

"It wasn't good enough."

"What do you want? Blood?"

"Don't tempt me."

I hissed under my breath then, blowing out a sharp exhalation, snapped, "Savannah, I'm sorry that I ignored your text messages and didn't check in with you. It was very cruel of me to leave you in the dark, especially when I know you love me and want what's best for me."

Savannah arched a brow. "See? You can do it when you try." She shuffled forward, dragged me into a hug I didn't want, then grumbled in my ear, "Hug me back, bitch. You're in 'Pack' O'Donnelly now, where you allegedly want to be. *We hug.*"

"I don't like hugging."

"Me neither. But you get used to it."

With a disgruntled grunt, I slipped my arms around her waist and embraced her. "I want you to know this is under duress."

"Tough shit."

The hug went on for a long time, neither of us admitting that it was comforting, neither of us pulling away.

Then, in my ear, she informed me, "I got the notification that Katina is on her way. Maverick wanted to confirm the guards' IDs."

So, he was taking her security seriously—thank fuck.

Anticipation filled me at Vana's news though. "Good. I miss her."

"I'm looking forward to meeting her again."

"Again?" I questioned, finally retreating so I could read her expression. "She didn't visit you as well, did she? I know you and Conor share the same building. Did she give you the laptop?"

"No. I was pissed at Aidan. Long story short, I felt like running away for a little while so decided to go to the Sinners' compound. I met her there. She gave me the laptop and I gave it to Conor."

"She never mentioned that she gave it to you." I frowned, surprised by the news. "When was the kidnapping?"

"Late last year."

Before I could wonder about Katina's silence on that subject, Savannah was back to scowling at me and shoving me in the shoulder again. "You could have just sent it to him instead of potentially dropping me in deep Shinola with the Sinners."

"I could have but I…" I pulled a face. "I wanted him to have access to it if I died. It didn't matter when you got it. I knew he'd be able to use the contents to avenge me."

Her mouth rounded. "You totally thought you were going to die?"

I hitched a shoulder. "I wake up each morning thinking today could be my last twenty-four hours on this planet."

"Lord, that's depressing."

"Nah, it's my reality. I like it, makes me appreciate the smaller things in life."

"Like watermelon Jolly Ranchers but not family and friends?" she mocked, obviously scenting the candy on my breath.

"I apologized. Twice. That means I don't have to say it again and it means you can't bring it up in future arguments."

She sniffed. "Where, in the terms and conditions of our friendship, did I ever agree to that?"

"Bitch."

"Asshole."

We smirked at each other.

Family—*it didn't have to make sense.*

50

CONOR

Conor O'Donnelly

FINN CLAPPED me on the back when I walked into his man cave and dragged me into a hug. "I didn't know how much I'd miss you until you left. You're the only one with any sense, I swear to fuck."

Brennan punched me in the arm. "What's going on?"

Grumbling, I rubbed my bicep. "That's your idea of a greeting?"

"You're pulling moves without discussing them first with the family."

With an eye roll, I retorted, "What am I supposed to do? Drop everything and teleconference with you before we make important decisions?"

"You should consult us. Aidan said you want to alter our plans. That's something we should be discussing together."

"Brennan, calm down," Finn clipped. "Since when does Conor do anything that doesn't take the family's best interests into consideration?"

My older brother didn't appear to have an answer for that, but that just made his scowl darken. "We're in this together. If we start pulling apart, then everything will go to hell."

"You're just pouting because I got to leave the country and you didn't. Trust me, Bren, I haven't been on a fucking vacation."

"What has Sullivan gotten you involved in?" Aidan queried, his tone quiet as he stared at his whiskey glass.

"*Sullivan,*" I mocked, "is going to be your sister-in-law—"

"You asked her to marry you?" Finn inquired.

"You barely know her," Brennan ground out.

"Fuck off, Brennan. It's been two goddamn years! Like you knew Camille when you married her. So sit the fuck down."

"I didn't have a choice. She forced my hand—"

"And is the best thing that's ever happened to you," Eoghan inserted, his tone low. Measured.

I shot him a grateful look, but the shadows under his eyes stole most of my attention. I hated how he suffered. God, I wished I could provide him with relief from the mess the Forces had made of his brain.

"I'm not saying she isn't," Brennan spat. "I'm just saying, Conor, if you need help, we're here."

I didn't like how he consistently thought badly of Star but his words resonated—Brennan was our fixer. He wanted to fix this situation if I was in danger, yet there was nothing to fix.

Even though our situation was unusual and we were deep into a mission to bring down the Sparrows, all was right with my goddamn world now that Star and I were together. Nothing else mattered.

My temper dispersed some. "Brennan, how deep is the family's dependence on my skills?"

"Nose deep."

His admission further quenched my temper. "So, why do you think my judgment is compromised in relation to her?"

He ducked his head. "We're supposed to look after you."

"Says who? Da? Da didn't look after me," I retorted. "So you don't need to worry about that, and Star's who I want to be with. She isn't dragging me into dick. In fact, the opposite just happened. She cut ties so I didn't have to be involved, and that messed with my head more than anything.

"She's been through a lot, Brennan, and for the first time, she knows she's not on her own. That I'm with her. That I'll help. I won't let you make her question that, not when it's taken me so fucking long to ram that lesson home.

"If you have a problem with her, then I'm getting out of here. No disrespecting her, understood?"

"I wouldn't have disrespected her."

"Bullshit," I sniped. "You seem to think she's a problem of mine that needs fixing. The only thing that needs fixing is her ass on a seat next to me for the next forty years."

Finn chuckled. "You got it all wrong, Conor. You don't want her on a chair next to you; that's what your lap is for."

My lips quirked up in a grin when I thought about our time on the jet and how I'd teased her about being better equipped for her comfort than a La-Z-Boy. "I wouldn't be against that."

"What's the plan, Kid?" Declan asked, speaking up for the first time.

A knock sounded behind me. "Perfect timing," I said happily, dragging open the door and automatically sliding my fingers between hers, then tugging her into the room.

Both of us were dressed down in comparison to the others, more relaxed and less formal. Star didn't appear to care though. I figured that had everything to do with her past. She knew that you didn't have to wear Prada to own a room. It only took presence, and she had that in spades.

At the center of my brothers' attention, she ignored them to peer around the den, stating, "The first time I knocked heads with the Five Points, I never imagined I'd step inside one of the O'Donnelly boys' man caves years down the road." She arched a brow. "I'm Star Sullivan."

"He's Aidan," I said, pointing to him. "That dick is Brennan, you know Eoghan already, and he's Declan. The one grinning like he's crazy is Finn."

Her gaze darted over each of them even though I knew she could put faces to names without any help from me.

"Why are you a dick, Brennan?" she inquired, tone amused.

He folded his arms across his chest. "Because I don't trust you."

"Clearly smart but not wise."

"What the fuck does that mean?"

"It means you don't need to trust me to be wary of me. Whatever you've done, Brennan O'Donnelly, it's child's play to me." She bared her teeth and then bit them noisily, snorting when Brennan glowered at her.

"Mad bitch," he rasped.

Seeing that I was on the brink of decking Brennan, Aidan surged to his feet, asking, "Would you like a whiskey?"

"Please." Gently squeezing my hand, she released my fingers and strolled over to him. Leaning against Finn's desk, her tone cordial, she imparted, "Conor once told me you're a whiskey connoisseur."

"I'm more of a collector than an expert." He poured her a finger from the bottle he brought along with him every week. Finn was getting quite the whiskey collection of his own from the remnants of our Saturday night discussions. "Tell me what you think of this one."

It was only then I noticed he'd turned the bottle around so the label wasn't visible.

"What makes you think I'd know the difference between a good whiskey and a bad one?"

"I think you'll have made it your business to know how to speak with each of us."

Annoyance on her behalf filtered through me—were they trying to think the worst of her?—but she didn't deny it, just accepted the glass, swirled it around the tumbler, then inhaled deeply.

"Notes of burnt heather, cedar…" She closed her eyes. "Chocolate and oak. Vintage oak at that." She lifted the glass to the light and stared at the undertones. "Bronze. Unusual. *Old.*"

He took a sip. "Very old."

"Expensive." Not a question.

"Incredibly so. Rare too."

"You bring that around for dinner with the fam?"

Aidan just smiled. "Who else would I share the bounty of wealth with if not my brothers?"

"You're a kinder sibling than Camden was. He'd sooner put

expired creamer in Savannah's coffee than bring her something like this…" Her brow furrowed as she took a deeper sniff of the liquor. "Glenfiddich?"

He raised a brow. "You know your whiskies."

She took another inhalation. "It was the molasses top note. I didn't smell it at first."

"How old is it, would you say?"

"Is this an episode of the *Antiques Roadshow: Whiskey Edition*? Because I didn't sign up for this," Eoghan muttered with a yawn.

Star, her gaze still locked on Aidan's, ignored the interruption to answer, "Got to be at least seventy years old."

"More like nearly ninety." He twisted the bottle to show her then let her take it to study the label. "Only fifty remaining."

She whistled under her breath and then returned it to him. "You might as well drink it. My mouth still tastes of Jolly Rancher."

His nose crinkled. "What?"

"Star likes candy," I offered.

Aidan shrugged but accepted the glass and poured the rest of hers into his. "If it weren't seventy grand a bottle, I'd throw it out."

"Nice to know you can think prudently," she mocked.

His lips twitched. "Go on then. Tell us."

"What? Our intentions?"

"No. What you know about us?"

"Aidan," I argued. "This isn't a job interview."

"Yes, it is," he retorted, dismissing me entirely. "She's yours. You don't think we're going to make sure she's the right one for you?"

"Like you asked for permission with Savannah," I snarled. "Like any of your brides got this goddamn treatment—"

Star angled her head as she studied him. "Is this about making Conor feel like a child or out of a desire to protect him?"

"Conor isn't a child. Conor hasn't been a child since he was molested by that fucking priest. Finn and I stopped being kids that day too. This isn't about making him look like he can't make his own decisions. It's about us protecting him. About us doing what we've always done—watched his back and taken care of his demons."

"I don't need you to," I snapped.

Aidan's gaze was cool as it landed on mine. "I will never know what you went through at that bastard's hands. I will never know how it affected you because you won't share it with us. But *you* will never know what it meant for Finn and me to find you in that position. For us to see him do that to you. For us to witness it firsthand.

"We've been protecting you ever since. Who do you think told Da to fine you instead of beat you whenever you fucked up?" He pointed at Finn. "That was Finn's idea. Who do you think encouraged Da to let you move into your own apartment? Me, via Ma. Because he'd have kept you at home for the rest of your fucking life, Conor.

"We all know what Da was. A bully. A psycho. But with you, he was different. You were his wunderkind. That didn't mean he wouldn't have treated you like the rest of us. If anything, I think it meant he was harder on you in some—"

Star pressed a hand to Aidan's shoulder. "I have no desire to hurt him."

"You already have. You left him," Finn said flatly.

"You think you're the only one who wants to protect him?" Star argued.

"Jesus Christ," I spat, drawing their attention my way. "What the fuck about me made you think I need protection? Me, more than any of the rest of us? Because I'm a nerd? What is it that makes you think I can't handle my-goddamn-self?

"Okay, I can't kill someone from a thousand yards away and I have no desire to beat someone to death with my fists or string them up until they're swinging in the breeze, but it doesn't make me weak that I don't choose to do those things.

"I don't need you to grill my woman to ascertain whether 'she's right for me.' I'm the one who makes that decision, and I made it—years ago. The first moment I recognized her skills, her intelligence, and learned what her purpose was, she had me hooked.

"This has nothing to do with any of you. *Nothing*. Sure, we watch each other's backs because that's what we do. We always have and we always will. I appreciate that we'll always be that way, but I also have the fucking sense to recognize we alone know who's right for us and Star is that for me."

I knew they were surprised by my outburst, but Star broke the silence by saying, "I did do my homework on them, Conor. I don't feel grilled. Just…" Her smile was for me alone, but it had me frowning. "…respected."

"What?"

She shrugged at my splutter. "It's nice to walk into a room and for people to understand you're a loose cannon."

"That's *nice*?"

Eoghan raised his tumbler to her. "I know where she's coming from."

"That's because you look like you play golf for a living, Eoghan," Declan drawled.

"Impostor syndrome," Finn teased.

"Being underestimated is overrated," was all he said, sinking a sip of his whiskey back and sighing as it hit his bloodstream.

"Go on then. Tell us what you think you know about us," Brennan prompted.

"You collect rare coins. Not just rare, in fact. So unique that most of your collection consists of coins that are either one of a kind or have circulations of ten or under." To Declan, she said, "There was a rumor that you were involved with the Isabella Stewart Gardner heist."

He chuckled. "I wasn't involved with the heist. I was too young for it. Just enjoyed the spoils, but that's interesting you know that. Who did you get to? One of my dealers?"

"I pick up information like the garbage men collect trash.

"I know the CO Eoghan shot before he left the army will never walk again thanks to a particularly well-placed bullet in his lower spine. I also know that wasn't why he was dishonorably discharged, and I know that Finn's father-in-law is the President of the United States." Hellfire lit up her eyes. "But as I told Conor earlier, I'm keeping him—"

"And I'm keeping her," I inserted with a grumble.

"—so you're under no threat from me."

Finn scratched his jaw but the look he shot me was accusing. "How did you know about Alan Davidson?"

"As I said, I have my methods. I already knew that first time I tangled with your family." She peered at me. "I have no idea why Conor feels the way he does for me. I don't understand it, but I'm not going to argue about it. Even without Conor stating facts, I knew that you wouldn't have given your other sisters-in-law the third degree, but I accept that I'm different."

"You're not," I argued.

"I am. I come with baggage, Conor," she reasoned quietly. "And that's fine. I respect them for loving you and for wanting the best for you. That's what you deserve."

As my brothers watched her watch me, it was Aidan who broke into the conversation with a soft, "Conor indicated there is a new plan underway to resolve this situation with the Sparrows."

Acceptance—she shouldn't have had to earn it, but she'd received it nonetheless. That he invited her to join the conversation and didn't request for her to leave the man cave made that clear.

Fuming on her behalf, we continued staring at each other, the links between us strengthening and deepening as we stood in this safe space where lives were threatened and the promise of death were machinations in a wider game that no one knew they were playing.

I was a powerful man.

Surrounded by powerful men.

And yet, in this place, Star held her own.

Shoulders back, spine straight, no fear in her gaze, expression calm.

This, did she but know it, was a culmination of years of work on her part.

In this very house, we were affecting change.

We *would* change the world.

She was a part of the future now.

Not just entangled with the past, trying to free herself from the bonds that had caged her, but breathing life into a world riddled with poison.

We were the Irish Mob, but together, we'd be so much more.

The United States of America had no idea what was going to hit it.

51

VICTORIA

LIKE IT OR NOT - MADONNA

THE KITCHEN WAS PACKED, as always, with women and kids.

It was like something from the fifties, enough that it would have irritated me *if* they weren't always talking about something interesting that mocked the traditional gender roles they 'appeared' to portray.

Since Papa's death and moving in with Inessa and Eoghan, I was starting to realize that I didn't have to fit into the same mold as I always had.

Papa had scared me.

He'd forced us to adhere to strict rules, punishing us if we veered outside of those lines.

But now, there were choices. I had options. I didn't have to hide my books. I could explore the world, and my sisters-in-law aided and abetted me in that endeavor.

Since Christmas, after Shay and I had gotten into an argument about glass ceilings, Savannah had started showing up on Saturdays with books for me. Various topics that were seemingly unrelated except that she somehow knew I'd be interested.

Aela discussed art with me, modern and traditional, and explained the importance of analyzing artwork because it enabled a person to see beneath the surface and to understand the 'human dilemma' better.

Aoife, for all her homey traits, was a shrewd businesswoman. Last month, I'd asked her how to balance my checking account because my allowance never lasted longer than a week and I wanted to start saving because Savannah said that a woman should never depend on a man for a source of income.

As for my sisters, Inessa and Camille, they were like me—caterpillars still stuck in their chrysalises. Not that anyone would look at either of them and think they were ugly caterpillars, but their development was slow. Camille was content with her crafts but Inessa wanted to study, wanted to grow, and neither of those were traits Papa wanted to develop.

So it was with curiosity that I stepped into the kitchen, wondering what I'd learn today.

Last time, I'd sneaked in without anyone realizing and got to hear about how Aidan Jr. would tie Savannah to the bed and how Declan did this thing with his tongue that made me wonder if that was something you had to learn or if the knowledge was passed down via DNA.

It had *definitely* made me look at Shay differently.

There was, however, a new addition to the kitchen today.

She was thin, very angular, had scars on her throat and arms, and... she was the most beautiful woman I'd ever come across in my life. Her strength was compact and she vibrated with it. Her confidence brimmed over as she picked up a brownie even though Aoife didn't let anyone touch them until dessert. But what fascinated me was how Savannah was discussing the current political situation in Afghanistan with her and she spoke of the country as if she knew it.

She was a soldier.

Fascinated, I stepped toward her and realized we were almost the same height.

The stranger just appeared larger than life.

"Hello," she said cheerfully when she took note of me hovering by Savannah's elbow.

"This is Victoria, Cin," Savannah introduced me. "She's Camille and Inessa's sister."

As always, I adored her for not classifying me as the 'baby sister.'

She tucked her arm around my shoulder and I tipped my head against hers with an affection I showed to few people.

"I know you," Cin declared after she swallowed some of the brownie in her hand.

My brows rose. "But we've never met."

Cin—short for Lucinda?—shrugged. "Heard a less-than-lucid Russian mumbling about you."

"A less-than-lucid Russian?" I repeated, perplexed.

"Maxim Lyanov."

Despite my confusion, my cheeks tinged pink. "Maxim spoke about me to you?"

"He wasn't really speaking at the time. He was groaning."

"Groaning?" Savannah cleared her throat. "She's barely sixteen, Cin."

Cin snorted. "I don't screw mobsters."

The chatter screeched to a halt in the kitchen.

Utter silence.

Fitting, seeing as everyone in the room screwed mobsters on the regular…

Uncaring that she'd just offended the entire household, Cin continued, "He was talking about chopping someone's hand off."

Though I knew Savannah was bristling, she barked out a laugh and nudged me in the side. "Maxim and his penchant for butchery. I think we know what his love language is, Victoria."

Nudging her back, I grumbled, "Shut up."

"Whose hand is he chopping off this time?" Inessa queried, drifting over to us.

"I don't understand why he can't just break a wrist. Why chop it off?" Aela groused.

"It sends a message," Camille reasoned as she lifted her mimosa and took a deep sip. "The Bratva way."

"Nuh-uh. They're 'The Forgotten Boys' now."

Savannah's correction had me frowning. "The Forgotten Boys?"

"Well, the…" She cleared her throat. "I should have kept my mouth shut."

"I think you're incapable of that, Savannah," Inessa teased.

"Probably."

Camille reached over the counter and patted my arm. "There's a new Russian faction in town."

Panic stirred inside me. "Are we in danger?"

"Of course not. We're Irish now," Inessa declared, her words loaded with her satisfaction.

I had no idea where Eoghan came from—seriously, he was like a ghost sometimes—but he was there all of a sudden, his arm sliding around her waist, and he was growling something in her ear that made Inessa blush.

Eoghan apparently liked hearing that Inessa considered herself Irish now.

I'd have rolled my eyes if I weren't used to their PDAs.

"You're not in danger," Eoghan confirmed a moment later. His gaze was measured as he zeroed in on me, gracing me with every inch of his focus. For someone who'd been starved of attention from a male authority figure, he never ceased to reassure me when he looked at me this way. "I told you, Victoria, I will always keep you safe."

My throat bobbed. "If the Russians are—"

"Maxim is in charge of the new faction and the soldiers are separating from the Bratva. Nothing is really changing on this end. The men are no longer heeding Moscow's call."

His explanation was brisk and to the point and it both concerned me and put my mind at rest.

"Won't that anger Moscow?"

"Undoubtedly. Lyanov has our backing though, and Moscow is far away from here."

Was anything truly far away nowadays?

Unease settled inside me as the kitchen as a whole grew busier when the men waded in. Finn got his hand slapped when he tried to grab a brownie, and Declan burped baby Cameron while Brennan did something that made Camille turn bright pink. I didn't even want to know why Savannah's eyes were sparking with anger because whenever she looked like that and Aidan was in the vicinity, they tended to disappear.

It was amid that chaos that Cin shuffled closer to me. "I didn't mean to frighten you."

In the face of her confidence, I felt pathetic.

Did anything frighten this woman?

"Y-You weren't to know—"

"I'm used to speaking my mind and I'm not comfortable around kids."

"I'm not a kid," I grumbled.

"You are to me," she said simply, but it didn't offend me, oddly enough. Mostly because I knew she didn't make that comparison based on years on the planet but on experience.

There was no denying that I was a child to this woman, as I easily fell into both categories.

"Is Maxim okay? Why wasn't he lucid?"

"Do you care?" She tipped her head to the side. "You seemed scared when I spoke of him."

"No. I was confused. H-He's a friend."

"A friend." She smirked. "Do mobsters have friends?"

My scowl was immediate. "You shouldn't judge people you don't know. The O'Donnellys didn't have to bring me into their family, but they did. I'm here. I'm safe. I wasn't before. They saved me from people who'd have hurt me, and they protect me. I don't like that you've disrespected them twice now. And while you're under their roof too."

Cin's brows rose but she conceded, "I worked for the government."

"So? They're not exactly the good guys, are they? The newspapers prove that!" I scoffed, shoving a piece of hair behind my ear before I demanded again, "Why wasn't Maxim lucid?"

"Because he got injured trying to rescue my friend."

I stiffened. "How badly?"

"Bad." Her stare was intense. "He was worried about you. That was why he was babbling."

"Why are you telling me this?"

"I don't know." She shot me a grin. "Mostly, I suppose, because it was strange. I appreciate the strange things in life. Punishment via butchery is new to me. It's very medieval. And considering he routinely does this for a girl who isn't even related to him makes it even more curious."

"Maxim *is* medieval," I rasped. "Why was he worried about me?"

"He thought he was dying. He wasn't but he didn't know that at the time. He seemed to think that he was leaving you alone to face the lions, but from what I can see, the lions are biting at his door, not yours."

"Where is he?"

"He's in New York now after his men arranged an evacuation for him."

"From the head of the Bratva in Moscow?"

"Yes." She hummed. "He was in a small, private hospital, hiding out from the *Krestiy Otets* the last I heard. What are you to him?"

"I-I, nothing, really."

"Unlikely."

"What does that mean?"

"He thought he was dying and he was worried about your safety *while* he thought he was dying." She hitched a shoulder. "As much as you disapprove of my disrespectful undertones when speaking of the mafia, I'd watch myself if I were you. The minute you turn eighteen..."

She let her words drift away with her as she left me alone to retreat to the window where she peered out of the shutters. I watched her position herself just to the side, much as Eoghan did.

Not allowing anyone to take a direct hit at them through the glass.

I couldn't imagine living my life that way even though I was a pawn in a wider game I had no control of. As much as my life had changed with Papa's death, that truth hadn't altered any.

Daughters were the vessels of an alliance.

Two years...

Seven-hundred-and-thirty days until I was eighteen.

Inessa had gotten married on her eighteenth birthday. It had led us down a road that was the best thing that could have ever happened to us, but I wasn't her. I wanted options, just…

My hands balled into fists as I snuck out to use the restroom.

Locking the door behind me, I leaned back against it and drew out my phone.

Me: *I heard you were sick. Are you all right?*

As always, he didn't take long to reply.

Maxim: *Not sick, katyonok. Just managed to get into a scrape.*

Me: *From what I heard, it sounded serious.*

Maxim: *It was more serious than I'd have liked but I'm okay.*

Maxim: *Thank you for asking.*

Me: *If I'd known, I'd have asked sooner.*

Maxim: *Is that a reprimand I hear, katyonok?*

My cheeks flushed.

Me: *Yes.*

Maxim: *The kitten has claws.*

My other hand balled into a fist.

Me: *Do you have a problem with that?*

Maxim: *Why would I?*

Me: *My father would have.*

Maxim: *Your father was a mudak.*

Me: *You wouldn't have called him a shithead if he were alive.*

Maxim: *He isn't though, is he?*

Me: *No.*

Maxim: *And isn't life much better for it?*

His words should have hurt me, but they were true.

Me: *Why do you always answer my texts, Maxim?*

Maxim: *I like to know you're safe.*

Me: *I mean nothing to you. I'm no one.*

Maxim: *That's not true.*

Me: *It isn't?*

Maxim: *No.*

I had no idea why I typed my next message, but I needed to get the words out. Had to. It was imperative.

Me: *I want to go to college.*

Maxim: *Then go to college you will.*

Me: *You wouldn't have a problem with that?*

Maxim: *Why would I?*

Me: *I'm not naive, Maxim.*

Maxim: *I think you are, but I do not see naivety or innocence as a curse. My childhood was stolen from me, katyonok, at too young an age. As someone who starved, who hurt, who bled to stay alive, I wouldn't wish that on anyone. Certainly not you.*

Me: *What am I to you?*

Maxim: *I think you know this. Naive or not.*

Me: *Tell me.*

Maxim: *You are my future, katyonok.*

That he sent that message to me so easily staggered me. My father considered women to be a weight around his neck, and that he'd been cursed with three daughters had been his biggest complaint. More than taxes or his tithes to Moscow—we were the worst thing that had ever happened to him.

Maxim: *But you are young and I must wait until you see me in the same light.*

Me: *Why would you wait? You don't need me to cement ties in the Bratva anymore.*

Maxim: *You know about The Forgotten Boys?*

Me: *I do.*

Maxim: *Are you sure you want to know the answer to your question?*

Me: *Of course.*

Maxim: *It is complicated.*

Maxim: *But I will explain it as well as I can. Your sisters have the O'Donnelly brothers. Through them, you have protection until you are of age, but afterward, you are a pawn in a game you cannot win.*

That we'd used similar words to describe my situation made nausea swirl in my gut.

Maxim: *I have been a pawn, Victoria. Now, I can be your rook.*

Me: *Not my king?*

Maxim: *That is a title one has to earn. Maybe with time, you will allow me to be that for you.*

Me: *Do you believe I'm in danger?*

Maxim: *Yes.*

Me: *From?*

Maxim: *Moscow.*

Me: *And you're not in danger from them?*

Maxim: *Of course. But they would marry you off in an instant to a Pakhan under their control.*

Maxim: *I am a relative stranger to you, Victoria. Yet you know the truth...*

Me: *What truth?*

Maxim: *That I have killed to keep you safe.*

His words made my shoulders sag.

Beyond, I could hear the outer door slam and the rabble of voices stirring in the hall, but it was nothing to the chaos in my head.

I wanted to be the woman Savannah was cultivating—independent, strong, self-assured—but that was at odds with an archaic future that involved a marriage of convenience for my protection.

But... it wasn't a convenience for him, was it?

He could cut ties.

Marry whoever he wanted.

I was young. He had to wait for me to be of age, but he should marry sooner and have a family so he could prepare to cement his power base in the future with children who could forge alliances.

But he *was* waiting.

For me.

Maxim: *Katyonok?*

Despite his assurances, I needed to ram something home.

Me: *I want to go to college.*

Maxim: *That can be arranged.*

Me: *And I want to be courted. Inessa didn't even meet Eoghan until her wedding day.*

Maxim: *You have already met me.*

Me: *I want more.*

Maxim: *More is something I can try to give you but I'm not a pervert. These types of conversations need to happen when you're older. I would never have spoken about any of this.*

Me: *I forced the conversation.*

Maxim: *You did.*

Me: *I won't bring it up again.*

Maxim: *That is wise.*

Maxim: *I know that boy Harris has been sniffing around you... Take care of yourself, katyonok. You are aware of the consequences to those around you if you don't.*

The threat was both reassuring and annoying.

Everything about this conversation had been.

I liked Franklin Harris. He was cute. But the threat was clear. If he touched me, he'd lose a hand then his life just like Timofai Stepanov had last year.

I curled my fingers in on themselves and straightened up.

My choices might be limited, but I wasn't going to be like Mama or my sisters.

There was more to life than a wedding ring.

52

STAR

Star Sullivan

"OMG, Star, Link was riding behind us the *whhhhoollllee* way from Jersey! It was so freakin' cool!" Katina shrieked as she flung herself at me.

All thin arms and spindly legs clambered around me, holding me tight, so tightly it hurt, but it hurt *good*.

Some days, I was sure she was the only thing I'd ever done right, and I hadn't even made her, had just saved her life apparently.

Just.

Thinking of a world that didn't have this little girl in it made me realize how grim a place it would be.

Pressing a kiss to her cheek, I closed my eyes as I hugged her back, reveling in the sweet scent of her shampoo and the perfume she'd sneaked from my room to spritz on herself.

The notion made me grin. "Thief."

Katina gasped. "I'm not a thief."

"No? Who sneaked into whose room to use my perfume?"

"You weren't using it," she pointed out.

"She's not wrong," Conor said easily from his position in the hallway where he was leaning against the wall, watching us.

"I've got two people ganging up on me now," I grumbled as Katina released a giggle then let go of me and hurtled into Conor too. He released a choked breath as she… Well, somehow, she kicked him in the process of hugging him and maybe elbowed him in the gut all at the same time.

My kid, for someone so coordinated in gymnastics class, could orchestrate a calamity while walking in a straight line.

"You did it! You brought her back to me! Thank you!" Her cry of joy, of thanks, made tears prick my eyes.

Goddammit, D was right.

He *was* making me mushy.

Conor, still looking winded from the multiple blows, returned her embrace. "You don't have to thank me, Kat. My job is to always bring her home."

I clenched my jaw at those words.

Did he have to keep saying stuff that hurt but in a wonderful way?

Pressing a hand to my chest where an ache was forming, I watched my kid and, God, my *man* together.

It was too perfect.

So innocent.

Except it was nothing I expected and everything I'd never dared dream of having for myself. For *ourselves.*

Throat thick with emotion, I wandered forward, moving behind Kat and sandwiching her in a soft hug, needing to be a part of this small circle.

My family.

Not just pack.

Family.

I breathed into the notion, pressed my face into Conor's throat which prompted him to settle his hand between my shoulders to hold me closer, and accepted the rightness of this moment.

That rightness filtered through me, spreading through my veins, overtaking everything with the promise of hope—something I never dared allow myself to have.

"You okay, my love?"

Startled, I tilted my head back to look at him. "Yeah, I'm..." There was only one word for it. "...perfect."

And I was.

Nothing was resolved, everything was in the air, and tomorrow was not guaranteed, but at that moment, I really, truly *was* perfect.

He beamed a smile at me that was as earnest as it was genuine and I cupped his chin, knowing he could see the stars in my eyes and was unafraid to reveal them to him when he deserved each one.

"Star!"

Kat gained my attention by accidentally standing on my toe. "What, kiddo?"

"Who's he?"

I blinked down at her. "Who's who?"

She prodded me. "Him."

Following her pointed finger, Conor was the one who, spotting the boy in the family room, answered, "That's my nephew. Seamus."

Her cheeks turned bright pink. "How do you spell that?"

"S-E-A-M-U-S."

She frowned. "Why isn't it 'S-H-A-Y-M-U-S?'"

"You think *his* name is bad? Wait until you meet Aoife," Conor drawled, making me snort. "But we call Seamus 'Shay' for short. All the vowels together is kind of an Irish thing."

Katina absorbed that information like the sponge she was. "Who's Aoife?"

"My sister-in-law."

I cleared my throat and took it upon myself to do the unthinkable: "She's family now, Kat."

My kid arched a brow at me, looking as sassy as a seventeen-year-old and not a preteen. "Family like Alessa or family like Link?"

Pondering that a second, I answered, "Bit of both, but Aoife bakes brownies for a living and doesn't talk about motorcycle engines all the time."

Kat giggled. "He doesn't talk about them *all* the time."

I grinned. "Just most of it. But she's going to be your aunt."

Conor's eyes widened, but he didn't correct me.

"When? I haven't had an aunt in ages."

The words drew my attention. "When did you last have an aunt?"

"When I was really little. She was super nice," she said absently. "Do you think Aoife will give me a brownie?"

Tension filled me. "What was her name? You never mentioned an aunt before."

Her brow puckered but not in sass this time. A strange blankness filtered into her eyes as if she were shielding her thoughts from me, but I could sense it was outside of her autonomy. Like her subconscious was protecting itself.

Fuck, what was wrong with my kid?

I'd seen her do this before, seen her just check out, but never this deeply.

Blankly, she muttered, "I-I don't remember."

I dropped into a crouch and reached up to cup her chin. "How come? Because you were so small?"

"I guess," she whispered, her fear obvious. "Why can't I remember, Star?"

My smile was easy when, deep inside, I felt anything but. "You were so little, kiddo. I don't remember things from when I was that young. Do you, Conor?"

"No." He cleared his throat. "Aoife will definitely give you a brownie, Kat, but probably not until after we've eaten. Are you ready for dinner?"

She turned to reply to Conor, "I-I guess."

A dimness had settled in Kat's eyes, one that replaced the wall of before. It concerned me because it reminded me of the times when she woke up from a nightmare, and the idea of sending her back home with the potential for another episode—one we hadn't had to deal with in so long—put me on edge.

"Brennan and Eoghan's sister-in-law, Victoria, she's here too. She's younger than Shay. I know Shay brings a Switch with him if you want to play games?"

That seemed to perk her up some and, silently, I thanked him for easing her distress.

"If Seamus is your nephew, does that mean he's my cousin?"

He cast me a look. "Well, yes."

"He's really pretty."

I snorted at her wistful tone. "I thought you had a soul mate in your class."

Kat frowned. "You've been gone too long, Star. We moved on. It was time."

"Soul mates don't move on," I pointed out.

"Of course they do," she chided me like I was the idiot here. "Life's too short to just have one soul mate. That's why Camden is so perfect for me."

"It helps that he's about twenty-five years too old for you and doesn't know you exist as well."

"Savannah told me she'd introduce us," she crowed.

Apparently sensing we were going to start bickering, Conor chuckled. "I think your opinion on soul mates will change when you watch *The Notebook*, Katina."

I rolled my eyes. "Of course, you've watched that."

"Meaning you haven't?" he sputtered. When I shook my head, he gaped at me. "We're changing that. At some point, you *are* watching that movie with me."

"I can watch it with you," Kat declared, sounding more like herself. Thank fuck.

"I think you're too young, Kat." He pulled a face. "I don't know the age it's rated for. I mean, there's no…"

Stifling a laugh, I replied, "You'll just have to wait, Kat. It's like the rides at the amusement parks that are too big for you."

"No fair," she pouted. "I want to watch too."

"We'll find something to watch together, don't worry. Conor loves cartoons."

Her eyes lit up, and the joy overwhelmed the earlier episode of… What? *Dissociation?* How had I never seen how deep this went before? Because I was on the lookout for trauma, not something else like fugue states?

"We can watch those together!" she cheered, drawing me back into the conversation. "Do you like *Naruto*?"

I groaned. "Don't get her started on that weird fox dude. Only sociopaths grin like that—"

"Weird fox dude?" They both blurted that at the same time, their outrage unfabricated.

"Never mind that Kakashi weirdo." Because my brain was on a delay, I asked Conor a stupid question, "You know he reads porn?"

Of course, Katina picked up on that. "What's porn?"

Before I had to answer, someone called out, "Hey!" The three of us turned as one and found Seamus, Conor's nephew, standing there, wearing an easy, welcoming smile. "Uncle Con!"

Conor hooked Shay around the neck and hauled him in for a bear hug. "You managed to stay out of trouble since I've been gone?"

His nose crinkled. "Maybe. You blacking out half of my social media helped."

Chuckling, Conor drawled, "Be careful what you wish for and don't get..." He cast a quick glance at Katina who was staring at the older boy with stars in her eyes. "...you know. Don't be dumb."

"I won't. It was a party!"

Ah. *Party = drunk.*

"Anyway, I'm about to go and set up a game and wondered if you'd like to play with Victoria and me?"

Before my very eyes, my precocious brat of a kid blushed bright pink and turned timid as hell. "I'd like that. Thank you so much for including me."

Without another look at either of us, she drifted away, her usual social commentary on life put on mute which was a testament to her sudden shyness.

Shaking my head at her antics, I turned to Conor who was studying me. "I know we have to talk but I can't not do this," he mumbled, stepping into me, one hand settling on my waist, the other cupping my nape.

When his mouth pressed against mine, I sagged into him, knowing he'd take my weight, knowing he'd support me.

That he always would.

My lips parted, accepting the soft greeting of his tongue, the caress a 'hello.' A 'you make me happy.'

I'd never made *anyone* happy.

In fact, I'd always done the exact opposite and usually, I'd gone out of my way to ensure I pissed as many people off as I could. Bitter, discontented people did not make for nice humans.

But Conor changed that by being him.

I slipped my arms around his waist and clung to him, my head falling against his shoulder until he retreated, pressing his forehead to mine as we both caught our breaths.

"Retrograde amnesia like Cin said, do you think?" he asked quietly. It didn't come as a surprise that he'd taken note of what Kat had gone through.

"Could be. She had the same look in her eyes as when she had a nightmare. But worse."

He cupped the ball of my shoulder. "Do you want to spend the night here? Have her sleep over instead of going back to West Orange?"

For a woman who was used to depending on herself, who was slowly embracing that she wasn't just a team of one anymore, how he blew down my barriers continued to stun me. His offer was enough to make me tighten my arms around his waist and hug him in gratitude.

"Would you mind? Would Aoife and Finn?" I whispered.

"Why would they care? This place is massive."

"She might…" I grimaced.

"Wet the bed?"

"She used to when she had a nightmare."

Conor pursed his lips in contemplation. "Do you want to head back to West Orange? Have her spend the night somewhere she knows she's safe?"

"No. We're already delaying things by spending the night." I rubbed a hand over my face. "I have a bad feeling…"

"About?"

"Troy."

"I've accessed her phone records. We could call her and warn her that we're coming?"

I bit my lip, the need to—

Crap, I didn't even know.

I just had an uneasy feeling in the pit of my stomach.

Granted, it had only been triggered by Kat's visceral reaction to something as simple as being told she had some new family members, but…

"What is it?"

"Maybe Aoife has some sheets or something for Jake? For when he has accidents?"

He frowned at the abrupt change of conversation. "Yeah. Of course. If not, we can buy some."

"Right. I just don't want her to feel humiliated, and maybe," I muttered, "she could stay here while we go and visit Troy? She'd be safe here, right?"

"I installed the security system and you put the firewall through your paces during mock runs last spring. It's probably more secure than a vault."

A relieved breath escaped me. "Yeah. You're right. We locked your code up tight."

"We did, and I worked on the system with Eoghan too. It's pretty much a fortress. Plus, there are guards. We bought the building next door so they're on the ground."

"Really? That seems excessive."

He just shrugged. "The past year has proven we need to have guards."

"You don't have any."

"I have you," he teased, which made me laugh.

"Stop making me smile," I argued, wiping a hand over my twitching lips.

"It's true, isn't it?"

I huffed. "Yes, it's true."

His smugness made me punch him in the arm.

"Hey! Brennan just hit that fucking arm. Ouch."

"Don't be a baby." I sniffed when he grumbled under his breath. "If she's here, then I'll feel better."

"What is it, Star?" he questioned, still rubbing his arm but seeming to read beneath the layers and sensing my unease.

"I don't even know. Ovianar just got into my head, that's all. She said that the kids were in danger."

"I doubt it. I mean, at the time, sure, but they were just toys in the game back then. It's not likely they're in danger now, is it?"

"They witnessed their parents' murders, Conor. Sure, those murders were by ex-cons, but we figured they were tied to a Sparrow-backed operation through Jorgmundgander, so what's to stop someone else from connecting the dots too?"

He rubbed the back of his neck. "Shit."

"Yeah. Shit." I blew out a breath, suddenly torn now that he was on the same page as me.

It had made sense to catch up with family while we were in the US, because who the fuck knew where we'd be in thirty-six hours? Now, I just felt like each of these minutes were borrowed.

Stolen.

All because I'd seen the tangible effect of the past on my kid.

"We could leave now. Ask the questions that need asking. Get back in time for dinner?"

"They won't be eating soon?"

"No. There are snacks and we eat late."

"I should have left Katina at the compound," I muttered. "I can't leave her with strangers."

He reached out to knot our hands together. "It's not ideal, but she's already playing with Shay so that will keep her occupied. She's safe. *Physically*. Eoghan is here. He won't let anyone hurt her. Never mind the rest of my brothers."

Nodding, I swallowed. "I'll tell her we're heading out."

"Heading out? Where?"

Twisting around and finding Cin leaning against the doorjamb and listening in, I said, "I've got a bad feeling."

She straightened up—as aware as I was about the importance of following your gut. "About?"

"Troy."

"You think she's in danger."

I rubbed my eyes as that strange urgency continued to pound at me like fists to the head. "Yeah. Dumb but…"

"Not dumb. We've wended a path across the globe that has led us to Troy. That path is traceable and Reinier is MIA. That has to concern Smythe and Foundry. The original six are suddenly down to two." She peered at Conor. "Does this place have an armory?"

Her words weren't reassuring but at least I didn't feel like I was freaking out for no reason now.

"It's an O'Donnelly family home," he retorted. "Of course it does."

I didn't even have it in me to smile.

My cell buzzed as he guided D where she was most comfortable—surrounded by submachine guns.

Unknown: *How goes the search?*

My brows lifted at the uncanny timing of, well, it had to be Kuznetsov, didn't it?

Was the timing too uncanny though?

I peered around, wondering if he was spying on us, but like Conor had said, I'd troubleshot his network security before I'd taken off.

His code wasn't just perfect; it was crazy beautiful in its complexity.

Me: Kuznetsov?

Unknown: Yes. You know my name. You use it.

Me: Do you know someone called Belyaev?

Unknown: Knew of him. He's dead now.

Me: I know.

Unknown: Why do you ask?

Me: Do you know WHY he died? Or how?

Unknown: No.

Me: He died on the same day as your son.

Unknown: What?!

Me: Do you know that he was a Sparrow?

I purposely kept that cryptic. Whether or not his son was a Sparrow was something I didn't feel like dropping over text. Whatever I thought of him, he *was* old.

Unknown: I did. He was highly ranked.

Me: One of the highest.

Unknown: Was his death related to Aleks'?

Me: Yes. We're still ascertaining how.

Unknown: Belyaev was feeding us intel.

Me: On?

Unknown: Art trafficking from looting during Operation: Enduring Freedom.

Whatever I'd expected him to say, it wasn't that.

Unknown: For obvious reasons.

My breath hitched.

Me: Me?

Unknown: Yes. That was why you were swallowed up by their trafficking operation, no?

Well, that and the double agent in our ranks, but I wasn't about to share anything of that nature with him.

Me: You were trying to find me?

Unknown: Yes. Belyaev was an old friend of Aleks'. From school.

Me: They were friends?!

Unknown: Yes. Aleks, like your mother, was a double agent.

Me: You knew he was a Sparrow?

Unknown: Yes. He was a Brother first.

Unknown: Belyaev had a bride from the Sparrow slaves. When Aleks learned that she died, he suspected Belyaev was behind her death and used it as leverage against him.

Unknown: Before that point, Aleks was well-positioned but not highly ranked.

Me: Why didn't you tell me this when we started?

Unknown: I wanted to see what you'd uncover on your own.

Me: And what I'd share with you?

Me: You were testing me.

Unknown: This comes as a surprise?

Me: It shouldn't. You didn't know their deaths were linked?

Unknown: I don't see why. Belyaev was visiting Ohio at the time of his death. He passed away from a heart attack in a hotel room in Cincinnati.

Me: He didn't. He died in a car crash. Where
did you get that information from?

Unknown: It's irrelevant.

Me: It isn't if someone fed you false intel.

Unknown: I'll deal with it.

Unknown: Are you close to finding his killer?

Me: Closer to finding your granddaughter.

The opposite was true but he didn't need to know that.

Unknown: This is fantastic news.

Me: I have to go.

Unknown: Whatever you need to facilitate
this investigation, you can have.

Me: Now that I've proven myself?

Unknown: Yes.

Me: Okay, so who fed you the dirty intel?

Unknown: As we speak, Interpol is creating a
place within its infrastructure for a
department dedicated to the Sparrows and
their trafficking.

So it was going to be like that, huh?
I hated stonewalling.

Me: Even though I haven't provided results
yet?

Unknown: Results or not, they are scum and
scum needs eradicating.

Me: Were you always going to create this
department?

> Unknown: It has been in the cards for the past two years. I saw little point when the public had no knowledge of the corruption in their governments, but now, it's different.

> Unknown: A department of this nature is costly. It's only affordable if public outcry is strong.

Me: Which it is.

> Unknown: Never been higher. Find me my granddaughter, Star. She lost her family, too, and she might be alone and has no need to be.

Me: I'm doing my best. I have to go.

Not wanting to accept that his words had worked their way into my conscience, I shoved my phone into my back pocket.

Seeing that Cin and Conor hadn't returned from the armory yet, I headed through the family room and toward a smaller den where two teenagers and Katina were playing *Mario Kart.*

Stepping over to her, I placed a hand on Kat's shoulder. "Kat, I have to go out."

"I don't need to come, do I?"

My lips curved—she was back to being precocious. Thank God. "No. I'd hate to ruin your game."

"I'm winning," she preened.

"Keep at it, slugger," I teased, pressing a kiss to the crown of her head. "I'll be back later, okay? If they serve dinner without us, will you be all right?"

"She'll be fine," the girl, Victoria, assured me with a kind smile. "We already said we're going to watch a movie after we've finished up here."

Appreciating that they were including her, I returned the smile. "I hope you guys have fun."

With a lingering look at Katina, who not once had turned her gaze away from the screen, I left them to it, feeling better about abandoning her here when she'd already made friends with Seamus and Victoria. I knew she was more comfortable with older kids because of how many adults she spent her time with, and this just confirmed it for me.

Upon my return to the hallway, Cin was packing semi-automatics into one of two black duffel bags and Conor was slipping a gun into a holster on his shoulder.

My brows rose at the sight, mostly because that was hot as fuck *and* unexpected.

He smirked at me. "See something you like?"

"No, none of that," Cin groused. "I'm too young for this kind of behavior."

"You were talking about orgies earlier," Conor grumbled.

"Yeah, I'm plenty old enough for that."

Rolling my eyes at her, I ducked down and pulled open one of the bags, studying what we had. "We're packing for war?"

"Prevention is better than the cure."

"Not sure that works with weapons," I mused.

"The Whistler's here," she prodded. "He'd be good to have on-site instead of hacker boy."

"I want him guarding this place. Just in case. Plus, this isn't his fight."

"It's *our* fight," Conor disagreed. "You want him on this, I'll get him. I already told him that we're leaving and to be on the lookout for trouble while we're gone. He's always prepared for war anyway. He's probably got a dismantled AK-47 tucked into his pockets."

Cin snorted. "Impossible."

"I was being facetious. Can't you take a joke?"

Not wanting them to start sniping at each other, I shook my head. "Let him stay here. If Cin's complimenting him then I know he's one of the best and that's what I want protecting the family."

Cin clucked her tongue but kept a lid on it, and Conor just watched me slip on a knife holster and two gun holsters.

Once we were suited and booted, we headed for the door, but not before Conor was pulled back by Brennan. Whatever they bickered about had Brennan scowling and Conor smirking, but he didn't say anything to stop us from leaving, just watched us go.

When we were on the road, I felt better. Proactive. Veering toward a goal instead of wasting time. Not that meeting up with Kat had been a waste of time, but the cloud of anxiety I was existing in at the moment had definitely been stirred up by her.

For the whole of the hour-long journey, I drummed my fingers against the armrest, agitated and uncertain about what we were walking into.

Troy was as neurotic as anyone in the business, so I knew it wouldn't be easy speaking with her. Especially if she didn't want us there, and I couldn't see her being welcoming.

Conor's hand kept a firm grasp on my free one and I let our fingers bridge, allowing the connection to stop me from feeling like I was going to burst out of my skin.

When he offered me a Pixy Stix, I shook my head. The thought of eating made me nauseated.

After we crossed the state line and approached Stamford, I turned to him as a thought occurred to me. "Are you in contact with Dagda? I'm going to assume you are, seeing as you negotiated with him?"

He sighed. "Is this really the time for that argument?"

"No. But I'm not arguing. He could be in danger too."

"You're freaking out about this, aren't you?" D muttered, staring at me in the rearview mirror of our SUV.

"I am. I spoke with Kuznetsov via text before we left—"

"And you're just telling us this *now*?" she snapped.

"I had to let it percolate," I retorted.

"Less bickering, more explaining," Conor reasoned, tone calm.

"He knew his son was a Sparrow. He was a plant. Belyaev was passing information to him about..." I swallowed. "The CIA was involved in looting important artifacts in Afghanistan, D. It was one of the reasons why I was taken. Kuznetsov confirmed that Belyaev was feeding Aleks information about that deal." It came as a pleasant surprise to be able to say, "Kuznetsov was looking for me."

Conor's hand tightened around mine in silent support, undoubtedly recognizing how much that meant to me.

"I'm glad," was all he said though.

My smile was shaky. "He believed that Belyaev died of a heart attack in his hotel room in Cincinnati, so someone fed him bad intel."

"What about that makes you think Dagda is in danger?" D questioned.

"I don't know," I said uneasily. "But what harm would it do to call him and check in?"

Nodding, Conor reached for his cell phone, and I watched as he hit connect.

"We're about ten minutes away from Troy's homestead," Dead To Me informed us.

"Great."

Tapping my toe now, I watched as Conor waited for his call to be picked up, but when there was no success, he shrugged.

"Keep trying," I rasped.

"I will."

Minutes later and exiting the highway, D decelerated as we approached a large parcel of land which, according to Google Maps, had a house in the center of a massive spread of corn fields.

Unlike other homesteads in the area, this one had an electric fence around the perimeter and a large gate that had more cameras on it than a Hollywood star on the red carpet. The defenses were more fitting for government-owned property than private land.

When we pulled up in front, Dead To Me tapped the buzzer.

"Still no answer from Dagda," Conor muttered.

"State your business," a crisp voice demanded on the intercom.

"Troy? It's Dead To Me."

"What the fuck are you doing here?"

"We need to speak with you."

"Who's we?"

"Lodestar's with me, plus her man."

"That bitch has a man?" Troy hooted. "Now I really believe today is doomsday."

Though I huffed under my breath, I stayed silent.

"She does, but we've come because we think you're in danger."

Troy snorted. "Ain't we always?"

"No. This is different. Let me in, Troy. We're on the same side."

"Doubt it. Look, this ain't a good time."

Before she could give us more attitude, I leaned forward so I could project my voice, snapping, "It's about Jorgmundgander, Troy."

There was dead silence, then the gates pulled inward.

That boded well.

The moment we were on the driveway, the gates closed behind us. Dead To Me didn't set off until the latch clicked and the area was secured. As we drove toward the house, Conor kept trying Dagda, but that he'd been trying for ten minutes fucking straight was a portent we didn't exactly need right now.

Disquieted, I twisted around, scanning the land for only God knew what. For as far as the eye could see, however, the remnants of corn season laced the horizon.

That meant the corn rows provided no shelter for anyone sneaking around, but it also gave us no cover from the highway, which only amped up my agitation.

I was always good under pressure, but this was hitting differently.

I didn't know if that was because *I* was different or what, but if I'd had a gun in my hand instead of in a holster, I'd have a hair trigger.

When we made it down the ridiculously long driveway, it was with relief we pulled up outside the house.

It was a regular farmhouse—to laymen's eyes. But the structure was clearly reinforced with security protocols that didn't belong on farmland.

More CCTV and, undoubtedly, a ton of other measures that weren't visible to the eye—heat sensors, pressure monitors, and the like kept it locked up nice and tight.

The farmhouse was also surrounded by trees, deciduous, which made me reach for my weapon when we were on the ground.

Dead To Me peered at the trees too, and that was when I saw it—*a glint.*

"She's in the trees," I called out, moving behind the car and keeping it as a meager shield, motioning to Conor to do the same.

"What do you want?" Troy hollered, unafraid to reveal her location now that we were staring at the tree she'd picked for a nest.

"We told you—to talk."

Her Kentucky accent was thicker than ever as she spat, "Ain't no one who wants to talk about Jorgmundgander with me that don't have trouble on their mind."

"Then why the hell did you let us in, Troy?" D retorted impatiently, plunking her hands on her hips.

"You armed?"

I scoffed. "Of course we fucking are."

"I wanna see your weapons before I come down."

"I thought she was visually impaired?"

D answered Conor, "She is."

"Then how the fuck is she up a tree and trying to shoot us?"

"She either lied or she can see better than she let on."

"What are you bitching about?" Troy hollered. "Less talking, more showing."

"This is ridiculous," I grumbled, but I flashed her my holsters. D did too.

"What about him?"

"I don't carry weapons," Conor lied.

My cell buzzed. Spying Ovianar's number, I frowned but turned away from Troy to pick it up.

"Hey, what the fuck do you think you're doing? Hang up the phone!" Troy snarled.

Hearing the click of the safety on her weapon ricochet around the otherwise silent clearing, I just flipped her the bird.

Showing my back to someone armed with a sniper's rifle wasn't smart, but this was total BS and we all knew this was her trying to establish some control over the situation.

"Ovianar, what—"

"STAR!"

Minerva's scream had me freezing up. "Minerva? What is it?"

Her sobs echoed down the line. "She's gone. Oh, God, she's gone." Her wail hit me straight in the heart. "How could you do this to us? How?"

The anger and the fear and the grief coalesced into one mass that she hurled at me. For a moment, it choked me. I had no words. Nothing to say. *What could I say?*

"I didn't..." My mouth worked. "W-What happened? Where are you?"

"We needed milk," she cried. "I-I went out, came back, and she... Oh, God. She's gone. She's fucking gone. Dead. She's dead." The sob she released made me realize I did have a heart and it was breaking.

We'd fallen out years ago, but I never wished ill on them. *Ever.*

A shiver worked its way up my spine. "She can't be!"

"She is. She goddamn is," she shouted.

"The cops—"

"They're here. Tryn too and—"

"How?" I rasped.

"How? That's all you can ask me? You got her killed, you fucking cunt."

"I need to know," I snarled, willing to take her insults on the chin but needing answers nonetheless. "Did she... Could she have..."

"This wasn't suicide," she spat. "It was to the back of her head." This time, the wail that keened from her had me shuddering in response to her grief. "She— Her— Oh, God. How am I supposed to live without her? How? Brady—what am I going to tell him?"

When she started sobbing again, the purest dose of guilt hit me like I'd snorted a gram of fentanyl. I closed my eyes as I whispered, "I'm so sorry, Minerva."

But she didn't want to hear it, and I couldn't say that I blamed her.

"Fuck you," she spat. "You did this. You brought this to us. She's dead *because of you.*"

My mouth trembled as I turned to Conor when a hand cupped my shoulder. "What is it?"

"Fuck you, Star. Fuck you. I hope they do to you what they did to her, you fucking bitch."

When she cut the line, I was almost relieved. I couldn't do it, couldn't hang up on her. Not after…

Swallowing, I whispered, "Ovianar was executed."

53

CONOR

Conor O'Donnelly

"DID I HEAR THAT RIGHT?"

The question didn't come from me or Cin, but Troy.

I stared at the tree where her scope was glinting in the sun, wondering how the hell she'd heard Star when she'd practically whispered what had happened to the woman we'd only just left in London.

Fuck—was her blood on our hands?

It seemed likely.

We showed up years after the murders of Kuznetsov and Belyaev and she was dead the next day?

"They're cleaning house," D intoned, ignoring Troy.

"Yeah," I rasped, watching Star with concern.

"Try Dagda again," she ordered, rubbing her brow.

Deep in her eyes, I saw her misery and guilt. I wished I could do something to take away the pain, but I knew too well that nothing did that. Only time, and even then, that didn't always work.

Needing to help her, I nodded and hit dial on my phone again. Barely a couple rings sounded in my ear when a bullet shot at the car, inches away from Star's feet.

Automatically, I grabbed her and dragged her to the ground. Cin slipped into a crouch too, her scowl deep, her anger growing.

"It's Troy," she clipped, but she remained stationed behind the SUV. "She's fucking around."

"Answer my question. Ovianar's dead?" Troy spat.

"You remember her, then?" D snapped.

"Of course I goddamn do. This is about Ohio, isn't it? Fuck."

"O'Donnelly?"

Amid this ridiculous conversation, the sudden appearance of Dagda's voice in my ear came as a shock, especially as he sounded breathless.

I cut to the chase, "Ovianar's dead."

"Fuck," he hissed.

"We think the Sparrows are cleaning house. There might be someone on their way—"

"They're not on their way, O'Donnelly. They're fucking here. I'm going underc—"

The blast of another bullet had me looking up, thinking it was Troy again—it wasn't.

It had been in my ear.

"Dagda?" I demanded. "Are you there?"

Dead air.

"Fuck."

"Dagda? You're talking to Dagda?" Troy hollered, suddenly leaping from the tree she'd been hiding in and striding over to us like she hadn't been letting off bullets to see us dance to her tune a couple minutes ago.

She wore camouflage, her face was painted, and she'd have made G.I. Joe seem underdressed—she was prepared for an ambush.

"His line just went dead. He said they were there already," I informed Star.

"Holy fuck," Dead To Me blurted, eyes wide with disconcertion. "This is a coordinated effort." She turned to Troy. "Have you been threatened? You must have been to get dolled up like that. What happened?"

Before she could answer, an alarm sounded from within the house.

It echoed around the barren fields, seeming to grow in volume with every pounding beat of my heart.

Troy, wearing an eyepatch like a boss-ass bitch, gritted her teeth as her head whipped to the side to study her house. "That's my perimeter alarm." Another alarm blared. "The rear gates."

As one, Dead To Me, Star, and I rasped the same goddamn words: *"They're here."*

That was when a ball of fire surged toward us from the highway.

BOOM.

AUTHOR NOTE

Hope you're ready for the Filthy Truth.

You can preorder the second half of the duet here: www.books2read.
com/FilthyTruthSerenaAkeroyd

You'll also find a deleted scene that didn't fit into the timeline of
Filthy Lies here: https://dl.bookfunnel.com/sv06kgjd0e

It's dark and has sexual assault in it from Star's time as a sex slave.

**Don't forget the second FILTHY LIES hits 500 reviews, I'll be
dropping a bonus scene in my Diva reader group!**

You can join here to read it when it happens: www.facebook.com/
groups/SerenaAkeroydsDivas

AND...

I'm so pleased to announce that I'll be co-authoring a project with
Cassandra Robbins!! A character from her Disciples will be falling for
a Fecker!! Can you guess who?!

You can preorder here: www.books2read.com/FilthyDisciple

Much love to you all,

Serena

xoxo

THE CROSSOVER READING ORDER WITH THE SINNERS & VALENTINIS

FILTHY
FILTHY SINNER
NYX
LINK
FILTHY RICH
SIN
STEEL
FILTHY DARK
CRUZ
MAVERICK
FILTHY SEX
HAWK
FILTHY HOT
STORM
THE DON
THE LADY
FILTHY SECRET
REX
RACHEL
FILTHY KING

<u>FILTHY DISCIPLE</u>
<u>THE CONSIGLIERE</u>
<u>THE ORACLE</u>
<u>LODESTAR</u>
<u>SILENCED</u>
<u>END GAME</u>
<u>FILTHY RICHER</u>

FREE BOOK!

Don't forget to grab your free e-Book!
Secrets & Lies is now free!

Meg's love life was missing a spark until she discovered her need to be dominated. When her fiancé shared the same kink, she thought all her birthdays had come at once, and then she came to learn their relationship was one big fat lie.

Gabe has loved Meg for years, watching her from afar, and always wishing he'd been the one to date her first and not his brother. When he has the chance to have Meg in his bed—even better, tied to it—it's an opportunity he can't refuse.

With disastrous consequences.

Can Gabe make Meg realize she's the one woman he's always wanted? But once secrets and lies have wormed their way into a relationship, is it impossible to establish the firm base of trust needed between lovers, and more importantly, between sub and Sir…?

This story features orgasm control in a BDSM setting.
Secrets & Lies is now free!

CONNECT WITH SERENA

For the latest updates, be sure to check out my website!
But if you'd like to hang out with me and get to know me better, then I'd love to see you in my Diva reader's group where you can find out all the gossip on new releases as and when they happen. You can join here: www.facebook.com/groups/SerenaAkeroydsDivas. Or you can always PM or email me. I love to hear from you guys: serenaakeroyd@gmail.com.

ABOUT THE AUTHOR

I'm a romance novelaholic and I won't touch a book unless I know there's a happy ending. This addiction is what made me craft stories that suit my voracious need for raunchy romance. I love twists and unexpected turns, and my novels all contain sexy guys, dark humor, and hot AF love scenes.

I write MF, menage, and reverse harem (also known as why choose romance,) in both contemporary and paranormal. Some of my stories are darker than others, but I can promise you one thing, you will always get the happy ending your heart needs!

9 781915 062833